Between a rock and a hard place . . .

Just then the Iranian jets paid another call. This time they were only 200 feet over the ground. The SEALs felt the wind whiplash around them as the jets sucked air after them.

Murdock scowled. "In about fifteen minutes, we're going to have more trouble than we need. A hundred and forty troops with a mad on, one machine gun on that AP Carrier, and those two damn jets rigged for air-to-ground fire."

Jaybird grunted. "Yeah, but then that's about our usual odds . . ."

SEAL TEAM SEVEN
Flashpoint

By Keith Douglass

THE CARRIER SERIES:

CARRIER
VIPER STRIKE
ARMAGEDDON MODE
FLAME-OUT
MAELSTROM
COUNTDOWN
AFTERBURN
ALPHA STRIKE
ARCTIC FIRE
ARSENAL
NUKE ZONE
CHAIN OF COMMAND
BRINK OF WAR
TYPHOON

THE SEAL TEAM SERIES:

SEAL TEAM SEVEN
SPECTER
NUCFLASH
DIRECT ACTION
FIRESTORM
BATTLEGROUND
DEATHRACE
PACIFIC SIEGE
WAR CRY
FRONTAL ASSAULT
FLASHPOINT

SEAL TEAM SEVEN
FLASHPOINT

KEITH DOUGLASS

BERKLEY BOOKS, NEW YORK

This is a work of fiction. Names, characters, places, and incidents are either the product of the author's imagination or are used fictitiously, and any resemblance to actual persons, living or dead, business establishments, events or locales is entirely coincidental.

Special thanks to Chet Cunningham for his contribution to this book.

SEAL TEAM SEVEN: FLASHPOINT

A Berkley Book / published by arrangement with the author

PRINTING HISTORY
Berkley edition / June 2000

All rights reserved.
Copyright © 2000 by The Berkley Publishing Group.
SEAL TEAM SEVEN logo illustration by Michael Racz.
This book may not be reproduced in whole or in part,
by mimeograph or any other means, without permission.
For information address:
The Berkley Publishing Group, a division of Penguin Putnam Inc.,
375 Hudson Street, New York, New York 10014.

The Penguin Putnam Inc. World Wide Web site address is
http://www.penguinputnam.com

ISBN: 0-425-17503-0

BERKLEY®
Berkley Books are published by The Berkley Publishing Group,
a division of Penguin Putnam Inc.,
375 Hudson Street, New York, New York 10014.
BERKLEY and the "B" design
are trademarks belonging to Penguin Putnam Inc.

PRINTED IN THE UNITED STATES OF AMERICA

10 9 8 7 6 5 4 3 2 1

SEAL TEAM SEVEN

THIRD PLATOON*
CORONADO, CALIFORNIA

Lieutenant Commander Blake Murdock. Platoon Leader. 32, 6'2", 210 pounds. Annapolis graduate. Six years in SEALs. Father important Congressman from Virginia. Murdock recently promoted. Apartment in Coronado. Has a car and a motorcycle, loves to fish.
WEAPON: H&K MP-5SD submachine gun.

ALPHA SQUAD

Willard "Will" Dobler. Boatswain's Mate First Class Senior Chief Petty Officer. Platoon Chief. Third in command. 37, 6'1", 180 pounds. Married. Two kids. Sports nut. Knows dozens of major league records. Competition pistol marksman. Good with the men.
WEAPON: H&K MP-5 submachine gun.

David "Jaybird" Sterling. Machinist Mate Second Class, Lead Petty Officer. 24, 5'10", 170 pounds. Quick mind, fine tactician. Single. Drinks too much sometimes. Crack shot with all arms. Helps plan attack operations.
WEAPON: H&K MP-5SD submachine gun.

Ron Holt. Radioman First Class. 22, 6'1", 170 pounds. Plays guitar, had a small band. Likes redheaded girls. Rabid baseball fan. Loves deep-sea fishing; is good at it. Platoon radio operator.
WEAPON: H&K MP-5SD submachine gun.

*Third Platoon assigned exclusively to the Central Intelligence Agency to perform any needed tasks on a covert basis anywhere in the world. All are top secret assignments. Goes around Navy chain of command. Direct orders from the CIA.

Bill Bradford. Quartermaster First Class. 24, 6'2", 215 pounds. An artist in spare time. Paints oils. He sells his marine paintings. Single. Quiet. Reads a lot. Has two years of college. Squad sniper.

WEAPON: H&K PSG1 7.62 NATO sniper rifle or McMillan M-87R .50-caliber sniper rifle.

Joe "Ricochet" Lampedusa. Operations Specialist Third Class. 21, 5'11", 175 pounds. Good tracker, quick thinker. Had a year of college. Loves motorcycles. Wants a Hog. Pot smoker on the sly. Picks up plain girls. Platoon scout.

WEAPON: Colt M-4A1 with grenade launcher.

Kenneth Ching. Quartermaster's Mate First Class. Full-blooded Chinese. 25, 6'0", 180 pounds. Platoon translator. Speaks Mandarin Chinese, Japanese, Russian, and Spanish. Bicycling nut. Paid $1,200 for off-road bike. Is trying for Officer Candidate School.

WEAPON: Colt M-4A1 rifle with grenade launcher.

Harry "Horse" Ronson. Electrician's Mate Second Class. 24, 6'4", 240 pounds. Played football two years at college. Wants a ranch where he can raise horses. Good man in a brawl. Has broken his nose twice. Squad machine gunner.

WEAPON: H&K 21-E 7.62 NATO round machine gun.

BRAVO SQUAD

Lieutenant (j.g.) Ed DeWitt. Leader Bravo Squad. Second in Command of the platoon. From Seattle. 30, 6'1", 175 pounds. Wiry. Has serious live-in woman. Annapolis grad. A career man. Plays a good game of chess on traveling board.

WEAPON: The new H&K G-11 submachine gun.

George "Petard" Canzoneri. Torpedoman's Mate First Class. 27, 5'11", 190 pounds. Married to Navy wife Phyllis. No kids. Nine years in Navy. Expert on explosives. Nicknamed "Petard" for almost hoisting himself one time. Top pick in platoon for explosive work.

WEAPON: The new Alliant "Bull Pup" 20mm 5.56 attack rifle.

Miguel Fernandez. Gunner's Mate First Class. 26, 6'1", 180 pounds. Has wife and child in Coronado. Spends his off time with them. Highly family-oriented. He has family in San Diego. Speaks Spanish, Portuguese. Squad sniper.

WEAPON: H&K PSG1 7.62 NATO sniper rifle.

Colt "Guns" Franklin. Yeoman Second Class. 24, 5'10", 175 pounds. A former gymnast. Powerful arms and shoulders. Expert mountain climber. Has a motorcycle, and does hang gliding. Speaks Farsi and Arabic.

WEAPON: Colt M-4A1 with grenade launcher.

Les Quinley. Torpedoman Third Class. 22, 5'9", 160 pounds. A computer and Internet fan. Has his own Web page. Always reading computer magazines. Explosives specialist with extra training.

WEAPON: H&K G-11 with caseless rounds, 4.7mm submachine gun with 50-round magazine.

Jack Mahanani. Hospital Corpsman First Class. 25, 6'4", 240 pounds. Platoon Medic. Tahitian/Hawaiian. Expert swimmer. Bench-presses 400 pounds. Once married, divorced. Top surfer. Wants the .50 sniper rifle.

WEAPON: Colt M-4A1 with grenade launcher.

Anthony "Tony" Ostercamp. Machinist Mate First Class. Second radio operator. Races stock cars in nearby El Cajon weekends. Top auto mechanic. Platoon driver.

WEAPON: H&K 21-E 7.62 NATO round machine gun.

Paul "Jeff" Jefferson. Engineman Second Class. Black man. ~~23~~, 6'1", 200 pounds. Expert in small arms. Can tear apart most weapons and reassemble them, repair, and innovate. A chess player to match Ed DeWitt.

WEAPON: Colt M-4A1 with grenade launcher.

This book is sincerely dedicated to
Kathleen Tucker who stays the helm, who
keeps the household afloat and who
dedicates her time and effort to the care,
comfort and well-being of Rose Marie.
May she always be on board.

NOTE TO THE READER

Welcome to the land of the U.S. Navy SEALs and
their remarkable exploits on land and sea and in the
air. We hope you're excited about the SEALs and
their exploits. I'd like to hear from you to get some
input about how you feel about the series, the
characters, and the types of actions they have been
involved in.

Take a minute out of your busy day to drop me a line
or a whole letter. Send it to:

Keith Douglass
SEAL TEAM SEVEN
8431 Beaver Lake Drive
San Diego, CA 92119.

You bet, I'll make sure to read and respond to every
letter. Why not stop reading right now and send me a
letter? I'll appreciate it.

—Keith Douglass
San Diego

1

Gulf of Oman

The fifteen members of SEAL Team Seven sprawled in the comparative spaciousness of the Pegasus Class Mk V (SOC/PBF). It was a Navy patrol boat specifically designed to insert and withdraw SEALs and other Special Forces on covert operations.

Lieutenant Commander Blake Murdock checked his men. This was a surprise flashpoint kind of a mission. They had no notice, just orders to get moving. No time to rehearse or plan out in detail what they would do.

Senior Chief Will Dobler grinned at his commander. "No sweat, Cap. We've done little ones like this a dozen times."

Murdock lifted his brows. "Yeah, but some more planning would have been good. Now we just go in and do it, the first time."

The Pegasus was eighty-two feet long and had an extremely low profile that was loaded with radar-absorbing material on its forward and rear cabin areas. Even the low-slung bow had the radar-absorbing material.

Now it slammed through the calm waters of the Gulf of Oman off southern Iran at its top speed of forty-five knots.

Commander Murdock had to shout to be heard over the rumble of the two MTU twelve-volt diesel engines that turned out 4,506 horsepower to work the two Kamewa water jets that jolted the slender craft through the water.

"You know most of it," Murdock said. "We go in at first dark, have all night to recon the place, plant our charges, and get ready for the big show about 0800 tomorrow when the curtain goes up. At least that's the way it's set up. We know nothing of current guards around this complex. Not one damn thing."

"Sure we got enough goop?" Radioman First Class Ron Holt asked. "Sounds like we got one shit pot full of junk to blow sky high."

"True, lots of stuff out there, but we're covered. That's why each of you has a drag bag loaded with C-4 and TNAZ."

"What if somebody spots us doing our work?" Engineman Second Class Paul Jefferson asked. "Hey, us black guys don't blend in too damn good with the fucking Muslims."

"We play it cool if we can. We want as few of their dead bodies out there as possible tonight. It could be a warning and get their guard up. Remember, all of these fuckers out there are terrs. We take anybody out, we have to tonight or early in the A.M., but we do it silently. Your knives will be best here."

"This sale yard is a half mile long?" Quartermaster's Mate First Class Kenneth Ching asked.

Boatswain's Mate First Class and Senior Chief Petty Officer Willard Dobler took that question.

"Yeah. Alpha Squad has the right-side quarter mile and Bravo Squad works the left four forty. We spread out over the length of the place, and when activity slows down about midnight, we move in, take out any guards we have to, then plant our goop and get the hell out of there. No timers to set. All will be detonated with radio signals."

"All this work for a damn rummage sale?" Machinist Mate First Class Tony Ostercamp asked. "Hell, couldn't six

F-18s off the carrier do just as much damage in less time?"

"They could," Murdock said. "The only trouble is world-wide public opinion would be against us on this one. We maintain that the mother of all flea markets of terrorists' favorite weapons and other missiles of war and terrorism should not be held. It's such an array of weapons that terrorists want that it's caused an uproar in several countries. Our satellites have been printing out pictures for two days of a glut of terrorist treasures. We want to destroy all of it we can.

"We knew that such a sale could not benefit the world in any way, yet could arm hard-core terrorists and hate mongers for ten years. That's why we go in covertly, do the business, and get out without anyone tagging any country as the hit men."

"Hey, glad for the work," Torpedoman Third Class Les Quinley said. "I can use the overtime pay."

That brought a chorus of wails and cheers.

"Somebody say that the old fox Osama bin Laden is behind this full table?" asked Electrician's Mate Second Class Harry Ronson.

Murdock looked at Ronson. "That's the word we have. Bin Laden is the multimillionaire who promotes terrorism on a worldwide scale. He recently moved from Sudan to Afghanistan, where he has his headquarters and training camps for terrorists. We raided him back in 1998 with Tomahawk missiles after who we think were his men bombed the two U.S. embassies in Africa earlier that year.

"It's reported that every year, bin Laden pumps millions of dollars of his inherited fortune into terrorist groups and supplies them with weapons. This huge fire sale of everything the terrorists want is believed to have been arranged and highly subsidized by the bin Laden millions."

"What if we miss something, don't get it planted with a bomb?" Machinist Mate Second Class and Lead Petty Officer David "Jaybird" Sterling asked.

"We won't," Senior Chief Dobler said. "When you go in, you'll be in pairs. You start planting your charges and move away from each other, planting your bombs on everything in sight. When you meet another SEAL working toward you, you'll know that you have covered your fifty-yard area. The two of you finish and shag ass out of there."

The snarl of the diesels slowed, then came close to stopping. The slender boat coasted to a halt in the water. One of five crewmen on the craft came into the compartment. He wore the stripes of a Lieutenant (j.g.).

"Men, we're ten miles off the objective, Chah Bahar, Iran. Their radar can't pick us up from here. We'll wait here until first dark and then move in slowly to your disembarkment point a half mile off the beach. The last mile will be at five knots. Any questions?"

"You'll be picking us up, Lieutenant?" the senior chief asked.

"That's not clear yet. It could be a sub, might be choppers, or it could be me. That will be worked out, and you'll be informed by SATCOM before you get wet coming back."

"Good. Otherwise, it's a long swim to the carrier," Dobler cracked, and the SEALs laughed, glad for something to break the tension.

"We estimate we'll be under way again in about fifteen minutes. Then we'll need about forty minutes to get you ready to splash."

"Thanks, Captain," Murdock said, using his title as captain of the small craft. The officer nodded and left.

"Double-check your gear again," Murdock said. "We'll use the rebreathers all the way as soon as we splash. Last report was that this beach was a gentle slope and sandy, but a recent storm may have turned it a dozen ways from there."

The SEALs did as they had dozens of times before on missions and on training runs. All the men, even the officers, had undergone the six months of rigorous training that became a boot camp hell of cold, water, explosions, more water, long hikes, no sleep, working the problems, and live

fire exercises, until they wanted to scream and run somewhere that they could get warm, dry, and go to sleep. More
than 60 percent of the Tadpoles who started SEAL training
quit and went back to regular Navy duty.

Murdock watched his men. He had been blooded with
all but one of them on the last two missions. His one new
man, George "Petard" Canzoneri, had been a find. He was
the top demolition man in the whole of Team Seven. He
could make C-4 and TNAZ do work that nobody else could.
Lieutenant (j.g.) Ed DeWitt had found him as they searched
for a man to replace Al Adams.

For a moment, Murdock was worried about DeWitt not
being along on the mission. He still hadn't recuperated
enough from his chest wound in Iran to get back into training. Senior Chief Dobler had been leading Bravo Squad
through the last two months of training. If Ed didn't make
it back into the team in another two weeks, he'd have to
be replaced by a new squad leader.

Murdock heard the big diesels stir, then turn out more
power. They were moving at what he figured was twenty
knots. Four of his SEALs had finished final checking on
their gear and were sleeping. He grinned. Yeah, they were
loose. This was a simple little mission that Don Stroh had
briefed them on two days ago.

"Directly from the President and the CIA chief," Stroh
had said. A day later, they were on the plane and then to
the carrier and now a half hour from Iran. But it would be
only a twenty-four-hour mission, if that long.

Fifteen minutes later, Murdock looked out the slanted
front windows of the Pegasus's cabin and saw lights onshore.

"Two miles off, Commander," the captain told him.
"We're at seven knots now, coming down to five. How
close do you want me to take you?"

"Half mile should be safe for you. Dark as hell out there
tonight. What happened to the moon?"

"It's on the wane," the Lieutenant said. "Don't think it
comes up until over the horizon tonight.

"Good."

Ten minutes later, the SEALs splashed into the Gulf of Oman, tied on their six-foot-long buddy cords, took their compass sightings, and headed for shore, swimming fifteen feet below the surface. The first man to touch land would wait for the rest, staying submerged.

Ken Ching found Iranian soil first and put down both feet, then backed up so he'd stay underwater. The rest of the men assembled, and the squad leaders counted heads. All present.

One by one, the SEALs surged shoreward with the waves, coming to rest on the beach sand, looking like long, motionless black logs. Murdock went first, using two waves to get in just out of the heavy surf. He unhooked his re-breather and, without moving, checked the shoreline.

Yes, sandy, no habitation. It had been cleared years ago of shacks and houses when they built the military air base; then the Iranian Air Force moved to a better location. The land remained undeveloped.

When First Squad hit the sand with its weapons pointing shoreward, Murdock came up to a crouch, then ran with his wet cammies pasted against his legs. On such a short swim, they elected not to wear wet suits. He pulled on his wet, floppy hat and slid in behind a small mound of sand that had been half claimed by hearty beach grass.

He sensed the other SEALs leaving the wet and lining up ten yards apart down the beach on both sides of him. Slowly, he lifted up and peered over the small dune.

Yes, he could see lights, lots of lights, as if it were a carnival or a huge outdoor display area. Which is what it was supposed to be. He heard some small motors running, generators probably, for some of the individual display areas. Then the flat snarl of an AK-47 jolted through the air with six rounds, then six more.

Someone slid into the sand beside Murdock.

"Somebody checking to see if a weapon fires," Operations Specialist Second Class Joe "Ricochet" Lampedusa said. He was the platoon's best tracker and lead scout.

"How far to them?" Murdock whispered.

"Half a mile, maybe a little more. A long flat space to come back across in daylight with them fuckers shooting at us."

"We fix it so not many of them are able to shoot at us," Murdock said. He took the Motorola out of his waterproof pouch on his combat vest. The Motorola was a person-to-person communication radio for short distances. Each of the SEALs had one. A belt pack contained the operational transceiver and battery. A wire led to an earplug and attached lip mike. When Murdock had his radio in place and saw that Lampedusa did as well, he spoke.

"Radio check, Alpha."

One by one, the seven men in Alpha Squad checked in. Then Murdock heard Senior Chief Dobler call for a radio check on Bravo Squad. All present and accounted for.

"Half mile to our objective. We'll move in our usual twin diamonds, but at half speed. No rush. Full dark now, and our job planting the explosives shouldn't take more than two hours, even if we run into some opposition. Drag bags. Let's dump them here and hang the goodies around your neck, in your belt, any way you can. We don't want to pull those fuckers over the ground."

Only Murdock and Lam had NVGs, Night Vision Goggles. Murdock pulled his down from where they had perched on his head and checked the objective. The pale green glow gave him a clear look at the sales area. They were at the back of it. Evidently, there was one long line of booths and display areas that faced the other way. There could be an old runway they were working on. He watched for security.

It was barely 2100. Many men still milled around, evidently working on their displays, getting them ready for the rush of customers in the morning.

Now and then, a light blinked out, and Murdock figured they should stay put for a while. He hoped the place would be deserted by the time they got there to place the explosives.

He frowned as he saw a soldier walking what must be a guard post. He went behind two shapes that must be tents, then moved thirty yards north and went back between displays.

Lam groaned beside him. "See that fucking guard?"

"Yeah. Complicates things."

Murdock used the Motorola. "We've spotted some Army guards patrolling. Changes things. We'll hunker down here and wait until all the lights go out. By that time, we'll figure out what to do about the guards and our whole timing operation."

They moved forward slowly for a quarter of a mile and found a small ravine a hundred yards from the display that would hide them. The SEALs spread out and settled down. Murdock, Dobler, Lam, and Jaybird talked it over.

Jaybird had watched the sales area and reported what looked like a series of guards who were on the whole layout.

"No chance we can get in and get out without being spotted," Jaybird said. "If we take out three or four of the guards, they'll find that out in a rush, and we'll have to fight our way in and out. They might not want to give us a hell of a lot of time to booby-trap all of those goods."

"How about a diversion?" Lam said. "We can use the forty-mikes to cause a problem for them two hundred yards the other side of the strip. They bug out over there, we put down the charges and haul ass out of there before they get back."

"Yeah, but would all of the guards go out there, or do they have a company of troops somewhere waiting for trouble?" Dobler asked.

"Probably," Murdock said. "We've got to count on them having a good-sized force here. Iran doesn't want a black eye, especially on bin Laden's show. So we go with the worst scenario. If it doesn't happen, we're glad and get the job done and get our asses back in the water."

They all looked at the objective again through the glasses.

"I figure about twenty guards," Lam said. "They each seem to have a zone about twenty-five yards long. They go around and around."

"We move in and take out ten of them," Dobler said. "On their next round, we take out the other ten. Then we dig in and plant our bombs and TNAZ and get the hell out."

"How long to plant all the goods?" Murdock asked.

Jaybird shrugged. "Each of us has fifty yards. That's maybe twenty bombs. I've got thirty. By rushing and having the detonators in first, we should be able to do it in twenty minutes."

Murdock rubbed his face with one hand. He needed a shave.

"So, say we try it that way. We snuff half the guards, and ten minutes later, they make the second round and we get the rest. If all goes right, we have twenty minutes to lay down the explosives and haul ass.

"If things get out of hand, say there's a shot or two fired by the guards, that would alert the rest of the forces and a jeep or two. Then we send out our forty-mikes on my command and create our diversion. We hope to drain off the manpower there until we get done with the goop."

"They'll know they've been hit by then and come right here to the prize and start checking," Lam said. "No way we can wait until morning to blow the bombs."

"Why they give us that time line, anyway?" Dobler asked.

"Said they wanted to catch the buyers in the area and snuff as many of them as possible."

"Probably won't go down that way," Jaybird said.

Murdock looked back at the target. "Fewer lights now. One generator must still be working."

"By 2400, that place will be dead black," Lam said. "I hope."

Murdock called up Petard Canzoneri.

"Yes, sir, all ready to go. Each man has enough explosives for twenty bombs. He also has twenty detonator

receivers. They will be handed out in groups of sixty, working from one end of the line to the other. Each group of sixty detonators will have a separate frequency to explode the bombs."

"Not all at once?" Murdock asked.

"No, sir. I don't have that many hands. This way I can work from one end, or from both ends, or from the middle outward, depending which will do the most damage."

"Sounds like a good plan, Canzoneri. Get some rest. We won't be moving for some time."

The plans made, they waited. Murdock knew they had five grenade launchers. On command, each man with a carbine would launch four rounds across the target and well inland to maximum range.

He had posted guards, one on each end of the SEALs' gully, and one in the center, all watching the target. None of the Iranian Army men had even looked outward toward the SEALs' location.

They waited.

At midnight, Murdock checked the target again through the NVGs. He had trouble finding any lights. At last he made out two, both small. Next he searched for the guards. Yes. There was one. He timed the man's circuit. It was fifteen minutes before a guard appeared at the same spot. Probably the same man.

Lam slid into the sand beside Murdock.

"I make their rounds every fifteen minutes," Lam said.

"Agreed. Senior Chief, are you awake?"

"Ready," came the sound over Murdock's earpiece.

"Work with Canzoneri and spread out the men so we can take the guards. Also have him give the men the twenty detonators in the sequence he wants. Have them put the detonator-receivers into the bombs. Do it now."

"That's a roger."

Ten minutes later, the radio earpiece spoke.

"All men in position," Commander. "All detonators given out in the proper sequence. We're ready."

"Good, Senior Chief. Let's move up slowly. Everyone

will stop twenty yards from the tents and displays. When the guards come, dispatch them silently. Let's move."

Murdock checked the line with his NVGs. The fourteen other SEALs were in line and moving forward.

They were twenty yards from the target when the men began dropping to the ground. Murdock went with them. Directly ahead, he saw a guard come around the corner of a bright blue tent. He didn't even look toward them. Instead, he stopped and lit a cigarette, cupping the glow of the smoke. Murdock was closest to the man. He waited until the guard turned away, then Murdock unsheathed his KA-BAR fighting knife and moved silently forward. The last four steps, he ran. The Iranian must have heard his footsteps. He started to turn just as the blade drove deeply under his left arm into his heart. He went down, dead, like a head-shot steer.

Murdock took the AK-47 and checked it. Loaded. He looked down the line and saw two other SEALs moving up to the tents and display tables. He heard no sounds. Good. He waited four or five minutes, then used the radio.

"Alpha Squad, how many guards down?"

He knew the voices. Four responded. His made five. That left fifteen. "Bravo Squad, how many terrs down?" Six different voices answered. That made eleven. Maybe they could pull it off. Another ten minutes, and he saw more guards through the NVGs moving around the backs of the displays.

He saw one man go down, then a second.

Before anything else happened, a piercing scream shattered the Iranian night, then the flat blasts of a dozen AK-47 rounds ripped through the air. Another voice shrilled. He heard the chugs of a silenced weapon near him. Somewhere a siren went off.

Murdock hit the mike. "Shoot those forty-mikes. Four rounds each. Fire now. Everybody plant those charges."

Murdock ran to the front of the tent and ducked inside. The tent was filled with 105 rounds and stacks of bags of gunpowder. He pushed two charges under the gunpowder.

Sympathetic explosions should wipe out all of the rounds as well. He ran outside and began working to his left.

By now, he wasn't sure that the double teams were intact. They would plant what bombs they could and haul ass when the fresh Iranian troops arrived.

He had heard the forty-mikes being fired and exploding well inland. He hoped that drew most of the others on hand. More sirens wailed. He saw a pair of headlights racing up the old concrete runway toward them.

Before the rig came into the range of Murdock's MP-5, a longer SEAL gun knocked out the lights and the rig itself with six rounds.

Murdock kept placing the bombs and checking the detonators. He'd never seen such a variety of weapons and ammunition. He had a glimpse of a jet aircraft of some kind and several armored personnel carriers down the way.

Machinist's Mate First Class Tony Ostercamp and Paul Jefferson had killed the guard they surprised and now came to the white tent. To the left side, they found tables piled high with assault rifles, machine guns, and boxes of ammo.

Jefferson worked there. Ostercamp waved and headed the other way to the tent. Jefferson wrapped charges around two AK-47s at the bottom of the pile. He moved to his right to an orderly layout of RPGs, rocket-propelled grenades. It took him only a few seconds to bury a quarter-pound charge of TNAZ under the stack and push in more securely the electronic detonator. He looked to his right.

Something moved.

He waited. The shadow he had seen stepped forward cautiously. Jefferson was glad his black face and hands wouldn't show in the darkness of the moonless night. The figure took two more strides forward, then turned to look behind. The guard held an Ingram submachine gun.

Jefferson froze in place, waiting. Another four steps. The man checked behind him again, then came forward.

Jefferson leaped upward at the last moment before the guard would have stepped on him. His KA-BAR knife drove out at the end of his stiff arm like a spear. It slashed through soft cloth, glanced off a rib, and penetrated deeply into the Iranian's heart. The man slumped forward, dead without a sound.

Jefferson caught him before he fell. The Ingram came between them and wedged in as Jefferson dragged the man behind the table of weapons. He found a canvas and hid the body under it, cleaned off his KA-BAR on the dead man's shirt, and sheathed it.

He could hear small arms fire inland. He hoped that the forty-mikes drew off some troops. He knelt and looked around. He saw no more guards. They were either dead or hiding. A grenade blew up fifty yards down the long line of arms.

Jefferson went back to his work on the weapons. Next he came to an armored personnel carrier, a small, fast almost-tank that could haul eight to ten men into battle sporting a fair amount of armored protection. He pried off the fuel tank filler tube, pushed an eighth pound of TNAZ into the tube, and reset the electronic detonator.

Jefferson put a quarter pound of TNAZ on the underside of the engine block where it wouldn't be easily found.

The next display was inside a tent. He unzipped the doorway and went in. A sleeping man jolted upright, lifting a pistol. Jefferson's boot slammed into his jaw, pivoting his head upward and backward, breaking his neck in a millisecond. The pistol fell out of his hand before his death spasms could jerk his dying finger on the trigger.

Jefferson found nobody else in the tent. Inside were six tables loaded with radios and simple radar equipment, enough to outfit at least a battalion. Jefferson strung primer cord around a dozen of the most complicated units, then put three one-eighth-pound chunks of TNAZ on radios, under tables, and in various spots where they might not be easily seen. He hoped the first man into the tent in the morning figured the primer cord was large electrical lead wiring.

When he finished, Jefferson dragged the dead man outside and put him behind the tent. Jefferson broke off some desert brush and covered him, then continued his work to the right. He heard more weapons fire. Far down at the end of the display, he saw some winking lights as weapons were fired his way. He could hear no rounds hitting.

His sector here was fifty. By then he should meet another SEAL working toward him from the other direction. He left the white tent and had started to look at the next display of shoulder-fired missiles when he felt something jab into his back.

"Do not even twitch, American SEAL. I have seen you people work before. Don't even think about moving or breathing, or I'll blow you in half with my machine gun."

2

Chah Bahar, Iran

Paul Jefferson knew what a gun muzzle in the back felt like. This was the real thing. He didn't have a clue who held it.

"What the hell's the matter with you, muthafucka? I'm here on security just the shit like you is. Take a good look at me. Hell, I'm black as a burned-out hutch. Get that stick outa my back."

There was a soft laugh, then the man whose speech had a trace of English accent came again.

"Oh, yeah, you're good at acting, too. Now, turn your ass around real slow, so I can watch your bastard eyes as I gut shoot you and see you learn what real pain is. Now, turn slow, slow, and don't get near that weapon in your hideout. Easy, now."

Jefferson turned with short, shuffling steps until he faced the man. He was six inches shorter than the SEAL, but the Ingram with a long magazine made him just as tall and twice as ugly. He wasn't black, but he wasn't white, either. Some kind of Iranian, maybe.

"Now, shithead, how many of you American SEALs here, a whole platoon?"

"Like I said, I'm on guard duty here for some special friends. We don't got to tell you bastards nothing."

The gunman slammed a pistol down across Jefferson's head, and he staggered back a step.

The *pfffffttt* came softly. The short Iranian in military cammies standing in front of Jefferson staggered to the left. Something blasted out the side of his head and took bone, blood, and gray matter with it. The small desert animal sounds shut off at once when the silenced weapon spoke. The terr collapsed to the left, dropping the Ingram from dead fingers before he hit the ground.

"Jeff, you all right?"

The whispered words came from the front, where a dark figure crouched near a stack of missile boxes.

"Oh, yeah, dandy now that this dude is dead. Mahanani?"

The big Tahitian/Hawaiian rushed forward and touched the dead man's throat for a moment, then grabbed the Ingram and with one hand, and dragged the corpse back between the displays.

"What took you so long?" Jefferson asked.

"Playing with this bang-bang shit is not my forte," Mahanani said. "You do the missiles yet?"

Jeff shook his head, and they both worked bombs into unlikely places where they wouldn't be seen come daylight.

"Look at these things," Mahanani said. "A whole damn stack of Stingers. Even these with the two-point-two-pound warhead can bring down a fighter or a commercial airliner. They'll do Mach one for three miles. Damn, where do these fuckers get this kind of shit?"

"Buy them or steal them," Jefferson said. "We done here?"

"Yeah, I come up to you just at the right time. I saw another guard, but I went around him." Mahanani looked closely at Jefferson. "Man, you been under a gun before. He really spook you?"

"He said he knew I was a SEAL. How the hell he know that? Who was he?"

"Iranian, from the looks. I've seen them before. Now, let's get those last missile stacks over there. Shit. Look, Sidewinder air-to-air missiles. Almost ten feet long, with twenty pounds of warhead. They'll do Mach two at least and reach out for ten to twelve miles. Man, where do they get this shit?"

They heard AK-47s stuttering to the north of them. An MP-5 answered on full auto.

"Getting hot in here, brother," Mahanani said. "We better do these two and split."

"I'm with you, buddy."

They put two quarter pounds of TNAZ on the inside boxes of the missiles. The blast would create a sympathetic reaction and should explode each of the Stinger warheads. Their propulsion systems also might ignite, and they could take off like twisted snakes in a circus.

The two SEALs moved away from the missiles, working straight back for fifty yards, and joined the other men who had finished planting their bombs.

Ten minutes later, all the SEALs were there.

Lampedusa had come back from a scouting mission. He talked to Murdock a few minutes, then the leader gathered them around him.

"Any casualties?" He paused and looked around in the darkness. Nobody spoke up. "We ran into more security than we figured. I'd say at least a company is working up the street. They won't think to look for bombs, but we'll need to blow them as soon as we get back a safe distance. So our job is half done. Better shag it out of here.

"Lam has found our new home. About three hundred yards over, there are some small dunes that get up to fifty feet. Highest ground around here. We'll get on the far side and work out our firing positions. Squad order, ten yards apart. Soon as we get into position, Canzoneri is gonna blow them. Let's go do it."

Ten minutes later, they had their firing spots picked out

and customized as much as possible. They would fire over the top of the dune from the safety of the reverse slope as necessary and have a clear run for the beach, which was now about 600 yards behind them. The tide would change that one way or the other.

"Okay, Canzoneri, you ready?"

"All set, Commander."

"Then do it. Any sequence you want."

"I'll start down where the troops were and work up toward us. We should be clear back here."

Canzoneri took a black box from his combat vest and lifted a two-foot telescoping antenna and looked at Murdock. The commander gave him a thumbs-up.

Canzoneri pushed the toggle switch, and at once the far end of the display line erupted in a series of explosions. They were followed by sympathetic detonations that lit up the countryside for half a mile.

The SEALs ducked below the dune.

Canzoneri walked the explosions up the display half mile. As one died down, he triggered the next one.

"Incoming!" somebody shouted.

One of the missiles launched itself and made a winding trail a hundred feet into the air, then slammed straight at the SEALs but kept the altitude and went all the way into the Gulf of Oman, where it detonated.

Now they could see other missiles bouncing across the land. In flashes of light they saw the tents burn away, saw one six-by truck explode, and the fuel from the tank set two other trucks on fire.

The jet fighter went up in a huge mushroom cloud as the aviation fuel exploded, showering blazing JP-3 over a hundred yards of displays.

Two minutes after Canzoneri triggered the first bomb, the last section exploded in a roiling gush of flames and nearly white-hot light. The 105 artillery shells detonated with withering *karumph* sounds and dirt, tents, and displays flew every which way.

"Holt," Murdock bellowed. "Get your big ears on, we're

hauling ass now. Move it, everyone. Straight for the wet. We get SATCOM going before then. We're bound to have company soon."

"Captain, we've got some trouble." It was Jaybird.

Murdock caught the message in his earpiece. "What, Jaybird?"

"Spotted a vehicle with lights on patrolling behind us. He made two circles, then stopped and conferred with three men in front of his headlights."

"So?"

"I used my glasses and I saw him use a radio, a handi-talki type. My bet is he called for some more troops or maybe some air support to work this area."

"Possible. We keep moving, we should be wet before they can find us. Holt, where's the damn SATCOM?"

"Need to stop a minute and get the antenna aimed," Holt said. "Take about two minutes. Can we do that?"

"Hold it, troops," Murdock said on the radio. "Move to the reverse slope of this small dune so we're out of sight of the blast. For a few minutes it's SATCOM time."

They stopped behind the dunc. Jaybird crawled up so he could watch the smoke and destruction of a few million dollars' worth of useless rubble. Holt aimed the antenna and passed the handset to Murdock.

"Set for voice, Commander."

He hit the Send button. "Floater, this is Petard. Read me?"

They waited a moment. It stretched out. He sent out the message again. On the third try, someone replied.

"Petard, this is Floater. You're early."

"Change in plans. Blew the field early. We nailed the whole half mile. Nothing left out there but smoking rubble. They had the army guarding the place. Total destruction. Rounds still exploding. On our way for a swim. Time is 0115. Need a wet pickup in thirty minutes."

"Understand. Stay dry if possible for now. Will reply in five."

Murdock gave the handset back to Holt. He still marveled at the SATCOM system. The SATCOM radio worked with the Milstar satellite in geosynchronous orbit 22,300 miles over the equator. It was officially the AN/PRC-117D, and it weighed fifteen pounds and was only fifteen inches long and three inches square. It had voice, data, or video transmission capability and could squirt out an encoded message in a hundredth of a second, foiling any enemy trying to triangulate its position. It could broadcast at a strong 10 watts of power for longer range or drop down to .1 watt for short distances and dangerous situations.

"Commander, we may have some trouble," Jaybird said. He had taken the NVGs to watch the blast scene. Murdock went up to the top of the dune and looked over. Murdock saw a line of four six-by trucks on their side of the destruction. One truck stopped every hundred yards and dropped off ten men, then moved on.

Lam moved up to the top of the dune with the other NVGs. "Three trucks, twenty men to a truck, about sixty of them," Lam said.

As they watched, they saw the men fan out in a line of skirmishers in a perimeter defense pointing at the SEALs. The Iranian soldiers went prone and some began digging in with entrenching tools.

"Too little, too late," Murdock said into his mike. "Nothing to guard anymore." Murdock took out his field glasses and scanned the ruins before him. He saw the shells of six trucks, both the blown-apart jet fighters, and skeletons of other equipment that had all been blasted and burned beyond any possible use. He looked at Holt.

"Holt, how long has it been since their last transmission?" Murdock asked.

Holt checked his wristwatch with the timer. "Two minutes, sir."

"Yeah, it goes fast when you're having fun."

Nobody heard the visitors until they were almost overhead. Then two Iranian jet fighters thundered across the scene. They came in at less than three hundred feet and scattered the smoke and ashes in the display. They made sharp turns and returned with throttles back for a slower look, then raced away to the north.

"They must have been baby-sitting the display, watching for any kind of an air attack," Murdock said.

"Commander, we've got company," Senior Chief Dobler's heavy voice said on the Motorola.

"Where and how many?" Murdock asked.

"Coming around the end of the display. Still about five hundred yards away, but they're heading straight for us. Two armored personnel carriers."

"I see them," Murdock said. "Must be doing thirty miles an hour. Bradford, you see them with your fifty?"

"Lined up in my sights with armor piercing, Cap'n. Locked and loaded."

"Take them."

The heavy crack of the big .50-caliber McMillan M-87R sniper rifle blasted into the darkness of the Iranian coastal desert. The first round was followed by four more. The second heavy AP slug bored through a chink in the front armament and splashed the radiator and continued into the engine itself before it exploded, shredding wires and lines, dumping the vehicle to the side, dead on the sand.

The second vehicle came closer. Two .50-caliber rounds on the driver's section made the rig veer to the left, but it kept coming. The fully tracked vehicle looked like a small tank. Inside, it could carry eight to ten fully equipped combat infantrymen.

Men sprayed out of the downed machine. They were 300 yards away.

"Let's take them down," Murdock said.

Up and down the line of SEALs, the carbines spoke along with the two machine guns and sniper rifles. Within ten seconds, the last of the ten Iranian soldiers spun and died in the sand from the accurate fire by the SEALs.

The second rig kept coming, angling now directly at where the firing had erupted against it. The rig had one side turret-mounted machine gun. Murdock figured it was a

12.7mm, which could do the SEALs a great deal of damage.

"Make up some impact bombs with your TNAZ," Murdock said into the lip mike. "Tape the impact fuses around the quarter-pound chunks. We need to blow that sucker's tracks off."

The AP carrier continued for the center of the SEALs' line but slowed and stopped when it was fifty yards off. Bradford had fired five more times at the rig but couldn't find a weak spot that his rounds would penetrate. He saw three of them bounce off the slanted armor.

"What the hell's he doing?" Jaybird asked on the Motorola.

"What would you be doing?" Senior Chief Dobler asked.

"Hell, I'd be wanting to know what was behind these dunes. Who my enemy was and his strength and weaponry."

"About what he's up to," Murdock said. "Maybe waiting for some help. He could call those jets back to make a strafing run. Now they know where the target is. Spread out, twenty yards between us. Holt. Get your electronic ass up here."

Holt had the SATCOM ready to go when he slid in beside Murdock and gave him the handset.

"Set for voice," Holt said.

Murdock took the mike and let out a deep breath. "Petard here. We've had visitors. Now more are showing up. Your five minutes are wasted. Time we got wet. Any air support over here? Come back."

The transmission went out in a thousandth of a second in a burst that was impossible to trace.

To Murdock's surprise, an answer came back at once.

"Floater says no chance of any friendly air. Get out of there as soon as practical. Wet pickup will be ready in thirty."

As they spoke, Murdock saw more Iranian army troops come from in back of the ruined display, form up into twenty squads of spread-out infantry, and begin a slow march toward the dead armored personnel carrier only fifty yards from the SEALs' cover.

"More company," Lam said. "Looks to be about a hundred and forty of them, all small arms, no heavy stuff or MGs. They have five hundred yards to go to get to the armored rig." He could barely see them through the pale darkness.

Just then, the Iranian jets paid another call. This time they were only 200 feet over the ground. The SEALs felt the wind whiplash around them as the jets sucked the air after them.

Murdock scowled. "In about fifteen minutes, we're going to have more trouble than we need. A hundred and forty troops with a mad on, one machine gun on that AP carrier, and those two damn jets rigged for air-to-ground fire."

Jaybird grunted. "Yeah, but then that's about our usual odds. Looks fairly simple to me. We take out the ground troops when they get close enough. Hell, they're in the open. Then we blast that junior-sized tank with TNAZ and hightail it for the wet."

Murdock lifted his brows with wonder. Jaybird was always the optimist. Just then, the Iranian jets came blasting over again, evidently taking one more look before they started shooting.

"Net check. You homies spread out? I want twenty to thirty yards between your SEAL bodies. Sound off."

All fourteen men responded. Murdock looked up. The Iranian troops were within 200 yard of their position. The armored personnel carrier started its engine and began to move forward slowly. Just then, he heard the Iranian jets. Something had to give. In another two hours it would be daylight.

3

Chaa Bahar, Iran

Murdock watched the armored personnel carrier moving forward, it's 12.7mm machine gun swinging slowly side to side, searching for a target. In the distance he could hear the jets making their high-speed turns. The Iranian infantry had come out of their prone positions and moved forward at a deadly pace.

"Jaybird, what's the universal signal to mark a target for fast-moving jets?"

Jaybird grinned. "Oh, yeah, Commander. Red flares."

"So, Lead Petty Officer, drop three red flares on those advancing troops out there damn quick."

The words went over the net, and the whole team knew the plan.

"I got one," Jaybird said. "Sound off as you load. Who else?"

"Yeah, one in the hole," Mahanani said.

Jaybird fired. A moment later, Murdock heard another flare launched and then a third. Two flares hit just in front of the advancing troops. The third one was right beside the personnel carrier, and glowed in the darkness.

Then the jets came storming in. Murdock wondered at the surprise of the pilots at the target designation. They'd make split microsecond decisions and follow their training.

Before Murdock turned to watch for the jets, they thundered overhead, having launched their payload seconds earlier. Three air-to-ground missiles jolted into the Iranian soil and exploded with a deadly rain of shrapnel. One took out two squads of the infantry. The second one blasted the armored personnel carrier into a flaming mass of twisted metal. The third round hit behind the advancing troops.

The entire line of Iranian soldiers hesitated.

"Let's get them," Murdock said and slammed off three rounds from his H&K MP-5 submachine gun. The high-speed 9mm and .223 zingers pounded the Iranians from all guns. They were joined by the machine guns and the H&K G-11 caseless rounds.

Ten seconds into the firing, Murdock called on the net.

"Bravo Squad men, put forty-mikes out there." The men in Bravo Squad with the 40mm grenade launchers switched to the small bombs and scattered them along the line of march by the Iranians.

Half of the force fell and didn't get up. In places, a squad of seven moved unhurt through the storm of lead. Another twenty seconds into the fight, and the Iranians began to waver, then one squad turned and ran to the rear. Two men from another squad tried to run back, but Horse Ronson picked them off with his NATO round machine gun.

Ten seconds later it was all over. Forty of the 140 who began the fight ran flat out to the rear. Only a few of those still had weapons.

"Cease fire," Murdock said, and the SEALs' weapons silenced.

"Lets go get wet," Murdock said. He heard some cheers over the radio net, then the SEALs pushed down the reverse slope so they could stand without being seen and jogged toward the surf some 500 yards away.

"Lam and I will pull rear guard, Mueller, get the men into

the water with rebreathers and head ninety degrees away from the shoreline, due south. Go, go, go."

Lam and Murdock lay in the sand, their camouflaged floppy hats barely showing over the top of the dune. A few more stragglers hurried to the safety of the burned-out display. Murdock saw half a dozen wounded struggling to get to the rear as well.

"The jets didn't come back for a second shot," Lam said.

"Maybe they figured they had finished their job," Murdock said. "Or maybe somebody used a radio and told them to get lost." They watched for five minutes, and nobody moved toward the dunes. Murdock slid backward and motioned to Lam. They went downslope far enough to stand up without being seen and then jogged toward the beach.

Ahead, Murdock saw his men taking off their radios and putting them in the waterproof pouches; then they slung their weapons across their backs. Dobler checked each man, then slapped him on the back, and the SEAL went into the water. Dobler waited on the beach for Murdock and Lam.

When they ran up, Dobler waved. "Told the others to swim out for fifteen minutes, then surface and we get together."

Murdock nodded.

Murdock and Lam were ready. The three ran into the surf just as they heard shots fired behind them. The shooters were out of range. The SEALs dove under the first wave and let the rebreathers work their magic. They left no telltale trail of bubbles for an enemy to follow. The SEALs didn't take time to tie their buddy cords but stayed together as they stroked outward from the land.

When they could, they went down to fifteen feet and kept on their compass course.

Later, Lam touched Murdock's shoulder and pointed to his watch. Murdock looked upward, and he and Lam surfaced. Dobler was just ahead of them. They checked around the choppy blue waves. Murdock whistled sharply between his teeth and waited.

He grinned when they heard another whistle to the left.

They swam that way and found the twelve SEALs floating, talking, and treading water.

"Is that sonar beacon out?" Murdock asked.

"Yeah, Cap," Jaybird said. "Fact is, I've got two of them trailing from my vest."

Murdock looked back at the breaking waves.

"Less than a quarter of a mile off the beach. We better do another half mile, then come up for a peek. Buddy cords this time. Anybody get hit back there?"

Nobody reacted.

"Hell, Cap'n, don't think we took a single round of incoming," Yeoman Second Class "Guns" Franklin said. "Us and their own fly boys kicked shit out of them Iranians."

"That we did. Now, let's get some distance from the Islam republic back there."

They swam.

They checked at half a mile, then swam again for half an hour and came up at what Murdock figured was about three miles offshore. They had seen no patrol boats searching for them. Murdock knew that Iran had some patrol boats. He'd seen some of the ten Kamin class boats, 150 feet long with harpoon missiles and a three-inch gun. He didn't want to see one now.

They kept on the surface, and Jaybird made sure that the sonar tracking balls were out and functioning. They waited.

"No sense to go any farther offshore," Murdock said. "Iran doesn't seem to want to come look for us. Figures. The sale wasn't their show, they just rented the lot to old Osama bin Laden. They knew he could afford to take the loss. He dumps millions into terrorist groups every year.

Lam heard it first. He usually did.

"Chopper from the south. Must be one of ours."

"How can a chopper find us?" Gunner's Mate First Class Miguel Fernandez asked.

"Easy," Ken Ching said. "Two of our submarines take a bearing on our sonar, get a cross-check fix on us, and radio the bird. Same way they hunt down enemy subs."

They all watched the bird come toward them. Murdock fired off a green flare.

"It's a Chinook," Bradford said.

"No way. It's a Sea Knight, a CH-46E," Quinley yelped.

It came straight for them, slowed, and stopped a hundred feet away. It was a Sea Knight.

"SEALs, welcome back. Do you have any wounded?" It was a bullhorn from the chopper.

The men shook their heads.

"Very well. We'll do a rope ladder pickup. By the book. We'll come around into the wind for a hover."

"You know the drill," Murdock shouted. "Flippers around your necks. Line up. Bravo Squad first. Dobler, get them moving."

By that time, the chopper came in and hovered. The rope ladder just touched the water's surface. Franklin went up first. When he was on the third of the six rungs, Quinley grabbed the bottom rung.

It went like a training drill. Nobody slowed or stopped or fell off. It took just over four minutes for the fifteen SEALs to go up the ladder and inside the rear hatch of the Sea Knight.

Murdock shook hands with the crew chief, who closed the hatch.

"How far from the carrier?" Murdock asked.

"The lieutenant said it was about twenty minutes out here. Should be about the same back. Your men need anything?"

"Hot coffee and hot showers would be nice," Murdock said, and they both chuckled.

Thirty minutes later, the chopper set down on the carrier deck, and the SEALs dismounted. They took all their gear and hurried to their quarters for coffee, hot showers, and clean cammies before the debriefing began.

Murdock checked with the new man, Canzoneri.

"How'd it go, Canzoneri?"

"Fine, Commander. Just fine. Except for that damn rope ladder. Our unit never got to train on it. Some foul-up and then we didn't get back to it. That was one hell of a climb."

Murdock smiled and went to his quarters. Yes, the new man was going to blend into the Bravo Squad and the platoon just fine.

4

**NAVSPECWARGRUP-one
Navy SEALs Training HQ
Coronado, California**

Lieutenant Commander Blake Murdock eased into his desk chair in the cubicle he called his office and gave a huge sigh.

Master Chief Gordon MacKenzie chuckled where he stood at the other side of the polished and empty desktop. "Well, laddie sir, looks like you're happy to have your feet under home territory again."

Murdock leaned back in the chair and let out another sigh. "Oh, yes, Master Chief, this is a bit of heaven compared to where we've been. Not our longest mission, but one I'm still glad we're away from. Our boys did good."

"I read your after-action report, Commander, and bucked it on up to our boss man. He can't be overdispleased."

"I'm not about to worry about Dean Masciareli. What I want to know is how is our super splinter coming along?"

"Working out hard. Been at it every day for the past three weeks, near as I can tell. Saturday and Sundays as well."

"Why don't you just ask me?" a voice said from the

hallway. Lieutenant (j.g.) Ed DeWitt came in the door and stood at an exaggerated ramrod attention.

"Lieutenant (j.g.) DeWitt, reporting for regular duty, *sir.*" He shouted the last word the way the Tadpoles did in SEAL training.

Murdock put his hands over his eyes. "I wanted to come home to this?"

"Sir, I'm ready for full-load duty, Commander, *sir!*" Again DeWitt bellowed out the final word.

The master chief broke up laughing. Murdock shook his head and waved at DeWitt.

"Shut up and sit down, Ed, before the master chief here has a case of apoplexy or gets a hard-on. Damn, you've got loud. If your body is as strong as your voice, you've got a go."

DeWitt relaxed a little as he slumped in the visitor's chair across the desk from Murdock.

"I'm fit and strong and ready for duty, Murdock. I don't want to miss another assignment, even a twenty-four-hour picnic. I got cut out of all the fun. I've been training like a Tadpole. That damn BB shot that hit my chest is gone and healed and forgotten. Hell, I can do the OC a full minute faster than ever before. I'm a gold-plated, absolute fit and ready SEAL, itching for some action."

"Medics clear you?"

"Hey, that was two weeks ago. Cleared me for regular duty, and I've been at it hot and heavy—"

Murdock held up his hand. "Okay, we'll have some more training work, you keep up with us, and I'll punch your ticket to get back on board."

DeWitt pushed a clipping from a magazine across the desk.

"What's this, some Buck Rogers blue-sky weapon?" Murdock asked.

"No, sir, Commander," Master Chief MacKenzie said. "The JG showed it to me. It's one hell of a weapon. We bugged Don Stroh about it, and he did some fancy footwork."

Ed DeWitt jumped in. "The weapon is the new infantry rifle, and it's the most advanced I've ever heard about. It has two barrels. One fires a twenty-millimeter explosive fragmentation round with a proximity fuze. Damn, that means we can in effect shoot around corners and hit troops dug in on reverse slopes. It's a real winner."

"How heavy is it?" Murdock asked.

"The M-16 with the added-on goodies weighs in at twenty pounds. This Bull Pup scorcher is only fourteen pounds. Get a load of this. The critter has a video camera built in with a six-power scope, laser range finder, and a miniature fire control computer. The laser range finder pinpoints the precise distance where you want the fragmentation round to explode."

"This thing does all the work?" Master Chief MacKenzie asked.

Ed DeWitt shook his head. "Oh, hell no. You have to be able to hit your target with a laser beam so the weapon knows where the target is. Then it automatically determines the range and sets the fuze for the airburst directly on target."

"Who sets the damn fuze?" Murdock asked.

"Read up on that last night," DeWitt said. "It uses a turn-count fuzing system. The weapon gets the target information, knows the tech data on the ammunition, then the fire control system calculates the number of turns it takes the round to reach the target. The laser in the fire control sends pulses out to the target. It then analyzes each pulse and calculates the exact range. The fire control communicates that information to the fuze before the round exits the barrel. Damn fast, that is."

"So what did Don Stroh say?"

"Our CIA contact said he'd get us six of them from the factory, handmade for field evaluation. The company is still testing it and making changes. Hell, the army isn't scheduled to get this weapon until 2005."

"All that electronics," Murdock said. "What happens if it gets wet?"

"Not sure, but we won't let it get wet. Oh, one more item. Those twenty-millimeter fragmentation rounds with proximity fuzes. They cost thirty bucks a pop."

"Hell of a lot more than even a fifty caliber," Master Chief MacKenzie said. "Stroh said he could get us two of these fancy Bull Pups within forty-eight hours and the other four would take a month."

"Until then, we go with what we have," Murdock said. "Oh, who makes this new wonder weapon?"

"Best part," DeWitt said. "The prime contractor and inventor is Alliant Techsystems Inc. of Minnesota. The basic weapon frame comes from H&K in Germany. An outfit from Pittsburgh, Contraves Inc., supplies the fire control system, and Dynamit Nobel AG has developed the twenty-millimeter ammunition."

"So this Bull Pup would replace our Colt M-4A1 and the grenade launcher?" Master Chief MacKenzie asked.

"Could, and it would give us a lot more range," DeWitt said. "The M-203 grenade launcher is good for not much more than two hundred yards. This Bull Pup can reach out a thousand yards with pinpoint accuracy. If you can get the red dot on the target, you can kill it."

"Fine," Murdock said. "That's downstream. It sounds good, and we'll wring it out in trials as soon as it comes. Thirty dollars a round? Now, that's expensive rifle fire. So, what about today and tomorrow? JG, you have any kind of a training schedule worked out for the troops?"

"Figured you'd want one, boss, so I made one out. It's only slightly slanted to the types of work that I want."

"Sounds good. We missed you on that recent swim. Want you back in the saddle for whatever comes next. How is Milly?"

DeWitt dropped into the last chair in the room and rubbed his face with one hand. "Yeah, she's good. You know she was uptight about my war wound. But, slowly, she's come around. Almost back to normal. She said to ask you to come to a barbecue Sunday afternoon. You too, Master Chief."

Murdock looked at the master chief.

"Well, sounds good, JG, but I've got a family thing planned for that day."

Murdock grinned. "Yeah, be glad to get some of that 'cue, just so Milly does the cooking."

"Oh, she will. Now, here is what I had set for today's training." The master chief waved at them and went back to what he called "work at the quarterdeck." Murdock waved back. He remembered that the master chief always turned down their offers to socialize. They usually asked him, but he said no. He once explained to Murdock that he had ten platoons to worry about. He couldn't let it look like he favored one over the other.

"The men all took three-day liberty and are back ready," Ed DeWitt said. "It's just past 0900 hours, and they are checking weapons and equipment. Ready when you are, CB."

Murdock looked up and laughed. "By CB, you mean C. B. DeMille, the old-time movie director? I got that one. Let's see, a six-mile soft sand run, then a six-mile ocean swim without fins, then live firing at the hole. What happens in the afternoon?"

The platoon had been home for a week when the first two boxes arrived by special jet to North Island, then by car directly to the Third Platoon's office. Third Platoon had just returned from a live firing run into the San Diego east county hills, and the men were checking out lunch.

Lieutenant (j.g.) DeWitt stared at the boxes for a full minute before he took out a pocketknife and cut the tape that sealed them.

Inside, he and Murdock found the first fully assembled and ready-to-shoot Bull Pup rifle. It glowed in its all-black splendor.

"Go ahead," Murdock said.

DeWitt picked it up and hefted it, then settled the butt plate against his shoulder and looked through the six-power scope.

"Wow, I love this shooter," DeWitt said. He caught up the thirty-round magazine for the 5.56mm barrel and rammed it home. He found the six-round magazine for the much longer 20mm HE rounds and pushed that into place near the butt plate.

Murdock found a pamphlet of instructions and handed it to DeWitt. The commander opened another sheet of paper from the box. He pushed it at DeWitt, who read it aloud.

"The company is sorry, but there is no ammunition for the twenty-millimeter part of the weapon available yet. We will ship you two hundred rounds early next week.

"As per our agreement with Mr. Stroh, we will expect frequent reports on the field use of this weapon. Please give us as much detail as possible about any malfunctions, jamming, misfiring of rounds, early detonation, or problems with the electronics, aiming, and fuzing systems. Send all correspondence to the above address."

Senior Chief Will Dobler came in and let out a whoop.

"It came. That's it, the Bull Pup? Damn, but she's a beauty. When do we start test-firing her?"

"No twenty-millimeter ammo yet," DeWitt said.

"Hell, we can use the five-five-six and the laser. Let's give it a workout this afternoon. What's on the schedule?"

DeWitt grinned and handed the weapon to Dobler. "Yeah, let's switch and go up to the pit and put some rounds through her."

Senior Chief Dobler winced. "Oh, damn, I'd love to. Commander, I came in here to ask for some personal time. I need the afternoon off. Can you spare me?"

"Urgent, Senior Chief?"

"Damn fucking urgent, Commander, or I wouldn't ask."

"Go."

"Thanks, Commander. I'll get back at you." The senior chief hurried out the door and up to the quarterdeck and out to his car in the parking lot in front. He started the three-year-old Buick Regal and whipped it out of the lot, heading left into Coronado. Less than two miles from the base, he parked in front of a half-block-long row of condos and apartments and hurried up the steps. The apartments had small balconies joining the steps, and he looked down the row at six more small shelves of the same size.

His next-door neighbor, Mrs. Jordan, sat on a chair in the shade, reading. She glanced up. "She ain't home, Chief."

Dobler stopped and went over to the end of his balcony that met the neighbors'.

"She's not here, Mrs. Jordan? She wasn't feeling well this morning when I left."

"Guess so. Ambulance came about an hour ago. I didn't know where to call you."

"Ambulance? Where did they take her?"

"The driver said to tell you the nearest emergency room was at the Coronado Hospital on Prospect Place."

He turned and ran. "Thanks!" he shouted over his shoulder and took the steps down, four at a time.

She was still in the emergency section of the hospital when he got there. He found the doctor who had treated her.

"Yes, you can see her for a short visit. She's still under some medications, so she's not totally lucid. It was a close thing. She called nine-one-one just in time."

"Why?" Dobler asked. He realized he was still in his cammies, floppy hat and all. At least he hadn't brought any weapons except the KA-BAR strapped to his right ankle under the cammies.

The doctor, who looked as if he hadn't slept for two days, sighed and rubbed his forehead.

"I thought someone had told you. She took about thirty sleeping pills and slashed her wrists before she called."

"Oh, damn. I knew she was feeling down."

"This was a lot more than down. Severe depression is more like it. I want to keep her here for three days for observation. We made the mandatory report to the police. Has she been under psychiatric care?"

"No, she said she didn't need it."

"That's like asking the pot if it's black. She needs it, and you may, too, trying to cope with her. I'm sorry. This sort of thing happens. Now, why don't you go in and see her. Children at school? You'll have to take care of that problem, too. Do you have relatives here?"

Dobler shook his head. "I'll deal with it."

The doctor pulled back the drape from around part of the bed, then closed it when Dobler was inside.

Nancy Dobler's eyes were closed. Will blinked as he stared down at her. Dark hair mussed on the pillow. No makeup, hands and arms outside the hospital-white sheet. Heavy straps bound each arm to the railing. Six-inch-long white bandages wrapped each wrist.

"Nan. Nancy baby, I'm so sorry. I knew you were upset this morning, but I didn't think that you would . . ." He stopped. Her eyes flickered, then came open to stay. Silent tears welled and ran down her cheeks.

"Baby, I'm so sorry." He brushed strands of loose hair back from her face and wiped wetness off her cheeks. "So sorry."

She cleared her throat.

"Water," she said softly, her voice scratchy. When he didn't move at once, she brayed the same word again, and a nurse moved back the curtain and looked in.

"She wants some water, nurse. Can you bring her some?"

The nurse said she could and hurried away.

"It's the damn fucking tube they rammed down my throat when they pumped my stomach." She glared at him. "Well, how the hell would you feel getting everything sucked out of your belly?"

The nurse came back in the middle of the sentence and she lifted her brows and frowned at the senior chief.

Nancy leaned up so the nurse could hold the glass for her, then the nurse put it on a table nearby and left.

"Look, Nancy. This is my fault. I should have been able to know what was coming and stayed home with you. I can do more of that. I'll take some time. I'm due two weeks' leave. Maybe we can fly to Chicago or New York and see the town."

"Mrs. Jordan told you I was here?"

"Yes. She really likes you."

"Bullshit. She hates me and the kids for making so much noise. She tells me so whenever you aren't around. Everybody in that whole shitty complex hates my guts."

"The doctor wants to keep you here for two or three days for observation."

Nancy laughed. "Oh sure, observation. They don't want me to try it again and do it right. I should have used that thirty-eight pistol of yours. No waiting time. Immediate results."

"Don't talk that way. You can't mean that."

"I do mean it, and you know I do, and you know that I'm probably going to try again. Maybe not this week or this month. But when that damn elephant gets on my back, there's no way to budge him off, except one. Why cry all the time and be miserable when I can end it with one goddamned thirty-eight slug?"

"Nancy, listen to yourself. You talk that way when the psychiatrist comes to see you, and they'll ship you down to the psych ward at Balboa Naval Hospital."

"Hell yes, lock me up and throw away the fucking key. Sounds about right. You have a nice day, too, fucking Boatswain's Mate First Class Senior Chief Dobler. I'm going to take a nap. Maybe I'll dream I'm half normal. Hell yes, a nap. Best idea I've had all day."

Nancy Dobler turned her back to him. She would be sleeping in a minute or two. He'd seen her do it a hundred times. He looked at his watch. Fourteen-thirty. Chuck and Helen would be coming home soon from school. No, this was Wednesday, that was cheerleader's practice. Chuck then. He had to figure out someplace for them to stay. Who this time? He'd been using up his welcome at some of his friends there in Coronado.

Mrs. Fernandez. Miguel's wife? A chance. He didn't know them well but had met them at a platoon fish fry last month. Could he ask her? He didn't know of anyone else. He drove home and called the base and talked to Miguel.

"That's the story, Miguel. My wife will be in the hospital for two or three days, and I'm in real need."

"Senior Chief, no sweat. Hey, you bring the kids over after school and with clothes for school and books and Maria can be there for them for as long as it takes. She's good with kids. Linda will love having a brother and sister. I'll call Maria and tell her you're coming."

"I owe you, man."

"No sweat. Just take care of your wife, Nancy, wasn't it? Just get her well, that's the important thing."

With that settled, Dobler checked the apartment. He found the blood in the kitchen and a trail into the living room and a dark red splotch on the rug where she must have fallen. The empty bottle of sleeping pills lay on the kitchen counter.

He tried not to think about it as he scrubbed up the blood. He never did get it all out of the carpet. How many times? He shook his head, remembering. Four, this was at least the fourth time. Her mother told him she had tried twice in high school, but no one knew if she was really serious or just trying to get attention. It got *her* attention, all right.

Was that still the problem? He spent too much time with the Navy and not enough time with her and the kids? Might be. Maybe he did need some counseling after all. Marriage counseling. That might help. At once he knew that she would never agree to it. She had told him many times before that she would never allow a shrink to dig into her brain.

It had been three years this time. Chuck wouldn't remember the last time, but Dobler was afraid that Helen would.

"Your mother's in the hospital and will be there for two or three days." He told them when they both came home.

"Why?" Chuck asked.

"She hurt herself. She'll recover and be just fine."

Helen looked at him, and when Chuck went to play with his computer, she asked him

"Again, Dad?"

"Yes, but don't tell Chuck. He doesn't need to know."

"Why does she do it?"

"I don't know. If I knew, I'd figure out some way to keep her happy."

"Hey, Dad. Don't even think about quitting the Navy. It's not that. You said she did it twice back in high school. It's not the Navy."

The kids were Navy. They adapted easily to new situations, new schools, new friends. They fit in nicely at the Fernandez place, and Maria and little Linda couldn't have been nicer.

That night, as Senior Chief Dobler tried to get to sleep back at his apartment, he wondered if his wife's troubles really were his being in the Navy. The Navy was a jealous mistress. Almost always she won. If the time came just right, he might have a talk with Commander Murdock. That was an option he'd think about.

He turned over and fluffed his pillow. Hell no, it couldn't be the Navy. Still, he wondered.

5

NAVSPECWARGRUP-one
Navy SEALs Training HQ
Coronado, California

All sixteen SEALs from Team Seven, Third Platoon, took turns with the Bull Pup rifle that afternoon at the pit down the Silver Strand toward Imperial Beach. The pit was where they used explosives in early Tadpole training and fired weapons there against the twenty-foot-high sand dune that bulldozers had piled up.

Murdock fired the 5.56 barrel in two-shot bursts. He held the weapon away from him and looked it over again, then pounded off four rounds. He turned the Bull Pup and aimed it down the beach at a file of SEAL Tadpoles packing a twenty-foot-long telephone pole. He touched the laser and saw through the six-power scope where the red spot touched the first SEAL.

"See the red spot?" DeWitt asked.

Murdock said he did.

"Right now, the chip is determining the range and figuring how many revolutions it takes the twenty-millimeters round to get to that point. Faster than we can say it, the device sets the fuze for an airburst before you would have had time to pull the trigger."

"Nice," Murdock said. "Nice. I like it. How many Colt carbines we usually carry?"

"Five, sometimes six."

"What would you think of trading in the Colts for five of these Bull Pups?"

DeWitt frowned. "Maybe. I'd want to see how they hold up in the field. We need a good three-day exercise with them and with live ammo for the twenty."

"Good. We'll also see what a little bit of rain and mud does to it. Remember how the first-issue M-16 rifles jammed? We don't want this one if it does that, even once. A jam could mean a dead SEAL."

"Amen to that. I'll give Stroh a call and see if he can shake loose that ammo any sooner."

"Go," Murdock said. "You need the road work, anyway."

DeWitt grinned, turned away, and took off at a six-minute-per-mile pace, heading north along the wet sand toward the SEAL HQ.

When all of the SEALs had fired the Bull Pup in the five-five-six mode, Murdock had them use the scope and the sights and the laser.

"Damn, if that works out to a thousand yards, we can cut hell out of a lot of the bad guys," Jaybird said. He handed the Bull Pup to the next man.

"Yeah, I like the feel of him when he's chunking off those two-round bursts," Harry Ronson said. "Seems solid, like it can do the job and get me home."

Twenty minutes later, they headed back. Jaybird carried the Bull Pup.

"This thing have an official name yet?" Ron Holt asked.

"Only thing I saw in the literature that came with it was that the army put out bids for an 'objective individual combat weapon,'" Murdock said. "They called it the OICW, which for sure isn't what we're going to call it. A writer in *National Defense* magazine called the weapon a Bull Pup, and the name might stick."

They slogged through the sand at a seven-minutes-to-the-mile pace on the three-mile run back to their quarters.

DeWitt was on the phone when Murdock came into his office.

"Yeah, sure, Don. We understand. We just want you to jack them boys up and send us some demo rounds so we can test this bird on more than the five-five-six NATO."

DeWitt listened for a minute.

"That's a roger, Don. Fact is, he just huffed and puffed in from a jog in the sand. Do you have an appointment?"

DeWitt laughed and handed the set to Murdock.

"Hey, slick, what's happening?" Murdock asked.

"Nothing right now, but we've got a move under way, and we want you and your platoon involved. Could be pretty hairy, and you better brush up on your Spanish."

"We can do that. What about the twenty-mike-mike?"

"They want to do some testing themselves. I'll see what I can do. How many rounds do you need?

"A couple of thousand would be a good start."

"Sure, when elephants do the backstroke."

"Really. We like the weapon, but we can't take it on a mission blind, hoping it works and have all five of them jam with the first twenty shots."

"All five?"

"Oh, yeah, we need three more for the squad. Thinking of replacing the Colt fourteen."

"You know that weapon isn't fully tested yet. There could be a lot of changes."

"We like what we've got. Get us three more of them if you have to sell the Pentagon to do it."

"Yeah, I'll try. How is fishing?"

"Wrong time of year to be good. Last time I checked, they were getting a few bonito, some barracuda, and lots of sand bass."

"Next time I'm out there and we have time, we're going to hit Seaforth."

"What about this Spanish trip?"

"Not sure just what your involvement will be. This one

is so covert that I won't even know about it until the day I call you."

"Gives you time to get those weapons and ammo to us."

"One-track mind. How is Ardith?"

"Not sure. Haven't seen her since we got back from across the pond."

"You probably will. So, brush up on your Spanish."

That night after chow, the men reported back to the day room for Spanish classes.

"That's right. A crash course in Spanish," Murdock said. "Miguel and Ching are your instructors. You two take your squads in separate corners of the room and get moving. This is conversation Spanish. Do it."

For two hours they worked at it.

"Buenos días," Miguel said to Bravo Squad. They chanted the phrase right back at him.

"That means good morning," Miguel said. "Polite conversation. To thank someone, it's *gracias.* If you need to fake it with some locals you can mutter, *¿Qùe pasa?* That means what passes or how's it going."

After he told them a word or a phrase, he had them say the words six times, then had each man repeat the word alone. Some picked up the words quickly. Others struggled.

"Where is a key word we might need. *Dónde.* You could say, *"Dónde es su casa."*

Murdock sat in with Alpha Squad, and DeWitt chanted the phrases with the Bravo Squad men.

They worked the Spanish classes for two hours every night along with their normal training schedule.

The third day, a special delivery came from North Island, where it had just landed on board an F-18 from Minnesota. DeWitt opened the wooden box and cheered.

"Five hundred rounds of HE twenty-mike-mike rounds. Let's go do some shooting."

That afternoon they drove thirty miles into east San Diego County into the bare hills to their unofficial long gun range. They had an agreement with the rancher who owned the property. He put up a signal to them when he was using this part of it for grazing. There was no signal this time. They went through the stretched barbed wire gate and drove into their range.

"Unload those ten three-foot-square cardboard boxes and open them, then lock the tops and bottoms in place," Senior Chief Dobler said. "We'll spot five of them here forty yards apart, then bring the other five back to the five-hundred-yard range."

When the boxes were placed, the SEALs rode their rig back to the firing position. Ed DeWitt had both the Bull Pup weapons ready. DeWitt took the first shot. He'd studied up on the procedure again. He loaded a six-round magazine and chambered a round.

He snapped on the laser sighting device and zeroed in through the six-power sight on one of the cardboard boxes at the thousand-yard range.

"Oh yes, I have a red dot on that box," DeWitt said. He pulled the trigger that worked both barrels. The 20mm round went off with a sharp report that none of them had ever heard before.

"Sounds like half a dozen thirty-ought-six hunting rifles going off at the same time," Jaybird said. A moment later, they heard the round explode in the air downrange. They could see the puff of smoke as the 20mm fragger detonated. DeWitt kept his prone position and checked through the scope.

"Be damned," DeWitt bellowed. "That box is shattered, ripped into half a dozen pieces. Jeeeeeze, but that's a beauty."

Murdock sighted in on one of the boxes at 500 yards and fired. Both men checked the box through their scopes.

Murdock came away from the scope smiling. "Hard to find any of that box left. The fuzing and trajectory is working just fine."

Ed nodded. "If these things are rugged enough to keep up with us, they're going to make one hell of a difference in how we operate."

The rest of the men used the weapons then. Soon they

were firing at chunks of cardboard. The last men in the squads had to pick out friendly rocks at the thousand-yard range to shoot at.

"Let's call it on the twenties," Murdock said. "No use wasting what could be our operational ammo. Remember, those twenties cost thirty dollars a shot."

They switched to the five-five-six NATO rounds.

"Won't quite reach out five hundred," Bradford said. "But I like the way it handles at three hundred yards."

They each fired a thirty-round magazine of rounds through the smaller barrel, then picked up their brass and policed the area. The owner of the land was never supposed to be able to find any evidence they had been there. That meant finding and grabbing all the pieces of the ten cardboard boxes.

They arrived back at their HQ just after 2000, and Master Chief MacKenzie waited for them.

"Commander, you're to call Don Stroh whenever you get in. He said he's at work, wherever that is."

"We getting employment?" Jaybird asked.

"Maybe. Hard to tell with Don. Usually he'd beep me if he was in a rush."

The platoon waited for Murdock to make the call. Jaybird and DeWitt broke down, cleaned, and oiled the Bull Pups.

"Two barrels to clean instead of one," Jaybird snorted.

Senior Chief Dobler paced the outer room. He wasn't sure what to do. He tried to plan ahead. If it was a mission, how could he leave with Nancy just coming out of the hospital? Could she manage the kids while he was gone? Would his fourteen-year-old Helen have to carry the load?

He heard Murdock contact Stroh and went up to the door to listen.

"Oh, yeah, Don, we're here. If I had a loudspeaker phone, the whole platoon would listen. What's up?"

"Remember I told you to brush up on your Spanish? You're going to need it. Down in Columbia they had an election today. The bad guys dumped out ballot boxes, stuffed others, kept hundreds of thousands of voters away from the polls with threats, shot down one whole election staff at one polling place. They in effect stole the election by wide-open fraud and violence.

"Tonight the winning presidential candidate has declared his victory. There was no international committee monitoring the election. One delegation from Germany and England went to Begotá but were kept prisoners in their rooms by armed men."

"So they can claim they have a legitimate government and nobody can rush in to save the country," Murdock said.

"Part of it. The rest is worse. The fraudulently winning president is Hector Luis Sanchez, known in this country as the second biggest drug cartel operator in Colombia.

"This went down the way State said it probably would. Now it comes to us. You are authorized to go in within a week. You will have three objectives. One is to disrupt the cocaine production, processing, and shipment from all Colombian ports. The second mission is to disturb and reduce the corrupt officials starting with the top man and working down. You realize this is not an instruction to assassinate anyone. We don't do that anymore. But if some of those illegally elected officials were caught in a crossfire by some drug traffickers, the U.S. could not be blamed."

"Hey, right. No blame on us. Is that's all? What about the army? As I remember, they have about a hundred and fifty thousand troops. Which side did they take?"

"Actually, they have a hundred and forty-three thousand men under arms. About two-thirds have stayed loyal to the new government and Sanchez. Mostly because Sanchez doubled their salary and paid them for two months in advance. The other third are centered in southern Colombia near the coast where the former President Manuel Ocampo has set up what he calls the real government of Colombia. Say he has about forty-eight thousand troops and half of the jet fighters and ten or twelve tanks."

"They have a navy?"

"Not much of one. Two submarines, four corvettes and about thirty-five coastal and river armed patrol craft. We don't know where any of them are, but some should be in Buenaventura on the Pacific side. We expect most of the fleet is on the Caribbean Sea side. This is a two-ocean nation."

"How long do we have?"

"We're making contacts now with the former president to clear the way for your landing by sea with tons of supplies, ammo, and various other goodies. Probably we can get it all arranged within a week."

"We got your twenty-mike-mike rounds and like them. We'll want those and three more over-and-under Bull Pups before we go and two thousand rounds."

"I'll try."

"Good enough. We'll go back to Spanish classes. Ed is in good shape and will be going with us. How will we travel?"

"You'll go by air southeast from San Diego. Bogotá is almost directly due south of the D.C. parkway. We'll have a carrier task force in the vicinity. It will be your floating base, and it will steam within twenty miles of your entry point.

"I'll download what we have on the two big cartels. You still at SEALsSeven@AOL.com?"

"Right, that gets us here in my office. Works great."

"You'll hear. The cartels are named after two large cities where they live: Cali, in the south, and Medellin, about in the middle of the country. Bogotá, the capital, is farther east in the mountains. Lots of mountains in Colombia."

"Okay, bwana. We'll be ready when you give us the word. Keep in touch."

Murdock hung up the phone and looked at the scrawled notes he had taken as Stroh talked.

"Get everyone together out there, Senior Chief, and I'll tell you all I just heard about our next assignment."

He went through it all. Murdock had always felt that the more the men knew about an assignment, the better. When he finished, the SEALs had some questions, then put away their equipment and headed out. All of them lived off the base.

Senior Chief Dobler tarried behind until everyone had left but Murdock. He went to the office door and knocked.

"Senior Chief?"

"Commander, do you have a few minutes? I've got a problem."

6

Miami, Florida

The whole scene irritated him. He'd been in worse, but this armpit section of Miami was right out of a horror movie. Deserted buildings, empty wine bottles rolling on the street in the sudden gusts of angry wind. Newspapers flying. Tough Tony Mitrango ducked his head and motioned to the man with him.

"That goddamned door is the one on the address. No lights. Where the hell is everyone?"

His partner, the one carrying the sleek suitcase filled with one hundred dollar bills, shrugged. "Hail, Tony, we've worked with these gents before. Good old boys from Colombia. No sweat, man. They ain't about to fuck us. We got clout with them now." Angelo Puchini snorted. He'd been on a dozen buys like this. Why should the family pay some middleman just to haul the goods from Miami to New York? The family did it and saved 30 percent.

Tony touched the door, turned the knob, and it opened. He thrust it inward and saw a dim light. He had his hand hovering over his belt where his old reliable Glock with seventeen rounds remained hidden.

He stepped halfway into the room and stopped.

"Ah, gentlemen. Good you have arrived."

Tony squinted. He saw a shape across the room. The sound of English with a stiff Spanish accent reminded him these were foreigners, assholes from Colombia. But they had the goods.

"There are supposed to be two of you." The same Spanish tilted words came sharply.

Puchini stepped into the room. The lights came up, and the two Mafia men saw two dark-complexioned men standing beside a small table. Both wore expensive suits, colored shirts with loud ties, and shirt-matching handkerchiefs in the jacket top pockets.

"Yeah, we're here," Puchini said. "Where the hell are the goods?"

"No rush, plenty of time. First we be sure you are who said would come. Then we see the money, and then we show you the goods and make the exchange. Good for business. Good partners, yes?"

Puchini wanted out of there. He wanted to make the exchange and get back to the car where he had two more soldiers. The Colombians said no more than two men on the exchange. The car was three blocks away, where two more Colombians waited with the Mafia car.

"Let's get on with it," Tony said.

"Yes. First we must go to another room. Please follow me, gentlemen."

Tony realized that the second foreigner had not spoken. Probably knew no English. Damn fucking Spanish assholes.

"This way," the Colombian said. He went first through a door into a normally lit room, then through that and up a stairway with no lights at all except at the top.

On the second floor, the four men stood in a bare room except for one table, a sturdy type, four feet wide and over six feet long.

The Colombian frowned. "You have firearms?"

"Damn right," Tony said. "Don't even get out of bed without my shooter."

"Suggest we all lay weapons on the table," the Colombian said. "Then no one tempted, all even-Steven."

"Hell no," Tony snapped.

"Easy, Tony," Puchini said softly so the others couldn't hear. "We put the pieces down and wait. Don't blow this. These guys are touchy sometimes. We never have any trouble."

Four automatic pistols soon lay on the table.

"What's your name?" Puchini asked the talker.

"Yes, confirmation. I am Pablo Ernesto. Yes, two first names. What name do you use?"

"Puchini is enough. I have the cash. Where are the goods?"

Puchini lifted the briefcase to the table and laid it down.

Pablo and his friend lifted a suitcase from the shadows and placed it carefully on the table. He unstrapped it and lifted the lid.

Puchini couldn't see inside.

"Come take a look, test it, one hundred percent."

Puchini made a small move with his head for Tony to stay near the money, then walked slowly toward the suitcase. He watched the man beside the cocaine.

The second man shot Puchini in the heart before he made it halfway to the suitcase. The silent Colombian jolted his weapon toward Tony, but he dove under the table, clawing at his right ankle for his hideout. He shot three times at the men's legs, had one hit above the knee on the first shooter before the man dove to the left and fired four times, drilling a line of lead slugs down Toni's right arm and across both legs.

The Glock fell from the Mafioso's hand, and he wailed in pain.

The two Colombians jabbered at one another a moment, then the one who spoke English bent and aimed his weapon at Tony.

"So, you do not want the goods. Fine with us. Your friend has made himself dead. We will take the money and slip away before anyone comes, no?"

"Bastards. Puchini said he trusted you shitheads. Why do you do this now? We have the money for the goods."

"Stupid. You are stupid. We make some money selling, true, but we make ten times as much stealing your two million dollars. Easy to figure. With two million, we could quit the drug trade, but when we go back with the money and the goods and tell our boss how you tried to double-cross us, we get big bonus and promotion. The Cali people are most generous."

They made Tony struggle out from under the table and put him on the table so they could treat his wounds. Instead, they tied him down to the table so he couldn't move. It happened quickly and before Tony's pain-dulled reactions could prevent it.

The two Colombians talked again in Spanish, then took a bottle of whiskey from the suitcase they had lifted to the table. They had glasses, cheese, crackers, a whole array of snacks. The man who hadn't talked downed his whiskey neat, then took out a switchblade knife and five inches of cold, sharpened steel and waved it at Tony.

"Oh, now you've made Rodolfo angry. He can be *muy malo,* when he gets riled up. His knife, his *cuchillo,* it can make you cry like a small *niño.* You should not shoot him in leg."

Rodolfo hovered over the helpless Tough Tony. The knife slashed, and moments later, the heavily muscled New Yorker was naked on the table, his cut-apart clothes in piles on the floor. The four gunshot wounds showed on Tony's arm and one leg.

Rodolfo grinned at Tony and sliced down his arm. The cut wasn't deep, but it brought a gout of blood. He sliced the other arm and then lifted his whiskey glass and drained it. The two Colombians watched Tony writhing on the table.

"Bastards. Fucking shithead motherfuckers. Gonna do you both good when I get off this table. Gonna cut off your gonads and make you chew them up and eat them."

Pablo slapped Tony's face one way, then the other, then

spat in his face. "Now you are making even me angry. I'm the calm one. I won't be able to hold back Rodolfo. He understands English; he just doesn't speak it so well. You in trouble, badass."

The knife came again and again. The slices were precise, so they would bleed but not seriously wound Tony. The two Colombians drank and laughed and sliced and drank again. When Tony passed out after a half hour of torture, they slapped him awake.

"You are missing all the fun, amigo," Pablo said. "Stay with us. You are not nearly ready to meet the angels yet." Rodolfo's knife came down again, and Tony wailed in terror and agony. Never had he hurt so much, never been so frustrated and helpless.

Later there came a time when he wanted it to end. He could see part of his body. It was totally smeared with his own blood. Slices and cuts on every part of his body bled. No one cut was severe enough to kill him, but over another hour he would surely bleed to death.

His voice was raspy from screaming. At last he swallowed and watched Pablo. When the man looked at Tony, he whispered his request.

"Slit my throat. Do it now. I can't stand anymore. Kill me quickly."

Pablo held up his hands. "Cannot do that, *mi amigo*. This is Rodolfo's party. I promised him two, but we have only one. It will be over soon."

A half hour later, the two drug traffickers sat on the floor, leaning against the wall, singing in Spanish. They hardly looked at the turkey meat of a man who lay on the table. The floor around the edges of the table was red and slippery with blood. They tipped the bottle again and sang another song.

It was two hours later that the two Colombians roused themselves and stood. Pablo had checked the briefcase of money and found the two million dollars in crisp $100 bills. They kicked aside the box that they had brought the booze and food in.

Pablo Ernesto turned at the door and saluted the two dead Americans.

"Vaya con diablo!" he said and guffawed as he and Rodolfo staggered out the door and down another set of stairs to the street below, a block away from the entrance that the Americans had used. Three blocks away, the two Mafia men from New York waited in their rented car.

7

NAVSPECWARGRUP-one
Navy SEALs Training HQ
Coronado, California

Lieutenant Commander Blake Murdock looked up from where he sat at his desk.

"Sure, Senior Chief, come in, sit."

Dobler had his floppy cammie hat in his hands, and that triggered a frown from Murdock. He killed the frown before it showed and put down the pen he had been writing with. Over the years he had learned patience when dealing with the personal problems of his men, and this sure looked like one.

Senior Chief Dobler sat on the hard wooden chair, squirmed a moment, then slapped his hat on his knee.

"Commander, you've met my wife, Nancy."

Murdock nodded.

"Unless you dug deep into my personnel file, you probably don't know that for years she's had some mental problems. Sweetest little lady you'll ever find, when she's feeling good. Lately she's been on a tear.

"I had to leave training yesterday to get home. When I

got there, I was too late. I knew she'd been feeling terrible. Yesterday afternoon she tried to kill herself. She's in the Coronado Hospital."

"Anything I can do, Chief, just name it."

"She hasn't tried anything like this for four years. They pumped her stomach, sewed up her wrists, but will keep her for three days for observation."

"Your kids?" Murdock asked.

"I asked Maria Fernandez to help. The kids went there after school and stayed the night. I don't know about tonight."

"Nancy wants you to quit the SEALs," Murdock said.

Senior Chief Dobler looked up in surprise. "How do you know that?"

"I've seen it happen before. The JG's woman goes up and down that same ladder, and they aren't even married." He watched Dobler a moment. "How old are your kids?"

"Helen is fourteen, and this is tearing her up. Chuck is eleven, so he isn't so affected, as near as I can tell. I just don't know what to do."

"You probably do, Chief, you just don't want to admit it. What's the first decision you have to make?"

Dobler took a deep breath, stared out the door, and fiddled with his hat. "Oh, damn, you're right again. I have to decide which is more important, my wife and my family or the SEALs."

"That's the big one, Senior Chief. Absolutely one of the hardest choices that you'll ever make. I imagine that you've been considering this choice for some time. You'll need some more time right now to get it worked out. I want you to take seven days' emergency leave. I'll have the master chief get your papers drawn up right now."

He reached for the phone and dialed. He gave the order in one sentence, cut off any question, and hung up the phone.

"Stop by at the quarterdeck. Your papers will be ready."

Dobler made a move to get up.

"Stay a minute if you can, Senior Chief. When the time

comes, I'd say that Maria Fernandez should talk to your wife. It should be easy and natural since she's been keeping the kids there. If you can arrange it, I'd like to have Milly there, too. She's the woman the JG lives with. Both have had the problem and worked through it."

"What about the training?"

Murdock shrugged. "Anything a SEAL can do that you can't do, Senior Chief?"

He let a thin smile brush his face. "Not that I can think of, Commander."

"If you get this straightened out with Nancy and feel you can leave her with the kids, you'll be on the flight to Colombia. If you decide that Nancy isn't well enough to stay with the kids alone, and you don't have any relatives who could live in, then you'll be free to ask to be excused from the mission."

Dobler sat there, turning his cammie hat around and around in his big hands. After what Murdock figured were two minutes of dead silence, the sailor nodded. "Yes, sir, Commander. I've never heard of anything in the Navy that was fairer and straight arrow. I appreciate it. Like I said, I have a decision to make."

Murdock stood and held out his hand. "Senior Chief Dobler, I'd hate to lose you. You're getting this platoon whipped into shape. But I know what a tough decision you have to make. It involves the three most important people in your life."

Coronado Hospital

Nancy Dobler sat up in her hospital bed in a rush. Her eyes opened and she looked around. A small nod, and she eased back on the bed and tried to relax. Her hands had been unstrapped from the railings. They trusted her a little. There was a TV camera watching her all the time. She knew it was there. It didn't bother her.

She knew they had her on some kind of relaxing medication. She couldn't work up a good mad at anyone, not even the nurse who took three stabs to draw her blood earlier.

Nancy blinked back tears. She had blown it again. What the hell was the matter with her? Yes, a bitching childhood, but that was over long, long ago. She was an adult now. She had to act like it. Partly the booze. Earlier that morning, she started feeling sorry for herself, and had one drink, and then another one, and before long she had blown the whole thing all out of proportion.

That's what the shrink told her earlier that afternoon when he stopped by. Procedure, he had told her. He said suicide failures were his meat. She had laughed at that. At least he didn't try to hide the *S* word.

Helen.

She thought of her daughter, and tears sprang to her eyes. Oh, God, she hoped that she hadn't traumatized her wonderful Helen. Why? Why? Why?

She pulled the sheet up over her head, closed her eyes, and cupped her hands over her eyes so she could see absolutely nothing but blackness.

Damn it to hell.

Yes, she knew why, but she would never admit it, never even think about it. She had tried to forget it for so long. There must be something or someone who could help her remember it one more time and accept it for what it was and put it forever behind her. Who?

"Hey there, sleeping girl. Are you in there somewhere?"

It was Will.

She let the sheet down gently, then uncovered her eyes.

"It's so damn bright in here," she said, flailing out, covering her eyes again.

"True," Will Dobler said. He reached over and snapped off the room lights.

"Better?"

She looked at him and smiled a yes. Will sat down beside her bed. The side railings were gone. He picked up her hand and held it.

"Missed you, sweetheart, we all have. The kids have

been staying with the other married SEAL in our unit, Maria and Miguel Fernandez. Wonderful lady."

"Good. The kids deserve—"

He cut her off. "Now stop that. Hey, we love you and want you home soon. Day after tomorrow, the nurse says. They have made some recommendations."

"A shrink?" Nancy said with more anger than she felt.

"Matter of fact, yes. Seems they got your chart from Balboa Naval Hospital."

"In all its ugly reality. Oh shit."

"True. Now, I have a decision to make. I want you to help me."

"About the shrink?"

"No. About SEALs."

Nancy looked at him. The tears had dried on her cheeks, leaving little splotches. Her eyes squinted for a moment, then her brows lifted. "Meaning what, Will?"

"Meaning you and I and the kids are going to decide whether I stay in the SEALs or go back to regular Navy service."

"Wouldn't they ship you out right away on a carrier?"

"Par for the course. I don't have enough years in to have much clout."

Someone came to the door and stood there. Will looked at her. She was a nurse in her forties. She checked his rank on his sleeve.

"Chief, I'm afraid that visiting—"

He turned suddenly. "Ma'am, this is a top secret discussion, and unless you have top secret clearance, I'll have to respectfully ask you to retire and close the door." Then he grinned.

The nurse smiled. "Chief, I did my twenty-five and sometimes don't quite feel that I'm out. This is as near as I can come. Take all the time you want."

She closed the door.

When Will looked back at Nancy, she had her old cock-eyed grin on, and he relaxed a notch.

"We'll decide over the next week. The commander gave

me a week of emergency leave time. We can drive up the coast or go down Baja and hunt for clams or just mess around in the apartment. In the end, we decide what we're going to do for the rest of our lives."

Nancy twisted some strands of hair around her finger. "Now a six-month tour of duty overseas on a carrier, that I could understand. I could plan for it and deal with it. This home and gone and home and gone is something that always takes a lot of adjustment."

She held up her hands. "Hey, I'm not arguing one way or the other. Just getting some facts on the table."

"Yeah, we're going to be kicking a lot of facts around. For right now, how about some rummy?"

"No cards."

He pulled a pack from his pocket and broke the seal. "Brand-new and never been stacked. I'll shuffle, you deal."

Nancy smiled softly, wiped at the dregs of new moisture in her eyes. They had met playing rummy, so long ago. He had remembered. It touched her in an important way. Her smile brightened.

Navy SEALs Trainings HQ

Third Platoon trained hard the next four days. The third day, their new supply of ammo and the three new Bull Pups arrived. They went on a special night maneuver in the mountains of the Navy Bomb Range in the desert. They dropped the weapons, skidded them through dirt, simulated rain on one for two hours. Through it all the Bull Pups performed flawlessly.

The second night after Nancy Dobler came out of the hospital, Maria Fernandez and Milly stopped by for a talk. Will had told Nancy they were coming, and she welcomed them. It was a frank and tough discussion. Will was booted out to watch TV in the kids' room.

Two hours later, the three women were crying when Dobler checked. Milly waved him in.

"Will, I think we're about done. We've had a good cry. We've ripped the male species apart and torn him limb from limb, but then tenderly put him back together again."

After the women left, Nancy and Will talked.

"Yes, Will. I want to go to Balboa to a psychiatrist there. I've been approved for two sessions a week starting tomorrow. I've made your decision for you. I don't want you to quit the SEALs. I see you more this way than if you were on a damn cruise."

He sat beside her and kissed her cheek, then her lips.

"Now that you mention it, why don't we get to bed early tonight and get all naked and see what happens?"

Her face glowed. "Maybe, but only two or three times."

8

Airborne Over the Caribbean Sea

Commander Blake Murdock leaned back in the first-class type airliner reclining seat. He could get used to this. The Third Platoon of SEAL Team Seven had been pulled out of station a day earlier than planned. The situation in Colombia was getting worse. More of the troops loyal to the former president were deserting to the new, fraudulently elected man owned by the drug cartels.

Murdock looked around at the aircraft. He knew it was an Air Force C-22, an adaptation of the Boeing 727 passenger liner. It had been set up for twenty-four occupants and was used mostly for VIP passengers in staff movements and getting vital military and high-level civilian personnel to the proper location quickly and with a minimum of danger.

They had taken off from North Island on twelve hours' notice. Senior Chief Will Dobler had talked with Nancy for two hours and had come back ready to travel. Nancy would meet every three days with Milly and Maria Fernandez to trade news and gossip and to cry on each others' shoulders if necessary.

All of Murdock's men were fit and ready. The big plane held the platoon easily, and the cargo bay carried all their personnel gear and weapons, including the five new Bull Pups and five thousand rounds of HE automatic fuzed ammo. They were ready.

Murdock wasn't sure what route they were taking. He heard something about a fuel stop in Texas and another one in Miami. He knew they would land in Panama City. This bird should have a range of over 2,600 miles. From Panama they would take a Navy COD for transfer out to a carrier somewhere in the Pacific Ocean.

Lieutenant (j.g.) Ed DeWitt snored softly in the seat just ahead of Murdock. He could go to sleep almost on call.

They had been airborne only two hours when one of the crew brought them hot meals from the plane's kitchen. It turned out to be standard first-class airline dinners, which the men appreciated.

"Damn lots better than MREs," Ostercamp bellowed.

They had left North Island at 1600. Don Stroh said that would make most of their trip in the dark, especially the stop in Panama City and the transfer to the COD and then the run out to the carrier.

"No sense telegraphing our punch," Stroh said on his last talk with Murdock. He said he'd follow them the next day and be on the carrier *Gerald R. Ford* CVN-81 and on call there.

"This one is still a little tricky," Stroh had said that afternoon on the secure line. "We're not completely happy with the former president. He may be sharpening his teeth to take over as a dictator himself. So protect your back at all times. We know that we want the bastard drug cartel operators out of power now, and we want to smash a huge hole in their drug trafficking."

Murdock mulled over the conversation. They would do what they could. Hit the growth area of the leaves of the cocoa tree. Or were there many in Colombia? As he remembered, most of the leaves came from Peru and Bolivia, high up in the mountains. They processed it halfway into cocaine paste and exported that. The Colombians processed that into cocaine. So they would take down the production plants that manufactured the cocaine and then burn up as much of the export pipeline to the States as they could. The puppet president might or might not be on their agenda.

He woke up when they landed. When he looked out the window, he saw all U.S. planes and guessed it was either Texas or Miami.

The C-22 had an extra crewman on board. He was a sharp-dressing corporal with a thick Southern accent.

"Best duty I had in a year, sir." He told Murdock all he had to do was play attendant. He served the meals, was on call, and said he could provide anything but alcoholic drinks.

"Our captain got orders that you folks was to be considered just a notch below generals and admirals, and we was to treat you with the utmost respect. You SEALs. What's a SEAL?"

Murdock explained to him.

"Oh, and this is some sort of secret mission. Yeah, I dig. Never heard of you, but then lots of things I ain't never heard of."

They took off, and the corporal served anyone who wanted it coffee, juice, or soft drinks. Most of the men slept through the landing.

It was dark when they came down in Panama. Murdock wasn't sure what relations were with Panama, but they had no trouble transferring their gear to the Navy Greyhound, the CA-2A. The Greyhound is a slightly altered model of the Navy's E-2C Hawkeye Airborne Early Warning aircraft.

It was a tighter fit, with the plane designed to carry thirty-nine troops. They climbed on board, stowed their gear and essentials, and took off at once.

By that time, Murdock was wide awake. He talked with the pilot who told him it was 0400 local, if he wanted to set his watch.

"We'll be well away from Panama by the time it gets

light and anyone gets curious," the pilot said. "Now we have to hook up with the carrier *Gerald Ford* about three hundred and seventy-five miles almost due south."

"That puts us off Colombia?" Murdock asked.

"About two-thirds of the way down. Not sure how far the carrier will be offshore by then, but should be out a ways."

Murdock thanked him. The flight engineer told Murdock he had an ETA of about 0520 local, give or take five minutes.

Murdock found half the men sleeping again. Good. They might not have a lot of time to sleep once they hit dry land. This could be on the hairy side. No real enemy, unless they tangled with the federal troops who remained loyal to the new regime. Even then, he wasn't sure how well equipped they were or how dedicated. Give them a 10 percent casualty rate, and they all might turn and run. Time would tell.

The speaker in the rear cabin came on a short time later.

"We will be landing in ten minutes. There are no flight exercises on, so we have a straight in. Get your gear together for a quick exit."

Five minutes later, the SEALs were ready. It wasn't quite daylight when the COD touched down with one bump, caught the number-three wire, and jerked to a stop. After the wire was unhooked, the Greyhound rolled to its assigned parking spot and the flight engineer opened the door.

Murdock was the first man out and on the deck. There he met another two and a half striper who held out his hand.

"Commander Murdock. Welcome aboard. I'm Lieutenant Commander Emerling. I'm your contact while you're with us."

"Good to meet you, Commander. Understand we are to have a meeting with your XO as soon as we arrive. Sounds like a quick turnaround."

"That's what I've heard. We're heading for the Colombian coastline, but I'm not sure how far offshore we are.

We have a secure compartment for your men's equipment right next to some six-bunk areas."

"Thanks. We'll see the men settled in, then you and I will go see the XO. What's his name?"

"That would be Captain Ingman. Let's get your men off the flight deck."

A white shirt motioned to them, and they followed the safety officer across the edge of the flight deck and down four levels to the assigned compartment. It was about forty feet square. The SEALs claimed spaces and put down their personal gear and weapons.

"What about the supplies we brought?" Senior Chief Petty Officer Dobler asked.

"I put a detail on that before we left the flight deck," Lieutenant Commander Emerling said. "All your goods should be here within ten minutes. If not, I'll twist some tail."

"Thank you, sir," Dobler said and went back to his combat gear.

Murdock looked around, signaled to Ed DeWitt that he was in charge, and then waved at Emerling. "Let's go see Captain Ingman."

Five minutes later, Emerling went down the last companionway and pointed to the doorway ahead. "This is it. The captain can be a bit crusty at times, but he's fair, and a lot of people say brilliant. He'll brief you, and I'll make any arrangements that need to be made for transport, onshore backup, support, communications, whatever."

He knocked, then turned the knob and stepped inside. Murdock followed.

"Captain, Emerling here, sir, with Commander Murdock. His SEAL platoon is on board."

Murdock took in the office compartment at a glance. All Navy, nothing personal except two framed pictures on the metal desk. The man who sat behind it had pilot's wings on his blouse and captain's insignia on his collar. His face was wind-weathered, tanned, and showing worry lines around his eyes. Probably three more years on his star chase to get his own carrier command and his admiral rank.

"Lieutenant Commander Murdock reporting as ordered, sir," Murdock said.

The captain stared at him a moment, then his face softened for just a flash of a second and he pointed to a chair.

"Good. Don Stroh has been calling me damn near every hour checking to see if you're here. He says he's on his way. Now, we have specific orders for you. Specific and yet open-ended. I imagine that you're used to that sort of thing."

"Yes sir."

"All I have is your first assignment, in case Stroh didn't get here in time. We are now about forty miles off the Colombian coast from the port city of Buenaventura. This port and much of that region is currently being held by Ex-president Manuel Ocampo. It's a sloppy civil war but not called that. Ocampo has about forty thousand men, a company of tanks, six jet fighters, two light planes, and the rest in infantry and one battery of one-oh-five artillery pieces.

"He's being harassed by troops loyal to the new so-called elected government."

Captain Ingman frowned and rubbed his jaw with one big hand. "Tough situation. Your main assignment now is to advise the president and his one one-star general on his situation, tactics, whatever. We will be doing some resupply to the president with some munitions and other items he has requested. We can get almost anything you want, except those new rifle-fired twenty-mike-mike exploding rounds you have.

"You are to proceed to the port at the earliest possible time. That means helicopters. We'll send you in a Super Stallion, and two more with equipment and matériel for the president. The air boss tells me he's now scheduled your takeoff time in a little over three hours. Give you plenty of time to get your men to chow and check their gear. You're going into a friendly situation, but it could turn ugly at any moment. Any questions?"

"I'll want my platoon to be fully armed, locked, and loaded as soon as they get on board the choppers. Will that be all right?"

"That's a roger, Murdock. Frankly, I've never seen an operation like this on a U.S. Naval ship. The fucking CIA is pulling the strings. My orders are directly from the CNO and the director of the CIA." Ingman shook his head. "Hell, I'm just a blue water sailor not used to this kind of high-level clout."

"Yes, sir. I know the feeling."

"I bet you didn't know that just so there won't be any Navy brass out of joint, you've been given temporary rank of captain for this mission."

Murdock hadn't heard that. "Sir, I'm sure that Commander Emerling and I won't have any problems with any of your crew."

"Just wanted you to know. Anything else?"

"No sir. Some chow would go good. Thank you, sir. I hope we don't interfere with any of your operations."

Ingman chuckled. "Hell, Murdock, for the next two weeks or however long it takes, you are our only scheduled operation. Wishing you all the luck, Captain."

Murdock grinned and the two junior officers left the compartment.

Emerling stopped in the companionway. "So, do I call you captain now, or what?"

"Murdock will do nicely. Let's get the troops into a mess hall."

"We've got a spot waiting. They've been on standby for twenty meals ever since you landed. Like the captain said, you and your team get the VIP treatment all the way."

Two hours later, they were on the *Gerald R. Ford*'s flight deck, checking their gear.

"Counted them damn boxes of twenty-mikes six times to be sure we got all of them," Jaybird told Murdock. "Damn, we don't want to lose any of those."

All of the weapons, ammo, combat gear, and matériel

they brought with them were accounted for. Murdock had them send up from the ship's arsenal two hundred rounds of .50 caliber, half AP and half HE.

Bill Bradford let out a long sigh when he signed for them and added them to the stack of boxes. "Keeeereist, I thought they was gonna short me on them babies," he said. "Can't get along without my Mama Eighty-Seven."

The platoon had set up parameters for the twenty-mike rounds. They would not be used except on orders of the squad leaders. If an emergency came up and contact couldn't be made, the shooter was given the decision to use the exploding rounds or not. The whole idea was to expend the rounds where they would be effective and not spray them around just for the hell of it.

"Yeah, and remember that's thirty bucks every time you pull that twenty-mike trigger," Senior Chief Dobler said.

The choppers rolled up on schedule. They were loaded with the SEALs' gear and two big stacks of more ammo and supplies, then the SEALs filed on board the first bird and within two minutes they were airborne.

One of the pilots came back and found Murdock.

"Captain, we're about fifteen minutes from this landing field at the side of the port at Buenaventura. We've been in there before. Commander Emerling told me to let you know that you'll be met by a Captain Gilberto Orejuela. He's been assigned to you evidently for the duration of your stay. Good luck." The young JG looked at Murdock for a moment in awe, then went back to the flight deck.

A short time later, Murdock felt the chopper come around and slow. Before it made it to the landing area, they heard explosions below. The craft jolted upward and then slanted down again as it took evasive maneuvers and whipped back out over the bay. Murdock thought he heard some rounds of shrapnel hit the bird.

"We're going to wait out here and see what's happening in there," the speaker over their heads said. "Looks like some kind of a local attack by some elements of the federals."

"Oh, God, I think I'm hit," Joe Lampedusa said. Then his eyes glazed and he fell forward, sprawling on the chopper's floor, blood making a stark red pool beside him.

9

Buenaventura, Colombia

Jack Mahanani, the platoon medic, dropped on his knees beside Lampedusa before Murdock got there.

"No wound on his back," the medic said. Gently they rolled Lampedusa over.

They both saw the head wound. Blood ran from the slice across Lam's forehead. Mahanani pushed a compress over the part bleeding and wiped off the rest of Lam's face and head.

"Just that one, looks like, Skipper," Mahanani said. "Head wounds bleed like sons of bitches. This probably looks a hell of a lot worse than it is."

"Only scraped across his forehead instead of penetrating his skull?" Murdock asked.

"What I'm hoping. But even that way, the shock of the slug hitting him could have knocked him out." Mahanani lifted the compress. Fresh blood oozed out but at a slow rate. "Oh, yeah. The furrow across his thick head is about a quarter of an inch deep. Two inches long. Lots of fucking blood but shouldn't be much damage."

"A concussion?" Murdock asked.

"Have to wait and see. He shouldn't be out long."

The medic quickly wiped off the rest of the blood smudges and put a bandage over the wound, wrapping the gauze around Lam's head. Lam's eyes flickered, then opened.

"What the hell? Who hit me?"

"Head hurt?" the medic asked.

"Like a damn steam engine is roaring through it. I get shot?"

"Just a little scratch, Lam," Murdock said. "Somebody had a landing greeting for us. Mostly, they missed."

"We have an all clear in the LZ. We're going in," The pilot said on the speaker. "There should be protection down there. Hope you guys are locked and loaded."

Murdock looked at the small window but couldn't see much. They were the first down.

"Shoulder those packs and chamber a round. When we hit the asphalt out there, it will be running. I have Lam's weapon. Somebody get his gear. If we have a guide, we follow him. Otherwise, we head for the closest building that looks like it has some kind of protection. Read me?"

He heard a chorus of responses.

The wheels touched down, the copilot rammed the hatch open, and Murdock led the way out of the bird. No one came to meet them. He bolted for the closest building, a two-story frame affair thirty yards away.

Just before Murdock made it to the building, a man dressed in green cammies and fisting a .45 auto ran out and waved them down the side of the structure to the door he had just opened.

"SEALs?" the dark-skinned man asked.

"Yeah, you our contact?"

"Right. Sorry about that little inconvenience. Turned out to be two men with three sticks of dynamite, a K-47, and two magazines. We got both of them."

"We've got a wounded man. Doesn't look serious."

Murdock and the captain moved indoors and waited for the SEALs to run inside. The last two in were Lampedusa with his head bandage and Mahanani carrying half his gear.

Lam sank to the floor just inside the door. Mahanani checked with him. "Commander, is there a doctor around here anywhere?"

Murdock looked at the Colombian. "You're Captain Orejuela?"

"That's right, Commander. There are doctors in town, but we are supposed to load up the trucks with all the matériel you brought and your men and proceed directly to camp Bravo near Cali."

"How far is that?"

"About forty-five miles."

"How long in the trucks?"

"An hour and a half."

Mahanani had been checking Lampedusa. He came over. "Cap, looks like he might have a mild concussion. Lost quite a bit of blood. He can do the ride if we pump him full of chocolate bars. I'll make a survey."

The big room they were in had folding meal cots, blankets, and at the far end what looked like some kind of a closed-up kitchen.

"We stay here for about half an hour," the Colombian captain said. "By then they should have the ammo and weapons loaded and we can put two or three SEALs in each rig."

The SEALs had dropped to the floor and waited. Those who had a routine used it. Harry Ronson took out a small harmonica and tried to play. He was terrible. Ed DeWitt and Les Quinley worked at a peg chessboard on a game they had started in the chopper. Half the men took a nap, not sure when they might sleep again. Will Dobler sat on one of the bunks with his eyes closed, thinking about his wife and daughter back in San Diego. Ken Ching wondered what the off-road bikers were doing this weekend. He wouldn't be with them.

Mahanani came back with five chocolate bars. "Eat up, Lam, do you good."

"Four ibuprofen pain pills would do a lot better," Lam said.

"You're bitching," Mahanani said. "Now I know you're not hurt as bad as you wanted us to believe. I'll take back one of those chocolate bars."

Murdock eyed the Colombian. "Tell me about the attack. Just two men, you say? How close did they get? Inside the complex? Who were they?"

"They sneaked into the enclosure. Yes, dedicated but now just dead. I shot one of them myself. Both men were under twenty. Probably some offshoot from the regulars. Definitely not from the federal army."

"Might be more of them out there?"

"Always more of them. That's why I'm glad you're along on this munitions run."

"You expect trouble?"

"No. My guess is they hit us too early. They hoped to get the munitions, but the choppers hadn't even landed when they struck. Bad timing. No, the colonel and I don't expect any trouble."

"We'll be locked and loaded all the way," Murdock said. He wiped sweat off his face and realized he was still sweating from the run in there from the chopper. Then he remembered. Cali was less than two hundred miles north of the equator. At anywhere near sea level it would be hot all day.

He took out his Motorola and hooked it up.

"Senior Chief," Murdock called. Will Dobler came away from where he sat in one swift move and took a dozen fast steps to his commander.

"Let's get the men ready to travel. We want their Motorolas on, all combat gear ready to go. The men with the Bull Pup should have their issue forty rounds. All else as usual. We should be moving out in fifteen."

Dobler gave a curt nod and talked to everyone awake, then went around waking up the rest.

Ten minutes later, the Third Platoon was combat ready. Twenty minutes after that, the convoy of eight six-by trucks with soft tops rolled southwest along the paved high-way toward Cali. There were two SEALs in each truck that was loaded with boxes of ammunition, weapons, and war supplies. Murdock and Senior Chief Dobler were in the first truck right behind the lead jeep with the colonel and Captain Orejuela and his driver. Both SEALs in the first truck had their issue H&K MP-5 submachine guns.

Only a few miles from the coast, the road slanted upward into lush, green mountains. The highway was narrow and made many turns and climbed up some grades slowly.

"Dozens of places along here are ideal for an ambush," Murdock told Senior Chief Dobler.

"If they're out there, they'll pick the best spot. My guess is it will be on a sharp rise where the trucks slow down to fifteen or twenty miles an hour to grind up the hill." ·

Ten minutes later, Murdock had just sat down from where he'd been watching out the front of the rig through a folded-back flap of the roof canvas, when a rocket-propelled grenade went off. It exploded on the side of the second truck, stalling it.

Murdock was glad the trucks had kept a good interval between them, about forty yards.

He hit the lip mike at once. "Bravo Squad, move to the right side of the road, Alpha Squad on the left. Come up through cover to the second truck."

Murdock forgot which two SEALs were in the second truck. He could only hope they were still alive. He and Dobler jumped from the back of the first truck and darted into the brush at the left side of the road. They heard some small-arms fire but didn't know where it came from.

Both men lay flat in the growth of ferns and weeds under the trees. Murdock pointed toward the second truck. They worked ahead slowly at a crouch, their weapons ready. Twenty yards ahead, they saw movement. Too early for his men to get there. Murdock dropped into the growth, and Dobler went down with him.

"Saw it," Dobler whispered in his mike. "Two of them. Young. No uniforms."

They moved forward again. "I have the one on the right," Murdock said. Dobler was to his left.

Ahead of them, the green brush near a small tree moved, then bent down, and a man lifted up and stared at the road ten yards away. Murdock had his MP-5 on single shot and with the silencer on. He moved slightly upward and got off one shot. The attacker took the round in his side, where it bored quickly through light bone and tissue and plunged into his heat, dumping him dead in the lush growth.

Brush moved six feet away from where the man died. A voice called a name that Murdock couldn't catch. The man screamed, lifted up, and ran straight for Dobler. A three-round silenced burst from the H&K chopper knocked down the Colombian in mid-stride. One round hit his chest, the second his throat, and the third his forehead.

"Two terrs down near the second truck," Murdock said on the net. "If anybody has spotted any more terrs, sound off." Silence. Murdock and Dobler lifted up at the same time and ran for the second truck, which still burned, but the flames were not near the fuel tank. They paused at the edge of the brush and checked out the truck again. The whole side had been blown off and the top had burned away. Boxes of small-arms ammunition lay scattered around the floor of the rig and on the ground.

"Bravo, any of you up near the truck they hit?" Murdock asked.

"Oh, yeah, and I need new drawers."

Murdock frowned. "Quinley?" Murdock asked.

"Yeah, Cap. I was in the damn second truck. My luck, right? All of a sudden I'm in the air flying into the fucking brush. Hit a tree damn solid, but didn't bust nothing. I think everything works."

"Who was on board with you, Quinley?"

"Who? Yeah. Who was it? Not sure. Not remembering too damn well. Oh, now I have it. Yeah, Ostercamp."

"Where is he?"

"Don't know."

"Cap, Fernandez, the Motorola said. "Just arrived.

Didn't see anybody else. We'll search the brush around here. Oster ain't on board this side of the truck. It's burning now. Hope to hell there ain't no HE rounds in there."

A grenade exploded on board the truck.

"Keep back. There'll be more of them if there was one," Murdock said.

"Found Ostercamp," a new voice said.

"Ed. Where is he? Is he wounded?"

DeWitt came back at once. "He's not bleeding, doesn't seem to have any broken arms or legs. He was wrapped around a tree and he's talking but not making much sense."

"Get him away from that truck and bring him up front. Get all of his gear you can find. Some may still be on the truck. Take your squad up ahead near the jeep. See you there. Alpha Squad, on me at the jeep in front. Move now."

Murdock and Dobler hit the shoulder of the road and ran forward to the jeep, where the Colombian captain waited. Captain Orejuela called to Murdock.

"You get them? Is it safe now?"

Murdock stopped beside him and scowled. "Where the hell have you been? Go back there and get your drivers to go around that burning truck. It's a complete loss and no way to salvage the ammo until the fire goes out. You can come back here with a squad of riflemen to protect it until you can salvage it. Now, get those trucks moving so we can get away from here. If there were two shooters, there might be fifty nearby. Move it, Captain."

DeWitt came up, leading Ostercamp. He seemed dazed to Murdock, not injured.

Mahanani had been on the other side of the SEAL, trying to talk to Ostercamp. "Yeah, man, come on, tell me where we are. Colombia, right? Yeah, we're here in Colombia. Some fucker put an RPG up our asses and we're trying to work out of it."

"RPG?" Ostercamp said.

Mahanani's face erupted into a big smile. "Oh, yeah, man, you're coming along. You hurt anywhere?"

"Hurt?" Ostercamp said. "Yeah, head hurts. Scraped my damn arm."

"Hey, buddy, we'll get you back on a truck, and you'll be doing fine."

Murdock heard the exchange. The jeep and the first six-by moved ahead to make room for the other rigs behind them as they drove around the still-burning truck.

"No chance to find their weapons, Murdock," DeWitt said. "We're missing Ostercamp's MG and Quinley's G-Eleven."

"We'll get some replacements flown in from the ship," Murdock said. He used the lip mike. "Let's mount up, same rigs as before. Mahanani, you take Ostercamp in your truck. Quinley, come on the first truck."

He waved at Captain Orejuela, who stood up in the back of the jeep at the head of the column.

"Let's move it, Captain," Murdock shouted. The line of trucks drove away from the still-burning rig behind them.

The rest of the trip went without incident. They wound higher into the Cordillera Occidental, the sharp range of mountains that worked north and south along the coast of Columbia. Just the other side of the peaks on the Cauca River, they came to the key southern city of Cali.

At one time, Cali had been one of the two huge drug cartel operations in the country. They traded punches with the Medellin people far to the north. Now the power had been usurped by the Medellin people, and they held a rigid, army-protected control over all of the drug business in the country. That made the Cali area safer for Ex-president Manuel Ocampo.

Twice on narrow mountain passes, the convoy had come to army roadblocks. These were what President Ocampo called his Loyalist Forces, those 40,000 troops who had remained loyal to him and the principles of democracy.

At the first roadblock, Captain Orejuela told the officer in charge about the attack, and he sent back ten men in a truck to push the burned-out rig off the road and to recover

the undamaged ammunition and weapons before the guer-
rillas stole them.

They drove into what Captain Orejuela told Murdock
would be an army compound five miles from the city. Cali
was the size of San Diego, 1.9 million people. Most of the
ex-president's men were in camps around the city, with
defensive postures facing north and east.

As soon as the trucks stopped, the SEALs off-loaded and
asked what to do with their supplies.

Captain Orejuela hurried up and apologized.

"A detail was supposed to meet us here," he said. "I'll
go find them. We have quarters for you and your men and
all of their supplies. Just a minute."

The SEALs relaxed.

Ostercamp was on his feet but not moving quickly. The
rest of them took his gear and his supplies off the truck.
Murdock and Mahanani looked at him.

"How you feel, Ostercamp?" Murdock asked.

"Sir, feel good, sir."

Murdock frowned. It was the chant from the Tadpole
training Ostercamp had taken three or four years ago.

"Where are we, Ostercamp?"

"On the grinder, sir."

"Sit down and stay put, Tadpole," Murdock said. "I'll
get back to you." Murdock and the medic moved away.

"Not good, Captain. That concussion must be worse than
I figured."

"We'll find out what kind of medical treatment they have
here, then I want you to get Lam and Ostercamp checked
out. I'll find you as soon as I have the others straightened
away.

It was ten minutes before the English-speaking Captain
Orejuela came back.

He apologized again, got them back in the trucks, and
drove two miles across the camp to a barracks set apart
from the others.

It took them a half hour to find and unload the SEALs'

part of the munitions and ammo that hadn't been on the second truck.

"Figure we lost about 10 percent of our goods," Senior Chief Dobler told Murdock.

The wooden barracks hadn't been used for a while. The captain called his jeep and told the driver to take Lam, Ostercamp, and Mahanani to the hospital. They had just left when Murdock heard explosions.

"Bombs," he said and darted outside. He saw two jet fighters swing around, drop their bombs, then head his way using 20mm cannon on a strafing run.

"Take cover," Murdock bellowed. One of the two jets turned in to a low-level attack directly at their newly found barracks. Murdock dove behind a low rock wall and ducked his head as the rounds jolted into the wooden building and exploded.

10

Camp Bravo
Cali, Colombia

Even as he heard the rounds exploding, Murdock estimated the damage and casualties. The fighter came in low and flat. That meant the rounds from his cannon would hit the ground and anything in the way once every twenty or thirty yards. All the rounds might miss the barracks.

He dumped that thought when he heard another round explode somewhere nearby. He wondered if the Bull Pups could have adjusted range fast enough to hit the plane. He decided the laser operating unit couldn't react fast enough with the target moving at 500 to 600 miles an hour.

The jet slammed overhead and vanished.

Murdock pulled up his head. No fire. He saw a soldier down in the company street a half block north. He ran to the barracks door.

"I just hate it to fucking hell when some asshole is shooting at me and I don't have a chance to shoot back," Jeff Jefferson said. He wiped one hand over his black face and said it again.

Murdock took in the large room in one swift glance. Two

holes in the far wall about the size of baseballs.

"Anybody hit?" Murdock called.

"Hell no, that was just a wake-up call," Jaybird shrilled. Somebody laughed.

"Joke's on that bastard, cause on accounta I wasn't fucking sleeping," Guns Franklin brayed.

"We got a break, guys," Murdock said. "At least he was out of bombs by the time he found us. No reason he singled us out. Just another target. Ed, check out your squad." Murdock used his Motorola. All of his men checked in except Lam, who was on his way to the medics.

"Clean up any damage, and we'll try to find out where a mess hall is and what the hell we're supposed to be doing here."

Someone came in the front door and cleared his throat.

"Commander, may I have a word with you?"

"Attention on the bridge," Senior Chief Dobler bellowed. The men jolted to their feet and stood at attention.

In the doorway stood a tall man in cammies with silver eagle insignia on his shoulders.

Murdock walked over to him and saluted smartly.

"Lieutenant Commander Murdock, sir."

"Put your men at ease and come outside."

"Yes sir." The man was darkly Colombian, spoke perfect conversational English, and had a demeanor that Murdock liked at once.

"At ease, carry on," Murdock said and hurried out the door.

"Commander, I'm Colonel Paredes. Commanding officer of Bravo. Welcome aboard. I spent a year in the States at two war colleges and training schools. I'm delighted to have you here. I understand you had two casualties. We have good medical facilities here."

"Thank you, Colonel Paredes. I want to go see my men, then get my troops settled in. I'm hoping one of your officers can give me a briefing about exactly what you want our mission here to be."

"I can do that, Commander, on our way to the hospital.

My car is right over here. Would now be convenient?"

"It would. I put top priority on taking care of my wounded."

"Good. We can talk as we drive. It isn't far."

The car was a three-year-old black Mercedes sedan. Murdock wondered if it had been liberated. Once inside the car, the colonel began.

"Your mission here. Partly up to you, partly our requests. Right now, we have a column of about four thousand men moving in and harassing our northern blocking force. If you could somehow discourage them, we would be relieved. You know that I'm outmanned almost four to one."

"I also hear you have only a few jet aircraft. That could be a problem."

"It's a huge problem, but you probably can't help me there. First, I want you to help me push back the federal column, hit and run probably. Then we'll talk about some more missions you can do here and elsewhere in Colombia."

The car stopped, and Murdock waited for the colonel to get out first. Military courtesy. Colonel Paredes studied Murdock a moment. "We have heard good things about you and your SEALs. You have our complete cooperation. I'll have Captain Orejuela here with a jeep, which will be at your command. Is the captain a good liaison officer for you?"

"Has he ever been in combat?"

"No, he's unblooded, but his English is excellent. That probably is more important. He won't go with you on most of your missions."

"We'll try him, Colonel. Now I need to get in there and see my wounded men."

Murdock saluted the colonel, who returned the courtesy, then the SEAL hurried into the hospital.

He found Lampedusa in the emergency ward. His head graze had been treated, stitched up, and a small bandage attached. Captain Orejuela was with him.

"Good news on Lampedusa," the captain said. "The

graze did not give him a concussion, and there should be no lasting damage. He's released for duty."

"About fucking time I got out of here," Lam said.

"Where's Ostercamp?" Murdock asked. He was two curtains over. A doctor talked with him in broken English and Spanish. Ostercamp responded.

Orejuela chattered with the doctor in Spanish, then turned and smiled. "Yes, the doctor says the concussion was not serious. It disoriented him for a few hours, but he's almost back to normal. They want to keep him here overnight for observation and will release him to duty in the morning."

Murdock frowned. "You sure he's okay? He was totally confused coming in. Thought he was back in SEAL training four years ago."

"No, he should be fine. This is one of our best doctors. I've seen him work many times with our wounded."

Murdock talked to Ostercamp just to be sure.

"Where are we, SEAL?"

"We're in Colombia, doing what the hell I don't know."

"What's your name?"

"Machinist Mate First Class Anthony Ostercamp, sir."

"What's your current duty?"

"With Bravo Squad, Third Platoon, with SEAL Team Seven, Coronado California, a part of NAVSPECWAR-GRUP-One." Ostercamp frowned.

"Hey, come on, Cap. I'm ready to go. Tell these funny-talking people I'm back to normal."

"Yeah, you sound like it. Take a rest in a good bed, and we'll see you in the morning. Get some good food and some sleep."

Ten minutes later, Captain Orejuela's jeep had taken Murdock and Lam back to their barracks.

Murdock had talked to the captain about some food. That was the next stop. A mess hall had been provided for the men less than three hundred yards away.

The SEALs ate together on steak, mashed potatoes and gravy, two vegetables, and ice cream for dessert. The coffee was strong and black. When they returned to their barracks, Murdock found a messenger waiting for him. The envelope held a brief message: "See me as soon as possible. The messenger will bring you here." It was signed by Colonel Paredes.

Murdock took Ed DeWitt and Senior Chief Dobler with him. He explained it to the Colómbian.

"Colonel, if this involves a mission for my men, I need these two with me to help evaluate and plan. It's the way we do things in the SEALs."

The colonel frowned for a moment, then rubbed his chin.

"Very well." He introduced them to two of his aides. Murdock couldn't remember their names. Both were majors.

"This is the situation. With our Loyalist Forces, we control most of the Cali area, from the coast to the mountain range to the east. The north flank is our weak spot, and that's where the so-called Democratic Forces are poised, ready to strike south.

"We are strong up the Cauca River Valley all the way to Tulua, which is about a hundred miles north. Beyond that, we have some control up another forty or fifty miles. Above that is the force we estimate at about four thousand men. They have armor and artillery and can call in fighter aircraft with air-to-ground missiles.

"That point is about two hundred miles south of Medellin, the headquarters of the drug syndicate and the second capital. The new president spends most of his time there."

"Do they have plans to move south with their troops?" Murdock asked.

"It's a threat. I'm not sure of their plans. We try for intelligence, but have lost six good men trying to infiltrate their planning section."

"There are good roads along the river, I would guess," Ed DeWitt said.

"Yes, good hard-surfaced roads, and the enemy has enough trucks to move his troops quickly down those roads."

"What about the river?" Dobler asked. "Sir, can it be used by large ships to move his men?"

"Not a factor. We have few ships we could use, and he has none that we know of."

"If we took out his transport, it would be a huge setback for any attack plans," Murdock said.

The colonel brightened. "Yes, good. I understand that he has more than two hundred trucks in the area, many what you Americans call six-by-six trucks."

"How would we get to the general area?" DeWitt asked.

"We could move you at night with one truck to within twenty miles of their outposts. From there on, it would be up to you how to proceed."

"Could we use the truck without your driver beyond that twenty-mile point to ram through their outposts and drive in as far as possible before we went on foot?" Dobler asked.

"Yes, we could sacrifice one of our trucks. But would it be wise to let them know someone was infiltrating?"

"Colonel, if you had that strength, would you worry about one truck trying to break through an outpost or two?"

The colonel chuckled. "No. You're right. They could write it off as a probe, a reconnaissance mission. I see. Yes, it should work. That way, you could get yourselves and a quantity of ammunition, supplies, and explosives in with ease."

"Maybe closer," Murdock said. "Once we break through the first outpost or roadblock, they'll come looking for us. We expect that."

The colonel stood and walked to a large wall map of Colombia.

He touched the area they were talking about. "You can always vanish into the mountains. There is a high range of mountains on both sides of the river valley. Yes, they are high, rugged, and tough. But they could be your salvation."

"How long have that many troops been in this threatening position?" Ed asked.

"As near as we know, they have built up to their present strength in the last six months."

"Do they have buildings or is it in a bivouac situation?"

"They have taken over many buildings so they are inside, have good food, and even entertainment."

"Good. They must be getting a little soft and used to their easy living," Murdock said. "That could be to our advantage once we start working against them."

The colonel went back to his desk. "There may be some urgency. We have heard rumors that the troops up there may be planning on moving within two weeks. They have been doing some training they didn't do before."

"So the quicker we get there, the better," Dobler said.

"Exactly."

"Can we draw some equipment and rations and goods we may not have?" Murdock asked. "We lost some of our matériel when the truck was hit on the way in here."

"Anything we have you need, is yours," the colonel said. He nodded at one of his majors.

"Let us work over some plans tonight and in the morning," Murdock said. "We will want to leave here so we hit their checkpoint just after dark. I'll leave the timing up to you."

"Is there anything else?" the colonel asked.

"We'll need a good, detailed map of the area," Dobler said. "A half dozen would be good, especially if they are waterproofed and the size that we can fold for our pockets."

The colonel said something in Spanish to the major, who made a note.

He looked at them again.

"That should do it for now," Murdock said. "We'll need an H&K machine gun in the NATO round size, and another long automatic rifle. We'll work through Captain Orejuela for those."

"Thank you, Commander. Anything we can do we will be glad to do. Let me or the captain know."

They drove back to the barracks, talking about the mission.

"Captain, we want you in on our planning session. We may be at it late tonight."

"Yes. I want to be there."

At the barracks they pulled the men around and told them about the mission. There were some questions, then Murdock outlined the general plan to get to the adjacent area.

"Once we get within striking distance of the main camp, we'll have to decide what we can do and how to do it."

"Man, we don't want to get into a land war with four thousand troops," Franklin said.

"Amen to that," Bradford said. "So we get in, hit them hard, and vanish into the mountains?"

"Sounds possible. There isn't any lack of mountains around here. How high do they go?" They looked at Captain Orejuela.

"The peaks go from thirty-five hundred feet up to fifty-five hundred. That's coming out of a valley by the river that could be no more than six or eight hundred feet above sea level."

"Lots of trees and brush up there?" Lam asked.

The captain nodded. "Lots of timber type trees and brush. A rain forest. Easy to hide in."

They talked for two hours about how they could get in, blow the motor pool into rubble, and then get out.

"We send in sappers to get as many trucks as possible," Jaybird said. "Then we go with our twenty-mike rounds and riddle the place with the proximity fuses and hope to hit some more gas tanks."

At midnight, Murdock called a halt. "Captain, can you be here at 0800 hours tomorrow? We'll have a list of items we need, including the two new weapons and some more explosives if you have any C-3 or C-4."

"I'll be here."

As they broke up, Murdock called on Holt. They went outside the barracks and set up the SATCOM antenna. It took three calls to raise anyone at Home Base, the carrier.

"Yes, Roamer, this is Home Base. ¿Qué pasa?"

They used voice, but it was all automatically encrypted both ways.

"Don Stroh. You finally made it. We're on site in Cali,

going on a move soon to short-circuit an invasion force. We could use some more of those twenty-mike-mike rounds."

"Sorry, can't do it," Stroh said. "We've had a cease and desist order from the maker. They say not to fire the Bull Pup weapon even in testing. They have found cracks developing in the receiver after two hundred rounds. One of the on-bench test weapons fired automatically actually exploded at 280 rounds."

"So we're not supposed to use them?"

"That's what the maker says."

"Yeah, I hear you. We'll let you know how our first go-round goes here. This is just the beginning. Glad you're on board way out there."

"The weapons, you won't use them?"

"We got the message, Stroh. We got the message. Out."

11

Camp Bravo
Cali, Colombia

Ron Holt looked at Murdock with surprise flooding his face.

"What the hell Stroh mean, we can't use the Bull Pup? Our whole attack plan is formed around those twenty-mikc-mikes."

"Pretend you never heard him," Murdock said. "I didn't hear him say anything about our not using the Bull Pup. We've got them, and we're going to use them. We'll check for cracks in the receiver, but we haven't fired any of ours more than ten times, let alone two hundred and eighty."

"Yeah, take our fucking chances."

"Don't tell anyone what you just didn't hear," Murdock said.

The next day, they left the camp promptly at noon after a heavy meal at the mess hall. They had the two new long weapons and another ten pounds of C-3 they would use on the trucks.

The six-by they rode in was not new, but the engine sounded good, and Tony Ostercamp pronounced it fit for

the 240-mile jaunt. Tony would be driving when they let
the Colombian army man out and went on their own. Murdock rode in the front seat along with Captain Orejuela.
He'd keep them on the right road.

The highway was two lanes, blacktopped, but not built
for speed. The best they did was 45 mph, and that was
down a slight grade. They arrived at Tulua about 1650 and
stopped for the box lunches that the mess at Bravo had sent
with them. It would be MREs from there on.

They passed the second friendly outpost and roadblock
about twenty miles north of Tulua, and the Colombian
driver moved to the side of the road and got out. He chattered with the captain for a moment, then ran back to the
outpost.

Tony Ostercamp took over the wheel. At fifteen miles
beyond the last outpost, Tony turned off the lights. There
was almost no traffic on the road. He managed it in the soft
moonlight. The road hugged the river and went gently
downhill with the flow of the stream.

Five miles farther along, they saw lights ahead.

"Headlamps, of two rigs," Ostercamp said. "They must
hear us coming."

"Turn your lights back on and slow down, then slow
again like you're getting ready to stop." Murdock lifted the
H&K MP-5 he had put on the floorboards and told the men
in back to be ready to shoot at the roadblock as they
rammed through.

The two rigs were positioned so there was room between
them for a truck to get through. As they came closer, Murdock saw that both roadblock rigs were sedans.

"Clip one of them as you ram through," he told Ostercamp. The race car driver and ex–destruction derby driver
grinned.

Fifty yards from the roadblock, they could see six troops
standing beside the cars. Half of them showed rifles. Tony
slowed again, then shifted into second gear and let the engine grind down.

The guards relaxed. Twenty feet from the roadblock,

Tony rammed down on the gas pedal, and the six-by jolted forward in second gear, gaining speed as it covered the ground. He hit the left front fender of one of the sedans, spinning it around as they boiled through the poorly planned roadblock."

Just before they hit, Murdock slammed a dozen rounds from his submachine gun into the gawking troops. Three of them went down.

As they rammed past the cars, the SEALs in back used their Bull Pups on the small barrel and riddled the rest of the men and the cars with the 5.56mm rounds. Tony shifted into high and raced down the road with the headlights on full.

There had been no return fire.

"Anybody hurt?" Murdock asked on the radio.

"Hail no, Cap," Fernandez said. "They didn't know what hit them. We didn't take a single round of return fire."

Ostercamp pointed at the odometer. "Fucking kilometers," he said. "That's point six two percent of a mile. Ten kilometers say six miles. Thirty kilometers, about nineteen miles. We'll watch for thirty kilos on the old dial for the next roadblock."

"Didn't look like they had radios back there," Captain Orejuela said, "so there should be no warning for the next roadblock. I've heard that it's larger, heavier, better manned than this first one."

"So we get past it if we can," Murdock said. "How far from the next roadblock on to the enemy camp?"

"We figure it's about thirty kilometers," the captain said. "There may be more installations leading into the camp."

"So if we get through number two and then drive twenty kilometers more, we should have run through our luck. We stop and set the truck on fire and haul ass into the mountains."

Murdock frowned at the Colombian. "Hey, thought you were heading back with the driver."

"I decided to stay, learn what I can from you. I have my own weapon, a NATO round rifle."

Murdock shrugged. "What the hell, you stick with me and Lam when we go on our look-see. Have to scout out the camp before we wade into it. Want to know what to expect and where to hit them."

Later, Ostercamp gave them a readout. "That's fifteen kilometers, and I don't see any lights ahead. Why no traffic along here?"

"They stop traffic at night for better security," the Colombian captain said.

"So they know we're not supposed to be here," Murdock said.

"Maybe they see an army truck, they wonder if it's one of theirs," Ostercamp put in. "Yeah, that might help us."

Ten minutes later, they saw lights ahead. Ostercamp blinked his lights as if to identify his truck as friendly.

"I want the MG and long guns through slits in the top pointing front," Murdock said on his mike. "As soon as we see any sign they don't like us, we blast them. Everything. This way we don't have to stop and ambush them. The long guns. Maybe two or three minutes. Look alive, stay alive."

They were still two hundred yards away when Murdock saw the winking lights of rifle fire.

"Do it now," Murdock bellowed. He had the Bull Pup out the window and fired the small barrel on two-round bursts. Half a dozen weapons overhead chimed in, and he could see hits on the men ahead. They had a six-by-six truck blocking the center of the highway. A sedan nosed up to the truck on each side, covering the two-lane highway.

"I'm taking the right-hand sedan," Ostercamp said as he gunned the engine. He was doing almost fifty miles an hour when the heavy bumper of the six-by smashed into the grill of the sedan and rammed it fifteen feet off the road into the ditch. The weapons in back of the six-by kept yammering as the truck plowed past the rest of the roadblock and slammed down the highway, picking up speed. This time there had been return fire.

When shooting stopped in the rear, Murdock used his radio again. "Check for casualties. Anybody hit?"

"Yeah, Cap, Jaybird took a round through his left arm below the elbow. Don't look too good. Anybody else hit?"

"Mahanani, check each man, we don't want a KIA not saying anything back there."

A minute later, the radio came on. "Okay, Skipper. No KIAs back here."

That's when Murdock saw the bullet hole in the windshield. The round had missed him. He felt Captain Orejuela slump against his shoulder. In the pale moonlight coming in the windshield, Murdock saw the round, purple hole in the captain's forehead. Carefully, Murdock touched the back of the Colombian's head. It was wet and sticky with fresh blood.

"Men, we do have a KIA up here. The captain took one in the forehead. I didn't notice until just now. He died without making a sound."

The men were quiet. Only the roar of the big engine and the whine of the tires on the road came through.

"How much farther can we go?" Murdock asked Ostercamp.

"Another five miles, and we better look for a lane we can pull off the highway and hide the truck. Come daylight, they'll be scouring this road for it."

"What about the captain?" DeWitt asked.

"We'll have to take time and bury him," Murdock said. "Least we can do. Get his dog tags if he has them. We'll make a map for his family so they can find the grave later."

Ostercamp looked over at his leader. "Commander, looks like we lucked out. Could have been you or me in front of that slug. Damn lucky. Hey, there's a lane to the right. Let's take it and get rid of this truck."

"Go."

A half hour later, they had the truck a quarter mile off the highway. They found a spade strapped to the truck and used it to dig a three-foot-deep grave. They piled rocks over

the fresh earth when they had the grave filled. Murdock
made a map on the back of the area map.

"Back to business," Murdock said. "We have about two
hundred pounds of extra goods we can't carry. We'll move
them a mile forward and hide them."

"We going to burn up the truck?" DeWitt asked. He hurried on. "Figured a fire here would be a beacon to anybody
out looking for us. There had to be a radio in one of those
roadblocks."

"Good," Murdock said. "We won't burn it. Disable it.
Flatten all the tires, mess it up proper. Ostercamp, your
job."

It was just past midnight when Murdock checked his
watch. They had the extra C-4 and TNAZ they couldn't
carry planted near a tree and covered with brush. It would
be easy to find if they needed it to do the job.

"How far we from that camp?" Jaybird asked.

Lam looked up from the map he'd been reading with a
pencil flash. "Looks like about ten miles, maybe twelve."

"Mahanani, how is Jaybird's arm?"

"Slug went on through, missed the bone. Hurts like hell.
Gave him morphine. Wrapped it up damn tight. He's fit for
duty. He made me say that."

Murdock chuckled. "Bet he did at that. Let's move out.
Five-yard intervals, single file so we don't leave too much
of a broad trail. We'll keep to the shoulder of the road until
we get some traffic. Easier than hiking through this damn
rain forest."

An hour later, they had not met any traffic nor had any
come from the rear. The military roadblocks evidently
choked off everything. Another four miles, and they saw
bright lights ahead.

"Roadblock," Lam said after he made a quick recon.

"We go around it to the right," Murdock said. "We don't
want them to know where we are."

Two hours later, Murdock and Lam edged up to a small
ridge top and looked down at the lights.

"Has to be it, Cap," Lam said. "Small town setup. Looks

like a bunch of civilian buildings taken over by the military. I've got some interior guards doing their beats. Military vehicles all over the place."

"So where is the motor pool?"

"Don't see it."

Murdock agreed. "Let's move around to the far side and see what they have there."

Thirty minutes later, they eased up to the side of a road and looked slightly downhill at the rest of the military complex. It had swallowed up nearly half the small town. Barbed wire fences circled the buildings and open spaces. Beyond the fences, the houses and small business buildings looked strangely out of place.

"Oh, yeah," Murdock said putting down his field glasses. "There they are. At least a hundred trucks lined up nose to tail on that lot."

"Got them," Lam said. "Could be another fifty in that big warehouse. It has a drive-through door."

"Any trouble getting inside the fence and planting about twenty charges?" Murdock asked.

Lam chuckled. "Not unless all of our guys go blind and deaf."

"Time is our problem. Not a chance we can get the troops over here and get the charges planted before daylight."

"So we pull the men over here tonight, find a safe hideout, and wait out the white light."

"About the size of it," Murdock said. "Let's move."

It was a little after 0400 when Murdock looked at his lighted-dial watch again. Lam had found them a hide hole a mile back in the mountains from the camp. There were no roads nearby, no trails, farms, nor coffee plantations.

They kept two guards out, and the SEALs went to sleep. Murdock took the first guard until 0600, then would rouse Jaybird. It gave him some time to think.

His mistake so far on this mission was letting Captain Orejuela come along. A lucky shot? Sure, but somehow hot lead had a way of picking out the most vulnerable. It would be his last mistake on this detail.

He thought of the SATCOM. No use in contacting Stroh. He'd yell again about not using the 20-mike-mike, which they most certainly would. It was the most amazing small arms weapon Murdock had ever seen. It would soon set the standard worldwide for the best infantry weapon. He wondered if the makers of the system had the patents on the various components or if the U.S. Defense Department held the patent, since they had probably paid R&D money for the development.

Or had they? It was a competition. Were those financed by Uncle or not? Murdock didn't know. He'd have to find out. Be damned uncomfortable if the Bull Pups went for sale on the open market. If so, he and his men would be fighting against those damn 20-mike-mike exploding rounds before long.

That brought up the wonder of how long he'd be in the SEALs. He had no desire to be in upper management. If he couldn't be in the field, why be a SEAL? Sure, he could probably get to be XO of some team, then eventually the CO. That might fill out his twenty years. He had no aspirations to move up into NAVSPECWARGRUP-one or -two. So, he would be a field SEAL or back in the blue water Navy.

He was sure he could keep his field status as long as he stayed a lieutenant commander. If he ever was promoted to full commander, it would take a direct order from the CNO to keep him working as a field platoon leader, especially in this current platoon.

He had no idea when the sunrise would be in Colombia a few hundred miles north of the equator. By 0530, it was starting to look a little bright in the east, but it didn't get much lighter by 0600 when he rolled Jaybird out of his slumber.

"Time to go to work," Murdock told Jaybird. He mumbled something and tried to turn over, but Murdock sat him up.

"Come on, Jaybird. Rise and shine and smell the coffee.

Only we don't have any coffee and no fires so we won't have any. You awake now?"

"Yeah, damn it." Jaybird shook his head and pulled on his floppy hat. "Now, what's the picture?"

"No change from when you sacked out. We hold here for the day, get all the sleep we can, and get into gear at first dark tonight. You have this end of camp. A Bravo Squad guard should be down there. Let the men sleep in as long as they want to. All they have to look forward to is MREs for breakfast and lunch. Do a two-hour watch and pick the next guard. We'll want somebody on alert all day."

Murdock waited until Jaybird made it to his feet, pulled his MP-5 submachine gun over his shoulder, and started looking around.

Then Murdock slept.

Ching woke up Murdock just after 1030.

"Sorry, Commander, but looks like we have some company not more than three hundred yards down this little canyon. Can't make out what the hell they're doing."

Murdock took out his field glasses and worked up where he could see the visitors. The six soldiers he saw had long rifles, maybe AK-47s or the newer ones from Russia, the AK-74, which fired the smaller 5.45-caliber whizzers.

"What the hell they doing, Commander?" Ching asked.

Murdock set his jaw and squinted at the invaders. "That's what we have to find out before they blow our whole mission," Murdock said.

12

Jungle Area
Colombia

Murdock heard something behind him and saw Lampedusa sliding in beside him with his field glasses up.

"Thought I heard something down there," Lam said.

"How many troops?" Murdock asked.

They both studied the area.

"I've got six," Murdock said.

"Three more just came from behind that brush," Lam said. "Hey, these three have axes and a crosscut kind of saw."

"That's a stand of cedar they're in," Murdock said. "They aren't after wood. Seems like they're sizing up the cedars. Must need some long, straight trees, telephone poles or such."

A moment later, the sound of an ax cutting into wood rang out in the forest. Ed DeWitt dropped down beside them. Murdock handed him his glasses.

"Company," he said.

"Engineers," DeWitt said. "Maybe they want to put up a quick bridge over a creek or small stream."

"I'm not going to stop them," Lam said. "I'll bird-dog them. If they come this way, I'll use the Motorola.

"Yeah," Murdock said. "I could use a few more hours of sleep while I can get it."

"That was an easy one," DeWitt said as they walked the fifty yards back to their temporary camp.

"Yeah, if that's all there is to it. What if they need more cedars and come up to this bunch we're sleeping under?"

DeWitt grunted. "No way. They should have all they need right there, at least for those nine men to drag down the hill."

The JG was right. The lumbermen cut down three cedars, trimmed them, and used a small tractor to drag them down the hill. Two hours later, the men were gone, and the forest took on the natural quietness of a few birds singing and the wind sighing through the treetops.

Murdock had the men up, MREs eaten, and ready to move a half hour before dark. Lam had drawn maps of the motor pool and set up the routes into the place.

Canzoneri took the drawings of the trucks parked close together and worked out a plan to bomb every fourth truck with a quarter pound of C-4 or TNAZ.

"We hit the trucks on the outside all the way around, and they should ignite the ones in the middle. At least no one will be able to drive them out."

"How many men you need with the bombs?" Murdock asked.

"Say we plant forty charges, each man does five, that would be eight men. We'll use the regular timer detonator. Set the first charges at thirty-five minutes, then work down a minute for each new charge to thirty minutes. Then get the hell out of there the same way we went in."

"I want the men with Bull Pups to stay back with me," Murdock said. "We'll be in support if you need it, and as soon as the first blast hits, we'll be using the twenty-mike-mike to raise all sorts of hell."

"What about inside the big garage?" Lam asked.

"Sounds too dangerous to go inside," Canzoneri said.

"We'll play it by ear, depending on the time and the number of guards we have to waste. If we can get some charges inside, we will. Otherwise, the proximity fuses on the twenties could do the trick."

"Agreed," Murdock said. "Timing. We'll move down closer and wait until 2300 before we move in. That will leave us six hours of darkness to make our exfiltration."

"Which direction in case we get split up?" DeWitt asked.

"Like we talked, up the river road we came in on. Our objective is that first Loyalist roadblock up the river about forty miles away."

"Walk in the park," Ronson said.

"I want all of the Bull Pup shooters over here," Murdock said. Jefferson, Mahanani, Franklin, Ching, Lampedusa, and Canzoneri came over. Murdock took Canzoneri's Bull Pup and gave him his submachine gun.

"Pick your sappers from the rest of the men. Take the MP-5 guys. We don't want anybody packing a heavy MG in there."

The men were chosen, and Canzoneri gave them each their five bombs with the detonator/timer inserted. All they had to do was dial in the time and leave the bomb.

"We'll put the charges in the fuel tank filler tube or on the gas tank when we can," Canzoneri said.

When it was fully dark, Murdock marched the SEALs away from their hideout. It was less than two miles when they arrived at the brushy section just across from the motor pool. The whole truck park blazed with lights, and two dozen men worked in and around some of the trucks.

"Not normal maintenance," Ostercamp said. "That they would do during the day. They seem to be checking the oil, tires, like they might be getting ready to move out."

"We wait."

Lam came up with a suggestion. "We could send the men into the motor pool from both sides. It would take a fence cut on each side, but I doubt if any of it is fixed with alarms."

Murdock and Lam talked to Canzoneri, who agreed.

They dug out two wire cutters, and Canzoneri gave one to each squad. He led one four-man detail and Will Dobler led the other one. He volunteered to go in.

They waited.

By 2200, half the lights had been turned off, and only two men still worked on trucks. By midnight, the last flood-lights snapped off and only what must be the normal night-lights remained. Murdock watched the scene and nodded.

"Remember, go back out the hole in the fence you went in. Any shooting must be with the silencers. Get outside the wire and get back here where we'll be throwing in the twenty-mike-mikes."

Murdock watched them move away through his NVGs. The fence didn't need cutting. They simply lifted up the bottom barbed wire strand and crawled under it. Then he lost them in the gloom of the trucks.

A jeep rolled around the area, snapped on its lights, and Murdock could see one man jump off the jeep and run toward the trucks with a weapon up. The man stumbled and fell. He didn't move. The driver in the jeep stepped out of the rig and promptly fell backward onto the seat and didn't move.

Murdock nodded. Those sound suppressors were great little gadgets.

He checked his watch. The men had been inside for fif-teen minutes. It was taking longer than they had figured. Then he spotted two shadows running for the fence. They were joined by two more. He checked the other entry point and saw three of his men there, crawling under the fence. Where was the last man?

He waited as the three men vanished into the brush. Just as he was about to call Ed DeWitt, the fourth man stumbled away from the trucks and limped toward the fence. He fell down as he reached it and crawled under it. On the other side, two men appeared and helped him up, and they all ran into the brush.

"Canzoneri, I have eight men out of the wire. One is hurt. Are you on your way back here?"

"That's a roger, Commander. I'm the one hurting. Had a small argument with a guard over a knife he wanted to give me. The guys tied up the leg slice. I should be mobile. See you in about ten. The charges have another twelve or thirteen to boom boom."

"Take it easy, Canzoneri. Good job. No rush getting here."

Murdock brought his Bull Pup shooters up. He spotted them ten yards apart. "As soon as the charges go off, we start shooting into the open door of the big garage. Two on the right concentrate on the trucks in the center of the park. We need to get those burning as well. If any group of ten or more men charge into the area, use the twenties on them. For now, let's do ten rounds each, then see what happens."

The eight sappers had not returned to the firing line when the first charge went off. It must have been in a fuel tank. The crack of the near air explosion slammed through the air, followed at once by a gush of flames and then a roaring of fire as gasoline from the tank caught on fire, splattering twenty yards away and burning furiously.

Seconds later, five more explosions rocked the motor pool. Sirens wailed below. Men ran from one building to another. As more and more charges detonated, the trucks parked on the outside row erupted in flames and created secondary explosions as more gas tanks went off. Less than a minute after the first charge, Murdock saw that almost all of the trucks on the outside ring around the park were on fire, and the flames were spreading to trucks parked next to them and all the way to the center.

"Now," Murdock said and fired the Bull Pup's 20-mike-mike round through the black entrance of the large garage. As he hoped, the laser dot had affixed somewhere inside the structure, and his round went through the open door before it exploded. He fired two more through the door, then looked at the trucks inside the circle of fire. Too many of them had not caught fire.

"Get the trucks," Murdock shouted. The gunners shifted their target, and the trucks began taking the exploding

20-mike-mike rounds. Some merely pulverized the windows, windshields, and tops with the deadly shrapnel. Others took direct hits on the engine or gas tanks, sparking a fire and then an explosion.

By the time Murdock had fired eight rounds, he couldn't find a truck that wasn't on fire. He looked farther down the camp. A formation of twenty to thirty men marched toward the fires. He put one round just ahead of them, and they walked right into the rain of flesh-shredding hot steel. A dozen went down, the rest scattered. For his last round, he picked a building well beyond the motor pool and fired. It was a wake-up call, something for the brass at the camp to think and wonder about.

When Murdock finished his last round, he saw that most of the others were through as well. Two more shots fired, then the men looked at him.

He used the mike. "Canzoneri, what's your position?"

"Making it, Cap. We're about fifty yards from you and moving. How did the bonfire go?"

"Beautiful, Canzoneri. Just like you laid it out. I don't think a truck parked outside escaped. Not sure how much hurt we did them inside, but they won't be transporting four thousand men anywhere for a long time."

"Commander, we've got some visitors," Mahanani said. "Beyond the motor pool."

Murdock checked in the string of lights below. What looked like a company of armed men double-timed toward the motor pool.

"Two rounds each into the formation," Murdock said. They used the proximity fuzes, and the rounds would detonate ten or fifteen feet over the marching men. Three rounds hit almost at the same time, and Murdock was amazed at the result. It was like dropping in a half dozen 40mm grenades. Twenty or thirty men slammed to the ground. Most never got up. Others screamed and ran away from the formation, dripping blood. More rounds hit and slaughtered another twenty. By the time the last round exploded in the area, there were few soldiers standing and none coming forward.

"My God!" Colt Franklin said. "This Bull Pup should be classified as top secret and our new top weapon. My God! Did you see what we did down there with twenty rounds?"

The other SEALs were quiet.

"You said it all, buddy," Jefferson said. "I just found my true love: this damned little Bull Pup."

They heard noise to the left.

"Hey, Canzoneri coming in," the Motorolas whispered. The sapper came in, limping badly. Mahanani was the first one to him. He took off the temporary bandage made from a shirtsleeve. He had Canzoneri behind some brush to screen him from the camp and hovered over him with a pencil flash in his mouth.

He washed the four-inch slice in Canzoneri's thigh with disinfectant, then used some cinch bandages and pulled the sliced-open flesh together until it matched. Then he treated it with ointment and put a bandage around it to keep it clean and help hold the cut together.

Ed DeWitt came up, and he and Murdock talked about the route out. Lam knelt down with them.

"Back this side of the river, same way we came in," Murdock said. "Mahanani, over here." The medic came, putting his kit back in place.

"How's Canzoneri?"

"I'd say he can make the forty miles. But not all in one chunk. Some transport would be nice."

"Roger that. Let's get put together and move out. Lam out front. We'll do a column of ducks unless it gets too hairy. My guess is that they will send out at least six patrols trying to track us down. We need to get ahead of them."

DeWitt put Canzoneri right beside him on the move and kept a tight watch on him. "Canzoneri, I know your leg is hurting like hell. You'll get another morphine in an hour. If we're going too fast, give me a yell. We go the rest of the way at your pace."

"Hell, no sweat, JG. Just a fucking scratch. I can keep up with these bastards any day."

DeWitt stared into Canzoneri's eyes a moment and saw the determination there. He moved out again with the rest of the men.

They were what Murdock figured was five miles from the smoking ruins of the motor pool when Lam held up his hand for a stop. Murdock moved up to see the situation.

"Figure there's about ten of them," Lam said. "Must have taken a radio call and come up from somewhere down this way. How would they know we were on this side of the river?"

"Where we fired from," Murdock said.

"There," Lam said. They saw two men run across an open space about thirty yards ahead.

"I need six men up here on a company front," Murdock whispered into his mike. "They're too close for the twenties. Use the rifles or the 5.56 on the Pup. Quietly."

The two men ahead who ran across the open space went back the other way.

"What the hell they doing?" Lam asked.

"Scouts," Murdock said. He felt rather than heard men coming into a line on both sides of him and Lam.

They heard a loud click, then a greatly amplified voice boomed across the open space and through the woods.

"U.S. SEALs. We know you have invaded our sacred Colombian homeland. There is no way you can escape. We have you completely surrounded. You will die here, SEALs. Your blood and your bodies will fertilize our fine Colombian soil. You will die, SEALs. Every one of you will be cut down and dead within an hour."

13

Forest Area
Southern Colombia

Murdock chuckled softly. Into the mike he said: "Don't pay any attention to the voice. It's an old trick the Japanese used hundreds of times in World War Two. The Colombians probably do this with every patrol that goes out. They set up in a blocking position and tell us exactly where they are. I do wonder how they know we're SEALs or that we're even in the country. That will keep.

"Lam and I'll go take a look, see who they are, and reduce them if practical. Lam, get an MP-5 with suppressor on it. Let's see how good we are."

Lam and Murdock moved out silently, working ahead slowly, not rustling a leaf. They worked slightly to the right of the open space and then forward a tree at a time. After forty yards, Lam was five yards ahead. He looked back at Murdock and motioned him forward.

They looked through a screen of trees and spotted a cluster of six soldiers. They had taken off their helmets and sprawled on the grassy mulch under the tall trees. Both Lam and Murdock had their NVGs. The soldiers drank from canteens and talked quietly with each other.

Murdock looked for any insignia. Dumbest thing an officer can do is wear his rank on his uniform or helmet in a combat situation. He found one. A single bar that could have been silver or gold. A lieutenant.

As they watched, three more soldiers came into the area. They dropped their weapons and helmets and sat on the ground near the other men. The officer stood to one side near a packboard that held a large, square object that Murdock decided was a battery. The Lieutenant picked up a microphone, turned a switch, and trumpeted his brave words into the night again. Now Murdock saw the two-foot-square speaker.

Murdock patted his silenced submachine gun and switched it to single shot. He showed Lam the weapon.

"Pick off the outsiders one at a time. When they panic, we throw in two grenades each."

Lam nodded and switched his MP-5 to single shot. He gave Murdock a thumbs-up, and they settled in. Lam would take the left side and Murdock the right.

Murdock saw one man at the far right. It looked like he had curled up and gone to sleep. Murdock zeroed in on his chest and fired. From thirty yards away, the effect was immediate. The man jolted with the entry of the bullet, then lay still. Lam found two targets on his side, then Murdock checked for the officer. He had sat down beside the loudspeaker. Murdock caught him with a round in the chest, but he shrilled out a warning scream as he dove for his rifle. Murdock's second round silenced him.

The troops scrambled for their weapons and helmets. Lam had out his grenade and threw first. Murdock's came a quick second later. Both exploded almost at the same time, the shrapnel slicing into half the Colombian soldiers. Two men lifted up and darted toward the woods. Lam caught one of them with a three-round burst, but the other one vanished into the woods.

Lam pointed toward the runner. Murdock shook his head.

"We'd never catch him. He's running for his life, and he

knows the territory." Murdock hit his lip mike. "Clear in front, move out, and we'll meet you just past the cleared zone."

"Roger that, skipper," Ed DeWitt responded.

Murdock looked at Lam. "Let's go down there and make sure everyone is dead."

They checked. Lam fired one shot from his MP-5, then the two SEALs went forward and toward the far end of the cleared space. The rest of the platoon was there when they arrived.

"One got away," Murdock told the troops. "If he gets back to his unit and if they have a radio, the rest of the damn army will know where we were. We better shag ass out of here." He looked at Canzoneri. "How's the leg?"

"Fine, Skipper. Just fine."

Murdock put Mahanani beside him, and they took off in a column of twos through the woods and angled toward the valley ahead of them and the road. It would be much easier marching along the shoulder or on the blacktop than through the thick brush.

Murdock led them out at a four-mile-an-hour pace. He checked with the medic after a half hour.

"He's keeping up, but he's hurting, Commander," Mahanani said. "Probably should drop it down a notch. I'd just as soon not have to carry him."

"Done," Murdock said. He sent word to Lam, who was out in front of the main body by fifty yards. The pace slowed.

They kept two hundred yards from the road, crashing brush as they went. Just when Murdock thought it might be safe to go to the blacktop below, a vehicle came boiling down the road. It had a machine gun mounted on it and every hundred yards, it blasted a dozen rounds into the brush. It worked alternate sides, then sometimes hit the same side three times.

When the rig was opposite them, the gunner turned the weapon toward their side of the road and fired off two six-round bursts.

The singing lead went high over their heads, but the SEALs had flattened to the ground with the sound of the first round. They stayed down as the jeep moved on down the road, the MG yammering again and again with wasted rounds into the brush.

They had been up and moving for ten minutes when the speaker came on in Murdock's ear.

"Skipper, I need ten minutes with our Petard guy. The wound broke open."

Murdock stopped the march, spread out the troops, and went back to see how Canzoneri was doing.

"No sweat, Commander," Canzoneri said. "Just a little blood came out and doc here got in a panic. Hell, I'm good for another thirty miles."

After the hospital corpsman had rebandaged the knife slice, Murdock talked to the medic.

"Mahanani, you still do that hypnotism?"

"Sure. You think now is a good time?"

"The farther we can get away from the federales out there before daylight, the better. Would Canzoneri be a good subject?"

"Never can tell. I'll ask him. He's smart enough to know how it would help him."

Canzoneri grinned when they told him.

"Hell, yes, give it a try. Never been put under, but I've heard a lot about it. Then I could hike normally and it wouldn't hurt at all?"

"About the size of it."

"Let's do it."

Canzoneri seemed to struggle against the hypnotic suggestion, but after five minutes, Mahanani had him under.

The march continued. They moved back to a four-mile-an-hour pace. When Canzoneri kept up, Murdock moved the speed up a notch.

A half hour later, the machine gunner on the enemy truck came past. This time, he fired on the other side of the road and the SEALs breathed easier.

Murdock took them down to the road, and they jogged for

two miles without meeting any traffic. The nighttime curfew on travel worked to the SEALs' advantage here. An hour later, they saw the machine-gunning rig headed their way, and they slipped into the brush and behind a small hill for cover.

Ed DeWitt dropped down beside Murdock. "Hey, you been thinking about that roadblock up ahead?"

"Some."

"Seems like a good time for a little share-the-ride time. We should be able to move in and take out the personnel, then borrow one of their vehicles and charge right through that second roadblock down the way."

"Sounds good, JG. Your idea, your mission. How far you figure the roadblock is?"

"My guess is about four miles out. I'll stay with Lam out front and watch for it. We should hit it from both sides at a forty-five angle. Be surprised if they have more than six men on the block. We'll tell the men not to shoot up the vehicles."

"Let's move it," Murdock said on the Motorola. "Same formation. The JG will be out front with Lam."

They saw the roadblock after three miles hiking on the blacktop. There had been no more motor traffic. Lam took them into the woods a quarter of a mile from the block, and they made their plans.

Ed DeWitt took his squad to the left-hand side of the lights on the highway, and Murdock kept his on the right. They stopped forty yards from the block and set up firing positions.

"We're looking for one of those rigs for transport," Murdock told his men. "Lots faster than walking."

"Then we blast through the next roadblock?" Ronson asked.

"That's the plan, unless we can fly over it. We'll fire on Ed's first rounds. Remember, don't damage the vehicles."

There were three of them. Two sedans and an older-looking six-by that blocked the center of the road. Murdock hoped it would still run. It must if they drove it out here.

Ronson had his H&K 21-E machine gun set up and ready. Bill Bradford had his PSG1 sniper rifle ready. The Pups would be on single-round fire.

"Let's do it," DeWitt said on the radio and fired his G-11 caseless-round submachine gun. A heartbeat later, the rest of the SEAL weapons opened fire.

Murdock made five men at the site. All five went down in the first volley.

"Hold," Ed called on the radio.

One man dove out of the cab of the six-by and ran for the brush. He didn't make it as three SEAL rounds dug into his body and sprawled him in the leaves and grass.

"Quinley, take a look," DeWitt said. The smallest man in the platoon at five-nine held his caseless submachine gun at port arms and charged into the scene. He kicked two of the bodies, fired into two more, and checked out the two sedans and the truck.

"Clear front," Quinley said.

Ostercamp ran ahead of the rest of the squad to the six-by and checked it out. He tried to read the gauges in the dark, then turned on the key and tried the engine. It ground over twice, then on the third try kicked over and settled down into a gentle roar.

"Pick up any weapons and ammo you can find and put them in the six-by," Murdock instructed. "Somebody search those two sedans."

Two minutes after the first rounds hit the men at the roadblock, the SEALs were loaded into the truck and Ostercamp drove it south down the road.

Murdock sat in the front seat with Ronson's NATO round machine gun. "Cut slots in that canvas so you can fire to the front over the cab," Murdock said on the Motorola. We'll need all the firepower we have when we roll into this last roadblock. They might have been alerted by radio from the main camp."

"We figured it was about twenty miles between the road-blocks," Ostercamp said Dufim. Murdock asked him.

"We're doing about forty miles per hour. So, should take us about a half hour to get there."

"Good, we'll be ready."

They drove without lights. Ostercamp said it was no problem.

Murdock used the mike. "Hey, Canzoneri, how are you doing?"

"He's sleeping right now," the platoon medic answered. "I told him to get some rest. He's still under. I can bring him out any time you want."

"Let's keep him that way until we see if we can get through this next roadblock with our wheels intact."

"That's a roger, sir."

Twenty minutes later, Ostercamp motioned ahead. "I can see the roadblock. Looks like they've got a fire going and some headlights on. They can't see us yet. Because of the lights, they're night blind up there."

"Turn on our lights and keep going. Start slowing down like last time when you're about two hundred yards off. Then, at a hundred yards, floor it, and we'll open fire."

"Roger, that. Not sure if they have a truck or not up there or maybe three sedans. Yeah, that's more like it. One sedan right in the middle of the road. I can take out the one on the right and blast it back off the road."

"Coming up on it," Murdock said to the lip mike. "Get all the firepower we can out the front. No twenty-mikes. I don't know how they would work from a moving rig. We'll open fire a hundred yards. Hit anything that moves."

Murdock had the machine gun locked and loaded, ready to push out the window and whale away at the roadblock. He heard the men getting the other weapons ready.

"Two hundred so I'm slowing down. I see three guards, probably that many off duty sleeping. Slowing more. At a hundred and fifty." He paused, then hit the throttle. "A hundred yards. Open fire."

Murdock saw his rounds slam into the three sedans and some of the men. He pounded off six-round bursts until the belt ran out. By that time, they were on top of the defenders. He heard the weapons over his head slamming dozens of rounds at the roadblock. He couldn't see anyone standing.

Then the heavy six-by rammed into the sedan on the right, which bounced off the thick bumper and jolted backward into the ditch. The big truck slammed through the opening and gunned on down the road.

Behind in the six-by, the SEALs turned around and fired at the roadblock they had just come through.

"No return fire," DeWitt said on the radio.

"Cease fire," Murdock said on the net. "I want a casualty report. Was anyone hit? Alpha Squad." His six men checked in as okay. DeWitt took a roster rundown and found no new wounds.

"Ostercamp, how much gas we have left?" Murdock asked.

"Don't think the gauge works, Cap. I've been watching the needle, and it says half full, but it hasn't moved since we started. All we can do is drive her until she quits."

"How far to the first Loyalist roadblock?"

"As I remember, about twenty-five miles. It's a wide no-man's land between the enemy lines down here."

Ed DeWitt came on the radio. "Commander, how do we get into the Loyalist's roadblock without getting ourselves blown to hell? I saw a rack of RPGs there when we came up. One of those rocket-propelled grenades into this rig, and most of us are going to be flying home in body bags."

"No sweat," Murdock said. "It's about 0230 now. Another hour at most, and we should be there. We'll stop off five hundred yards with our lights out and send Fernandez up to work past the checkpoint in the brush and come back to the road on the other side. Then he walks into the roadblock and with his Spanish tells them who we are and that we're driving in with an enemy truck."

"Yeah, I can do that," Fernandez said. "These jokers have a weird accent, but I can understand them."

It went just that way.

By 0400, Murdock dictated a statement to Fernandez who

translated it for the radio operator at the Loyalist roadblock. The message went to Colonel Paredes, informing him of the success of the campaign with an estimated 150 six-by trucks destroyed. He also reported that Captain Orejuela had been killed in action during the drive through an enemy check-point.

The radio operator nodded that he had sent the message and Fernandez looked at Murdock.

"What now, Cap?"

"Now we take a leisurely hundred and fifty mile ride back to Camp Bravo, have a big meal, and catch up on our sleep."

The SEALs were all back in the truck and Ostercamp had just started the engine, when the radio operator came running out of the shack beside the roadblock. He handed a message to Murdock. It was written in Spanish.

"Fernandez, front and center," Murdock bellowed.

Fernandez read the message in the headlights.

"Congratulations on your mission accomplished. Sorry about Captain Orejuela. Must ask you to make all possible speed to return to Camp Bravo. Have had a disturbing and threatening development here. We will expect you some-time this morning."

The message was from Colonel Paredes.

Murdock looked at Ostercamp. "Did you get some gas from the trucks here?"

"Did that, Commander. The tank is full, and the gauge still reads half."

"Good. We'll need it. We have to get back to Camp Bravo as fast as we can. Don't spare the horses."

Murdock climbed in the cab, wondering what the hell had happened that involved them.

14

Camp Bravo
Cali, Colombia

It was just past 1100 before the truck turned in at the main gate at Camp Bravo. Murdock had Ostercamp drive directly to the base hospital.

"Ed, get the men settled and weapons cleaned. Then they can hit the mess hall before they sack out. I'll get Canzoneri and Jaybird treated and see you as soon as I can. Then we go see the colonel."

Canzoneri winced but didn't cry out as the medics in the hospital took off the bandages. They cleaned the wound, asked how old it was, and after treating it, stitched it up. The doctor didn't speak English, and Murdock's Spanish was as sketchy as the other SEALs'.

"¿Quando tiempo?" Murdock asked. The doctor frowned. A nurse going by paused. She said something to the doctor who brightened. He spoke to her and she nodded.

"He says he wants to keep your man here for at least three days to watch the healing," she said in English. The wound was open for a long time."

"Thanks, my Spanish is not good. Could I hire you as my personal interpreter?"

She was slender, in her mid-twenties, and with darting brown eyes. Her pretty face broke into a smile. "Afraid not. I have a lot of other work to do. Sick people, wounded men."

The doctor spoke again. She listened and interpreted. "He says that your man will be fine, but he can't go charging around like a wild man for a few days."

She smiled. "Are you American SEALs wild men?"

"Does everyone in Colombia know that we're here?"

She nodded.

"Well, to answer your question, usually we aren't wild men. Now, I need to go see your Colonel Parades."

She waved. *"Hasta luego,"* she said.

"That's something about going in health. I'll try."

Murdock checked where a doctor had looked at Jaybird's shot arm. He had cleaned the wound, treated it on both sides, and bandaged it again. He said Jaybird should check back in the hospital in three days.

At the colonel's office, Murdock was shown in at once. Ed DeWitt and Jaybird Sterling sat in the outer office waiting for him.

"They stitched up Canzoneri. He's on the shelf for three days."

A lieutenant opened the inner door and ushered the men inside. One army major worked over the camp map at a side table.

"Gentlemen. Glad you're back, and congratulations on your mission," the colonel said. "I have sent condolences to Captain Orejuela's wife. This new problem is a nasty one.

"Late last night, a small force broke through our exterior guards and attacked and captured our communications center. It is the heart of our operation. Without it we have only a few radios like the one we contacted you on.

"The insurgents may be rebels working with the federal troops or they may be an elite force of the federal commandos. We don't know which. Come to the table."

He waited for them to move over.

"The communications center is here in this concrete-block building. It is a fortress and was designed that way. It is three stories high, easy to defend, nearly impossible to penetrate.

"Heading the incursion is a man who calls himself Colonel Rafael Cardona. He is holding forty of our men and civilian employees inside the building as hostages. He has made demands, unreasonable demands. If they are not met, he says he will kill a hostage every four hours. This morning at 0800 he pushed a dead lieutenant out the front door and allowed our medics to pick him up. He had been shot. We're not sure if he was killed during the takeover or executed."

"What are the demands?" Murdock asked.

"First, he said I had to surrender my whole army to the legitimate president. I told him I didn't command the army, President Ocampo does. Then he said I had to surrender Camp Bravo, at once.

"When I refused, he pushed the dead lieutenant out the door. That was almost four hours ago."

An aide came in the room with a message. The colonel read it and he sagged against the table.

"I have word that a corporal was released by this Colonel Cardona. As he walked out the door of the communications center, he was shot in the back six times and died instantly. Cardona says the corporal is the second hostage to die. I must act quickly."

"How many men does he have?" Ed DeWitt asked.

"He claims he has a hundred. Some of our people saw him enter the building late last night. They say they saw twelve men."

"Is there any underground access to the building?" Jaybird asked.

"No, only the surface doors. It does have a small basement."

"Are there windows?" Murdock asked.

"Yes, but now they have blinds drawn on all of them."

"Metal blinds?"

"No, fabric."

"You have a helicopter?"

"Yes, three of them. One will carry six men."

"You have some tanks?"

"Yes, two."

"Let us talk a minute," Murdock said. He and the other two SEALs went to the corner of the room and threw out ideas. Murdock grabbed them and formed his plan.

They went back to the map.

"Colonel, bring your tanks up to the least sensitive part of the building, say where they keep records, files, the non-communication part."

"I can do that."

"Order them up now and have them manned and ready to fire."

The colonel nodded to his aide, who left the room.

"Now, we'll want to get our equipment, then your chopper will put six of us on the roof. The rest of my men will be situated around the front of the structure. Where would he keep the hostages?"

"Probably in the basement behind a locked metal door."

"Good. Our men will fire into the windows. I want you to put one tank round into this side of the building at the exact time that we land on the roof in the chopper. My men will fire special rounds through the window that will explode inside. Then we will come down from the roof through the access door and clear the building.

The colonel frowned. "Will this work?"

"Yes. The shot into the wall will confuse them. Our special twenty-mike-mike rounds exploding inside the rooms will paralyze them. Then we swing down the stairs with our submachine guns, and they will be easy targets."

"Let's give it a try. I don't want to lose any more men."

"We need an hour to get set up. Have your chopper land as close to our quarters as possible. We'll also need a truck for transport."

"Yes, easy. Right this way."

An hour later, the chopper circled a block away from the communications building as the two tanks swung into place fifty yards from the back wall of the structure.

DeWitt had Bravo Squad in firing positions fifty yards from the front of the building.

"When we hear tank fire, we shoot out the windows with the 5.56 rounds," Ed DeWitt told his squad. "Do your assigned windows. Then at once aim your laser through the broken window so the round will go inside and detonate there. Everyone with me?"

A chorus of yeahs came back.

Murdock saw the tank operator give the signal he was going to fire. The chopper wheeled and headed for the rooftop.

The tank fired one round that exploded against the back of the building. By then, Murdock couldn't see the results. The bird had touched down on the roof, and he and his Alpha Squad boiled out of it. Bill Bradford was the first one to the roof access door. It was the built-up kind, probably with steps leading down. It was not padlocked on the outside.

Bradford caught the handle and tried to turn it. Locked. He blasted the area just below the handle twice with his MP-5 silenced sub gun and the door swung inward. He jumped to one side. No shots came through. He looked in, then stepped inside and vanished.

"Clear down here on the third floor," Bradford said on the lip mike. "Looks deserted."

The other SEALs went down the steps quietly. They heard shots from the outside, then muted explosions downstairs.

Murdock looked around. There was a staircase to the left next to the wall. They moved that way. He waved Jaybird to take a look. He carried a borrowed MP-5 submachine gun and eased down the steps one at a time. Then he swung the weapon around and pulled off a three-shot burst of silent rounds. He jolted down the rest of the way to the second floor.

"Hold fire on the second floor, twenty-mike shooters," Murdock said on the lip mike. "Alpha Squad's now on floor two near the back. Hold your twenty fire here." The rest of the squad raced down the steps and found Jaybird checking out a man in green and brown cammies.

"Dead," Jaybird said. "Only one up here. The rest of them must be on the first floor. This one was a lookout, I'd guess. He doesn't look more than about twelve years old."

The stairs didn't continue to the first floor. On the far side of the big room they found two doors and beyond them more space with desks and cubicles with snapshots of family on them. Through another door they could see a stairway leading down.

The squad checked three more rooms but found no one there. Murdock took the lead at the stairs. He edged up to them and looked down. There was a landing halfway down, then the stairs turned for the next run to the ground floor.

Murdock heard an explosion and lunged back away from the shrapnel of the 20-mike-mike. "Hold the twenty fire on the first floor," Murdock said to the Motorola. "Alpha Squad soon to be in residence." Then he surged downstairs to the landing. His MP-5 was on full auto, and he sprayed a dozen rounds in one direction, whirled, and fired six more the other way. Ching lunged down the steps to back him. He saw four men huddled in one corner. Their weapons had been abandoned and they held up their hands. Three men on the other side lay sprawled where the 20-mike-mike rounds had caught them in the open and laced their bodies with shrapnel wounds, killing them.

Two shots blasted into the silence from directly ahead of them. Both were high. Ching swung his MP-5 around and sent a dozen silent rounds slamming into a desk and thin partition where he had seen movement. A high, snarling yell pierced the big room, and slowly, a man stumbled out from the partition, a rifle falling from his hands as he took one look at his executioner and pitched forward on the floor.

"No dispare!" a voice called from behind them. Murdock turned to see a figure stand. She was short and he guessed no more than fourteen. She wore cammies and her long hair had been bound up and hidden under a floppy hat. She held both hands high over her head and she had no weapon.

Ching yelled something at her in Spanish, and she lowered her hands.

Ching asked her something and she shook her head. Then he shouted in Spanish, but there was no reply.

"The rest of Alpha Squad come on down," Murdock said in the Motorola. "Let's clear this place and find the hostages."

The girl motioned to Murdock. "Hostages this way," she said in English. She led them to the far corner of the room where a stairway went to a basement.

Murdock used the Motorola. "Holt, get the front door open, but be careful until we get this floor cleared. The rest of you get it cleared quickly."

The girl pointed down the steps. He saw a steel door with a pair of steel bolts.

"Hostages down there," the girl said. He motioned her forward. She went to the door and pulled back one of the bolts. Murdock opened the other one and swung the door outward.

People lay on the floor, sat against the walls. Two women cried silently, men sat talking. All stopped and looked up when the door opened. The girl spoke rapidly in Spanish and the people in the room began to cheer and cry for joy.

"Tell them to stay here until we're sure the first floor is safe," he told her. Then he ran back up the steps.

"Clear right," Sterling said.

"Clear left," Bradford chimed in.

"Clear front and back," Ronson said. "All clear, Commander."

As soon as the front doors opened, Colonel Paredes and a squad of heavily armed soldiers rushed inside. They took the four men in cammies prisoner and marched them outside. Murdock called to the girl to let the workers come up.

Later that day, Murdock found out that the four terrorists were executed by a firing squad on Colonel Paredes's orders. The young girl sent to a women's prison for six months. The commander of the raid, self-styled Colonel Cardona, was one of the men killed by the deadly shrapnel of the exploding 20mm rounds.

Murdock called for a radio check on casualties. There were none. They found the truck they came over in and drove back to their barracks.

"Damn, did those twenty-mike-mikes work good," Jefferson said. "We could see the rounds go through the window and then explode inside. Must have been hell on wheels in there when we put ten rounds through the windows in less than a minute."

DeWitt laughed. "Oh, yeah, those twenty-mike-mikes are going to be on my wish list for every mission we go on. I have a suggestion, though. We should get more weapons. We had to borrow some of the MP-5s you guys had. We need it so about half of us can use either the MP-5 or the Bull Pup. Those old widow makers still come in damned handy in a room-to-room situation like Alpha Squad had."

Murdock agreed with him. Murdock had just finished cleaning and oiling the borrowed MP-5 when Holt came up with the SATCOM.

"Figured that I better leave the receiver on," he said. "Seems Don Stroh has been trying to get us now for a day and a half."

Murdock took the handset. Holt nodded. "Lost Sheep calling the Shepherd," he broadcast and grinned.

"Lost Sheep? That you Murdock?"

"Not anymore, you found us. Thanks, Shepherd."

"Quit clowning around on government time. Had some signals from the CNO. He wants a report. What the hell you doing in there with Colonel Paredes?"

Murdock gave him a quick rundown but didn't mention the 20mm rounds.

"Yeah, sounds like you earned your keep. The CNO says

he's getting pressure for you to do something on the drug front. He says there are half a dozen big cocaine labs right near Cali that turn the coca paste into cocaine. That's your next assignment. To tear up some of those labs and put them out of business."

"Are the labs illegal?" Murdock asked.

"Damn right. At least they were under the old regime. This new bastard president is living off cocaine. We shrivel up their payroll, and they won't have so much clout."

"We need a contact who knows where these labs are."

"Talk to Colonel Paredes. He works closely with Ex-president Manuel Ocampo. They can tell you."

"Stroh, I have a bad feeling about this one."

"Oh, yeah? You don't get paid to feel, Murdock. I've got pressure on this I can't even tell you about. Just get in there and blow up a few labs, and we'll get you out before the locals lynch you."

"We love you, too, Stroh."

15

Camp Bravo
Cali, Colombia

Two hours after the talk with Stroh, Murdock had an order to report to the colonel's office for a briefing. The message said to come alone.

Murdock took the jeep that they had left for the SEALs' use and drove to the commander's office. He was escorted directly to the colonel's lair. Murdock saluted smartly.

"Lieutenant Commander Murdock reporting as ordered, sir."

The colonel returned the salute.

"Sit down, Commander. This may take a while. First, our thanks for your good work on our commo center. It's almost back to normal operation. The rebels didn't try to smash the equipment. I'm not sure what they wanted to do. At least that's over with, and we lost only two men. Did you have any casualties?"

"None, Colonel."

"Good." The colonel looked at the ceiling for a moment.

"Commander, we knew when we asked for help from you that there would be a favor or two we'd need to do in

return. I received orders from my president an hour ago.
I've been trying to make sense of them ever since.

"As you may know, Colombia has been the world's leading processor of cocaine for years. It's not a record that
I'm proud of. Our president had worked as best he could
to fight the drug problem. The drug cartels won when they
trashed our recent election and, by fraud and outright hoo-
liganism, took over the federal government.

"Now I'm instructed to help you find and destroy cocaine
processing plants in the Cali area, and then plants in the
Medellin area." The colonel sighed. "This is most difficult
for me. I'm a military man, not a social or political re-
former. But when my president gives me an order, I carry
it out.

"What do you know about the cocaine trade, Commander?"

"Very little, Colonel."

"Some basics. Cocaine is derived from the leaf of the
coca tree. There are two varieties, and both are grown in
the Andes mountains of Peru and Bolivia from altitudes of
fifteen hundred to six thousand feet.

"Growing coca leaves is legal in these countries. The
shrubs can grow to twelve feet tall, and after four years,
they bear leaves, which are harvested four times a year.
The leaves are then dried in the sun and taken to a processing plant.

"This initial processing breaks down the leaves and eventually leads to a product called coca paste. A thousand
pounds of dry leaves yields ten pounds of coca paste.

"At this point, most of the Peru and Bolivia coca paste
is shipped to Colombia where it is processed further into
cocaine. It's a complicated and intricate process that is
used, with the end result producing crack cocaine or pure
cocaine powder. This is the product that's sold around the
world on the black market illegally. Most of it goes to the
United States.

"The key here is economics. The hill country farmers in
Peru and Bolivia, the *campesinos*, can make four times as

much growing coca leaves as they can any other product. Here in Colombia, the cartels have become so enormously wealthy that they have now bought themselves the whole nation. It's obscene. It's deadly. It's almost certainly the worst state of affairs in a nation I have ever heard of.

"There are two keys to disrupting the cocaine traffic. One is to stop the processing plants from turning out the finished product. The other is to stop the flow of ether to the processers. Huge amounts of ether are used in the final stages of cocaine processing. Colombia produces almost no ether. All of it is shipped into this country through legitimate vendors. Stop those shipments for sixty days, and the cocaine industry is paralyzed."

"My orders are to assist you in locating the incoming shipments of ether and the cocaine processing plants near Cali. I'll need the rest of today and tonight to gather information, to locate guides, and to establish contacts."

The colonel looked up.

Murdock could feel the strain of the colonel's duty.

"Colonel, are these processing plants in industrial or populated areas?"

"Up to now they have been clandestine operations at the edge of the jungle, usually with a four-wheel-drive truck needed to get in to them. Now I understand the new government is setting up huge processing plants near the cities and making them legal. Here they are still out in the brush. That's why we need to have trusted guides to lead your men to some of these plants."

"I'm getting the picture, Colonel. I need to say that I'm no more pleased with this assignment than you are. But like you, I follow orders. My men will look at this as any other military assignment. We will make one major change. We will do this destruction without the loss of any Colombian lives. We're not policemen, so we don't know who is doing something illegally. We'll go after the hardware, the processing equipment, the raw stock, and the finished product. The people involved will be safe unless they resist. Colonel, I'm sure you understand that if these people shoot at us, we will respond in kind with overwhelming firepower."

"Yes, Commander, understood. Now, I have a lot of work to get done. I'll see you here tomorrow morning at 0800 for a final briefing and to provide your contacts and guides."

Murdock stood, came to attention, did a perfect about-face, and left the room.

It took Murdock two hours to brief his men on the situation and their new assignment.

"So we're fucking drug cops?" Jaybird wailed.

"About the size of it, Jaybird."

"Who sent us on this shit-faced job, anyway?"

"Who? Your boss, Stroh, the CNO, the President, and probably his drug-fighting czar, whoever it is this week."

"Hey, Cap. Say we bust this processing plant and find some pure white cocaine," Mahanani said. "We get to snuff a few rows before we leave?"

A cheering broke out, and Murdock grinned. "Sure, anybody can who wants to. All he has to do is hang up his trident and go back to the scrub-and-dub Navy."

"No way out of this detail?" Ed DeWitt asked.

"Not a prayer," Murdock said. "Which means we have some planning to do. Ed, you were right about the weapons. We need a selection on our trips so we can adjust our type of weapon for the job. The Pups wouldn't have done the work inside that commo building today. But then the carbines wouldn't have done the work the Bull Pups did with those twenty-mike-mikes. We'll talk with the locals and then see what we can get brought in from the carrier. Ed, make out a list of what we need."

"So what now, Cap?" Will Dobler asked.

"We just take it easy until tomorrow when we get back into action." Murdock paused. When the men had dispersed, Murdock turned to his lead man and asked quietly, "Chief, you want to send an E-mail to your wife?"

Dobler hesitated, then shook his head. "No, I told her no special treatment. Better stick with it. I think those two ladies are going to help her stay straight."

"Okay, Master Chief. You need anything, you let me know."

Cocaine Lab Near Cali, Colombia

A short way outside Cali, Jaime Pardo Leal drove the big stake truck through the track of a road. A bulldozer had been through there two days ago, but sometimes he couldn't be sure where the trail went. He couldn't guess. Not with ten fifty-five-gallon drums of ethyl ether in back. The price had gone up again. Now it was almost a thousand dollars a barrel. It took seventeen liters of ethyl ether to make one kilo of cocaine.

If his supply of ether failed, his plant would be out of business. After a four-mile run up the rough trail, he came to his operation and made a stop at the first shed. Six men came out of it and began to roll the drums down a pair of planks to the ground, then roll them inside the building.

It was little more than a shed with a raised wooden floor. It was one of fourteen sheds around the jungle site. There was no airstrip here. That made the plant too easy to find. Instead, all work came in and went out by truck.

He nodded at some of the people. Most were *lavaperros,* dog washers in Colombian slang. They had been street people in Cali and were brought here to work and get fed and were provided with a bed to sleep in. They were essential. He had fifty of them and could use another ten or twelve.

Jaime had a smooth-running operation. Every day, trucks came in and went out for the long run into the civilian airport near Cali. There was almost no control over the planes that landed there or took off.

He had been working here for more than three years. They had everything for a small city: food, clothing, washers and dryers, generators, a huge kitchen, and twelve tanks for processing the paste into cocaine.

He walked into his office in one of the sheds at the far end of the complex and made an entry in his log. He had brought in 550 gallons of ethyl ether. That would last him for some time.

He checked his entry of coca paste. So far, the total read 14.23 metric tons of paste he had taken in. Yes, it was going to be a good year. A makeshift trail circled the drug lab and buildings. Every ten minutes, a guard with an Uzi submachine gun on his back circled the area on a dirt motorcycle. Security. Twice he had caught men trying to slip into his complex. He had questioned them. Both had been dog washers, and he had put them to work. A third one a month later had been from a rival cartel, and when it was proved who he was, he was shot at once and thrown into a shallow grave. Security was a must.

Jaime called in his second in charge, a man who went by one name, Montanez. The man was short, solidly built, and had been a boxer in his youth. He had lost an eye years ago in a knife fight and now ran the lab with a delicate hand that was needed.

"Had to slap around two of our dog washers this morning. They claimed they were sick. After the lesson, they worked well all day. I'll watch them."

Jaime finished with Montanez and walked his domain. Not his, really, but he had come to think of it as his own. He worked for the people in Cali who used to run the Cali syndicate before the big brothers from Medellin had squashed them with twenty-three assassinations. His boss had been on vacation at the time and missed the party. Now he was making a comeback but keeping a low profile. All of his goods went out of the country by boat. Slower but safer, and there was no battle with Medellin regarding air space and landing facilities. At one time the two cartels had shared those things. No more.

He checked the shed where the finished cocaine powder was stored in thirty-three-gallon plastic garbage cans. He needed to make a shipment. His benefactor had told him never to have more than six or eight of the big cans filled in the shack at any one time. Medellin was not beyond raiding them if they knew where this lab was. Yes, he would set up a boat tomorrow and have the load gone within a week. Now with the old president holding court in Cali, he had to be more careful than ever. In this area his was still in an illegal business.

Back at the shack that held the ether, he checked his supply. The ten barrels brought him up to fourteen. He was definitely still short. He'd make another run into Cali tomorrow. His supplier said he had plenty now that the demand was down. This indicated to Jaime that there were not more than two big labs working around the area. Five years ago there were ten or more.

Jaime went to his quarters. He had assigned one of the dog washer women to keep his rooms clean and to cook for him. She was the only pretty one from the last batch. He had made her wash and cut her hair and brought her good clothes. Now she was almost presentable. When he came into the room, she stopped polishing his silverware and took off a colorful blouse so her breasts swung free.

"Is there anything I can do for you today, Mr. Jaime?"

She had learned quickly what he wanted after a hard day's work, and she was always ready. This duty was much better for her than working in the factory on the vats of coca paste and the foul-smelling chemicals.

He motioned to her and she ran to him, put her arms around him, and pushed her bare breasts hard against his chest. He spanked her soft bottom, then lifted her up. She wound her legs around his waist and locked them. Jaime carried her that way into his bedroom and the king-sized bed. He dropped her on it. Then he told her to get on her hands and knees.

Jaime smiled. It was going to be another good romp before dinner. Yes, he had it all right here. For just a moment he thought of his wife and three children in Bogotá. They were well taken care of. Colombian women were not naive. They expected their husbands to have a mistress. He pulled her skirt off and dropped her on the bed. Oh, yes, he had it all right here. Besides this, he had been paid slightly more than a million dollars last year. Most of it was in a bank in Bogotá. He gave his wife ten thousand dollars a month to spend. That alone was enough to keep her happy. He'd go home again at the end of the month on his twice-yearly trip.

Camp Bravo
Cali, Colombia

When Murdock awoke the next morning, he wasn't at all enthusiastic about the prospects. He had an 0800 meet with Colonel Paredes. That would result in an assignment to go out and destroy a cocaine lab somewhere in the area. Yes, knocking out some of the cocaine supply was a good thing. But it wasn't exactly the type of mission he and his men had trained for. Okay, he thought it was beneath their talents. The truck parking lot and the commo center, that was more like it.

He shaved carefully, removing two days' growth of beard, and reported on time with Ed DeWitt in tow. At least Ed could help backstop the bleats of wonder they would get from the men.

There were four military men in the room beside the colonel. Murdock was surprised to see two enlisted sergeants. That was a good sign.

The colonel nodded at them and began. He pointed to a large map of Cali on the display table.

"Gentlemen, here is the target for tonight. It's an unusually large cocaine production laboratory from the old days. It's twenty-five miles outside of Cali, in a rugged section of the mountains. There are no known residents in the general area. Anyone found there can be considered a lawbreaker or someone working for a lawbreaker. Captain Herrera will give you the details."

His English was scratchy, but they could understand the captain.

"My friends the SEALs. It is good to have you here. Congratulations on your two missions here so far. They have been exemplary and effective. Now to the problem.

"The president has commanded us to take out every cocaine processing plant we know of in the Cali region. This is the longest one. It has been in place some day for more than fifteen years. So it goes back to the days of the huge Cali cocaine cartel. That no longer exists.

"We have two men who will lead you to the site. It is an armed camp, with guards, weapons, and men who can use them. Inside the camp will be from twenty to sixty civilians, workers from the streets of Cali. Many were homeless and work there for food, clothing, and a place to sleep. They should be spared as innocents.

"We estimate that there are about twenty guards there. They do not have guard dogs. The area is not fenced or protected in that manner. There are six supervisors and one general manager by the name of Jaime Pardo Leal. We know little about him. Our suggestion is that we go by truck to within a mile of the site, then off-load and march to the lab area. Would a night or daylight attack be most beneficial to the SEALs?"

Murdock looked up. "A night attack is preferable for this type of operation."

"Then it will be a night assault. Our primary objective is to capture as many of the guards and supervisors as possible. To release the civilians, and to totally destroy the facility so it never again can be used as a cocaine processing plant. Fire will be one of our tools."

"Will you be along, sir?" Ed DeWitt asked.

"Yes, unless that would conflict with your procedures."

"Glad to have you along, sir," Murdock said.

"Will you want any of our troops to back you up?" the captain asked.

"No sir," Murdock said. "If you had your men there, we wouldn't know who to shoot at."

"Will you need any additional equipment, ammunition, or explosives?"

"Yes sir. We'll confer with you on that. When is the operation planned?"

"For tonight, Commander. We'll be moving as soon as all is ready."

Hills South of Cali, Colombia

The one six-by truck left Camp Bravo just after two that afternoon. They had on board the SEALs, the two Colombian sergeants, both of whom could speak limited English, and Captain Herrera, who rode in the cab and acted as native guide. Ostercamp drove.

The route soon left the city and traveled up a small valley with only a few farmhouses. Then it turned left up another small stream where there was no real road.

"The lab is six miles up road," one of the sergeants said.

They drove four miles, and Ostercamp pulled off the road into a lane that ended in a heavier growth of trees that completely concealed the truck.

The two Colombian sergeants left the truck and hurried back to the turnoff where they covered up the tracks the truck made in the turn so no one traveling by would know a truck had left the main trail. They came back and reported to their captain.

"If the man in charge has driven into Cali today, he will be coming back well before dark," Captain Herrera said. "We'll wait here and see if he drives by. If he doesn't show up by four o'clock, we'll move toward the lab."

"When will it be dark today?" Murdock asked.

"Yes. Good. By five-thirty, or 1730, it will be dark. That will be extremely dark since we have a cloud cover and no moon."

They waited. The SEALs had attached additional bags of explosives to their combat harnesses. They all had regular weapons except the Bull Pup men, who were given MP-5s as better for this venture. Murdock had the only Bull Pup and twenty rounds.

It was just after 1645 when they lined up and moved out. They used the road with Lam out front a hundred yards and one of the Colombian sergeants in back, listening for a truck.

Nothing happened before the captain and Lam went to ground two miles later. Murdock moved up with them.

"We're about two hundred yards from the lab," the captain said. "The shacks are spread out for three hundred yards and all camouflaged on tops and sides. Almost impossible to see from the air except by a chopper at a hundred feet."

They had moved up well dispersed and stayed in the heavy brushy and woods cover. It wasn't dark yet, and Murdock had a good look at the layout. It ran up the small creek for about 300 yards and had cheaply built shacks and sheds all over. One of them must be the lab. They would burn everything in sight.

"You said there might be a roving patrol," Murdock said. "Would that be by jeep or truck?"

Just then they heard the growl of a motorcycle. It came down from the far end, circled around behind the buildings, and then moved toward the watchers. It turned sharply north and behind the nearest buildings, then up into some brush and vanished. A moment later, the engine sound cut off.

"I think that's their roving patrol," Captain Herrera said.

DeWitt looked at Murdock. "How do we play this? We don't know where those civilians are."

"No crossfire," Murdock said. "We'll all get five yards apart and move across the complex. We take out any guards we find and herd the civilians into one of the structures. All weapons suppressed. We'll move out as soon as it's fully dark."

Murdock gave the same instructions on the Motorola, and the SEALs settled down to wait for darkness.

It came less than a half hour later, and Murdock waved at the captain. "Time to rock and roll, sir."

He used the Motorola. "Okay, we spread out and move into the area. We take out any guards with silenced shots if we have to. If they surrender, we put them down and cuff wrists and ankles. I think we're about ready to move out."

A new generator kicked in somewhere ahead of them. In

an instant the entire three sides of the cocaine factory showed brilliant pink bars of light.

"It's a three-bar high laser fence," DeWitt chirped into the Motorola. "What the hell are we going to do now?"

16

Hills South of Cali, Colombia

"How far away from us is that laser fence?" Murdock asked.

"Maybe fifty yards," Lam said in his Motorola. "Look, it's just a warning laser. I'll go up there and break the beam, and we'll see what happens."

"Go," Murdock said. "Everyone else, let's move up slowly. Stay out of the beam until we see what their reaction is."

Lam fisted his MP-5, brought it up to port arms, and ran forward. He came to the beam and ran through it, then back and through it again before he went prone. The beam snapped off when it was broken, then came back on and snapped off again and stayed off.

A siren wailed somewhere among the buildings.

The beam remained off only where it had been broken. The rest of the sectors remained a three-strand pink glow. Murdock heard an engine snarl, then race, and he knew it was the motorcycle.

"The bike is coming. Lam, take him out with a silenced

round, then we all surge forward and move in five yards apart."

They waited.

A moment later, the single beam of the motorcycle's headlight cut through the night, bouncing toward the fence break where Lam lay. The bike came directly for the spot and bounced over a ditch of some kind. They heard the rider swearing. Then the headlamp's beam grazed across Lam, and the rider shouted what could have been a warning.

Lam's three-round burst from the silenced MP-5 jolted the rider out of the seat, exploded the headlight, and sent the bike into a spin to the side where the engine coughed and died.

"Let's go forward," Murdock said into his lip mike, and the fifteen SEALs and their three locals surged across the field, rushed through more sections of the barrier, and came to Lam. He checked the bike rider. Dead. He jumped up and ran with the others forward toward the low-lying buildings.

Murdock heard loud voices near one shed, then he saw the muzzle flashes of at least three guns and heard the hot lead streak past him well over his head.

Six SEALs fired at the flashes, and they heard one loud cry, then the dark shadows ran behind the building.

Murdock pulled the three-cell flashlight from his webbing. Each SEAL had one for this mission. They were tied to the webbing on a stretch cord.

"Ed, move your squad into that first building and clear it. We're on backup."

The Bravo Squad surged forward. Quinley opened the door and jolted to one side. No shots came through. He poked his flash around the doorjamb and looked where the beam went. It looked like a storage area. Sacks and bales and boxes.

"Clear first building," he said.

Ed DeWitt came up beside him and confirmed. "Yes, first building clear."

The line of SEALs swung to the left and advanced on the next structure. It was an open-sided shed with a floor built up two feet off the ground. Inside they found twenty large plastic garbage cans with covers in place.

Captain Herrera opened one and confirmed. "Coca paste. The raw stuff waiting to be processed. No people here."

Bill Bradford heard the captain and repeated his words over the Motorola.

Just as they swung around the second building, gunfire erupted from the shadows around the third structure.

"Cover," Murdock snapped into the Motorola. The SEALs dove to the ground and returned fire. Within seconds, two hundred rounds slammed into the area where the guards had fired. They heard one scream over the gunfire, then the muzzle flashes slowed and stopped ahead.

"Hold fire," Murdock said into the radio.

A moment later, all was quiet.

"Holt, Ching, check them out. See if any of them are still alive up there."

Two forms lifted off the ground and zigzagged on a run the thirty yards to the next building. They went to the ground at the spot and found two bodies.

"Two dead here, and two extra rifles. Look like AK-47s. Holding."

"Move up," Murdock said, and the SEALs surged forward to the near side of the building. "Ronson, Sterling, check inside."

Ronson rushed to the door, turned the knob, and pushed it inward as he twisted away from the opening. No shots came though. He dropped to the ground and shone his flash through the door from the floor level.

"Cap, looks like a barracks. Lots of people in there. Better get a Spanish speaker up here."

Murdock sent one of the Colombian sergeants to the door, and he began shouting in Spanish.

"Move around it to the next building," Murdock said. "Easy. They must have some more guns here somewhere."

The line of SEALs moved around each end of the barracks and forward. In front of them they saw in the dim light an open space where two trucks were parked. Beyond that was what looked like an office building. It was better made than the rest with glass windows and a chimney. It also was built two feet off the ground.

Without warning, a weapon on full automatic cut loose in front of the building, spraying bullets in their direction, but most of them went over the SEALs' heads. They hit the ground and returned fire. The automatic fire ceased, and a door slammed.

"Move up slowly," Murdock ordered. "Who has a Willy Peter?"

"Got me one," Holt said on the Motorola.

"Get up there and put it through that window. Bravo Squad, move around to the back to cover any rear entrance. Go, Holt."

Holt ran forward, pulled the pin on the white phosphorous grenade, and threw it through a two-foot-square window. Four seconds later, they heard the pop as the grenade went off, then saw the streamers of furiously burning white phosphorus through the broken window.

Inside, somebody screamed. When exposed to air, white phosphorus burns instantly and so hot that it burns through cloth, flesh, and even bones. It is impossible to put out and usually creates an instant fire when used in a building.

Less than a minute after the WP grenade exploded, the SEALs saw fire taking hold of the all-wooden building.

Ed DeWitt reported from the rear of the place. "We have three men coming out the back. None seem armed."

"Capture them," Murdock snapped.

DeWitt fired over the men's heads. Miguel Fernandez had heard the orders from the platoon leader, and he bellowed at the startled men in Spanish.

"Hold it right there, or you're dead meat. Hands up and stand still." Fernandez fired over their heads, then ran up with two other SEALs and put plastic cuffs on their wrists and ankles. Fernandez told them not to move if they wanted to stay alive.

"Any of you Jaime Leal?" Fernandez asked in Spanish.

All three denied that they were the lab boss.

"Secure here, Commander," DeWitt reported.

The rest of the SEALs came around the burning building. It was about twenty by thirty feet, and soon fire shot out the windows. They moved quickly to get out of the firelight. Ahead were two more buildings, larger than the rest.

They heard a generator purring contentedly and saw low-level lights in the first building.

"Night shift?" Murdock wondered on the net. He saw two doors, one at the side and the other at the front. This building was better made than the others and had sides and what looked like a good roof.

Murdock worked his way to the side of the place, then forward to the door. It had no windows. He touched the door and felt it give. Not locked. "Dobler, Ching, Lam. On me at the door, now."

He sensed the men lined up behind him. "We go in soft. Anyone here probably is one of the dog washers. Innocents. Don't shoot unless fired at."

He rammed the door open, and the four SEALs stormed inside. They were in a processing shed. More than a dozen large vats took up the entire area of the one hundred-foot-long building. Murdock could see no workers.

They filtered through the spaces around the vats, discovered no one hiding, and went out the door on the far side. Murdock had sent the rest of the SEALs around the building toward the next one.

When the SEALs were in the open, rifle fire erupted from windows of the next building thirty yards away. Return fire came at once from the SEALs. Murdock heard a groan and figured one of his men was hit.

"Scatter," Murdock ordered on the radio. "Ed, see if you can get half your squad behind them. We'll keep firing here." He thought of the 20-mike-mike rounds but knew the range was too short. The explosive rounds wouldn't have time to arm. He fired with the 5.56 half of the Bull Pup and was pleased with the way it functioned.

He hit the dirt and rolled, fired, and rolled again. The return fire had slackened off.

"Hold fire in front," Murdock said on the Motorola.

A moment later, a strange silence hovered over the scene. "Who got wounded?" Murdock asked.

"Yeah, just a scratch, Cap. Nothing serious."

"Senior Chief?"

"Yeah. Picked up one in my right leg. Thigh. I'm still mobile. Carry on."

"Mahanani, you copy that?"

"In front, I'm coming back. Hold it right there, Dobe."

Murdock held up any movement until he saw that the medic was talking with Dobler.

"Let's move up to that building. Find out where the shooters went."

There was no fire from the structure as they charged it. Murdock and Jaybird went through the door, one diving left, the other right. It was dark inside. The two men waited without moving or breathing, listening.

Suddenly a shadow stormed out of the blackness, a weapon in hand, firing on semiautomatic. Jaybird threw up his MP-5 in a reflexive action, his finger on the trigger at full auto. He saw fifteen rounds jolt into the black figure. Then the Colombian's finger went slack on the trigger as the form fell forward just past Jaybird and in front of Murdock.

The SEAL commander kicked the weapon away and then kicked the man in the side. He didn't move or make a sound. Murdock bent down and checked his carotid pulse. Dead. Murdock sat down quickly. His head pounded and he began to sweat. *What the hell?*

"Hey, Cap, you okay?" Jaybird asked.

"Not sure. Yeah. Okay, took a round in my left arm. Now it's hurting like hell. Where'd that guy come from?"

"Cap, you stay put, I'm going to clear this place. Looks like an office or storeroom, maybe a little of both. You hold steady there, and I'm back in about a minute."

Jaybird ran down an aisle, back up another one. He

stopped near the front windows a minute, then came running back.

"Can you walk, Cap?"

"Yeah and talk and chew gum. I'm not hit that bad."

"Let's get outside. We've got two more dead bodies over there by the windows. I only saw three shooting out of here, so I think we have them all."

Jaybird watched his commander stand, weave a little, then walk steadily out the door they had come in.

"Jack, we need you over here near the front door," Jaybird said.

The medic was there before Jaybird got Murdock sat down. He motioned at the commander. "His left arm, take a look."

Mahanani held a pencil flash in his mouth as he examined the officer's left arm. "About halfway up, and the slug went on through. Gonna hurt like hell for a few days, Commander. I think it missed the bone. I'll wrap it up and take a better look at it as soon as it's daylight."

Jaybird hit the lip mike. "JG, we need you back here. Can you bring your squad around?"

"That's a roger. What's the problem?"

"The Cap took one in his left forearm."

"We're on our way."

The SEALs called a halt to the clearing job. They heard no more gunfire but weren't sure the place was safe yet. DeWitt had the SEALs and Colombians in a perimeter ring around the two casualties. Senior Chief Dobler was growling and feeling better.

"Damn it, I can still walk and run and fight and piss and fuck, so let's get on with it."

They told him about Murdock's wound and he settled down a little. Captain Herrera talked with DeWitt.

"Can the commander finish the job here?"

"Hell, yes. We're a team, Captain. We function as a unit, and one or two men down doesn't mean we fall apart. If I get the word from Murdock, I'll take over command for the rest of the mission. If he can carry on himself, he will.

My guess is he's in a little shock, but he'll be raring to go in a half hour."

Murdock called DeWitt over. "Send Lam out and find out how many more buildings we have to clear. Don't bury me yet, Ed. I'm not about to cut and run."

"What I was telling the captain. Let me find Lam."

The corpsman treated Murdock's wound, bandaged it up tightly, and gave him three pain pills.

Lam came back fifteen minutes later with his report.

"Cap, there are five more buildings we need to clear. One is a barracks, one a kitchen/mess hall, two more processing sheds, and a big storage building that looks like it's loaded with raw product, finished cocaine, and a lot of fifty-five gallon barrels."

"See any more hostiles?"

"Not a one."

"Let's get on our feet and clear the rest of the buildings," Murdock said. "Moving out."

DeWitt looked at Murdock and watched him take his first few steps. He touched Mahanani on the shoulder. "Stay with the skipper," he said. The corpsman nodded.

They spent an hour clearing the rest of the structures, found one more dormitory filled with workers and the storehouse with the barrels and large plastic garbage cans filled with a white powder that the corpsman said he was sure was cocaine.

They had come back to the storage building, and Murdock surveyed it. "What's in the barrels?" he asked.

Two SEALs checked them out with their flashlights.

"Ethyl ether," Franklin said. "What's ether doing way out here?"

"Ether is a vital element in the final phase of cocaine production," Ed DeWitt said. "It's also a colorless, volatile, and highly flammable liquid."

Murdock swayed a moment, then caught his balance. "Looks like we have some of our fireworks right here. Captain Herrera, can you get your men to wake up all of the workers and get them a quarter of a mile away from the buildings, back along the road?"

"That we can do, Commander. Yes. At once."

Murdock waved him on. "Ostercamp, I want you to get those trucks and cars we passed and drive them all down away from the buildings. We'll use them tomorrow."

Ostercamp took off at a trot.

"Now for the fun part. Ronson and Jefferson. Grab one of those barrels of ether and roll it down to this next building and push it up against the wall."

Jaybird grinned. "Regular Fourth of July fireworks, Cap?"

"Could work out that way. We don't want to waste all of our goodies in one bonfire."

The building the barrel of ether rested against was one of the labs, about a hundred feet long and thirty feet wide. Murdock pulled the troops all away from the building and lifted his Bull Pup. He fired six 5.56 rounds into the middle of the barrel. The whizzers ripped through the metal and a waterlike liquid poured out. He fired two more rounds into the barrel, hoping for a ricochet and a spark.

"Ronson, hit the bottom of the barrel with two of your NATO rounds."

It only took one. There was an instantaneous explosion as the vaporized ether gushed into a ten-foot-wide fireball and splattered the flaming liquid across the length of the lab building. The SEALs moved back from the sudden heat.

After that, it was a matter of logistics. The SEALs rolled barrels of ethyl ether down the slight grade to seven of the other buildings. When they were sure all of the workers had been moved away, the barrels were punctured and set on fire by rifle rounds. Within ten minutes, the landscape for half a mile around was lit up like noontime by the fires.

They had used WP grenades to set on fire the six buildings above the storage area. Now the last building to be fired was the one with the twelve large garbage cans filled with pure cocaine.

"Will that stuff burn?" Jefferson asked.

"It'll melt," Bradford said. "Is that freebasing?"

Nobody knew. There were four barrels of ether left. They rolled them around the cocaine, took off the plastic covers of the garbage cans, and moved back. They punctured all four barrels and then one caught fire and another one exploded. They moved back another fifty feet.

The fire was intense.

"So we wait for dawn and see how we did," Murdock said. He had the Colombian soldiers guard the workers and went to question the three prisoners they had captured. Captain Herrera handled the interrogation.

They knew little. Two said they had been hired as guards just a week ago and this was the first problem. The boss was here, but they didn't know if he had stayed or run away. They would look at the dead men in the morning and see if the big boss was one of them.

Murdock put two men on guard and let the rest of the SEALs get some sleep.

Mahanani had been shadowing him ever since he took the hit. He waved the big Tahitian/Hawaiian off. "You don't need to baby-sit me anymore, Mahanani. I'll live. Get some shut-eye."

Murdock took two more pain pills the corpsman gave him, then stretched out on a grassy place, and slept before he knew it.

He came awake suddenly and heard rifle shots. It was dawn and nearly full light. He grabbed his Motorola he had taken off and hit the mike. "Who the hell is shooting?"

"Yeah, Cap. Lampedusa. Two big, ugly birds were starting to have breakfast on one of the dead Colombians. Figured a couple of shots would scare them off."

"Yeah. Good. Want to take a look at the coke?"

They walked up the rise to the former storage area. Every building they passed had burned to the ground, including the wooden floor. At the storage area they found the same. The plastic garbage cans had melted and let the white powder spread out on the ground.

"Looks like 90 percent of the cocaine is still here," Lam

said. "Damn stuff is hard to burn in this quantity."

"Would it melt in water?" Murdock asked. "Seems to me I remember guys trying to melt down stash in the toilet when they were raided."

"Worth a try."

Murdock took his canteen out of the pouch and grabbed a handful of the cocaine powder and poured water on it. It slowly melted.

"Yes," Lam said. "Now we need the local fire truck and a high-pressure hose."

Murdock looked at the small stream that ran through the complex. He grinned. "Lam, see how many shovels you can find. There must be some around here somewhere, unless we burned them all up."

Lam looked at him strangely. "Shovels?"

"Yes, shovels, go."

Murdock walked upstream and decided it would work. He hit the mike. "Men, I need the platoon up here above the cocaine stash. If anybody finds a shovel or pick, bring it along."

Lam found five shovels and two picks. He had it figured out before he made it back to where Murdock stood by the small stream.

"It's not ecologically correct to alter the course of a natural streambed," Lam said.

"No problem," Murdock said. "We'll use it and then lose it."

17

Cocaine Lab Near Cali, Colombia

Murdock laid out the route of the small ditch and all of them with tools started digging. It went from an upstream point across twenty feet and down about fifty feet to the white mound of cocaine.

"We melt the damn stuff," Quinley said. "Damn, I wonder how much that would be worth on the street in New York?"

Jefferson lifted his brows. "I'd say between forty and fifty million bucks. Lots of money."

"Damn, really?" Quinley said. "Too bad we can't cash in on that some way."

"You do every time you cash your paycheck," Murdock said. "Dig."

He put three men at the cocaine, pushing it to the near side with boards until it was in a small depression. The mound of white powder looked much larger out of the garbage cans than it had inside them.

They dug the ditch a foot deep and rapidly moved it down the hill, angled for the white powder. Before it was done, Murdock had three men lugging rocks from the area to build a small dam across the four-foot-wide stream. Once the rocks were in place, he had them pile dirt in front of them to seal off the damn.

"Ready with the ditch," DeWitt called. Lam dug out the foot-wide section to open it up to the stream, and the water flowed rapidly downhill toward the cocaine. Two men filled in the last of the dam, and more water surged into the canal.

Two SEALs poked the mound of cocaine a little at a time into the water. It swirled and at last overflowed the small depression. When the white powder hit the water, it dissolved at once. The coke-loaded water ran under the burned-out floor and down the side of the hill.

It took them two hours to melt down the mountain of cocaine they had. When the last of it fell into the water, the SEALs let out a cheer, and Murdock shoveled dirt into the canal to shut off the water supply.

Murdock watched the water drain out and cheered with the rest of them.

"Treats are on me, men. I'm a big spender. MREs for everyone."

They hooted him down, but most of them flaked out and had a meal ready to eat.

Captain Herrera came up to Murdock.

"The workers. What about them?"

"Put all of them you can on those two trucks and the one car I saw and drive them into Cali or let them off along the way if they want that. Otherwise, it's a long walk."

"The three prisoners?"

"Turn them loose and let them walk back."

"They looked at the dead men this morning and said the lab boss and his assistant were not there. They must have run away at the first sound of gunfire."

"Figures," Murdock said.

"We need to take a walk," Captain Herrera said.

They went to the first lab building and viewed the destruction.

"One problem here," the captain said. "Somebody else could come in and use the vats. They are made of metal and some kind of coating to withstand all the chemicals, and were not hurt a bit by the fire."

"Looks like we'll have to use our explosives and blow them up," Murdock said. They went back to the combat vests, and Murdock took a quarter pound of TNAZ and a detonator/timer and they moved back to the first lab. Murdock placed the bomb under the lip of the vat halfway down so it would ruin the structure even if it didn't shatter it completely.

He set the timer for five minutes, and the two men walked away.

The blast came right on time and jolted most of the SEALs who didn't know what had happened.

"Relax, SEALs," Murdock boomed in his parade ground voice. "Just a little experiment."

Half the SEALs looked at the results. The ten-foot-square vat had a two-foot hole blown in it, and the near side crumpled until it touched the far side.

"Should be sufficient," Murdock said. The Colombian captain nodded his agreement.

"Senior Chief," Murdock called. Dobler hurried over, showing only a hint of a limp.

"Senior Chief, we need to blow all of the vats like this one. As I remember, there are something like twenty of them. Check out our supply of explosives and get the job done. After that, we'll be heading back for hot chow and showers.

"Aye, aye, sir," Dobler said and moved away with more of a limp now that he wasn't thinking about it. He called the men around him, and they went to their gear and gave him a total on the quarter-pound charges they had. They were short.

"A whole case of C-4 in the truck," Jaybird said. Dobler told him to go get it.

For nearly thirty minutes the hills rang with the sound of explosions. The SEALs set them off one at a time until the last vat was punctured and twisted beyond all repair.

The trucks had pulled out an hour before with all of the

workers. They were packed in tightly but didn't mind. They were being freed of a kind of slavery that only the homeless and truly destitute know.

It was just 1000 when the destruct job was done, the dead men buried, and the SEALs and Captain Herrera pulled away from the former major cocaine processing plant.

"Somebody in Cali is going to be angry," the captain said.

"I'd like to meet him face-to-face," Murdock said. "He wouldn't be angry long. He'd be dead."

Herrera put on a crooked smile, and Murdock wasn't sure what he believed about the cocaine traffic. He was following orders, but that might be the extent of his anti-cocaine feelings.

The truck was two miles from the burned-out cocaine lab when Murdock asked Ostercamp to stop so Holt could key in the SATCOM.

"It's set up to receive, Cap," Holt said. "How long you want to wait for a message?"

"We'll cool it here for ten minutes and see if anything urgent is popping," Murdock said.

It was just past five minutes when Murdock thought he saw something move in the brush a hundred yards down the little valley. He was about to say something about it when a shot snarled in the deep green and a round slammed into the overhead canvas covering on the back of the truck.

"Down!" Murdock bellowed. "Sniper moved to the left front about a hundred yards out. Long guns, do it."

The sniper rifle responded first, but not before another round came smashing into one of the roof struts. Bill Bradford sent six rounds into the general area, then saw movement and changed targets and fired six more times.

Ronson got his H&K NATO round machine gun up and working and sprayed the same area with hot lead. The 5.56 weapons scattered shots into the same spot, but Murdock figured the sniper had moved on by that time. It would be impossible to find the man, let alone track him in the heavy brush.

"Cease fire," Murdock boomed to get over the sound of the weapons. "Get us out of here fast, Ostercamp."

The truck jolted forward on the narrow lane and soon passed the spot where the sniper had been. Another half mile down the trail, and the men relaxed a little.

"Anybody get hurt on that last go-round?" Murdock asked. He was thankful that no one had. He looked at his own arm. He had forgotten about his wound. Proved it wasn't much. He grinned. This would be his thirty-seventh purple heart if he was receiving them.

He had four men with semiserious wounds already, and the mission was just getting moving. He hoped this wasn't going to be one of those times when every man in the platoon came home and reported at once to Balboa Naval Hospital.

The rest of the ride was uneventful, and they came into Camp Bravo a little after 1400. Murdock and Dobler went to the hospital. They had their wounds checked, treated, and were released. They went up a floor to find Canzoneri.

When they came to his bed, he was sitting up talking to a pretty little nurse. He chattered some Spanish words at her and she giggled and shook her head and said them the correct way.

"Hey, slugger, looks like you're feeling better."

"Told them I was fine. Conchita here is teaching me some Spanish. So far I know *perro,* which is dog, and *qué lastima.* That means what a pity."

"So, what she's telling you is that it's a real pity that you're a dog," Dobler said.

"Hey, that's not it. So you guys were shot up, huh? You guys here professionally? You get nicked?"

"Just a scratch," Murdock said. "I need to find that nurse that speaks English." He found her and she looked at Canzoneri's chart. She smiled.

"He can go back to his unit now, but he should come in

after two days for us to change the bandage and look at the wound."

"Good," Canzoneri said. "Where are my pants?"

Back at the barracks, Holt had the SATCOM on receive. He handed Murdock a note.

"Stroh called a half hour ago. He says get you on the horn as soon as you get here. He says this is flap city, and he's the fucking mayor, whatever that means. Should I get ready to transmit?"

"Probably. Maybe we should have some chow first."

"He seemed insistent that you get back to him ASAP."

Murdock snorted. "He's always in a rush. Yeah, beam me out, Scotty."

Stroh answered as soon as Murdock's message went out.

"You're back. Good. We've got a problem."

"I have no problem except having a big supper, a hot shower, and about twelve hours of sleep. We just came in, Stroh."

"Good, glad you made it. What I want to talk about is a serious situation. The American embassy in Bogotá has been invaded and captured by Colombian military forces. They used three tanks and a flamethrower. Your job is to go in and get the hostages out before anything else happens."

"How? We're a hundred and seventy miles from Bogotá. If you come in from the Pacific, it's about two hundred and seventy miles. That's an RT of five hundred and forty miles. We don't even have a bird that can do that."

"So, it'll take some planning. From Cali up and back would be only three hundred and forty miles. You're directed to talk to the captain and air boss here on the carrier. They have some ideas. We don't have a hell of a lot of time. They took over the embassy this morning just before noon. The ambassador figured some trouble was coming, so they flew most of the personnel out. The ambassador is still there, and he says they have only twelve Americans left there. You get in touch with Captain Ingman here on the carrier. He's the man you'll have to coordinate things with. I've talked to him, but you'll need to do the overhead planning."

"Yes sir. We better go through Lieutenant Commander Emerling. He's my contact. Can you phone him and get him up there and have him set up a time for me to call the captain?"

"Can do. Soonest. Talk later. Stroh, out."

18

Camp Bravo
Cali, Colombia

Murdock, Jaybird, DeWitt, Lam, and Dobler sat on bunks at the far end of the barracks, thinking through the problem.

"Makes more sense to go and come from here," Jaybird said. "We're only a hundred and seventy miles away, maybe a hundred and twenty of that over hostile territory. We can resupply from here. The chopper could come in here from the carrier with no sweat."

They had agreed that a chopper rescue was the only reasonable way to get the remaining twelve Americans out of the embassy.

"Yeah, if they're still there," Dobler said. "Remember the embassy in Iran? They had our people out of the embassy almost at once and scattered all over the city."

"From what we know so far, the Americans are still at the embassy," DeWitt said.

"So which chopper has the range and capacity to go in and back three hundred and forty miles and carry up to thirty passengers?" Murdock asked.

"Old reliable, the Sea Knight, the CH-46E," Lam said. "We've used them before."

They looked at Jaybird, the statistics man.

"Sea Knight, okay. Most of them are out of service now, but some are left in the fleet. They can do a hundred and fifty-four miles an hour cruising and get up to fourteen thousand feet ceiling. Range is four hundred twenty miles loaded with up to twenty-five fully equipped Marines."

Murdock stood and walked two bunks down and came back. "So the Sea Knight would do it, if this task force has one. What about protection? They have two .50-caliber chatter guns on them, but that's not much against a few fighter jets."

"Bring along some air cover, like a pair of F-18s," Lam said.

"Overflight of a sovereign country," DeWitt said. "Will the Navy and the U.S. State Department let us do it?"

"Hell, Colombia violated international law by capturing our embassy," Murdock said. "A little technical matter like an overflight to rescue the Americans isn't going to raise any eyebrows. Colombia probably expects it."

"So they'll be waiting," Jaybird said. "Maybe it's a trap to send all of their aircraft after the rescue chopper and escorts."

"That we can let the brass figure out," Murdock said.

A short time later, the SATCOM came to life, and Holt handed Murdock the mike.

"Yes, Home Base, this is Rover. You have some suggestions on the embassy situation?"

"Yes, Rover. This is Captain Ingman. We have the CAG here with us. It obviously has to be a chopper rescue. Does that work with you?"

"Yes, Captain. We are talking about the Sea Knight. Do you have any in your task force?"

"Sea Knight," a new voice said. "This is the CAG. We have two that had been working PAV Low Three. We can pull out some gear and get it to you. Be best to go from Camp Bravo to the embassy?"

"That's our thinking, Captain. We figure a hundred and twenty miles over hostile territory to get to Bogotá. What about some fighter cover?"

"Getting touchy there," the CAG said. "State and Stroh tell me to do it with just a chopper. I don't like that."

"Won't work, CAG. No way. They can find the chopper with one fighter and knock us down going in or coming out. I'd guess at least six Eighteens or Fourteens would be needed. No sense getting the ambassador and his staff off the ground just to KIA them in the jungle somewhere."

"Agreed, Commander. We can request the overflight fighter protection, but State and the President will have to decide that one."

"What's our timetable?"

"Soonest."

"What we want, then, Captain, is one hot Sea Knight with six F-14s for cover in and out. Suggest you fly the Knight in here as of now and if you get a go on the Fourteens, they can catch up in a rush. Our troops are ready with sixteen for combat. We'll be at the Camp Bravo airstrip in two hours."

"We've sent a request through to the White House and to State and the CNO. We should have a reply in the requested half hour. This is number one on their list, so they'll decide in a rush. Flight time from Bravo to the embassy should be about an hour. You want a day mission or night?"

"Night would be better for us. Let's hope the Colombians keep the Americans at the embassy."

"We've launched a Sea Knight. They may remove some equipment and leave it there at Bravo. Flight time to you is less than an hour. Keep your set on receive and we'll call as soon as we get a decision one way or the other."

"That's a roger. Bogotá is a big place. Hope your pilots will know how to find the embassy."

"We have that pinpointed, SEALs. Good luck."

Murdock stood and bellowed at his men. "We have thirty minutes to pack up, get ready for a mission. Clean your

weapons and resupply regular loads of ammo. We're going
to fly into Bogotá for a quick little vacation. This is a room-
to-room clearing operation, so we'll take the MP-5s instead
of the Bull Pups. Move it."

"What about that chow and hot showers?" somebody
called.

"Hell, you fight better when you're dirty and hungry,"
Senior Chief Dobler called. "We'll try for some box
lunches for the one-hour flight to the target. Let's get hump-
ing."

Dobler ran to the jeep out front and drove to the mess
hall. They told him they could have box lunches ready in
twenty minutes.

A half hour later, word came through from Lieutenant
Commander Emerling on the carrier that approval had just
come in from the chief of Naval Operations that the President had approved the flyover of Columbia by the chopper
and six fighters to rescue the captured embassy personnel.
By then it was almost 1700. It would be dark by the time
they flew into Bogotá.

Twenty-eight minutes later, the sixteen SEALs were in
the air heading for Bogotá. Canzoneri had been released
from the hospital and was more than anxious to get in on
the next mission.

"This time I get to be in on some of the fun, too," Canzoneri said.

Once in the air, Murdock went up front to listen to the
radio chatter. It was in the clear, no encrypting, and he
wondered what Colombian operators who understood English would make of it.

"Slow Moe, this is Fast Duck. We have you on our magic
box. We'll circle you for a while, then will be replaced by
Fast Duck Two."

"Fast Duck, glad you're on board. Always use a little
help from our friends."

The chopper pilot, Lieutenant (j.g.) Anderson, waved at
Murdock. "Glad to have you with us, Commander. We're
forty minutes out from target. Bogotá is a big gunner, al-

most seven million people. We have a pinpoint on the embassy and good sight lines to it."

"Hate to drop in at the wrong embassy," Murdock said.

"No sweat. You want us to stay on the ground or drop you off and cut out?"

"We don't know what kind of forces they have at the embassy, so it'll be best if you cut and run. We'll call you back in on the SATCOM or if it goes out, we'll give you a red flare for when and where."

"Sounds good to me," Anderson said. "If we don't get company, we'll be spooling around at about ten thousand so our radar can get a good sweep."

Before Murdock could reply, a silver streak flashed in front of the low-flying chopper. The pilot had kept it to less than two hundred feet above the series of mountain ranges they flew over. The jet raced away, and they saw it make a slow turn.

"I have the local fly boy on my scope," the U.S. fighter pilot said. "That was evidently an ID run. He won't have time to make a second. I'm locked on and firing. One AIM Sidewinder away."

Murdock looked at the pilot, who shook his head. "We just have to wait and see. Those Sidewinders choggie along at Mach 2."

"Oh yeah, splash one bogie," the F-14 pilot said. "That one slipped in under our radar. We're moving our whole system down a few thousand to get better concentration. I'm rotating out. Number two coming in. He knows what went down. Good hunting, you Slow Moe guys."

"Thanks, Fast Duck, and take care," the chopper pilot said on the radio.

"Time left?" Murdock asked.

The pilot looked at his instruments and then his watch. "About twenty. Time to get your men ready. I know you'll get your troops out of there quickly. I don't want to be grounded more than twenty seconds at the most."

"Easy," Murdock said. "Thanks for the ride."

In the cabin with the men, Murdock told them about the

Colombian fighter that had been shot down. "At least they'll know we're here."

"If they admit it," DeWitt said. "They might pass the crashed jet off as an accident."

Ten minutes later, the speaker overhead came on. "SEALs, we're over Bogotá and about two minutes away from the objective. Do good work out there, and we'll be ready for a pickup on your call. The crew chief will get the hatch opened for you."

They made last-minute checks, chambered rounds into weapons, and stood ready to charge out. There was no plan. They would have to play it as it came. First objective was to suppress any guards on the site. Then to find the hostages if they were still on the embassy grounds. Then get the hell out of there.

"We're almost down, Commander. We're landing in the parking lot of the embassy. The gate has been smashed down, and we see two military vehicles out front. We saw no soldiers coming in. Ready, we're down. Opening the hatch."

Murdock was the first man out of the chopper. He hit the pavement and ran flat-out for the first cover he could see: a military half-track parked thirty yards from the embassy front door. He took in the scene in a second. Two-story building that looked like concrete block. Windows along the front mostly broken out. A fire smudge at the front door and through one window. That would be the flamethrower.

He looked behind and saw the last man, Dobler, exit the chopper, and it lifted off. He dove behind the half-track just as he heard the first sound of gunfire. Small arms coming from the embassy. There were some bad guys at home.

"DeWitt, where are you?"

"I've got four of my guys at the near end of the embassy. I saw you head to the front. Want me to swing around to the back door and see who's home?"

"Go. We have some shooters up here. Let me know if you get inside."

"Roger that."

Two more SEALs slid into the paving in back of the half-track. Murdock lifted his weapon over the front of the rig and put three rounds from his submachine gun into the nearest window. He thought he saw movement there.

A weapon fired out a window on the second floor halfway down the building. It was made like a southern plantation mansion with pillars in front. Two cammy-clad figures darted from the front door, heading for a civilian car forty yards down the lot. Two SEAL guns nailed the runners before they made their haven.

More firing came from the front windows. It was thirty yards from the half-track to the mansion. Murdock looked beside him.

"Ostercamp. Can you make this thing run? If you can, we can stay behind it all the way to the front door. Give it a shot."

Ostercamp opened the half-track door and crawled inside.

"No keys, Cap," he said on the radio.

"So jump it, like you used to do in El Cajon."

That brought a laugh. After two minutes of sniping and return fire with the windows the main target, Murdock heard the engine crank over, then roar into life.

"Hooooyah!" Ostercamp bellowed. "Let's roll." He got the rig in gear, and it rolled and clanked along over the paving. The half-track took fire from the building, but Ostercamp was on the floor, steering with one hand over his head.

A minute later, the front bumped into the embassy's side wall.

"Big window," Murdock said. Behind him, Harry Ronson agreed. Murdock put six rounds through the six-foot-square window, smashing the glass. Then he and Ronson ran forward and jumped through the shattered window into the embassy.

It was a conference room. A long table with fancy chairs sat around it in the middle of the room. Oil paintings decorated the walls, and at the far door, two uniformed men stared in surprise at Murdock. Both went down in one burst from Murdock's MP-5. Two more SEALs charged through the broken window, and Murdock used his radio.

"DeWitt, we're inside, through a window. Watch out who you shoot if you come in."

"Will do, Cap. We've found some stubborn ones back here. About ready to use some grenades on them. Busy. Out."

Murdock had checked through the door. He pushed the bodies aside and peered out. It was a hallway that evidently led to the near end of the corridor with two more room doors showing.

"Clear them," Murdock said. Ronson used his machine gun to cover the hall the other way. Lampedusa, Ostercamp, and Holt ran with Murdock to the first door. Lam had it low. Murdock reached across and turned the knob and rammed the door inward, then leaned back away from the opening.

Lam had a perfect view of the room from the floor level. Three men crouched at the window, looking into the front parking lot. All had rifles. Lam riddled all three with his Colt carbine on full auto, and they slammed against the wall and went down. One tried to sit up, and Lam hit him with three more rounds.

Holt ran into the room and cleared it.

Murdock hit the radio. "Ching, Bradford, Jaybird, and Dobler. Where are you? Get in the south wing at the broken six-foot window. We're clearing rooms. Move now. Sound off when you're inside."

Holt edged down the hall to the next door. He took the floor position, and Lam pushed open the door. The room was empty. Behind them, Ronson sent a five-round burst down the hall as two Colombian soldiers appeared twenty yards down the way. They darted back out of sight.

Murdock and his charges went down the hall the other way. Ronson stayed ahead of them, covering the hall.

Murdock rammed open the next door and leaped back as

six rounds jolted through the opening. Lam was at the floor
level and sprayed a dozen rounds into the room, chewing
up four men who had been at the windows. They went
down, and two tried to roll over to fire back. Murdock
slammed them into hell with three-round bursts.

Someone made a noise at the other side of the room.
Murdock looked over and saw a small man in uniform
holding both hands over his head.

"*¡Me rindo! ¡No dispare!*"

Holt swung around, surprised at the man, and fired six
times with his submachine gun. The small man's eyes went
wide, then he crumpled against the wall and slid down it,
dead by the time he hit the floor.

"What the hell did he say?" Lam asked.

"Probably that he wanted to surrender," Murdock said.
"Any more of them?"

"Room clear," Lam said after a quick look. This had been
an office, with big leather chairs, a huge desk, and fancy
lighting.

"Dobler, Ching, Jaybird, and Bradford inside," Murdock's radio said.

"Down the hall," Murdock radioed. "You'll see Ronson
in the hall."

In back of the embassy, DeWitt knew he had a fight on
his hands. He'd spotted six soldiers just getting out of a
truck when he and his squad rounded the corner. They fired
on the Colombians at once and took cover wherever they
could find it.

That was the trouble; there wasn't much: one car in the
lot, a low stone wall, and two stacks of wooden boxes.

Jefferson had pitched three grenades so far, and two of
them had been short. The six soldiers couldn't get in the
back door since Mahanani had it covered with his Colt
Commander carbine.

"Franklin, try a forty-mike. Use it almost point-blank,
bouncing it off the wall behind them."

Franklin waved and loaded a grenade and aimed. The
round exploded at what seemed the same second he fired

it. The deadly grenade splattered shrapnel over three of the defenders. Two of them went down dead before they could run. The other four took off around some boxes and two parked cars and ran flat-out for the far corner of the building.

Ed's men had no targets.

"Move up," Ed said in the radio. "Let's see what they were so keen on defending."

It was a truck behind another truck. The second one was loaded with furniture, TV sets, computers, everything of value they must have found inside the embassy.

They kept to cover and stared at the back door. They had seen no one firing from the rear windows. The place was bigger than it looked at first. There was a wide one-floor section back here before it went two stories.

"All at once," DeWitt said. "We storm the wall. Franklin and me at the door. Ready, go."

The six men charged the wall without taking a shot. DeWitt nodded. He had guessed right. The defenders must all be working the front of the building. He tried the door-knob. It was locked. He put three slugs into it from his G-11 with the caseless rounds, and the door swung inward. He jolted his head out and looked inside, then jerked it back.

Two shots slammed through the open space. He used the radio. "Murdock. We're at the back door. Have it open, some opposition. Check who you shoot at. We're some distance from you guys."

DeWitt jerked a grenade off his webbing, pulled the safety pin, and let the arming handle pop off. He delayed a full second, then tossed the bomb through the door and hugged the outside wall. The grenade exploded as soon as it hit the floor inside. DeWitt and Franklin charged inside one to the right, one to the left.

Not even the moonlight showed inside the room. Both men lay still, waiting for some enemy movement. After two minutes, DeWitt swore softly. He pulled down his forgotten NVGs and looked around the room. It was a storeroom.

Looked like they took in freight and supplies there and then distributed them. He saw one door leading away, then spotted the head and shoulders of a man sprawled behind some boxes. DeWitt checked. He was dead.

"Room clear," Ed said, and the rest of his squad rushed inside.

He pointed at the door, but the others didn't see it. A stream of light slipped under the barrier. He eased up beside the door and tested the knob. No lock. He edged the door open an inch and tried to look through. He needed more room with the NVGs. At six inches, he could see inside. More supplies, but these were seemingly laid out in some order and set in neat rows and piles. He edged the door on open and looked all around the room.

"Second room clear," he said and went inside. Two doors led away from there. He tried one of them and saw a long corridor. At the far end was something that looked like a chandelier. The whole place was lit up like day.

The other door led into a larger room that looked like part of a kitchen. Then he saw the kitchen through some open serving windows. No help, but no soldiers, either. He went back to the first door.

Quinley called to him. "Down here, JG. Something strange. There's a door behind a wall covering, but the door won't open."

DeWitt looked at it. A door with a handle but no lock, yet it wouldn't open. He stepped back and put four rounds about where the locking mechanism should be near the handle. Nothing happened. He fired four more times directly in front of the doorknob. The heavy door shuddered, then edged inward an inch.

Murdock waved his men back and pushed the door open slowly. Inside it was totally black. He pulled down the NVGs and looked again. He grinned.

Steps led downward. Directly in front was a rack that held a dozen full wine bottles.

"The embassy wine cellar," he said and pulled the door closed.

Back at the long corridor, Franklin and Fernandez took the first door on the left. They kicked it open, waited for gunfire, then charged inside. Nobody home. It was a dormitory room set up with four beds. A door beyond led to a bathroom.

The next door down the hallway was similar. The third on the other side of the hall responded with a dozen rounds through the door when Mahanani kicked at it. He put six rounds into the door lock and shoved it open, staying on the wall side and out of the line of fire. Four more shots came through.

Quinley leaned around the wall and drilled a dozen rounds from his caseless-bullet submachine gun. A strangled cry came and then silence. DeWitt looked around the door at floor level. A pair of rounds ripped through the wooden jamb just over his head. A splinter gouged into his cheek.

He pulled back, took a grenade off his webbing, popped the pin, let the handle fly, and held the bomb two seconds before he rolled it into the room. It exploded in two seconds, and he and Jefferson charged into the place when the shrapnel stopped flying. They found one soldier and a dark-eyed girl lying behind a low bed. Both were dead from the grenade.

The rest of the hall produced no surprises, and they edged toward the central room with the chandelier. They had heard gunfire down another hall before. Now DeWitt checked in.

"We're in a lobby of some kind," DeWitt said. "Lights all over the place, no bad guys."

"We're about four doors away," Murdock said. "Lots of activity down here. Any sign of the hostages?"

"None. They might not even be here. We'll hold here until you arrive."

Five minutes later, Murdock's crew cleared the last room, which turned out to be the ambassador's private office, and joined DeWitt in the lobby.

"You didn't tell me there was another wing to this place," Murdock said.

DeWitt shrugged. "Hey, you didn't ask."

A booming voice in English cut through the answer.

"Americans, you must give up your try at rescuing the hostages and surrender to us. If you do not, one hostage will be shot for each ten minutes you delay. You have no chance to get to us. The hostages are in the room immediately in front of us. We can fire over them at you, but you won't be able to fire at all without killing the twelve U.S. State Department officials. See how hopeless it is? Surrender now, or we will kill the first victim, the ambassador himself, in exactly eight minutes."

19

U.S. Embassy
Bogota, Colombia

Murdock looked at his men and the effect of the hostage killing on them. "Anybody see the electrical master switch?" he asked.

"Yeah, around back," Mahanani said. "Back by that door we came in."

"Run back there fast and turn off the power now," Murdock said.

Mahanani took off at a sprint.

"They have to be down this corridor in front of us," DeWitt said. "No place we've seen the other way could hold the hostages."

"Same on our wing. We move down here fast until we get some fire. Then we figure. Lam and I are out front. Five yards and use doorways for cover. Let's go, Lam."

Murdock and Lam ran across the lobby and down the new hallway one door each, then paused. No reaction. They charged down the hallway again, passing two doors this time. Ahead fifty feet they could see large double doors.

Murdock used the Motorola. "DeWitt, clear rooms as you

move up. We'll clear rooms from here on up."

Murdock twisted a doorknob and pushed the panel in. No reaction; the office was empty.

Suddenly, the hallway and the rooms went starkly dark. The contrast was total. Murdock pulled down his NVGs and let his eyes adjust to the night vision. The green hue came in slowly, then firmed. He went to the door on the right and motioned to Lam, then realized he could see. Murdock kicked in the door and scanned the room. One civilian held up his hands. Murdock raced into the room and fastened his hands and ankles with plastic riot cuffs and left him.

Back in the hallway, he touched Lam and pushed him forward. The next room on the left had two soldiers looking out the window. Before they could swing their rifles around, both SEALs fired. The soldiers went down and didn't move. Lam ran over and checked to be sure they were dead.

At the hall, the two paused. They were ten feet from the big double doors. The Colombian army officer who must be in charge had no power to run his PA system, unless he had a handheld bullhorn.

The sound came the same time as the thought.

"Clever, Americans, but it won't work. We still have your people and will execute the ambassador in exactly three minutes."

Murdock used the radio. "Take cover in the rooms or doorways. We're going to open or blow down the double doors you might have seen. Ed, you have the NVGs?"

"Affirmative."

"Use them. There may be some fire down the hall. We're moving up now."

He and Lam ran for the door. It was locked. Murdock took an eighth pound of C-4 from his webbing and pressed it firmly against the door handle where the lock should be. He saw well enough with the night vision goggles to put in a detonator and set it for two minutes. He whispered the time to Lam, pushed the activator, and both men ran for the first room and lunged inside.

A minute later, the cracking roar of the explosion shattered their nerves and turned the black hallway into noontime daylight. Then the roar swept past them down the hall. Murdock grabbed Lam's hand, and they went to the door. He looked down the hall and saw the door blasted flat on one side and hanging by a hinge on the other side. Beyond that he could see little.

A machine gun chattered from somewhere in the void. It was shielded by something down the hall that Murdock couldn't see over or through.

"No firing," Murdock said into his mike. "We don't know where those hostages are. They probably don't have them out as a human shield, but you can't tell."

The weapon down the hall ahead fired again. Then the bullhorn snapped on.

"You lose, American SEALs. We just killed the ambassador. Next comes the second man in command. You now have eight minutes left in your second ten-minute period."

"A green flare," Lam whispered into his mike. "I have two. I could put one into the wall thirty, forty feet down there and see what it will show us."

"Go," Murdock said.

Lam fired the flare from his Colt Commander. It was designed to lift high in the air and descend slowly on a small parachute. At least here it would burn. How bright would it be?

Murdock waited. Lam fired it a moment later, and it hit the far wall, bounced down the hall, and popped into a pale green light at once. Murdock saw the sandbags and a mounted machine gun. Directly in back were four soldiers. Even with the penetrating power of the night vision goggles he could spot no civilians.

"Take them out," Murdock said. "Lam and I are out of your firing line."

At once the SEALs' machine guns and two long rifles

cascaded a rain of fire against the sandbags and enemy gun. Two of the soldiers went down in the first barrage. The next one battered and riddled the top sandbags, and a round nailed the machine gunner, who had managed only a short burst before he died. Murdock saw the fourth man lift up and dart toward a door at the side of the hall. He didn't make it, spinning to the floor with two rounds in his chest.

"Cease fire," Murdock said on the radio. The SEAL guns fell silent. Murdock studied the area behind the gun again through his night vision goggles. Movement. Who? A man in a white shirt. A civilian.

"Everyone move up to closer cover," Murdock said. He and Lam darted ahead to the blasted door. The machine gun lay on its side, ten yards ahead. Murdock could see two hall doors open. A soldier ran from one, looked back down the hall, then fired a four-round burst and vanished again. The green flare weakened and soon burned out, leaving the hallway dark.

Now Murdock could see through the goggles more civilians being moved down the hall.

"No return fire. Civilians in the hall. DeWitt, take four men and run to what must be a back door down this wing. I think all of the defenders are with the hostages. We'll try to surprise them if they try to leave the building. The rest of you, move closer but maintain cover between moves."

Murdock touched Lam, and they ran into the wing and pushed into doorways on both sides just past the machine gun. Murdock cleared the room on his side with his goggles. They all had moved on. Why? Where were they going?

He checked for bodies. Only the three soldiers showed. No civilians. No dead ambassador. Was the army man bluffing? What good to kill a hostage if no one could see it?

Ahead, Murdock heard a door close. Where? He hadn't thought of the second floor. Nowhere had he seen stairs leading upward.

"Ed. If you can get inside that back door down there,

check to see if there's a stairs to the second floor. If so, block it and set up a fence across the hall."

"That's a roger, Cap. Almost to the door. We'll move carefully."

Murdock adjusted the NVGs and moved into the hallway with Lam in tow. They worked ahead on silent feet. Murdock checked both open doors they passed. No bodies. Where were they going?

The bullhorn blasted into the silence. "Well done, SEALs, but not good enough. We have the edge in manpower, and we know the terrain. You've found no American bodies? True. I made the living ones carry the two dead ones. Now for a final solution to our little problem. We are at a stalemate. I have the prisoners, you have the better weapons. However, to use those weapons, you run the risk of killing the reason you came in here.

"Oh, to add to your stress, we have a radio report from our commander that your helicopter and two of the fighters that came with it have been shot down and crashed in flames. That should make you think about your mission. You have no way to get out of here."

There was a moment of silence.

"No response? I didn't think so. This is the situation. Each of our hostages is holding a live grenade with the safety pin pulled. All that is keeping them alive is not dropping the grenade or letting the arming spoon flip off. Right? Soon some of them will become tired and one or more bombs will go off. None of my men are near them. You can't find them or get past us. Now you must surrender."

Ed DeWitt heard most of the talk as he and his four men slipped in the rear door. He had the other pair of NVGs. The things were heavy, clumsy, and not a favorite of the SEALs, but they did come in handy now and then. He looked past a doorway just inside the hall and listened. He heard movement in the room directly above him.

Where were the stairs? He looked along the hall again and fifteen feet ahead saw the steps leading up. One room on each side with doors closed. He took Franklin with him and edged up to the door. Silently, he twisted the knob and pushed it open. No response. He looked inside with the NVGs and saw no one. The other side door yielded the same results.

Ed looked at the stairs. Somebody was upstairs. The man on the bullhorn sounded like he was in the hallway. It extended far down ahead of him. He saw at least six or eight doors in the misty gloom of the greenscape.

He touched the other three men, and they all moved to the steps and slowly went up them. One flight with a landing on top almost against the wall. They all stopped and listened. Again there were movements of feet and some whispers. The civilians?

They paused on the landing in the dark. DeWitt could see the new hallway on the second floor. There were more doors opening off it as if this were a dormitory.

Before DeWitt could move, the door opposite him opened, and a soldier left, locking the door behind him. He felt his way toward the steps with one hand out in front. The other hand carried an automatic rifle.

As the soldier came closer, DeWitt grabbed Fernandez's sniper rifle and waited. When the Colombian soldier was a step away and still blinded by the darkness, DeWitt swung the heavy rifle like a club, hitting the soldier in the throat. The man dropped the rifle, and it clattered to the floor. DeWitt surged on top of the man as he fell. The soldier grabbed his throat, then wheezed twice and his head rolled to one side.

DeWitt certified that he was dead, then found a key in his pocket and went to the door the soldier had just left. He turned the key in the lock and edged the door open. With his NVGs, he saw that the people inside were civilians.

"U.S. SEALs here," he whispered. "Quiet. Is the ambassador here?"

A man stepped forward, tears running down his cheeks. "Yes."

"Murdock," DeWitt whispered into his mike, "I have the whole staff, all safe and well. No grenades. You are facing a force of one man."

"Roger that," Murdock whispered back. He began to edge forward. The bullhorn had been pushed out one of two rooms into the hall. It was silent now. Which room? Murdock picked the first one to clear or to kill. He moved to the very edge of the door and looked around. No one in the room.

He waved at the men to stay where they were, even though he knew they couldn't see him. The other room across the hall had the door open.

He stepped that way silently and started to look around the doorjamb. A figure stepped outward, nearly colliding with him. Murdock brought the butt of the MP-5 submachine gun upward in a vicious butt stroke that connected with the man's chin and rocked his head backward.

The man dropped the bullhorn, stumbled backward a step, and then fell to the floor, his neck broken. Murdock checked for a pulse at the carotid, then used the mike.

"DeWitt, troops. This thing is over. Holt, move outside through the back door and see if you can contact that chopper. He must be hanging around somewhere."

"Mahanani, go turn on the lights," Ed DeWitt ordered. "The hostages are all well. None was killed. Two have wounds from the assault and takeover. From what I hear, there were only about twenty soldiers here. We took out a lot of them, and the others ran for cover."

"Everyone just hold in place except Holt until we get lights. Then we'll move outside and find an LZ. SEALs, do we have any casualties?"

No one replied. "Alpha Squad, report in on hurts," Murdock said. All checked in as not wounded. The same for Bravo Squad.

The lights blossomed, and everyone was blinded for a minute.

Murdock heard the people coming downstairs. He looked at the last man he had killed. He was a Colombian sergeant and had two grenades in his belt, but both had the safety pins still in them.

Ten minutes later, outside near the spot where the chopper would land, a red flare burned brightly. The ambassador and the rest of his people stood to one side, hugging each other. Some cried. Others looked back at the embassy that had been their home for years.

They heard the chopper coming in. The SEALs were in an extended perimeter defense, lying on the blacktop of the parking lot. They saw no movement around the once again blacked-out embassy.

The bird came in and landed, and Jaybird and Murdock ushered the civilians to the chopper door and helped them inside. Once they were all on board, the SEALs piled in the door and found floor space wherever they could.

The Sea Knight was on the ground a minute and twenty seconds, then the crew chief slammed the hatch and it lifted off.

Murdock went up front and used the bird's radio. He raised the carrier and reported a success so far.

"Now all we have to do is get back to Camp Bravo, and we can call it a completed mission."

Don Stroh tried to talk, but Murdock cut him off. "Sorry, Stroh, can't talk right now, I have some people to take care of. See you soon."

Murdock grinned. Damned if he was going to get another fucking mission before this one was even completed. Twice during the next hour, Murdock heard reports from the F-14s flying cover that they had blips on their radar. The bogies tended to come forward to within about thirty miles of the chopper and then headed back the other way.

They landed at Camp Bravo and said good-bye to the Tomcats that went back to the carrier.

The civilians were met by two State Department officials who took them into Cali by bus. The ambassador shook Murdock's hand once more before he left.

The SEALs gathered up their gear and caught a ride back to their barracks. Murdock knew there was another job for

them out there in Don Stroh's little black book, but he'd
be damned if he was going to talk about it before he had
that steak dinner, a long, hot shower, and at least twelve
hours of sleep.

Damn, but he was tired. He didn't even think how long
it had been since he'd seen a bunk. Just like hell week.
Hooooooooyah!

20

Murdock and the rest of the SEALs slept in. Some put in twelve hours in the rack, some eight. Murdock came to the surface after ten and had a shower a big meal and was surprised to find that it was almost noon. He checked with Senior Chief Dobler.

"Weapons are all cleaned and oiled and equipment is repaired or replaced. Most of the men are up to regs and ready to go. Two are still snoring, but I'll move them along. You heard anything from Don Stroh?"

"Haven't given him a chance. Figure the men need a short break before we head out on another one of these small fires to put out."

"Holt asked me if he should turn on the SATCOM. I told him to wait and ask you. Sure as hell, Stroh is going to be yelling at you."

Murdock grinned. "I'm about to leave him off my next fishing trip." He rubbed one hand over his face. "Hell, we might as well find out what the spook wants. It won't be good. Where's Holt?"

Five minutes later, Holt had the SATCOM zeroed in on the satellite. A minute after he turned it to receive, the set spoke.

"Roamer, this is Home Base. We need to talk. You awake yet over there?" There was a pause.

"Oh, yeah, Home Base," Murdock said. "Awake. You sound rushed."

"We've been handed a new assignment. You're moving north to the Caribbean. The carrier *Jefferson* is floating around up there somewhere off Cartagena, a Colombian port town with a lot of shipping. We've got a COD warming up on deck. It will be at your location at 1300 to move you."

"North? Shipping?"

"Right. I'll be on the Greyhound so we can chat all the way up across the Pacific and a flyover of part of Panama. I think you'll like this one."

"Don Stroh, sir! You know we always love the assignments we get. We take all of our goodies?"

"Everything you took in with you. All your gear, ammo, and TNAZ."

"Thirteen hundred. We'll be ready."

"Any more wounded?"

"We're full strength again and raring to go."

"See you then."

They signed off. By then, half the platoon had gathered around the radio. "So, we're moving. Senior Chief, roust up the rest of the men and we'll have a quick talk."

The Navy COD, officially a Greyhound C-2A, took off from the small field at Camp Bravo near Cali at 1310. The COD is a Navy acronym for carrier on board delivery plane. It can land and take off from the larger carriers and is routinely used to deliver VIP personnel, mail, and important equipment and goods needed in a rush by the Navy.

It was derived from the E-2C Hawkeye aircraft It cruises at 300 mph, with a ceiling of 33,500 feet, and can haul thirty-nine troops or twelve hospital cases on litters. It has a range of 1,200 miles loaded, carries two pilots and a flight engineer, and is powered by two Allison turboprop engines.

Stroh talked to the men as soon as they loaded and before they took off.

"We're going to the Carrier *Jefferson* somewhere in the Caribbean Sea north of Cartagena, Colombia. There you will get more specific details about your missions. Roughly, it's a three-part assignment. You'll go ashore in the harbor and destroy any way practical the four tons of powdered cocaine loaded on two freighters due to sail in two days.

"Then you will destroy a pair of warehouses where more than a thousand barrels of ethyl ether is being stockpiled by the Medellin drug cartel. I understand ether burns well and when vaporized is volatile and extremely explosive.

"After that, you will get some sort of transport to the small town of Plato, where the Medellin drug cartel has just built a new airfield for its drug trade. Planes come in from Bolivia and Peru bringing in coca paste. There are several processing plants in this area as well as more stockpiles of finished coke ready to be sent out to the States by plane. Planes, trucks, processing plants, and stockpiles will be your targets.

"If you have time and personnel, you will proceed by your own devices to locate and eradicate from one to three of the top men in the Medellin cartel. They are supposed to be at the airport facility there for a planning meeting now that they own Colombia and have their government in power. Any questions?"

Just then, the turboprop engines turned over, and conversations inside the COD were limited. The flight engineer came back and told Murdock that they would have a two-and-a-half-hour flight.

They landed on board the *Jefferson* fifteen minutes sooner than that, and Murdock saw his men put in quarters and their equipment spread out in an assembly compartment.

"Commander Murdock?" an officer who walked up asked.

Murdock saw a short, thin lieutenant commander in a tailored uniform.

"Yes, Commander."

"I'm Lieutenant Commander Kenney, your liaison with the ship. You have the highest priority I've ever seen, Commander. The admiral says that anything you want, you get. Right now I can arrange a meal for you and your men. You have your quarters. There were some indications that you might need arms or explosives and ammo. All I need is a list."

"Thanks, Commander. You'll work with Senior Chief Dobler. We have an appointment with your XO in forty minutes. First we need to do some planning and figure out what we'll need. Sit in, if you like."

Murdock called his key people around a small table and they made notes on pads of paper as they talked.

First the coke.

"Can't blow it up or burn it," DeWitt said.

"How can we melt it the way we did down by Cali?" Jaybird asked.

"Fire hoses," Senior Chief Dobler said. "The goods will be packaged in plastic to protect it from the salt air and any spray or leaks. We'll need to slice it open and soak it down using the firefighting hoses and pumps on the ship."

"If we get the time," DeWitt added.

"So, we soak it down and melt it," Murdock said. "Sounds like the only way. Not even sinking the merchant ship at the dock would do it. The goods would just float."

They moved on the ether situation.

"Talk to Canzoneri," Murdock said. "Find out how much explosives we'll need to set the stuff on fire. If it's in a warehouse it will be best, one big bonfire nobody will be able to put out."

Dobler went to find Canzoneri.

"This Plato deal is going to be a tough one. First we have to get down there," Murdock said. "Stroh tells me it's about eighty-five miles south of the port city. They just said do it, not how we get there. Any suggestions?"

Jaybird swore under his breath. "The sombitches did it to us again. We're on the Caribbean, right. At this port city. So after we do the bonfire, we get into our rebreathers and fins and swim out a half mile where we meet a Sea Knight after dark for a ladder pickup and transport to Plato with our resupply of ammo and explosives the Sea Knight brings us."

Murdock looked at the others. "Any more suggestions?" Nobody said anything. "Well, it's a long swim up the river that runs through Plato and out at the port we'll be in. The resupply with the Sea Knight sounds like a good plan. How else could we get down there?"

"Long walk," DeWitt said.

"At Plato we have production vats, ethyl, stored coke. Why not do a few of their small transport planes as well?" Murdock looked at his watch. "Okay, the four of us are going to see the admiral. I told him I was bringing my staff, so look important."

"Oh, hell, yes," Jaybird said. "Admirals are always kissing up to me."

They arrived at the admiral's compartment early but were let in by a master chief. His brows went up when he looked at Jaybird with no rank showing on his cammies and Senior Chief Dobler.

"The admiral will be right with you." He indicated a conference table with five chairs. The SEALs sat.

A moment later, Admiral Tennant came through a door from another section of the large quarters, and the SEALs jumped to their feet.

"At ease. I'm Admiral Tennant. As you were." The admiral smiled. "Glad to see you men. I know a few ex-SEALs. You do good work."

Behind him came a captain and Lieutenant Commander

Kenney, their liaison. The admiral motioned to the second man.

"Gentlemen, this is Captain Wilson, the *Jefferson*'s XO. You know Commander Kenney."

Senior Chief Dobler and Jaybird stepped back from their chairs, offering them to the other two officers.

The admiral gave a curt wave with his hand. "No, SEALs, you sit. We do too much sitting around here, anyway. You'll be on your mission soon enough with no chance to take it easy."

The SEALs sat.

"Now, Commander, you've had some time to consider your assignment. Your suggestions."

"If you have a Pegasus in the task force, it could take us in to within half a mile of shore, and we'll go in underwater to the first objective. If no Pegasus, a Sea Knight could take us within a mile and we'll drop out and swim on in."

Murdock looked up. The XO nodded.

"We have a Pegasus, an eighty-two-footer. That would be the least intrusive."

Murdock then outlined in broad strokes their plans to wash down the cocaine in the freighters and be gone before the Colombians knew what was happening. "We understand there are two tons of cocaine on each freighter. That's over a hundred million dollars' worth in street value. That'll hurt them."

"What about the ether?" the admiral asked. "It's in a guarded warehouse in the port area."

"Ether is highly volatile, and if we can get one or two barrels of it burning, it can cook off the rest in a huge bonfire nobody could put out," Ed DeWitt said.

The admiral looked at DeWitt a moment. "What else?"

"Then we'd need some help, Admiral. Our plan is to go back to the water and swim a mile offshore. We'll contact the carrier by SATCOM before we leave dry land and ask for a meet a mile off with a Sea Knight chopper. We'll go up the rope ladder from a hover position. Then the Sea

Knight can take us about eighty-five miles upriver to Plato, where the rest of our mission is located."

"Ladder access. What if you have wounded who can't climb the ladder?"

"We carry them up or rope them up, Admiral," Senior Chief Dobler said. "No problem; we've done it before."

"When the Sea Knight comes, it would bring a preordered resupply for us of ammo, weapons, and explosives," Murdock said. "Some MREs would be good, too."

Captain Wilson cleared his throat. "After you do your work there, how do you get back to the water?"

"That one we didn't have time to work out. We could float down the Magdalena River. But that would be at least a ninety-mile trip with a lot of chances to be discovered."

"You'd need the Sea Knight and some fighter cover, same way you got out of Bogota," Captain Wilson said. "Will the President authorize it?"

"He did before," Murdock said. "We think he will again."

"If the chopper came in due west of Plato, there would be only about sixty miles of territory to cover, and it's less built up than the north."

"Noted. What about the Colombian navy?"

"As you know, Admiral, Colombia has only four corvettes in the one thousand five hundred–ton class," DeWitt said. "They have one larger patrol boat of a hundred and eighty-five feet, and about forty patrol and riverboat craft. We consider the navy's threat to us as insignificant."

The admiral peaked his fingers and looked at his men. "Any questions of the SEALs?" he asked. They shook their heads.

"All right, Commander. We'll go with the Pegasus and the Sea Knight. The CAG isn't here, but I'm sure he can spare one for a while. On the resupply and trip to Plato, give us a two-hour lead time so we can get your resupply on board and make your meet on time. We'll want another two hours for the trip in from the west coast toward Plato. Commander Kenney will coordinate your need for weapons, ammo, and supplies. Anything else?"

Captain Wilson cleared his throat again. "Commander, I hear you have a new army rifle. Is it as good as I've heard?"

"Senior Chief Dobler can fill you in on that, sir," Murdock said.

They looked at Dobler. "Sir, it's called the Bull Pup, at least for now. It's a dual-barreled weapon of about fourteen pounds. It has one barrel for 5.56mm rounds and another one on top to fire 20mm explosive rounds that are aimed and fuzed through a six-power scope, video camera, and a laser range finder. The laser is spotted on target, responds to the computer inside, and arms the round with the exact number of revolutions the spinning bullet needs to reach that spot.

"The rounds can be set to explode on contact or with a delayed fuze to shoot through sheet metal or light wooden walls. The rounds cost thirty dollars each. It carries a six-round magazine. The weapon is now under testing by the makers and will not be available to the army until the year 2005. We ordered specially made models because it's such an advanced design."

"So it will give a rifleman an airburst with a 20mm round," the captain said. "That's like shooting around a corner or over the back side of a building or hill."

"We have found it's tremendously effective, Captain," Murdock said.

"I'd like to see one, Commander," the Captain said.

"I'll arrange that, Captain."

The admiral stood and the rest of them came to attention.

"Thank you, gentlemen. We didn't touch on the timing. It's now about 1600. Your orders said at the first possible moment before those two freighters sail. Can you do it tonight?"

"Yes sir. We'd like to leave here so we can hit the port at first dark or as close to that as we can," Murdock said.

"We're about fifty miles off the Colombian port of Cartagena," the captain said. "That's about an hour and a half in the Pegasus so you don't get shaken to pieces. Commander Kenney, you better get cracking on that materiel these men need."

"Yes sir."

"Work with Senior Chief Dobler," Murdock said. The admiral looked at Murdock, then turned and left the compartment.

Two hours later, Murdock looked around the tightly efficient cabin of the Pegasus. The eighty-two foot craft had been specifically designed to insert and recover SEALs and other covert forces. It could rev up to 45 knots and had a range of 550 miles. A crew of five ran the boat. It wasn't designed as a fighting craft but did carry mounts for 12.7mm machine guns and one Mark 19 40mm grenade launcher. The boat jolted along through the darkening Caribbean Sea at a little over thirty knots, cutting down the slamming into the light chop on the water.

They were ready. Murdock had made one last check on Canzoneri to be sure that his leg wound hadn't opened up. It looked to him to be healing well. Mahanani gave the petard expert an okay for duty. Murdock told the corpsman to check the other wounded. Murdock's wrist took a new bandage. Dobler's round through his thigh was coming along well, not giving him any trouble. Jaybird's shot left forearm was starting to heal. All ready for duty. They all settled into the boat.

Murdock had brought along three extra MP-5 submachine guns. They would be in drag bags with their explosives and other gear that they wouldn't need at once. Their first job was to get into the water, then swim to shore and find the right ships in the harbor.

It was nearly 1930 when the SEALs rolled off the Pegasus and dropped into the warm Caribbean Sea. They had their buddy cords tied on and the eight two-man teams sank to fifteen feet, checked their compasses, and headed for the

port city of Cartagena, Colombia. They had a little over a
half mile to go.

At the entrance to the harbor, they all surfaced, and Murdock and Lam studied the situation. The brightly lit Navy
Station showed to the left. To the right they saw the docks
with six merchant ships tied up. Two of them were bathed
in floodlights and were being loaded with huge cargo containers.

Murdock motioned for them to swim that way, and they
went underwater again, using their rebreathers so they
wouldn't show any line of bubbles behind them.

The next time they came to the surface, barely breaking
the water, they were at the first in a line of freighters. They
could read the names: *The Montrose*, a Bolivian flagship,
and *The Mary Jane*, registered in the the Bahama Islands.
Murdock read the name on the bow of the big freighters
and waved his men around them. They found the ones they
wanted two down. The *Winddriven* and the *Alpha Marie*
were the targets. They lay side by side and were dark. Evidently, the loading was finished.

The plan was for each squad to take one ship, to move
up the side of the ships on ropes anchored by rubberized
grappling hooks on the rail, then to capture any crewmen
and guards on board, and then to wash down or otherwise
ruin the two tons of cocaine on each ship.

Murdock sent DeWitt with his Bravo Squad to the *Winddriven,* and he moved up to the *Alpha Marie*. He had his
men fasten their drag bags on the hull to the ship with large
magnets with hooks on them made for that purpose. The
waterproof bags rested just below the waterline so no lookout could see them.

The platoon leader threw the first grappling hook attached to quarter-inch nylon line that could hold more
than a thousand pounds on a straight pull. On the second
try, the hook caught. Murdock tested the hook by putting
all his weight on the rope. It held. He passed the bottom
of the line to Jaybird and began to go hand over hand,
walking up the side of the ship and pulling upward on

the rope. His MP-5 submachine gun was strapped over his back.

He had just cleared the side of the ship and climbed over the low rail when a shadow appeared in front of him. The shadow turned into a man with a submachine gun pointed directly at Murdock's chest.

"Well, look at this. Froggy, froggy, what have I captured here? Make a move at that weapon, and you'll be dead in a five-round burst."

21

Behia de Cartagena
Cartagena, Colombia

Murdock stared at the gun-wielding American. *"¿Qué pasa? Qué pasa?"* Murdock said, using his best Spanish accent.

"Oh, shit, you kidding? None of the greasers down here have frogman junk like you're wearing. Full wet suits, breathers, masks, gloves, and even boots."

"Inspección, inspección." Murdock shouted, not knowing what else to do. He held out both his hands in a pleading gesture.

Two silenced rounds drilled into the gunman's chest six feet in front of Murdock. The guard grunted and slammed backward, dropping the submachine gun he held and falling with dead weight against some pipes and pulleys on the deck.

Murdock charged forward and grabbed the weapon and checked the American. He was dead.

Jaybird climbed over the rail and grinned in the darkness through his camo-paint-splotched face.

"De nada," Jaybird whispered. Together they lifted the

body and carried it down a dozen feet along the rail and dropped it overboard. By then, two more SEALs were on deck, and they spread out as previously arranged. Murdock and Jaybird took the bridge; two more men cleared the area just below it. And two more took each of the other decks and areas where there might be crew or guards.

On the bridge, Murdock and Jaybird found one Bolivian guard sleeping. They knocked him out and tied his hands and feet with riot cuffs. The papers were all in Spanish. By the time they moved down the ladders to the holds, Senior Chief Dobler said the boat was secure.

"We found three crew and three more guards, all goofing off. No shooting. All contained and cuffed. Ching talked to all of them. One said the secret cargo was in hold four. He took us down to it. This way, Cap."

Hold four was in the center of the big cargo vessel. A mixed cargo was arranged around the heavy wooden boxes. Each one was four feet square and three feet high. Jaybird found some tools and ripped off the top of one. Inside, wrapped in triple heavy plastic, lay the powdered cocaine.

Lampedusa had out a fire hose, and Bradford waited at the valve to turn it on. There were ten boxes stacked three high. Ching and Ronson pushed the top ones off to fall to the deck, then the men began breaking in the tops of the other boxes.

The water came on, and Lam aimed it into the powder. At first they used too much pressure and the white powder flew all over. With practice, they figured out how much water to use and washed down one box after another until there was a milky flood over half of the hold floor. It took longer than they figured. An hour into it, they had half the boxes of cocaine ruined. All the tops were now pried off, and a second fire hose was watering down the coke.

Jaybird came running down a ladder and called to Murdock.

"We have some trouble, Cap. Four guys coming up the gangplank. Two in suits. Two look like gorillas."

Murdock took Jaybird and Dobler with their silenced sub

guns, and they ran up to the top deck. The men headed for the bridge.

"*¿Aye, qué pasa?*" Murdock called. The men turned. Two pulled out automatic handguns, looking for trouble. Murdock and Jaybird had shots. Both the big men went down with a pair of 9mm slugs in their chests.

Dobler ran up and covered the two suits.

"What the hell is going on here?" one of the suits yelled.

Jaybird checked both the gunmen. Dead.

"I said, what the hell is going on here?" the taller of the two men asked.

"You forgot to pay your insurance on the cocaine shipment," Murdock said. "As the shipper, you know damn well you have to pay the insurance."

"We paid off half the damn country . . ." The man stopped. "Hey, you're Americans. You divers or frogmen or what the hell?"

"We ask the questions," Murdock said. "You two want to live more than five minutes, you better start giving me some answers. Names and addresses."

"Joe Black from Miami," the taller one said.

"Phillip Bartlesman, Atlanta," the other said.

"Who do you work for?"

"None of your damned . . ."

Murdock lifted the silenced MP-5, and the man changed his tone. "We buy from the big guys, the Medellin. Figured we'd cut out a middleman and do our own delivery."

"Both ships?" Murdock asked.

"Yeah."

"Street value?"

"About a hundred and thirty mil. But we don't see a third of that."

"Nice profit."

The shorter man dove to one side, drawing a handgun. Dobler tracked him and put five silenced rounds up his back before he could roll. He never pulled out the gun.

"Keerist, you shot him down."

"He shouldn't play with guns," Dobler said. Dobler put

the still-hot muzzle of the MP-5 under the suit's chin. "Isn't his five minutes up, Cap?"

"Almost. Who do you work for?"

The suit shivered. "Art. Art Ridozzo. Miami. The Ridozzo Family."

"Some Mafia shithead doesn't scare me. Tell him he just lost his sixty million dollar investment and to get into another line of work. Can you swim?"

"Yeah, a little."

"Good, come over here to the rail."

"I can walk down the gangplank."

"Not yet. When we're done, you go for a swim. Cuff him, Jaybird. A gag, too. Then let him lie there until we're done. Dobler, see if you can find out what's going on at the next ship."

Murdock didn't want to use the Motorolas unless he had to. The Medellin cartel could have some serious receivers and scanners in this area. They could afford to buy the best in the world. Dobler trotted to the far side of the freighter. Murdock went back to hold number four.

The milky swamp on the hold floor was a foot deep by then. They were on the last two boxes of cocaine.

Murdock went back on deck and looked at the other freighter anchored fifty feet away. His earphone came on with three clicks. He clicked three back.

"Cap. We've got troubles. Thought we had it clean. Four gunmen jumped us. Fernandez is hit bad. Stalled on the meltdown. Could use five more guns. Come up the gangplank. Oh, Christ. Gotta go."

"Dobler, Jaybird. Finish the meltdown here. Rest of you top deck for the gangplank. Bravo needs some help. Move, now."

Murdock ran for the gangplank. He scanned the dock. He saw only one wandering homeless man with a plastic sack over his shoulder. It was sixty feet down a wooden and concrete dock to the next freighter. He saw no one on deck. Holt, Bradford, Lam, Ching, and Ronson came storming up to the plank. All had their weapons at port arms, ready for action.

"Trouble on the next boat. Ed might be pinned down. We go up the gangplank without a sound, search for the bad guys. Four of them. They must be in the hold or can look down into the hold. Let's go."

The SEALs moved swiftly but without a sound down the metal gangplank to the dock, then ran the sixty feet along the concrete to the next ship's plank. Lam went first with his eyes wide open, watching for any movement. Nobody was on guard. They all made it to the ship and hunkered down along the rail, listening.

Somewhere inside the ship they heard a shot, then another one. Muffled but not suppressed. The sound came from the aft section. They moved that way. More sounds. Some shouting.

A hatch was open halfway to the aft end. Murdock looked over the side and saw the deep hold with nothing in it but a dozen wooden crates identical to the ones they had in the first ship.

He could see no SEALs. A white milky flood on the hold floor showed some of the coke had been melted.

"How do we get down there?" Murdock asked.

Ching led the way to a set of steel steps leading down to the holds about halfway back. They moved down and worked a series of catwalks and ladders until they were near the open hold.

"Ed, where are you?" Murdock asked on the radio. "Where are the shooters?"

"All of us are pinned down behind the coke crates. Two of the shooters are to our left in some machinery. Two are behind some heavy boxes to the right."

"We can't see them," Murdock said. "We're halfway down. Can you use a grenade?"

"Afraid where it would bounce. Close quarters in here."

"Let it cook for two seconds, then throw it. Give it a try."

Seconds later, a grenade exploded in the hold. The confined space made it sound like a two-thousand-pound bomb going off in an elevator. Murdock and his men crawled forward for a better look into the hold.

Lam pointed to one side. Two men with automatic rifles hid behind wooden crates. Lam pointed right. Murdock took the one on the left. They both fired three-round bursts from the suppressed weapons. The men jolted backward. One tried to crawl around the box. Lam nailed him with three more rounds, and he lay still.

"Two down," Murdock said.

"I think the grenade did the other two," DeWitt said on the radio. "Franklin is checking."

"Two down here, Cap," Franklin said.

"Get back to the hosing down," Murdock said. "We're running behind schedule. How is Fernandez?"

"Not good. He took two rounds, one in the high chest, one in the shoulder. Mahanani got the bleeding stopped, but Fernandez is moving slow. Nothing vital. Mahanani is worried about the top of his lung getting hit."

As they spoke, Murdock saw his men turning on the hoses again. All of the tops were off the boxes. The millions of dollars of cocaine rapidly turned into worthless soup on the hold's floor.

Murdock put Lam on deck as a lookout. He checked his watch. It was nearing 2200. He had hoped they could be out of there and moving toward the dock warehouse and the ether by this time.

He found DeWitt. "How much longer here?"

"Half hour at the most. We're on the last boxes now."

"Rush it any way you can. How about Fernandez? Use two men to help him up to the rail across from the one you came in. Send any line you have with him. We don't want him jumping in the water. I'm going to check on top. Any chance those four clowns we offed had a radio?"

"Don't know. I'll have somebody check the bodies. Fernandez is on his way. He's bitching, so he might not be as badly hurt as it looks like."

Murdock was halfway to the open deck when his ear-piece spoke.

"Cap, looks like we have visitors. Two army trucks. Troops getting out of them."

"Roger that. Dobler and Jaybird. Get out of that ship and into the bay. Come over to the south side of this freighter and wait. Bring all of our drag bags with you."

"Aye, Cap. Will do." It was Dobler.

Murdock ran up the last ladder and slid to the deck so he could see over the rail. Looked like two squads of infantry, fourteen men, maybe sixteen. One squad approached each of the two freighters. They went to ground near the gangplank. What were they waiting for?

"Ed, get your guys out of there, now. Come up the far side if you can. Go over the side and pick up the drag bags. Any line? Can you get Fernandez down gently? Time for us to split. Visitors look like security guards, not anxious to get into a fight. Let's move, now. Everyone over the far side and into the wet."

"Yes, we have line. We'll rappel Fernandez down. We're moving."

They all still had on their full wet suits, with rebreathers and fins tied around their necks. The SEALS hung on the rail and dropped into the water twenty feet below.

Dobler and Jaybird waited for them at the side of the ship. The rest of the SEALs dropped in and moved underwater at the side of the ship, touching each other to stay together. Murdock and Dobler waited for Fernandez to be let down. He grinned at them, but there was pain in his dark eyes.

"Can you swim, Fernandez?"

"Think so, Cap. Might not keep up. Hurts like hell. One-arm swim time."

Murdock put Harry Ronson on Fernandez to buddy him and help him keep up. They would try to match their swim speed to the best that Fernandez could do.

Ed indicated by signs he was on his way with a man to get their drag bags on the other side of the freighter. He was back seven minutes later. Murdock had everyone surface along the side of the freighter, and he swam along, counting wet suit hoods. All sixteen accounted for.

Murdock signaled down, and the seals tied as buddies went to fifteen feet and swam around the freighters. Their intel said the ethyl was in one of a pair of old warehouses on the docks near an unused pier no more than five hundred yards from the freighters. Murdock hoped that they were right. Fernandez worried him. The chest shot could be bad. He could go sour and die as he tried to swim.

After enough strokes to cover 500 yards, Murdock surfaced with his tied-on buddy, Holt, for a sneak and peak. He barely let his face break the surface and looked around. They were thirty yards off the dock, a wooden affair that stilted ten feet into the water.

Around Murdock more SEALs broke the surface. He counted. Seven pairs of heads showing.

Where were Fernandez and Ronson? It had to be them. He waited two minutes by his watch, then another minute. To his relief, he saw two more heads surface slowly. Ronson's rebreather tube came out of his mouth. "Cap?" he whispered. Murdock was halfway there.

"Need to get Fernandez to shore pronto. He's hurting."

Murdock helped pull Fernandez along as they swam to shore under the overhead of the dock. They eased down on the rocky shoreline, and Fernandez took off his mouthpiece and goggles and shook his head.

"Gonna be a long night, Cap. Don't think I can hold up my end of the fight."

"You rest right here. This one should be a cakewalk. Just a little bonfire to start. Then we take an easy run down the channel and out to sea. Have you back on the *Jefferson* before you know it." Murdock found Quinley along the line of SEALs.

"Watch Fernandez. Stay with him. Get him some morphine and pain pills from Mahanani. Time for us to be moving up."

They left their rebreathers and fins on the rocky slope

just over the water and took out of the drag bags what they needed. More TNAZ and C-4 and extra ammo. The alert around the ship might have triggered more troops to come to the area.

Murdock went to the side of the pier and up to the top. He watched the first warehouse for five minutes. There appeared to be no roving guards. He couldn't be sure about fixed guard posts. Lam had come up with him and said he'd take a quick look around the place and see what he could find.

Lam moved a dozen feet toward the building. He was still thirty feet away from it when a siren went off, floodlights billowed on his side of the building, painting the whole scene as light as day. Lam surged back over the rocks beside the pier and out of sight.

The SEALs had taken out their Motorolas from waterproof pouches as soon as they landed. Now Murdock hit his lip mike.

"Snipers, get the hell up here. We have some fucking floodlights to shoot out. Looks like the party is starting."

22

On the Docks
Cartagena, Colombia

Murdock watched the warehouse area with the floodlights blazing. They had snapped on when Lam broke some beam or tromped on a movement or vibration sensor. These drug cartels could afford the best in protection. But what about personnel?

Bill Bradford slid in beside Murdock with his H&K PSGI sniper rifle with a suppressor. He began taking out the lights with the deadly cough of the NATO round.

Murdock worked on two close lights and snuffed them with his silenced MP-5 on single shot.

On the other side of Murdock, Jaybird began taking out lights with his MP-5. Two Colt Commander carbines came on line, and within two minutes, all the lights on their side of the building were shot out. When the firing stopped, Murdock and Lam listened to the silence. A dog barked far off. Some kind of a night bird shrieked as it dove on a mouse. They heard no trucks, no alarms. No men running. The siren had cut off when the first floodlight smashed.

Murdock used the radio. "DeWitt. Get your squad up

here and take the front of the building facing the water. Alpha, let's get the side in the dark and test the back. Go inside if you can, DeWitt, and see what our situation is. Let me hear. Go."

Murdock's squad boiled over the small berm and darted across the blacktop to the side of the now-dark building. They paused but could hear no opposition. The back of the building had not been lit up. Or had it and all the lights went out due to a short when the others were shot out? Probably. Murdock and his men charged around it to the dark far side and then to the front.

"Cap, we're inside," DeWitt said on the Motorola. "This is the place. Maybe two hundred barrels of ether in here. No interior guards."

Alpha Squad ran through the truck-sized door in the front of the building and stared in amazement at all the barrels. They were stacked four high on steel racks along the walls, three high on the floor. Dozens were in rows with alleys between them. Enough ether to run a drug cartel for a year.

"TNAZ on three locations would do the job," Canzoneri said.

"Go," Murdock said. "Set the timers for ten minutes, but don't activate them. Lam, Ching, out front and watch for any arriving cavalry. There must be some military here somewhere."

Canzoneri picked up TNAZ from two other SEALs and plotted out his charges. He put three quarter-pounders of TNAZ in one spot about a third of the way into the building. The explosives went under one barrel so the blast would be reflected upward from the concrete floor.

The second one he put a third of the way into the warehouse down a row of three high stacks of barrels. This one he put between the containers six feet off the floor for a spread pattern blast. Again he used three quarter-pounders. One quarter-pound chunk of TNAZ was enough to blow apart the average-sized three-bedroom house.

He put the last bomb closer to the door so the upward

blast would carry into the steel frames that held up barrels around the sides of the building.

Canzoneri came up to Murdock. "Charges set, Cap. Rigged them for ten minutes. I'm clear here. Haven't activated the timers yet."

The radios buzzed. "Commander, some native sons approach in trucks. Four trucks. Not sure how many troops. We have the fifty?"

"In a drag bag," Bradford said. "Back by the bay."

"No time," Murdock said. "Activate the charges. Everyone pull back to the water. This is one fight we don't want unless they cut us off. Go, go, go."

Canzoneri ran to the charges and activated the timers, then was the last man out of the big warehouse. The oncoming troops couldn't see the front door as the SEALs jolted through it and raced for the pier. Canzoneri had set a countdown watch on his wrist. He limped as he came over the edge of the rocks and underneath the rotted wooden pier.

"How did it go?" Quinley asked. He was with Fernandez, who lay on the edge of the bank. He had Fernandez's rebreather in place and his gear all on. Murdock knelt down beside him.

"Hey, man, how do you feel?"

Fernandez looked up at him and tried to grin. "Hurting like a bitch in heat, Cap. I'm not gonna be much on swimming."

"No sweat, Fernandez. Our job is to get you back into the wet and out the harbor." He turned to the others. "Suit up," Murdock said. "Rebreathers and fins and we hit the water."

"Six minutes," Canzoneri said. "Best if we can get off another three hundred yards or so. Gonna be one fucking big blast in another six."

"Jefferson, Bradford, over here," Murdock called.

They came up and looked at Fernandez. "Palm off your drag bags. You two are going to work with Fernandez until we get a pickup."

They tucked Motorolas in waterproof pouches, grabbed their drag bags, and slid into the murky water of the bay. They knew the compass course out of the bay, dug down fifteen feet to the usual SEAL water highway, and swam.

Bradford and Jefferson took turns towing Fernandez through the dark water. Two other SEALs took their drag bags, and they all swam.

As time for the explosion came, the SEALs popped out of the water two at a time to watch. They were about two hundred yards off the pier when the first charge went off. It was partly muffled, but the blast was stronger than they had heard for a while.

Murdock watched as one section of the roof blew off and a boiling cloud of smoke and fire streaked into the sky. The second blast came before the first had finished its havoc, and this one flattened the rest of the building, launching burning barrels of ethyl into the sky like rockets, some soaring out a quarter of a mile, Murdock figured. One landed behind the SEALs with a huge splash and created a massive cloud of steam as the burning ether barrel sank, putting out the fire.

The third blast eclipsed the other two. Building on the heat and open fuel, it sounded like a doomsday bomb. The SEALs instinctively dove underwater before the compression wave of hot air stormed past them. They came up a few moments later and stared in awe at the huge fire.

Murdock gave them some time to check their handiwork, then moved them back toward the bay mouth. He had to find some dry land and take out the SATCOM. He surfaced every five minutes and found his spot on the third lift. He grabbed Jaybird going by and had him swim forward and head the SEALs to shore. Most of them landed thirty yards down the bay.

Holt came out of the water and had the SATCOM out of its waterproof housing and ready to work in two minutes.

"Home Base, this is Rover."

The response came at once.

"Rover, location and requirements."

"Home Base, moving down the channel to the bay mouth. Suggest pickup in forty minutes about half a mile offshore with the Sea Knight. That should be the one with resupply of ammo and TNAZ. I show the time as 0110. That would put the pickup about 0150. You copy?"

"Copy, Rover. That bird is ready for takeoff. Resupply on board. Stay due west of the bay. Copy pickup in forty at about 0150."

"Home Base. We have one badly injured. Request change in mission after pickup to return wounded man to Home Base and continue the mission with first dark tomorrow."

"Rover. Will consult and have word for you at the pickup. Good swimming. Out."

Holt had the SATCOM turned off the minute the "out" was said, and had the fifteen-pound radio back in its waterproof house two minutes later. They walked down to the other SEALs, and Murdock checked on Fernandez.

Mahanani had given him another shot of morphine, and he was a little woozy.

"Fernandez, we've got a chopper coming. Hang in there for us. In a half hour, we should be out of the wet."

Murdock motioned the men back into the water. Jefferson and Bradford helped Fernandez into the wet. His buoyancy in the water made it much easier to move him than it would have been on land.

They swam. Murdock and Holt led the group at the usual fifteen feet. They surfaced twice to check their position, then felt the pull of the tide stronger as they went over a shallow bar and surged into the Caribbean Sea.

Murdock checked his watch: They had another twenty minutes to get offshore a half mile. No sweat. They all surfaced by arrangement at 0120 to help them keep together. Murdock counted thirteen heads. He pulled out his mouthpiece.

"Is Fernandez here?" he asked.

"Don't think so, Cap," Jaybird said. "They were falling behind."

"Lam, swim back surface and see if they have come up. Give me two short whistle blasts if you find them."

The rest of them waited. It was nearly five minutes on his watch before Murdock heard what he thought were some whistles. Jaybird nodded.

"Yeah, Cap. That was Lam. He's got them."

Nearly ten minutes later, the four SEALs came up to the rest. Murdock had Mahanani check out Fernandez.

"He's in rough shape, Cap," the corpsman said. "Must have lost a lot of blood. Not a damn thing we can do here. He's in and out of consciousness. Better keep him on top."

Murdock nodded. "Ching, Dobler, front and center and take over Fernandez. Keep him topside. We'll all stay on the surface for the rest of the swim. Anybody else hurting?" He received no response. "Let's move, due west. Don't worry about the time."

Murdock put Fernandez at the head of the line. They would swim at the speed that Dobler and Ching could move him. So they would be five minutes late at the meet; it wouldn't matter.

Murdock felt himself relax. He was at home again, in the water. SEALs always felt safer in the water where they were better than any enemy. Here he and his men were in their element. The swim went a little faster than Murdock thought it would, but they had fresh legs on the towing work.

Lam heard the chopper coming in before anyone. "Chopper to the east," Lam shouted. They all stopped swimming. Murdock took out a red signal floating flare, lit it, and thew it twenty feet to the side. The red glow blossomed on the sea.

The big Sea Knight came in gently, found the flare, and lit up a circle of light that pinpointed the SEALs. The first thing down was a basket from the side hatch. Dobler helped Fernandez into the aluminum basket. He strapped the wounded man in and gave a thumbs-up to the operator.

Once Fernandez was inside the bird, the rear hatch opened, and the rope ladder dropped down. Jaybird made

it to the ropes first and began climbing up. Two more
SEALs grabbed the bottom rung to hold it steady, and the
SEALs scurried up the ladder as if it were a set of steps
on dry land. Murdock was the last one up, and the ladder
swung free, making it twice as hard to climb. He came over
the lip of the rear hatch and bellied into the ship with the
help of two handy SEALs. Once he was inside, the hatch
swung upward, closing.

"Commander?" A youngish looking lieutenant (j.g.)
asked.

Murdock rolled over where he lay on the floor and nodded.

"Right. Any word on our direction?"

"You've been ordered back to the *Jefferson*, sir. Glad we
found you. Anything I can get you and your men?"

"What about some nice hot coffee and sandwiches?"

"Surprise, Commander. Somebody named Don Stroh got
all over my lieutenant until he took on board this special
box. Yeah, hot coffee and monster sandwiches. Enjoy. We
have about a forty-minute ride back to the ship."

Murdock laughed. There really was hot coffee and sandwiches. Not your usual Navy sandwich, but humongous
built things that looked like they came from the neighbor-
hood deli. Murdock had two of them and three cups of the
black, scalding-hot coffee.

Mahanani came over, shaking his head. "Don't know
about Fernandez. He doesn't respond. I had a radio message
sent to the carrier. They'll have an emergency team with a
gurney on deck when we get there. His vitals are all way
down, but he's fighting."

Murdock went over and sat beside the wounded man. He
was unconscious but breathing. Mahanani sat on the other
side, monitoring him every second.

Stroh tried to meet them at the deck of the *Jefferson*, but
the corpsmen and three doctors were at the door waiting
for a litter to bring Fernandez out. Mahanani had stripped
off the top of the wet suit before landing, and once Fernandez was on the gurney, the doctors and nurses began

working on him. They hung a bottle of blood and some clear liquid and put needles into his arm. They tested him with stethoscopes as the gurney rolled across the flight deck.

Murdock walked alongside; stripping off his combat gear and handing it to Jaybird, who trailed him. DeWitt had told Murdock he would get the troops back to their assembly room and quarters.

Five minutes later, Murdock paced outside an operating room as the doctors went to work. It took them over an hour. Murdock had downed three cups of coffee a steward brought him. Every time someone came out of the operating room, he questioned the person, but no one would tell him anything.

At last he sat down, exhausted. It wouldn't look good if he went to sleep on his feet, leaning against the wall.

"Commander?"

Murdock looked up and shook his head. He had dozed off. "Yes?"

"He made it. The boy should be dead. He lost a lot of blood. The bullet punctured his left lung, but somehow the hole closed up and the lung didn't collapse. His shoulder wound is actually more serious now. We did some rebuilding on one area, and he should have full use of the shoulder. Right now, it's broken and in a cast. We have his uniform and gear in a bag you can take with you if you wish, Commander."

Murdock stood and swayed a moment.

"Are you all right, Commander?"

"Yeah. I'll make it. Thanks for your work on Fernandez. He's a good man. I'll check with you in the morning."

"That's not long now, Commander. Maybe this afternoon."

Murdock found his way to the SEALs' assembly room. It was deserted. He went to his quarters and fell on his bunk as soon as he took off his wet suit.

Murdock heard someone get up from the four-officer compartment next to hers. Too bad didn't even check the time.

He went back to sleep at once. It was noon again before he came to reality. He showered and put on clean cammies and went to check on Fernandez.

The doctor shook his head. "Fernandez took a turn for the worse early this morning, but we have him stabilized again. The surgery is solid. His lung is responding. We pulled the last of the bullet out of his shoulder before we repaired it. Now it's mostly up to him." ·

"He has to make it, Doctor. He has a family back in San Diego waiting for him. Do your best." .

Murdock had lunch, then went to the assembly room. Half of the men were there. Dobler had taken Canzoneri to the hospital. His stitches had pulled out. They were sewing him back together.

"Don Stroh was in half an hour ago, looking worried," Senior Chief Dobler said. "Something about throwing his timing off. He said he has to talk to Washington, and then he'll be back."

"Not every operation goes the way we plan it," Murdock said. "Stroh knows that. If we hadn't brought Fernandez back here last night, he'd be KIA by now."

"You going to E-mail his wife?"

"Not until he's out of danger. The doctors are still worried about him. I think he's going to make it."

Don Stroh strode into the room with a frown clouding his face. He saw Murdock and sailed straight for him.

"You threw off our damn timing," he said.

"What timing? What are you talking about?"

"Today you were supposed to be raising hell at Plato, the airfield, production facilities, and storage area for the Medellin cartel. Right?"

"Yes."

"Today also was when there would be six or eight of the top men in the cartel meeting at a luxury residence in the complex. We had hoped that some of the men would have an accident. You were supposed to be the accident."

"You didn't tell us that on our briefing."

"Not the sort of thing we put on paper or over the air.

Our country has an antiassassination policy, remember?"

"But accidents are all right?"

"Who can predict an accident? They happen." Stroh chuckled. "But now I find out that we may have lucked out on this snafu. Turns out our source says that the meeting has been held over another two days, and a fresh crop of dancing girls has been flown in."

"Can we get some air support this time?" the platoon leader asked. "Say we go in with a Sea Knight. The most firepower it has are two fifty-caliber machine guns. How about a Sea Cobra from the Marines with its firepower? We fly in together. We drop off three hundred yards from the complex. Our Sea Knight's fifty shoots up the place, and then the Cobra hits them with its seventy-millimeter rockets. They can cause a whole hell of a lot of damage."

"Then you go in and clean up and dispatch any of the bad guys who haven't had the good manners to die?" Stroh asked.

"Sounds good to me. After that, we do in the processing plants and the storage areas and the planes and trucks, then we try like hell to get out of the place. It's only sixty miles to the water."

"Another incursion over a foreign nation without its permission? State and the Joint Chiefs will never go for it."

"Give them a try. Take along the CNO. He'll love it."

Stroh groaned as he pushed away from the bulkhead. "Now all I have to do is go fight with my chief and then the CNO and then talk to the President. Be glad you don't have my job."

Three of the SEALs working nearby went into a fit of crying. Stroh grinned and hurried out the door to make his radio calls.

"Think they'll go for it?" DeWitt asked.

"Depends how much they want these Medellin people dead," Murdock said. "And if they think we can get away with it."

Two hours later, Stroh was back.

"I didn't even get my chief. Small arms rounds they can't

identify. But those seventy-millimeter rounds they can. We don't want any worldwide uproar about a big power play here. We'll go with your guys, one Sea Knight in the dark, and hope nobody can spot it. Can we do it all in the dark?"

"Maybe," Murdock said. He looked at DeWitt, who shrugged. "Say we hit the coast at first dark. Sixty miles to the target, which is another twenty minutes. Say three hours to reduce the luxury residence, but then we don't have much time to do the rest of the mission in there."

"The cooking vats, the storage, and the planes and trucks," Stroh said. "Those were your first targets." They looked at each other.

"What the hell is going on here, Stroh? You want us to forget the first target and take out the brass or what? Tell me."

"That was the first thought of my chief. Then he backed off. He wants that facility burned down to the ground. We knock off the head men, they have twenty fighting to take each of the top spots."

"So, we're talking two days. We clobber the big house the first night and try for the production vats. We've done that before. Then we cut into the woods or jungle or whatever they have there and play hide-and-seek during the day."

"By then there will be at least a battalion of military there hunting us, guarding the rest of it," DeWitt said. "So how in hell do we take out the storage and the planes and trucks without getting ourselves killed?"

"Carefully, with the usual SEAL nerve, guts, and ability," Stroh said. "You do this all the time. Anyway, we have no reports of any army facility anywhere near this place. It was originally built away from the military because it was illegal. So why bring in military now? I think you have a good go at it."

"Tonight at 1730?" Murdock asked.

Stroh grinned. "Attaboy, knew you could do it. I'll alert the CAG and get that chopper ready. You need any more toys?"

"Yeah, the rest of our supply of twenty-mike rounds," Murdock said. He stared hard at Stroh. The CIA man lifted his brows, then shut his eyes a minute.

"I don't know what you said. I can't remember, but they will be on the chopper. Just don't blow up any of your people with one of those Bull Pups."

"No fear," DeWitt said.

"Let's get the men ready to rumble," Murdock said.

23

Pacific Coast
Near Plato, Colombia

The Boeing Vertol–built Sea Knight helicopter slammed across the Colombian coast at two hundred feet. Full dark had just covered the land, and the Navy bird with its cargo of SEALs powered through the night air at her maximum speed of 165 miles per hour. The pilots didn't want to be over hostile territory any longer than they needed to be.

The air distance from the coast to Plato was sixty miles. The pilots had planned a twenty-two-minute flight into an isolated area ten miles outside of the small city of Plato. They were told the spot would be easy to find. It was lit up like a birthday cake, would have landing lights on a concrete aircraft runway, and there would be more than a dozen houses, warehouses, and other sheds along with a half-dozen good-sized planes near the hangars.

The SEALs were ready. Six men had the Bull Pup twin-barrel weapons and sixty rounds each. Bradford carried the big .50 caliber sniper rifle with an MP-5 submachine gun strapped on his back. Each man had two pounds of TANZ and C-4, along with the needed timer/detonators.

"We do the fancy hotel-like mansion first," Murdock reminded the men. "When we get it cleared, we move on to the next closest target."

"We don't know where they are?" Jaybird asked.

"About the size of it. Not enough intel on this one, it came up too fast. We don't have a handy satellite assigned to Plato, Colombia."

The crew chief from the chopper came back from the cockpit.

"We're three minutes out, so get ready. The rear ramp goes down. You guys have done this before, right?"

"Three hundred and seventy-eight times," Lampedusa said. "Yeah, we know this bucket pretty well."

The crew chief grinned. "Good. You guys kick ass for me out there, you hear?"

Murdock checked out a small porthole window and could see light below, then water, and more lights.

A speaker came on in the cabin. "Thirty seconds to touchdown," one of the pilots said. "We'll be about a hundred yards from this big lit-up mansion. Biggest thing around here. After you exit, we lift off and give you support fire with our fifties. Good luck!"

The chopper touched down with a light thump, the crew chief dropped the aft hatch, and the SEALs charged out in squad formation.

Lam had the point on Alpha Squad, with Murdock right behind him. Ten seconds after the last SEAL hit Colombian soil, the chopper lifted off and pounded .50 caliber machine gun fire into the fancy mansion. Murdock saw windows shatter and round after round jolt into the place.

"Squads front for some assault fire," Murdock said on his radio. The SEALs spread out ten yards apart in a long line and kept running for the house, their weapons firing short bursts as they charged across the open stretch of land.

A few winking lights showed return fire, but nothing came close. They came in on the side of the place.

"DeWitt, take Bravo to the front and get inside it you

can. We'll go to the rear and try the same thing. If you get in, tell us so we don't shoot each other."

"Roger that," DeWitt said. "We're swinging that way as of now."

The flat crack of an AK-47 on full auto sounded from the mansion.

"Anybody spot that AK-47?" Murdock asked on the net. No response.

"Watch for him."

Alpha Squad went to ground thirty yards from the rear doors of the big mansion. It would be the kitchen, Murdock guessed. He could see garbage cans and food containers around the rear door. As he watched, the door slammed open and four men with rifles rushed out. SEAL guns cut down two of them, but the other two dove to the left behind a three-foot-high stone wall. They lifted up and fired over the top at the SEALs.

"Get the floodlights," Murdock said. The Bull Pup's 5.56 rounds on two-round bursts quickly blasted the bulbs into darkness.

Murdock pulled a fragger grenade from his combat harness and jerked out the safety pin. Not more than twenty-five yards to the two riflemen. He lifted up and threw the bomb, hearing the arming spoon spin off. The M-67 sailed through the air, hit on top of the rock wall, and bounced straight up before it went off in a deadly airburst.

"Move up," Murdock said into the mike, and the SEALs charged the rear door, jumping over the low wall and skidding to a stop against the mansion's rear wall. Lam pulled the door, and it swung outward. The room inside was lit. Lam made a quick look, saw nothing, and charged inside, diving to the left. The small room held only kitchen stores and food supplies.

"First room rear is clear," Lam said. Murdock and Jaybird rushed inside.

Near the front of the house, DeWitt found more protection. Three men had been on guard there as he came from the side. They fired on the SEALs as soon as they could see them, then ducked into planned defensive positions.

One guard huddled behind a rock fountain. Ed DeWitt used his Bull Pup and sent a 20mm round into the wall directly behind the man. The round exploded on contact, showering shrapnel backward on the hiding man. He bellowed in pain and ran for the front door.

Quinley cut him down with a two-round burst from the Bull Pup's 5.56 barrel.

The other two guards were behind a low rock wall that ran across the front of the compound. Ostercamp threw a grenade, saw it bounce against the mansion wall, then come back toward the guards. It exploded a moment later, and one of the guards screamed in pain, then went quickly silent.

They saw nothing more of the third guard. DeWitt figured the man crawled behind the wall to the far end and vanished into the night.

The front door stood open. "Let's get over the stones out there to the mansion wall," DeWitt said into his mike. The SEALs lifted up and ran for the front wall of the big residence. They took no enemy fire. DeWitt edged toward the front door. It was still open.

"Franklin, with me. I have the right, you go left. Now." The two SEALs charged the door, dove in left and right, their weapons up ready for any enemy.

DeWitt came up on his stomach and cleared his half of the room. It was an entryway with two soft couches and chairs and a table filled with liquor bottles and mixers.

"Over here, JG," Franklin said, his voice husky. DeWitt looked at the other side of the room. A man sat in one of the soft chairs. The whole side of his head had been torn off, probably by a fifty-caliber round. Beside him on the chair sat a shapely naked woman who looked up at them with a tear-stained face.

"You bastards, you fucking murderous bastards!" she screamed.

"We're inside at the front," DeWitt said into his mike.

"We have one DB, one naked lady alive. She speaks English."

"Shake the place down," Murdock radioed. "Careful on the shooting."

DeWitt brought the rest of his men inside and watched both doors leading off the entryway. He sent Franklin to one, and he took the other one. They both pulled the doors open at the same time. Shots boiled through Franklin's door. He had flattened against the wall, and the rounds missed him. He dropped to the floor and edged out to look into the room from that level. He spotted two gunmen standing with handguns up, waiting. He pulled back, pushed his MP-5 around the doorjamb, tilted it up, and ground off ten rounds. On his next look, he saw one man down, the second one sitting against the wall, holding his stomach. Franklin hit him with three more rounds, and he crumpled.

"Clear left," Franklin said.

Franklin took Canzoneri and Quinley into the room. It had one door leading out.

DeWitt took Mahanani, Ostercamp, and Jefferson into his room and eyed the next door. Suddenly, it burst open, and four women ran through it. All were young, all pretty, and all birth-naked. They stopped when they saw the cammy-clad warriors. One shrieked. Another one fainted and slumped to the floor.

DeWitt waved them through the room. He stepped around the unconscious woman and looked into the next room. Two men sat at a desk. Both were Colombian, both dressed impeccably, both with stacks of banded money in front of them.

"Gentlemen, it seems there has been a serious misunderstanding. We have no fight with the United States Navy SEALs. You are free to come here as you please. We ask you no more gunfire. Some of our people have been hurt, and we're seriously upset about this turn of events."

DeWitt stood openmouthed even as he aimed his Bull

Pup at the men. He found his voice. "You an American?"

"No, actually no. You see, I lived in Miami for several years, so I picked up the language. English is easy. But we're getting off the subject. Those of us here today wish to make a deposit in your retirement account."

DeWitt motioned with the Bull Pup muzzles. "Away from the desk, and keep your hands up. Move."

"Of course. We're reasonable men. We have cash for you, no wire transfers and no problems. On the table are eight million dollars in one hundred dollar United States currency bills. It's yours for the taking."

"Murdock. How far front are you? I have a non shooting problem here."

"About two rooms away. No opposition. Problem?"

"Eight million dollars, U.S., in cash."

"Cash?"

"Greenbacks. Get in here."

DeWitt motioned Jefferson to check the far door. He opened it and looked around the next room. "Clear," he said.

He looked again. "Right in here, Cap," Jefferson said.

Murdock came through the door cautiously. When he saw the situation was under control, he marched to the desk and looked at the stacked and banded bills. They were all hundreds in packs of what he figured were 100. Ten thousand to a bundle.

"Counterfeit," Murdock said.

"We couldn't stay in business a week if we used counterfeit bills," the Colombian said. "We would be cut down in a tornado of hot lead. You know that's legal tender. It's yours. Your platoon can split it any way you choose. Sounds like a half million each. Sailor, what could you do with five hundred thousand dollars, all tax free?" The Colombian had directed his question to Canzoneri, who stood closest to him.

Canzoneri grinned. "You fat pig, I'd take it all and jam it right up your asshole and laugh."

DeWitt and Murdock had a quick conference.

"We found one in the lobby," DeWitt said. "Then we nailed two more suits."

"We cut down three in a back room," Murdock said. "These are the last two."

"Suggestions?" DeWitt asked.

"We do our job." Murdock and DeWitt turned and fired six rounds each into the two men, who slammed backward from the force of the rounds and died against the oak-paneled wall.

"We take the money and turn it in," Murdock said. "That way these bastards can't buy more cocaine paste with it. Find a plastic garbage bag, a pillowcase, or a suitcase. Go now."

The SEALs split up and searched the rooms. Jefferson came back with a green canvas barracks bag.

Murdock nodded. "Stuff the bills in there and take it with us. Jefferson, it's your baby. You lose it, and it's a statement of charges out of your pay for eight million. Who has Willy Peter?"

Two men called out.

"Use them. One here, one farther back. Want to see this place burned to a crisp. We're out of here."

They were soon a quarter of a mile away, heading for a series of low shacks such as they had seen near Cali at the processing plant. Behind them, the mansion began to burn through the walls. The buildings they aimed for were what Murdock had figured.

The SEALs found no guards around the processing sheds. Canzoneri gave some instructions. "Put the charge at the center of one side of the tank. That will blast it inward and crumple it so the vat can't be fixed. A quarter pound of either TNAZ or C-4 should do the trick." He looked at his commander.

"Timers, Cap. How long?"

"We'll use the net. How many tanks here?"

"Twelve, Commander."

"Plant the charges, get a check by radio, then we'll set the timers, depending on where else we go. Lam, see what you can find out about some larger buildings for storing the finished product."

Five minutes later, Canzoneri had a radio check that the charges were all ready. Lam had not returned. "Set the timers for thirty minutes and get back up here pronto," Murdock said.

They had to find the finished cocaine storage area, and the one for the local ethyl ether, then the planes. A good night's work yet to come.

Lam caught up with them two hundred yards from the production facility.

"Two buildings up there beside the runaway," Lam said. "One of them has a loading ramp. We should check it out for the coke."

They jogged across the open ground toward the buildings that had a few night-lights on. They stopped in the darkness a hundred yards away. Now they could see more lights. A pair of floods snapped on.

"Why?" DeWitt asked. "They couldn't know that we're here. Half of them must be over at the big fire." They could still see where the mansion burned. It was really roaring now, with fire out the windows on the third floor. A fire engine had responded, but it was far too little and too late.

"We have twelve minutes to the first charge at the vats," Canzoneri said. The twin floodlights snapped off. Lam lifted his binoculars and watched the area. Three minutes later, the same lights flashed on.

Lam chuckled. "Some kind of a stray dog is wandering around up there," Lam said. "It's an intrusion sensor picking up the dog and turning on the light."

"So we'll have to shoot them out before we go in," Dobler said. He shifted his weight so it would be on his good leg. His right thigh still hurt where the bullet had gone through, but it was coming along. He could live with it.

Usually he didn't even notice it. He figured it might slow him down half a step in a fast forty-yard sprint.

"How close is the dog?" Murdock asked.

"He activates the lights at about fifty feet. It's set for a wide pattern. Silenced shots would be best." He paused. "Oh, damn. That little dog has some company, two full-grown Doberman pinschers with studded collars. Guard dogs running as a team. Problem is, I don't see any fence to keep the dogs in."

Dobler snorted. "The best-trained guard dog knows his limits. He won't go outside the area he's been trained to protect, and he won't let anyone inside that boundary. Must be damned good dogs."

"Too bad about them," Murdock said. "We have a silenced sniper rifle?"

"Yeah," Quinley said. "I got stuck with Fernandez's gun."

"Bring it up," Murdock said. "You and Lam move up. Lam, take out the dogs on their next pass with your silenced MP-5. As soon as they go down, Quinley, kill those lights. Go."

Well behind the SEALs the first of the processing tank charges went off, followed quickly by eleven more. They lit up the landscape for a few seconds with each blast. When the last finished, they heard a siren and could see headlights bumping across the land toward the tanks.

Quinley and Lam scurried toward the target, keeping low and hitting the dirt at about forty yards. A minute later, the lights came on and showed two Dobermans. Murdock could hear the cough of the MP-5 on three-round bursts. There were two of them, and the dogs went down whining, then quieted.

As the dogs died, Murdock moved his platoon forward. An instant later, Quinley killed the first light but took two shots to get the second.

The SEALs ran into the darkness around the building. The big truck door was down at the dug-in ramp. At the far side, they found a door with a padlock. Two silenced rounds slammed it open, and Murdock and Dobler darted inside. Murdock brought down his NVGs. Cumbersome, heavy, but damned useful. He scanned the forty-foot-square building, then saw a shed leading off this one.

There he found long tables, scales, sheets of heavy plastic on rolls, wrapping tables, and at the far end a large stack of kilo-sized packages of ready-to-transport cocaine.

The other SEALs came in behind them. Dim lights around the inside of the big room gave off an eerie half-light.

"No fire hose," Jaybird said.

"Look for any kind of plumbing and a faucet we can use," Murdock said on the net.

"Let's go to work on those packages. We slash them open with our KA-BARs. It's going to be work. Wish the damn stuff would burn better."

Mahanani found a hose and faucet halfway back on the building. There was enough hose to reach the first part of the stack of coke neatly arranged on pallet boards.

"Ronson, guard us out that side door. Watch just outside for any activity. Hope most of them are still at the fire."

Murdock took his turn slashing the kilos until his arm ached. Jaybird worked the hose, spraying the powdered cocaine, creating a pool in the middle of the stack to further the melting. There were ten pallet boards each loaded with carefully stacked kilos four feet high.

Ostercamp found another hose at the back of the room, and this one was larger. It evidently was a fire hose. It kicked out an inch stream of water. The melting went much faster then. They slashed and sprayed and before long, all of the SEALs had white spray all over their cammies.

"Company," Ronson said on his radio.

"How many?" Murdock asked.

"Looks like two truckloads heading this way. No way we can know if they'll stop here."

"Franklin, Ed, Lampedusa, Ching, get out there and hit them with the twenties with the laser if they come closer than five hundred yards. Use the airbursts, and knock them out before they get here."

"How about six hundred yards, Cap?" Ronson asked.

"Go."

The four men rushed out the side door and set up. DeWitt watched the trucks. They were on a road that led directly to the packaging facility. Ed had his Bull Pup on the target with the laser. The other four men did as well.

"Let's do it," Ed said and fired. He got the laser back on the target just as his round exploded over it. The rig teetered on the edge of the road but kept coming. Four more rounds went off in airbursts over the truck at almost the same time, and the truck veered off the road and tipped over.

They fired at the second truck now at five hundred yards. Ed didn't use the laser this time and saw his next two rounds explode on impact with the front of the truck. One round must have gone through the windshield; the other blew apart the radiator and part of the engine. The truck died in place, and the men bailed out just in time to greet three airbursts that riddled them with shrapnel and sent them screaming to the rear.

"If you see anyone out there move," DeWitt said, "pick a target and laser him for an airburst."

All was quiet for a minute, then two of the Bull Pups barked, and the airbursts shattered the stillness.

"Love this damn Bull Pup," Ed DeWitt screeched on the mike. "The bad guys are running back home."

"We need another fifteen minutes in here," Murdock said. "We've smashed the scales, slashed all of the plastic, and when we leave, we'll put some charges around just for good measure."

"How many you want, Cap?" Canzoneri asked.

"Don't waste them. We still have some ether to take out. Two should do this place."

"More company, Commander," Jaybird said. "Three big trucks coming around the back side. Too close for the laser. We need some help with the twenties, and we need it damn fast!"

24

Medellin Cartel
Plato, Colombia

Six SEALs charged out a back man-sized door and saw the problem. Murdock heard Jaybird firing already. He went prone and lifted his Bull Pup. Yeah, too close. The trucks were within two hundred yards of them. He aimed and tracked the first truck and fired a 20mm round.

"Thirty dollars' worth," he whispered.

The round hit the side of the truck and exploded. The rest of the twenty rounds were hitting now. One truck took a direct hit in the engine, and fire gushed from the hood as it veered to the left and ground to a stop.

The second truck kept coming. Somebody put a round into the right front tire, and when the tire blew, the truck careened in a sudden turn to that side, lifted high on those side wheels, and then settled back to the roadway and spun around to a stop.

Murdock watched the third truck try to turn away from the slaughter. It took two twenties at the same time, one penetrating the windshield before it exploded in the cab and the other one hitting one of the wooden bows holding up the canvas top and exploding with the shattering spray of shrapnel that cut down half the men riding in the back of the rig. The truck kept rolling with no one alive behind the wheel. Then it slowed and stopped.

Soldiers had been spilling out of the trucks as they were hit. Now they assembled and put down fire at the SEALs. They were only 200 yards away. Murdock burrowed lower behind an oil drum and considered. He touched his lip mike.

"We've got two CARs that can fire forty-mike rounds. Get them up front here fast."

Ron Holt had one, Ostercamp had one on his back. They slid behind some wooden boxes in back of the building, and Murdock talked to them.

"We need some HEs on those assholes out there. About two hundred yards. Drop in a few, and let's see what they do."

The SEALs fired two rounds each. The first one came in short, the next three walked up the line of winking muzzle flashes. The volume of rounds slowed from the Colombians.

"Four more each," Murdock said. "We have the rounds?"

"I have four," Holt said.

"Down to three, Cap," Ostercamp said.

"Do them." The other SEALs kept up their 5.56-round fire from the Bull Pup's smaller barrel. Seven more 40mm HE rounds dropped in on the soldiers and killed and wounded a dozen more. In the dimness, Murdock could see several men running back the way they had come.

"Keep them moving," Murdock said. When they were 400 yards away and he could barely see them, he caught one with a laser spot and fired a twenty. It reached the required turns and exploded with the proximity fuze fifteen feet off the ground. In the flash of the round, Murdock had seen three men running. He figured all three of them were not running anymore.

"Cease fire," Murdock said.

The silence closed around them like a thick audio fog. A man screamed from where in front of them. Another voice in Spanish harangued the first. Then all was quiet.

Murdock left two men on guard and took the rest back inside.

"Lam, where's our next target, the ether?"

"Not sure, Cap. There are two big buildings to the south about two hundred yards. Want me to check them out?"

"Go. We'll finish here and meet you halfway. Canzoneri, you ready with those charges?"

"That's a roger, Commander."

"Set them for ten minutes. The soup here is cooked. All the coke is melted we have time for. Ninety percent gone, I'd say. Maybe fifty, seventy five million dollars' worth."

"Let's get out of here, troops. South side. Now."

They assembled and moved out a hundred yards south and waited. Canzoneri told them there were two minutes to the blasts. They turned to watch the packaging and shipping building.

The explosions were an anticlimax after the others. The great noise and rush of air blasted past them, then one side of the big building blew out and half the roof caved in. The SEALs went flat on the ground as the brilliant blast of light flashed past them, then was gone.

Lam ran up and dropped. "Yeah, all this fun and fireworks, too. Found it, Cap. It's the second building down here. First one looks like a barracks, so I stepped softly around it. We're off maybe three hundred yards from it."

The SEALs took a short hike. Murdock rubbed his left wrist where the bandage was. It hadn't hurt him, but he knew the bullet hole was still there. It itched. Did that mean it was healing? In the heat of action, he didn't even realize he had a weak left wrist. Now it throbbed, but no real pain. At least the round had missed the bone. Hell, he'd get it looked at later.

They found the building with the ether inside. Lam said he had seen no exterior guards. The place didn't even have a lock on the door. They went in and found no guards. There were enough barrels of ethyl ether to keep the syndicate in production of cocaine for some time. It took seventeen liters of ether to produce one kilo of cocaine.

Murdock studied the storage area through his NVGs.

"I figured there would be more here," Murdock said. "Jaybird, give me an estimate on the number of barrels."

Jaybird ran down the rows of barrels and came back.

"Three rows of barrels three wide and two high. Each row is ten barrels long. That's one hundred and eighty barrels, Cap."

"Canzoneri?"

"Same as last time. Only six charges this time out. We'll use a half pound for each bomb. Give me five minutes, and I'll have them in place. Hey, guys, I need some donations of TNAZ."

"Go," Murdock said.

Four SEALs went outside, one at each wall of the building as guards. They saw only activity around the packaging building. A small fire had started, and they could see figures trying to put it out.

Lam was on the prowl to find the landing strip.

Seven minutes later, the SEALs left the ether building and hiked away five hundred yards toward some far lights. The big blasts came right on schedule. The TNAZ set some of the ether on fire, blasting the liquid ether around the place like burning torches, and soon the rest of the barrels cooked off, blew their caps, and erupted into a massive blast that flattened the building and sent a gigantic fireball and mushroom-shaped cloud into the sky. The SEALs could hear the drums raining down in front of them. Some were still burning like bright bonfires.

The SEALs shielded their eyes.

"You guys do good work," Lam said on the net. "Found the fucking landing field. It's about a mile to the west. Could be on our way out of this cocaine garden as well. Look to the west. You'll see a glow from the lights of Plato. I'll find you as you come this way. I've seen no security out here. They all must be fighting fires."

"We're moving," Murdock said as he touched the SEALs near him and they hiked toward the west in squad diamond formation. Murdock always thought of the diamond as a defensive/offensive setup. With it, half the squad could do assault fire to the front, and the other half could give protective fire to the rear. It was almost a perimeter defensive formation, and it was good for a lot of reasons. If all the men went to ground and pointed outward, they would have a perimeter.

They found nothing to slow them down as they jogged the mile toward the west. Lam picked them up at the halfway point and talked with Murdock and DeWitt.

"Couldn't see it all, but there's a couple of buildings and a windsock and what looks like a concrete runway maybe three-quarters of a mile long. Saw four twin-engine transports, like the old DC-3s. Maybe a little smaller."

"Sounds like a perfect setup for the twenties," DeWitt said. "We can stand off and blast them into rubble until we start a fire."

"I'll go with that. How close are the planes parked to each other?"

"Thirty yards apart, at least. Also in the area are two small Piper Cub type planes and three trucks, six-bys, by the look of them."

"Good, let's hold here a minute." Murdock used his Motorola. "Holt, we need to do some long-range talking. I'm in front."

Holt hurried up and pulled the fifteen-pound SATCOM radio out of its nest and aimed the antenna. He gave Murdock the handset. "We're on voice, Commander."

It took Murdock three tries a minute apart to raise the carrier *Jefferson.*

"Rover, this is Home Base."

"Home Base. We're in the ninth inning here. One more contact, and we're ready to exfil. What would contact time be if the chopper left soon?"

"Rover, we have a problem. Stroh wants to talk with you."

There was a pause, then Don Stroh came on.

"Yes, tall friend, we have a glitch. State is all over us

like a clawing tiger. They've been getting flack from Colombia for two days about incursions, invasions, air attacks, and acts of war. State has tromped on our toes and ordered the CNO not to allow any more air incursions of Colombia."

"No chopper pickup? Come on, Stroh, you're hanging us out to dry again."

"Hell, not me, it's the State Department and the President."

"They invaded us first, the embassy. Damn. You expect us to walk out?"

"It's only sixty miles."

"Oh, yeah, and across a range of mountains that make the Rockies look like anthills."

Murdock saw the SEALs crowding around, listening to the speaker on the SATCOM and his talk.

"No suggestions, Mister Christian in Action Guy?" Murdock asked.

"Steal a chopper and fly it out?"

"I'm not checked out to fly a chopper or anything else."

Murdock turned off the handset and stared at the radio. The speaker came on.

"Do the best we can to get the order lifted. Might take a day or two. Be ready to receive daytime at noon, three and six."

"If that's the best you can do."

Jaybird pushed through the men to the front. "Hey, Commander, we've got four DC-3 types out front. Why not steal one of those?"

"Can you fly one?" DeWitt asked.

"No."

"As I remembered your files, none of our men has a ticket to fly a DC-3 or any other aircraft," DeWitt said.

Murdock began to grin. "We can't fly them, but someone over there at the airfield sure as shit can. We don't blow up those craft, we move in and capture them and a pilot. We blow away a few of them until one says he'll fly us out rather than get his head shot off."

Jaybird let out a short cheer. "Damn, I'm good. I knew we had to steal one of those gooneys. So I forgot about a pilot."

The tactical plans changed. The SEALs came up on three sides of the administration building. It was medium-sized, and Murdock hoped it also housed the pilots. They went in silently. One guard on duty had fallen asleep. He would never wake up. They found the office, a records area, then a hall with a dozen doors. Lam listened to three of them and heard snoring at the last one. He tried the handle. The door was not locked.

Murdock went in with his NVGs on. Two men in a two-bed room. Both had pictures on the wall. Each showed a man beside a plane. Murdock clamped his hand over the first man's mouth and shook him awake. He pulled the man out of his bed. He wore shorts and a T-shirt. Murdock propelled him into the hall.

Ken Ching was there and questioned him in Spanish.

"We won't kill you if you stay quiet and answer our questions, all right?"

The Colombian nodded.

"Are you a pilot?"

"Yes."

"Can you fly the twin-engine transport outside?"

"Yes."

"Is it fueled and ready to fly?"

"Yes, all fueled full."

"Is the plane loaded or empty?"

"Empty, to be loaded tomorrow."

Ching told Murdock the gist of the talk, and they hustled the pilot outside. It took five minutes for the pilot to go through his preflight check. As he did, the SEALs examined the interior. It was set up to haul packaged cocaine in liters, but there was plenty of room on the floor for fifteen SEALs.

Canzoneri used the last of his TNAZ and C-4 and planted bombs in the three other transports, the two small planes, and three trucks.

"Ready to activate the timers when you are, Commander," Canzoneri said.

Murdock put all the men on board, told Canzoneri to set the detonators for ten minutes, and race back on board.

Ching held an MP-5 submachine gun on the pilot as he slid into the cockpit seat.

"When I tell you to, you start the engines, and at once taxi away from these buildings. You do it damn fast, understand?" Ching told the pilot. "Any problem, and you're dead where you sit." The Colombian had been sweating profusely since he was jerked out of his room. Now rivelets of sweat worked down his cheeks.

"All on board," Murdock bellowed as he closed the door and pushed the locking arm in place.

"*Vámonos,*" Ching said, and the pilot started the engines and almost at once began to taxi away. Behind them lights snapped on in the main building. Men ran out in their underwear, carrying long guns.

"Faster!" Ching told the pilot in Spanish.

They raced down the runaway, and Ching ducked as a bullet slammed through the cockpit side glass and buried itself in the roof. They kept rolling.

"Get us out of here," Ching's radio spoke. "We're taking rounds through the fuselage back here."

"Faster," Ching yelled in Spanish. There was no wind. They could take off in this direction. Ching watched the ground speed. He didn't know what speed the ship needed to get airborne. At last the plane shuddered, then lifted gently from the ground and turned at once to the left and climbed.

The pilot looked at Ching and nodded.

"We're in the air," he said in Spanish. "But we took a lot of rounds. The flaps don't respond. I'm not sure I can fly this machine very far."

"All you have to do is get us to the coast. Set a course due west."

The pilot looked alarmed. "That means going over the Montes de Marla. They are over ten thousand feet high."

"Ceiling on this crate is much higher than that," Ching said, hoping he was right. "We can get over them easy."

He switched to English on his radio. "Murdock, we have a small problem up here."

The platoon leader came into the cabin with a question on his face.

"Pedro here says we have to go over the mountains, something Maria to the west. Up to ten thousand feet. He's not sure if he can make it."

The right engine sputtered, almost died, then caught again. The pilot pointed to one of the fuel gauges and yelled in Spanish.

"He says the tank was full, now it's half empty. They must have hit the fuel tank with the rifle fire."

25

Airborne Over Central Colombia

Murdock looked at the fuel gauge. It was at the halfway level. The pilot could be lying.

"Ask him how far he can go on the fuel he has left," the platoon leader said.

Ching asked the pilot in Spanish.

"He says he isn't sure, twenty miles, maybe more."

"Fine. Tell him to head directly at the mountains. He must know of a pass through them that's less than the height of the tallest peaks. These aren't supposed to be the highest in the country. Tell him if he can't get over the mountains, we're going to crash into them."

Murdock listened and watched the expression of the pilot as Ching talked to him in Spanish. He was not an actor. What he felt showed at once. First it was stark fear, then the idea of the pass came, and he relaxed a little.

"The bastard was faking the fuel. Now, get out your MP-5 and hold it on him all the time. Tell him if he does anything wrong, he dies. Remind him we have two men who can fly the plane in case he comes up with a dozen rounds in his black heart."

The pilot had turned pale by the time Ching finished the small tirade at the man. He began sweating again. He looked at Ching, then at the submachine gun, and nodded.

"*Sí, sí. Paso, paso.*" He struggled then but said in English. "I know mountain pass. Maybe get through. Plane old, tired."

Murdock relaxed a little. There was a chance they just might make it over the hump. The mountains were nearer the coast than to Plato. Once over the mountains, they would have a chance to get to the coast.

Murdock could feel the plane climbing, not sharply but probably as steep as the old engines could go. The plane could have been built back in the 1950s or before then. The DC-3 was a workhorse, but even horses have to be shot at some point and put out of their misery. He hoped it wasn't misery day for this old DC-3.

The climb continued. Murdock caught his men up to date on the cockpit talk.

"So, if he can make the pass over the mountains, it will cut down the altitude needed. This old bird isn't exactly a spring chicken looking to cackle."

"This is the same bird the Air Force used to call the C-47," Jaybird said. "First ones came out in 1935. Let's hope this one was built a hell of a lot later than that. They should have a top cruising speed of a hundred and eighty-five miles an hour, so it shouldn't take long to get thirty or forty miles to those mountains."

They looked out the small windows but came up with nothing but blackness.

"We've been in the air for fourteen minutes," Canzoneri said. "Stopwatch counts up as well as down," he said before any challenged him.

Murdock went back to the small cockpit. Ahead, he could see a few lights sprinkling the ground.

"He says it's a small village, and the road leads sharply west into the only pass he knows of. He drove over it once and it was over twenty-seven hundred meters. That would be about eight thousand feet."

"I'd feel better if those mountain folks were much farther below us," Murdock said. "Now I wish we had our chutes."

"Everyone else had the same idea," Ching said. He turned and jabbered something to the pilot. The man nodded.

"Just reminded him that he lives or dies by getting us through that fucking pass. He gets the idea."

Murdock thought of trying the SATCOM. He wasn't sure they could hold a satellite with their antenna as they were flying. They'd never tired that before. He really didn't have anything to tell Stroh or the Navy. When they got down, if they could, he'd yell and scream at the CIA asshole. How could they hang the whole platoon out in the wilderness this way with every chance they would get their balls shot off?

The pilot yelled something.

"He says the pass is right ahead. He's been following the headlights of a few cars. He figures we need another three hundred feet altitude."

"Tell him to circle around until he gets the vertical feet that he needs," Murdock said.

The pilot frowned when he heard the orders. He shrugged and pulled the aircraft in a half-mile-wide circle, climbing as fast as the old engines would permit.

They made six circles, and Chin yelled at the pilot. "Nobody is coming to help you. We have the altitude, we're at almost 8500 feet if you set your altimeter right." He shouted it in Spanish at the man. "Now, get us over these mother fucking mountains or your ass is stretched and blasted and cut in half with nine-millimeter rounds. Does that sound good?"

The pilot wiped his dripping eyebrows, glanced at Ching and his leveled submachine gun, then stared straight ahead. He pulled the bird out of the circle and angled slightly to the northwest.

Ching looked out the cockpit window on his side, and he could see the loose string of lights below. Then a few miles to the side, he saw the pattern of streetlights that lit up a small subdivision of houses. No mistaking it.

He grabbed the pilot by the throat. "Are we heading west? What's a housing project doing up here on the mountain?"

Ching had screeched it in Spanish. The pilot pawed at his throat. The plane took a steep turn to the left. Ching let go of the pilot, who righted the plane.

"Yes, big government project. Need many men, so build houses. Mountains here. Look at compass. West." Ching looked closer at the floating compass and saw that the heading was generally west.

"The pass, can you find it?"

"Yes, ahead, three miles. Almost high enough. More power and maybe get over."

"Damn well better, or like I say, you die first, in the air, not in a crash." Ching clicked the safety on and off on the MP-5 sub gun and pushed the muzzle into the Colombian's side.

"Now fly us the fuck over this mountain."

Murdock watched the small drama play out. Ching was handling it perfectly. No chance to fake it on the pilot's part. If he did, he was dead meat. So were the rest of them in the plane, but he didn't know that.

Murdock looked out the window at the dark shadows ahead. The mountain or clouds? No clouds out tonight. It was solid Colombian soil, rock, and trees.

"Get us higher," Ching shouted.

The pilot grimaced and pulled the controls back a little more. The throttle was on maximum.

Murdock watched the mountain come closer. He could see the headlights crawling along below. Then all at once he realized the headlights were no more than a hundred feet below them. They were almost on top of the road. Now he could see the opening where the road went. It was a good three or four hundred feet below the peaks on both sides. Plenty of room for the wingspan of the old DC-3.

The sudden rumbling of the air and the screaming roar of a plane overhead slammed into the transport and made it veer to the left. The pilot swore and pulled the ship back on course.

"Fighter overhead," Murdock said. "He knows we're here, he's probably asking for permission to shoot us down."

"What was it, a MiG?"

"Heard they had a few."

"Yes!" the pilot shouted. Murdock looked out the cockpit windows to the front and couldn't see the mountain.

They were over it, through the pass.

"Now, get as low as you can go," Ching said. "We want to be right on the treetops all the way to the coast. Can you do that?"

"Yes, but not too low. Some small mountains out front. Lower, but not good to crash into."

"Was that a MiG jet fighter that buzzed us?" Ching asked the pilot.

"Oh, yes, my country has twelve now. And twelve pilots to fly them."

Ching checked the fuel gauges. One for each engine. He saw the one on the right was down to a quarter of a tank. That was the one he figured took a rifle round. The other one had the needle hitting the red line of empty.

"Fuel!" Ching brayed.

The pilot checked the gauges. He swore in Spanish before he looked at Ching. "One engine quit in two, three minutes. Fly some with one engine, not far."

"Find us a place to land," Ching said. "We'll belly land it with the wheels up. You understand?"

Sweat poured down the pilot's face again.

"Yes, long valley, maybe with grass."

"Good," Murdock said. "Can you find one in the dark?"

The pilot grinned, suddenly the man in control. "Yes, have flown this way before. Another five miles or so. Long valley, much farmers there."

Murdock wondered about the farming fields. There weren't a lot of options. He went to the cabin and told the men they would be making a belly landing without wheels.

"When I give the word, hold onto something. Brace against something forward because that's the way you'll be pushed as the bucket here stops suddenly."

"Just not too suddenly," Jaybird cracked.

Murdock went back to the cockpit. He saw that the pilot had slowed the airspeed and was turning to his left. Then he saw it out the window in the moonlight. An open valley maybe five miles long.

A few lights showed at the sides of the valley.

"No chance go around for second try," the pilot said. "First time. Slow as much as possible."

They came in over the valley, in a steep glide, then leveled out twenty feet over the ground. All Murdock could see were a few fences and land plots, and then a field filled with bales of hay. He couldn't see directly below, but they must be within fifty feet of touching down.

The pilot yelped and nosed the plane down sharper, then brought up the nose and flared out as he waited for the plane to stall out just before it touched.

The nose dropped a foot, then the whole transport eased to the ground and skidded along.

Murdock had glued himself to the forward cabin door and held on. Ching had strapped himself in the copilot's seat and had both feet on the instrument panel.

The plane jolted forward, rumbling and groaning. Murdock felt himself slammed against the door frame as the rig hit something that slowed it even more. Then it skidded again and slowed more and more.

Twenty long seconds later, it came to a stop.

"Open the hatch, everyone out," Murdock bellowed in the sudden silence. Both engines had shut down. Murdock ran into the cabin. The men were jostled about, but none looked broken up.

Ed DeWitt rammed open the side hatch and dropped to the ground.

"Out, out, out," Murdock roared. "This thing could explode at any minute."

The SEALs stormed out, most leaving their equipment

behind. Murdock pushed the pilot out and was the last man to clear the aircraft.

DeWitt came up to him, grinning.

"Lucky bastards. He set us down in a field of just-mown hay. Not raked or baled. The cut hay made a perfect slide for us. A plowed field could have killed us all."

Murdock saw the cut weeds and hay. The plane would never be able to take off.

"Anybody hurt? Casualty report, Alpha." His men all reported in. DeWitt made a check. His men were all in good shape.

"Let's get any gear out of the aircraft we left there. We just might need it before we get to the coast." He frowned. "What the hell ever happened to that barracks bag full of hundred dollar bills? Jefferson, that was your eight million dollar baby. Where is it?"

"Cap, it was too fucking heavy. We split up the cash. Every man 'cept you and JG got some bundles."

"I'm a rich son of a bitch," Franklin crooned.

They pulled weapons and two drag bags from the plane and then hunkered down, waiting for the decision where to go. Murdock checked his wrist compass. "Due west leads over that little hill. Anybody have any MREs left?"

"Hell, they been gone for a day or more," Ronson said. "Damn flight attendant on this bucket didn't even give us breakfast."

Murdock and Ching talked with the pilot.

"Where do the farmers live who work the land?" Ching asked.

"Small village, far end of valley. Two miles."

"We need some food," Murdock said. The pilot nodded.

"Village, we find food," the pilot said.

"Mount up, troops, short walk to our new mess hall." Murdock checked his webbing. He had one more WP grenade. He ran to the plane and tossed it into the cockpit. It exploded with streamers of white phosphorus arcing through the craft.

By the time they were half a mile away, they heard the

fuel tanks explode with what was left of the fuel.

Ten minutes later, Lam was out front of their column of ducks when he went to ground. Murdock hurried up beside him. Ahead in the moonlight, Murdock saw four good-sized one-story houses. All had small barns and sheds in back of them. No light showed. He checked his watch. It was almost 0400. He passed the word to send the pilot up with Ching.

"Go down there and pick the best-looking house and get them up. They have sixteen guests to feed. Ching, watch what the pilot says. Tell him he's dead meat if he tries to hurt us. Nobody leaves the house once you're inside."

Ching talked to the pilot a moment, then they both stood and walked quickly toward the houses. They all still had on their Motorolas.

"Lam, take a tour. See what kind of transport you can find. Two old cars or a farm truck would be handy. We came across a road back there, so there must be roads that lead all the way to he coast."

Lam nodded and took off at a trot toward the last house in the group.

Jaybird settled in beside Murdock. "Wonder why that jet didn't come back and blow us out of the sky. He must have air-to-air missiles and radar and guidance systems."

"Maybe he couldn't find us."

"Sure he could, with his radar."

"Maybe he wasn't sure if we were one of the smugglers' planes. The pilot said he'd flown through that pass before, coming this way."

"At least we're still alive."

Murdock watched through his NVGs as the pilot knocked on one of the houses' doors. It took several minutes of repeated knocking before anyone came. A light glowed inside, then the door opened.

Murdock could hear faintly some of the Spanish over his radio as the pilot spoke.

Then Ching's voice came on. "Yes, tell him there are

sixteen of us, and we will pay him well. We need food and water."

A minute later, Ching spoke.

"All set here, Skipper. Bring in the troops. We're getting food. We'll give him a hundred dollar bill, and he'll be delighted. Of course, if he tries to cash it in, he may be shot as a spy."

"Roger that," Murdock said. They lifted up and walked down the slight incline to the house.

The small front room in the house was sparsely furnished. Murdock liked the kitchen better. By the time they got there, women in their forties were starting a fire in a wood range and cooking. Two men came into the room and stared at the uniforms. Both talked with the pilot, and Ching monitored it.

"He's explaining how his plane crashed," Ching reported. "They seem satisfied."

The food came quickly. First a mush with milk and honey and coffee, lots of good, black Colombian coffee. Then chicken, which had been pan-fried along with sliced potatoes and half a dozen kinds of steamed vegetables. There were thick slices of homemade bread and more honey and lots more coffee.

Lam had slipped into the long table and reported to Murdock.

"There's an old farm truck out there with a stake body, ton and a half, I'd say. We can all ride on it. Has a full tank of gas and looks like it gets used daily."

"Lam, you have some of that drug money?"

"Sure, five hundred thousand dollars. Some guys have six hundred thousand. Jefferson figured it out."

"Let's buy the truck," Murdock said, grinning.

They later asked the pilot what the farm truck would be worth to the family. He looked at it in the dark and said maybe six hundred dollars, U.S.

Ching and the pilot talked to the local Colombian men and soon made the bargain. They paid them a thousand dollars, and the SEALs loaded up. Their canteens were full and their stomachs belching. It had been a weird breakfast.

The pilot climbed on board the truck. Murdock frowned. Ching saw him and asked him where he was going.

"Go with you. Guide you to coast for two hundred U.S. dollars."

DeWitt belched. "Yeah, bring him. He might get us through something we don't know is coming up. How far to the damned coast?"

The pilot asked the farmer, who said it was twenty miles. By then it was nearly daylight.

"Let's move," Murdock said. Ostercamp had checked out the rig. They paid the farmer for his truck and the meals and drove away. The road turned north and then west and held that line for five miles. By that time, it was fully daylight.

The dirt and gravel roads were not made for speed. Ostercamp was glad when they could average fifteen miles an hour. Just after daylight, they heard a jet fighter. It screamed overhead and followed the valley they had just left.

When it came to the burned-out transport, it circled several times, then went high and circled again before it turned and flew directly where the truck had been moments before.

Ostercamp had pulled the rig under three large trees that totally concealed it from the air. The jet made two more passes, then lifted up and raced away.

"We've been made," Murdock said. "Five will get you fifty that we have some ground troops heading our way right now. Let's get as far away from that burned-out plane as we can."

Ostercamp hit the gas but had to slow almost at once on a washboard section that jarred their teeth.

Murdock figured they were halfway to the coast when he saw the roadblock ahead.

"We can take it out," Ostercamp said. "Done it enough times before."

"No," Murdock said. "We hit a curve and get out of sight, then we abandon the bloody truck. It's an albatross around our neck. That jet must have reported we were on this truck. So we dump it. We hit the shank's mares and fade into the countryside. We can't be more than ten miles to the wet."

They ditched the truck and found a stream heading toward the coast. It had a friendly growth of brush and trees they could use for cover as they passed the roadblock half a mile over and kept right on going. When they were two miles beyond the roadblock, Murdock called a halt.

"Holt, let's do it."

Holt took out the SATCOM and aimed the antenna.

"Home Base, this is Rover. Home Base, this is Rover."

They waited, but there was no answer. The fourth time he made the call, the answer came.

"Rover. We read you."

"Figure we're about three miles from the wet. On a compass bearing due west of Plato."

"What's your ETA on the wet, Rover?"

"Not sure. Depends on our luck and the skills of the Colombian National Army. Will give you a definite ETA on our next call. Shall we expect a Knight or a rubber raft?"

"The Knight is our choice. Keep us informed."

"Let's rumble," Murdock said.

They hiked with renewed interest then. Lam was a quarter of a mile in front as they skirted farms, waded the creek twice, and stayed under cover as much as they could.

"Two choppers ahead, Cap," Lam said. "They're doing a pattern search. No way they can miss us if we keep moving."

"Come back, Lam. We'll go to ground in these trees and hope they pass over without spotting us. Odds are in our favor."

"Hold, Skipper. Now I see. There are two of them, and they are big jobs, with about twenty men each. They're leapfrogging over each other. Let the men out to search a half mile, then pick them up and jump them over the next group. They're working right up this valley. Could be a dozen units like this working all the routes up to that burned-out plane."

"Hold, Lam. I'm on my way."

Murdock ran the two hundred yards up to where Lam lay in brush on a small rise so he could see downstream. One big chopper had just lifted off and raced toward them a half mile, dropping off its load a quarter of a mile from where Murdock lay.

He stared at the soldiers spreading out in a search formation and starting up the valley.

"Oh, yes," Murdock said. "Now that does present us with a small problem."

26

Golfo de Morrosquillo
Colombia

The helicopter rested on the ground for a few minutes while the troops moved slowly toward the SEALs. Murdock and Lam now had their Bull Pups.

"Twenties on that first chopper," Murdock said. "You laser it, I'll try for a contact hit."

They both aimed and fired. Murdock watched as the airburst riddled the chopper with shrapnel. The rotor blades slowed, then stopped.

His round came in almost at the same time, hit the cockpit, penetrated, and exploded inside. A moment later, the chopper boiled into a fireball.

"Use the laser on the troops," Murdock said. He worked the Motorola. "Get the Bull Pup shooters up here. We've got company."

Murdock and Lam fired four rounds each, lasering the troops on the ground. They had stalled in place. When the proximity fuses exploded the 20mm rounds ten feet over their heads, the troops must have wished that they had scattered. They tried to then, but round after round followed them.

Jaybird nudged next to Murdock and got off a shot.

"Where's the other chopper?" Jaybird asked.

Then they saw it, climbing into the sky a mile off.

"Let's try it," Murdock said. Both he and Jaybird used the laser sight and automatic arming device built into the weapon, and when they had the laser on target, they fired.

The chopper came slowly toward them, perhaps to see what had happened to the other bird. The laser sighting was off only a little as the chopper moved. The first round exploded twenty feet behind the aircraft. The second one went off directly over it and smoke billowed from the helo as it settled gently to the ground. Two more rounds with the laser sighting brought gushes of smoke from the helicopter, and soon it burned furiously.

Murdock looked at the troops ahead of them a quarter mile. They were in a total rout.

"Cease fire," Murdock said on the net. "We may need the ammo later."

Lam motioned ahead. "Which way, Cap? We go down through the bodies? There may be more choppers on the other side of these small hills."

"True, and these guys must have radioed their problems before they got creamed. Straight ahead, straight west is our best bet. More farms and maybe a village we can slip through. Let's move."

A half mile along the small valley, they came to the bodies. They skirted them and the still-smoldering choppers.

Mahanani worked his way up to Murdock a short time later.

"Canzoneri is having some trouble with his leg, the one that got sliced up. Can we take ten while I rebandage it?"

"Let's hold it in place for five," Murdock said on the lip mike. "Lam, get a quick recon and see what's ahead of us. We should be within three or four miles of the beach."

Mahanani worked on Canzoneri. Some of the stitches had come out. Mahanani put on some bandages to cinch together the parted flesh, then tied the wound tightly. An ampoule of morphine helped.

Lam came back quickly. "Directly ahead not more than a mile there's some kind of an army camp. Don't know how big it is, but it sprawls out a ways. We better go south for about three miles. Then maybe we can make a run for the wet."

"Any activity that looked like they were coming after us?" Murdock asked.

"Not that I saw, Cap. Fair-sized camp."

"We better choggie. Let's go up and moving. Let's hope we can find some cover."

They had hiked for ten minutes when the net came on.

"I've got a chopper high and left," DeWitt said. "We better go to ground and not move. He should miss us."

"Do it," Murdock ordered, and the SEALs lay absolutely still.

Lam came on the radio. "Cap, do I need to find a hide hole for us for the rest of the day? A damn lot of army around here."

"Not yet. Let's see if we can break through into the water. My gut feeling right now is that the Colombian army is confused and doesn't really know where to find us."

Jaybird spoke up on the Motorola. "Hey, what happened to our friendly pilot guide? Where the hell did he go?"

"Did he get paid in advance?" Ching asked. "If he did, he took the money and ran. At least he won't cause us any problems."

They moved out again. After what Lam figured was three miles, he probed west again and saw that they were a mile beyond the last of the military buildings and the wire fence with concertina barbed wire on the top.

Lam settled in on top of a small hill and used his binoculars to check out the western route. He groaned.

"Cap, you need to see this. I don't know if the damn army is on maneuvers or just on a camp out. I'd say there are at least two thousand men in pup tents and company fronts and mess halls and kitchens out here in front of us."

Murdock worked up to his scout and scanned the area with his binoculars.

"Be damned. Look over there. Jeeps flying white flags. Men with white helmets on. Those are judges. The whole operation is maneuvers, and they're getting ready for a contest of blue against red or some such."

"Nice thing about maneuvers, Cap. None of them will have any live ammunition."

"But they could call in live ammo help in a rush if we tried to take them on. We go around them."

"Again?"

"Again, unless you have a better idea."

Lam looked at them again. "If we're going around them, we better move. Looks like one of the teams is getting ready to march out. Must be a whole fucking battalion of them."

The SEALs marched themselves. They picked up the pace to four miles a minute and angled straight south again, which they hoped would put them well out of the maneuver's area.

Two hours later, Murdock figured they were eight miles from the maneuver bivouac. They hadn't seen any troops or jeeps or white-helmeted judges for the past two miles.

"End run to the Caribbean?" Lam asked on the net.

"Let's give it a try," Murdock said. "Just past 1200. If we don't run into the damn new Colombian president and his staff, we should make it this time."

Murdock went to the head of the column with Lam out fifty yards in front as they turned due west. They had gone about a mile, Murdock figured, when they heard a clanking, grinding, and roaring in front of them.

"Tanks?" Lam asked.

Coming around a small valley and churning up the grass and weeds were six tanks. The first machine stopped, the tank gunner at the hatch rattled off six bursts of ten rounds each. The hot lead cut a swath through the brush just past where Murdock and Lam had been standing. They drove for the ground.

"They sending tanks after us?" Lam asked.

"Tanks don't mind 20mm rounds," Murdock said. "No way they could know where we are. They haven't had a spotting since those choppers, to hell and gone back there this morning."

"So why are they shooting at us?" Lam asked.

"They don't even know we're here. This must be a live firing range for the tanks. Let's pull back out of this firing range. We can deal with the war games better."

They moved back through the cover to where the rest or the platoon waited, then backtracked another mile toward the war games.

Murdock called a halt in a grove of trees near a small stream.

"Let's find that hide hole and take a break. We'll have more luck getting out of here after it gets dark."

"There's some high ground about five or six hundred yards up this stream," Lam said. "I looked at it when we came by. Want me to check it out?"

"Go," Murdock said. "We'll wander up that way behind you."

Just then, a series of rifle shots came from in front of them and not more than two hundred yards away.

"Down," Ed DeWitt whispered in the radio. The SEALs went flat in the grass and weeds in the brushy area. Jaybird crawled through the brush until he could see the shooters. He chuckled into his mike.

"Blanks. Don't you crackers know the difference in the sound of a blank and a live round? The troops out there are having a great time shooting blanks at each other. They're moving away from us now with three captives. No sign of a white-hatted umpire."

Twenty minutes later, Murdock figured the top of the hill they were near was three hundred feet above most of the rest of the swatch of green in front of them. They had burrowed into the brush and behind small trees to be completely out of sight. Sleep was the purpose.

Murdock and DeWitt took the first watch. They saw

some patrols of the cammy-clad Colombian troops, but none came near them. Twice they saw firefights between the two sides, but no prisoners were taken. Once they saw white-helmeted judges and referees moving along a hint of a road in a jeep.

Murdock brought Holt up with the SATCOM. Holt zeroed in the antenna and gave Murdock the handset. The transmissions went out in bursts so quick that triangulation was impossible. The words were also encoded so no one without the decoder could read them.

"Homeplate, this is Rover."

"Rover, we've been waiting. Are you held up?"

"That's a roger. Stalled and can't move until full dark. Will let you know what's happening after that. Possible we can get to the wet during the darkness. Will this give your birdman any problems?"

"Negative, Rover. Let us know, and we'll be there."

"We'll be in contact in about six hours."

Mahanani slid into the brush beside Murdock.

"Let me take a look at that left wrist. You probably thought I'd forgotten all about it."

"It's fine."

"Good, then it won't hurt to put some ointment on it and a new bandage."

Murdock held out his left arm. The corpsman pulled up the woodland green cammy sleeve and looked at the bandage. It was almost black with a large red stain on it. He cut off the bandage and checked the wound on both sides where the rifle round had dug through.

"Looks worse than the day you were hit," Mahanani said. He treated both sides of the wrist, put compresses over the wounds, then bandaged it tightly and wrapped the bandage with inch-wide 3M Transpore sticky tape.

"Should keep you until we get back in the wet. If that starts hurting, you give me a holler. Checked Dober's thigh, and it looks worse than your wound. Who fed you guys those indestructible pills, anyway?"

"Got them from you, corpsman. Now get some sleep."

DeWitt watched Murdock a minute. "That arm giving you trouble?"

"No, it's fine. Now you get some sleep."

Ed held his finger to his lips and pointed down the hill. They saw four men in cammies like theirs moving slowly upward as if following a trail. Murdock ducked behind a larger bush and waited. The four men kept coming, some chattering, some looking up the hill.

"We sure they have only blanks?" DeWitt whispered.

"We shoot beside them, they'll hear the lead. We don't let them use their weapons."

By then the four men were twenty yards away. They frowned, argued among themselves, then came on. When they were ten yards away, Murdock and DeWitt sprang out, firing two two-round bursts from the 5.56mm barrel of the Bull Pup. They shot beside the men so they could see the bullets.

Murdock and DeWitt charged the men. Two had dropped their rifles and held up their hands. The other two half lifted weapons, then lowered them. One chattered something in Spanish.

Ching ran down the trail to the group. "He said you're not supposed to have real bullets. You'll get in a lot of trouble."

"Tell them we're not in his game," Murdock said. "The game is over for them. Tie them up. We'll leave them here when we leave. Somebody will find them before they starve to death."

Half the SEALs woke up with the firing. They helped put the plastic riot cuffs on the four Colombians and stashed them at the side of the trail. They stacked their rifles neatly and went back to their improvised bunks.

"If anyone comes looking for them, we get the troops up and bug out over the hills to the south," Murdock said. He had Ching pull guard duty, and he and DeWitt vanished into the brush for some sleep.

One of the SEALs highest on the slope was Senior Chief Padden. He hadn't slept. He kept thinking about home and his wife and family. How was Nancy holding up? He wondered if the two women were meeting with her and helping her.

He hoped so. His family was tremendously important to him. He had been on the point of quitting the SEALs several times in the past year. Nancy was so insecure, so worried about him, about the kids, about everything.

Dobler remembered when they were first going together. He could remember the exact time when he first saw her at that little dance in the community center. He had been nearly twenty-two years old and sure that he would be a bachelor forever. It just seemed the best way to go. No responsibilities. No one to answer to every night. No one to explain what happened if he lost his pay in a poker game. No one . . .

That soon became unimportant. He saw Nancy, and she twirled when dancing with someone else. Her eyes lit up and her face was ecstatic. She was simply the most beautiful thing he had ever seen. He cut in on the couple and whirled her away and longed to see that same expression on her face. He had taken her home from the dance.

"Hey, pretty Nancy. I'm going to marry you. Did I tell you that?"

She looked up at him and laughed. "Hey, no offense, but I'm shooting for a higher goal. Some rich guy who can take care of me and buy me all sorts of diamonds and cars and furs and boats and we go to Las Vegas and drop a few thousand and we don't even notice it. Oh, my, yes. I want to marry a rich man. Now isn't it just as easy for a girl to fall for a rich guy as it is to fall in love with some handsome sailor boy?"

He said he figured it was. At her place there was a porch without a light, and he eased up close and looked at her, then lowered his face toward hers. She didn't back away or protest. He kissed her gently, then again. The third time, she had her arms around him and pushed close against him.

They went out every night for two weeks, then he had to go on sea duty for six months. When he came back, she was there, waiting for him, and two months later, they were married.

She hated his six-month sea duty, but it came and went. The first time after they were married, she was pregnant with Helen. She cried and asked him to quit the Navy. He explained it wasn't a job you could walk in and quit. He had signed for four years. Two were up, but he had two more to do. She begged him to quit after the hitch was up. He promised they would talk about it.

Somehow, they never did. Then one day he came home and found Nancy on the floor, nearly dead by her own hand. That was when he talked with her mother and discovered Nancy's sensitive nature and her suicide attempts when she was in high school.

This last one had been the worst. He thought he had lost her. Even now he wasn't sure. Yes, she had moderated, she had come down from her manic stage, but how long could she hold? Most important, would the two other SEAL women be a positive influence on her?

He stared himself right in the face and knew the way he was going. He had eighteen years in the Navy. He could do the last year and a half standing on his head. It didn't have to be in SEALs. He slammed his hand against the ground.

Damnit, if he had to, he would quit the platoon and go back to administration or some other nonfield assignment in the SEAL Team operation. With his clout, he could find a berth for a year and a half. Then he'd consider getting out of the Navy for good. It all depended on how Nancy reacted to this mission and his absence. He knew she'd go half crazy when she saw his shot-up thigh. No way he could keep that a secret.

But first, they had to get out of this trap. How could their own government write them off this way? How could they ignore fifteen U.S. citizens on foreign soil where the embassy had just been invaded, the diplomats held captive, and by now the embassy totally destroyed. How in hell could his own government do that to him?

Twenty feet below where Dobler worried, Murdock came awake and alert. He felt his lip mike in place. "Who's on guard duty?" he asked softly in the set. No one responded. It was almost dusk in the woodland. He rose silently and moved down the hill to the lookout point. Bill Bradford sat there with his weapon across his knees, looking through a bush down the hill.

"Bradford?"

The man turned. "Hi, Cap."

"Didn't you hear my last transmission?"

"Not a whisper. Try it again."

Murdock spoke into the lip mike.

"Damn, I'm down. Could be the battery. We have spares? Oh, yeah, that little package in the waterproof. Watch this spot for me for a minute, and I'll go get a new battery."

"Go."

Murdock studied the last of the landscape he could see. He could hear no guns chattering. Maybe the war was over until daylight for the game players. He hoped the tanks had gone back to their base. It was so frustrating. He knew they couldn't be more than three to five miles from the sea, yet somehow they couldn't get there.

Hell, they were going to head due west with dark and go around or through anybody or anything that tried to stop them. They had the firepower and the incentive. Besides, he was getting hungry.

He tapped his mike. "Wake up call, crew. Time to rise and shine. We're heading for the water. With any luck, we should be back in some warm, dry bunks before the night is over. Anybody want to take a hike?"

He got various comments over the net. Five minutes later, they were assembled and ready to move.

DeWitt came up to Murdock in the darkness. "We better cut these four soldiers loose, Cap. Don't see how they can hurt us. Somebody must know we're in this general area. We'll take their rifles and throw them away."

Murdock thought about it a minute. "Go," he said. The

men couldn't believe they were set free. Ching told them
they were lucky to be alive. That they should rush back to
their units and say only that they got lost and misplaced
their rifles.

Lam led them out due west, down the hill, over part of
the heavy tracks of the tanks, and along a small stream
heading for the sea.

Lights showed to one side a half mile away. Murdock
guessed they were the war games camp. They didn't have
out any patrols or security. Around a small hill they saw
more lights, and the clanking of heavy metal on metal.

Lam stopped for Murdock to come up. "Has to be the
tank company," Lam said. "They are working on tracks or
rollers, something with a heavy sound."

"Around them," Murdock said.

"You don't want us to steal a tank and ride in style to
the beach?" Lam asked.

"Not unless you can get fourteen guys hanging on the
outside of the rig."

They detoured and kept going. Murdock thought he
could smell salt air. Lam said no way.

Dobler realized with a start that he was limping. He
hadn't noticed it before. Just a little limp, a quick move
with his right leg so it wouldn't have to take his weight so
long. Damn. In the dark nobody could see it.

Nancy would shit purple if she knew he was wounded.
He had made Murdock promise not to let her know until
they got home and he could do the talking.

A mile on west, they heard loudspeakers. Ching listened
closely but could catch only a few words.

" 'Enemies of the people of Colombia,' that's all I can
understand, Cap," Ching said.

"What the fuck is going on up there?" Murdock asked.
DeWitt and Jaybird shook their heads.

"Could be a beach blockade," Dobler said. "Somehow
they knew we were SEALs in the other place. Who ___
___, too. They know we go to water. They knew where

we were. This must be one of the closest places to get to the Caribbean Sea."

"Lam, Jaybird, on me. Let's go see." They worked their way silently through the dark night along the stream, which had now grown into a good-sized river thirty feet across. Beyond the fringe of trees bordering the creek, they could see farmland and a few houses here and there. Most had lights on.

Six hundred yards from where they stopped, the three SEALs bellied down beside a fallen tree trunk and peered over the decomposing top.

They saw a highway, and beyond it the crashing surf of the Caribbean Sea. The highway was easy to spot. Two huge searchlights shone on it, turning the night into noon. Not even an ant could crawl across that blacktop road without being seen.

"The searchlights are easy," Lam said. "The twenties with impact hits. Then a charge."

"Where are their support troops?" Jaybird asked. "They must have a couple of hundred riflemen guarding the area with the searchlights."

"Just beyond the blacktop roadway, the beach drops off ten, fifteen feet," Murdock said. "They could have the troops down there waiting. A surprise party."

"The searchlights are reaching out about a hundred yards," Jaybird said. "So they cover a spot two hundred yards wide. We could shoot out the lights, with most of our guys down in the dark on the other side of that light. That way we'd go across at a spot they didn't think they would have to defend."

"Unless they figure that's what we would figure," Lam said with a big grin.

"We can't stay here all night. Lam, you have your Pup. You stay here with your ears on. We get the platoon in position down the way, I'll give you a go on the lights. You nail both and run your ass down to where the rest of us will be waiting. As soon as you get there, we go across the fucking road." Murdock whacked Lam on the shoulder.

"Give us twenty minutes to get into position." Murdock and Jaybird took off at a run to get back to the platoon.

27

On the Coast
Northern Colombia

Murdock moved his men as close to the highway as the terrain permitted. He had cover to within forty yards of the road. He and the rest of the platoon were fifty yards from the searchlight with the beam pointed the other way. It was dark on this side for as far as he could see to the south.

He used the Motorola. "Okay, Lam, take out the lights."

The sound of the 20mm round exploding on the nearest six-foot-high searchlight came almost at once. The light died. A moment later, the other light two hundred yards away exploded as well, and the beams of light coming toward where the SEALs lay snapped off.

"Let's move up slowly, watching everything," Murdock said. "Go now. Walk. We don't want any surprises. Over this highway and then we hope to make it to the beach in a rush. Easy now."

The line of SEALs spread ten yards apart moved toward the moonlit blacktop road. They heard some voices to the right where the searchlights had shone. No sounds came from directly ahead. They worked through a shallow ditch at the side of the highway and went up the shoulder. Murdock watched the far side of the roadway where it dropped off six or eight feet to the beach sand. He could see nothing.

The flat crack of an AK-47 on full auto slammed through the silence. "Get down," Murdock barked into the network. The fourteen SEALs went prone in the small ditch as a dozen weapons opened up across the highway, directly in front of them. They had just enough cover in the ditch to keep from being slaughtered.

"Grenades," DeWitt shrilled into the Motorola. The SEALs had started out with six hand bombs each. They had used some. Fourteen grenades sailed across the blacktop and vanished on the other side. They went off in a staccato of death against the gunmen defending the road. One grenade had been a WP, and its bright burning streamers of white phosphorus lit up the night sky for a dozen seconds.

The SEALs saw a few heads showing over the rim of the roadway. A barrage of fire barely skimming the road surface made direct hits on four of the curious heads. One Colombian soldier began screaming and couldn't stop.

The rifle fire from across the road ceased.

"Pull back," Murdock said into his lip mike. "Back to some cover. Those trees will be best. Go, now."

They sprinted for the trees and made fifty yards before the defenders could send more shots after them. Murdock took a squad check. Lam called in from behind them.

"Why didn't you guys wait for me?" he asked.

Murdock heard DeWitt get a net check. Five men came on the set. DeWitt waited a minute. "Quinley, are you with us?" There was no reply. "Quinley, can you hear me?"

As DeWitt called, the Colombians launched another round of rifle fire from their secure position in the drop-off across the highway.

The SEALs took cover behind trees and a small hump of land.

"Ed, we can't go look for Quinley now. We've got to reduce those forces over there."

"Yeah, how?" DeWitt asked.

"How close can these twenties explode in an airburst?" Jaybird asked.

Murdock frowned. Everyone had talked about long range on them. "Let's find out. We're back about fifty yards. I'll laser a round at the far edge of the pavement and see what happens." Murdock leaned around the tree, sighted in on the shadowy edge of the pavement, found the focus spot, and pulled the trigger. He still wasn't used to the heavy thump of the recoil from the 20mm round. The shell exploded in an airburst almost at once at the far edge of the pavement.

"Yes," shouted Jaybird.

"Two twenties for every Pup shooter," Murdock said. "Laser the far edge of the pavement. Should work."

They fired and the ten airbursts rained death down on the Colombians hiding behind the drop-off.

The return fire from the highway cut off. In the sudden silence they could hear some screams, an order barked out, and then no voices at all.

"Mahanani and I are going to find Quinley," DeWitt said.

"Go," Murdock said. He considered storming the roadway now. The chance that the Colombians had pulled out was good but not sure. How many men would he lose if there was even a squad left there with the AK-47s? Too many. He'd wait on Quinley. The man might be seriously wounded.

No firing came for three minutes.

"Murdock. Just found Quinley. He's gone. Took a round through the side of his head. KIA. Should I bring him back there, or are we going over the side here?"

"Have Mahanani check over the far side for any hostiles. Sorry about Quinley. We take him with us."

"Yeah. Take him. Mahanani is checking. Oh, he just went over the side below the highway. Must be clear. He's back up."

Mahanani bent low and ran back to where DeWitt lay.

"Yeah, slaughtered about fifteen of them. Spread all over.

Equipment, ammo, even food. Bugged out anybody who was alive. We should be able to get down there and then make a run for the surf. Figure it's about fifty, maybe seventy-five yards off. Almost no waves."

"Murdock, you hear Mahanani's report?"

"Yeah. Both of you go over the side and check each way for thirty yards. Want to be damn sure."

"On our way."

The two SEALs dropped over the lip into the sand and sprinted. DeWitt went right, Mahanani left. Moments later, they hit the net.

"Clear right," DeWitt said.

"Clear left," Mahanani said.

"Moving in. We'll bring Quinley with us. Set up some protection both ways."

"Skipper, there's some kind of a pier sticking out into the sea south maybe a hundred yards from where I am. A few boats along it. Look like fishing boats."

"Noted. Thanks."

Five minutes later, the SEALs dropped over the side of the highway into the sand. They moved twenty yards left to get away from the dead bodies and began to stow their radios in the waterproof compartments on their combat vests.

"Somebody coming from the right," Lam said. "Vehicle with no lights."

"Down, everyone," Murdock called.

The rig came closer, then a machine gun chattered from a mount on the vehicle. Lam put a 20mm round into the gun flashes. When the round hit, it detonated, silencing the machine gun and probably killing the driver. The jeep's engine sputtered and stopped.

"No more firing," Murdock called. "We'll see who else comes. Get your gear ready for wet. Set up in an arc around this spot. Lam, watch over the pavement to see if they bring anybody up that way."

All was quiet for a minute. Then they heard equipment rattling, jingling. The Colombians were coming. There were no gun flashes to give them away, but every SEAL on the beach knew they were coming. No time to get into the water. Someone would carry Quinley, and that would slow them all down.

Murdock watched to the right. They must have most of their men there. He checked his situation. They were hard against the six-foot drop-off from the highway for rear protection. Open on the other three sides. Water in front. Beach both ways. No way to see any terrain features.

They couldn't use the airbursts without some target to laser. They had no targets at all until the enemy began firing. Claymore? No time to rig one thirty yards in front of them.

"Anybody have any forties left?" Murdock asked the man next to him and the question flashed around the men. The answer came back quietly. There was one left.

"Fire it a hundred yards down to the right, and we'll see what happens."

Seconds later, the round was on its way. It arched up high and came down with a deadly explosion. In the flash of light, Murdock could see about twenty men advancing on them in a assault line.

"Everyone move to the right. Let's sweep the beach with hot lead. Fire when you're ready."

Gunfire erupted. Ronson's throaty machine gun chattered out five- and seven-round bursts. The sniper rifles whammed away and the MP-5s on three-round bursts cut in with more fire. They took some return rounds and that gave them better targets.

Lam had dropped down and used his Pup on two-round fire with the 5.56 ammo. Somebody sent a lasered round into the gun flashes and won an airburst. Then two more twenty rounds hit, and the gunfire from the right slacked off.

As it did, Lam listened. "Two more vehicles coming," he shouted into Murdock's ear. "My guess, two tanks."

"Bradford, on me," Murdock called. The big quartermaster dropped into the dry sand beside Murdock.

"Give me your rifle. You're on Quinley. We're heading for that pier to the left. Go now. The rest of us are coming."

Murdock sent them three at a time, the rest keeping up the fire. When they could spot the tanks in the soft moonlight, they dropped in 20mm impact rounds on them. The tanks responded with machine gun fire.

By then the last of the platoon had bugged out for the pier.

It was a fishing dock, which projected from a small point of land. In the dark Murdock saw six fishing boats. Two of them on the far side of the pier were large enough to hold the SEALs.

"Ostercamp. See if you can hot-wire the engine on that second boat. The quicker we know, the better. That tank can fire out to sea just as well as on land."

Murdock placed the SEALs in a defensive position around the end of the pier and on two boats on the near side. He doubted if the infantry would make another try, but the tanks would look for them. If they didn't fire, the tank commander wouldn't know where to look.

Murdock found Quinley and shook his head. He had been a good man. Always ready to do his part. The round had bored all the way through Quinley's skull. Not pretty. They wouldn't leave him. Murdock could count on one hand the men he had left on foreign soil. Two, maybe three. He checked over the fishing boat they were hijacking. It was no bargain, smelled like fish, but it looked fairly clean. He hoped the motor was working and that they had enough fuel for a mile or so ride to sea.

The tanks lumbered closer. They sent streams of machine gun fire around at random now, some into the water, others down the highway. The gunners had no idea where their enemy was.

"I can do it," Ostercamp called. "Give me about two minutes' notice, and we can get out and away before that tank knows we're moving."

Quietly, Murdock moved his men on board the boat. Ronson carried Quinley on and laid him on the short deck.

The boat was mostly masts to let down with fishing lines, and a big empty center to hold the fish. The men sprawled wherever they could find room.

Murdock, Ching, and Bradford with his machine gun took the guard posts.

The engine kicked over and roared into full-blown life. Murdock had two men ready to cast off the lines, and they were moving.

Ostercamp took the wheel and steered the boat away from the tanks.

"This ain't no hot rod, but we should be able to do about ten knots," Ostercamp called over the roar of the engine.

"Holt, let's do some business," Murdock called. They went to the back of the boat where the engine noise was weakest and made the call to the carrier. They connected on the second try.

"Home Base, we're in a fishing boat in the sea and heading due west. Had a few problems, including a couple of tanks, so we couldn't call earlier. We may be fading in and out due to our motion."

"Read you fine, Rover. We'll have the bird in the air in two minutes. Stay on that due west course. Our ETA a mile offshore there should be in about twenty minutes. Mark. Use a red flare when you spot our bird and go to TAC one for communication. Any wounded?"

"No wounded. We have one KIA."

"Sorry, Rover. We'll see you shortly."

Jaybird came out of the forward hold with a boy about twelve in tow. "Look what I found, Skip."

Ching looked over and said something in Spanish to the boy who grinned. He chattered back.

"Says he's the grandson of the boat owner and he goes out fishing with them. They were getting ready to go at five A.M."

Murdock chuckled. "Tell him he can drive the boat back to the dock when we leave it and have a wild story to tell his grandfather."

Ching translated.

Two minutes later, Lam called out.

"Fast boat coming up on our bow. Looks like a coastal patrol boat of some ilk."

"Can we hide?" Murdock asked.

"Don't think so, Cap," Lam said. "Most of these patrol boats, even the small ones, have good radar. This one must be making about twenty knots."

"Most of these patrol craft carry a twenty-five-to-forty millimeter cannon," Jaybird said. "Also a couple of machine guns."

"Range?" Murdock asked.

"Barely see her, maybe three thousand yards."

"When she gets to a mile, we test our Bull Pups on max range. My guess, we might be able to discourage her from getting too close."

"Then she can lay off and blow us out of the water with those forties," DeWitt said.

"If she has any," Murdock said. "How is that range?"

"Twenty-five hundred if the moon is right," DeWitt said.

"Get the Bull Pups up here. All five of them. We laser that patrol boat, and when we can see it, we try a round. How many rounds we have left?"

They sang out with numbers, all with more than fifteen rounds.

"Good, we might need them."

"Two thousand yards and closing," DeWitt said, looking through his binoculars.

"Let's try for a laser response," Murdock said, aiming his Bull Pub at the oncoming ship.

"She's at least a hundred feet long," DeWitt said. "Lots to shoot for.

"Range is at a mile," Jaybird said. He fired. They all waited and watched. Moments later, the round exploded on target over the top of the speeding craft.

"Fire for effect," Murdock said.

The first exploding 20mm round didn't get a reaction from the patrol boat, but when it took four more rounds raining deadly shrapnel down on the boat, it cut power.

"The captain is thinking it over," Murdock said. "Two rounds each, and let's see what happens."

"Eight minutes ETA on the chopper," Ostercamp said.

Murdock fired his two rounds and watched through his binoculars as they exploded in airbursts. Eight more rounds went off on or near the ship moments later. He could see that all of the forward windows had been blown out. The radar antenna must have taken a lot of shrapnel hits as well. There was no one on the decks.

The forty-millimeter cannon on the patrol boat fired. The first round hit short, the second walked up toward the boat. Ostercamp cranked the wheel and had the boat going directly away from the path of the oncoming patrol craft.

The third and fourth rounds hit well aft.

"Two more rounds each," Murdock said to the Bull Pup shooters, and they blasted away. This time Murdock saw that three crewmen were caught on deck. Two of them went down, and the third smashed into the rail and went over the side. The patrol boat kept coming toward them.

"Bradford, get out that fifty and some AP rounds. Hit the bridge on that craft if you can. We need some help here."

Bradford grinned and primed the big bolt-action, fifty-caliber weapon and pushed in a five-round magazine of armor-piercing rounds. He fired, swore, and fired again. The second round jolted through the plating on the outside of the bridge and exploded inside.

The patrol boat slowed, then swung sharply to the left and went dead in the water.

"Didn't think you needed me, right?" Bradford said.

"Three more, for good measure," Murdock said.

Two of the three rounds hit the bridge and gun mount and exploded inside.

"Two minutes to contact," Ostercamp said.

"Keep motoring west," Murdock said. "That wounded duck back there might still be able to fire his forty. We don't need any more casualties."

It was nearly five minutes before they heard a chopper. It came in high, then low when Murdock threw out a floating red flare. It swung around into the wind and settled toward the now dead-in-the-water fishing boat.

A speaker from the chopper cut through the sound of the rotors.

"Welcome, SEALs. We'll send down a litter for your KIA. He comes in first. Then, if we have time, we drop you a ladder. Anyone who can't climb the ladder?"

Murdock gave a thumbs-up gesture, and the aluminum litter dropped down on a line. They let the litter touch the deck and short out the high charge of static electricity it built up from the rotor wash, then they grabbed it and lifted Quinley in and tied him securely.

A moment later, the litter lifted skyward.

Ching talked to the Colombian boy.

"You tell your grandfather we needed to borrow his boat. We didn't hurt it any, and here is a hundred U.S. dollars to pay for the fuel. You understand?"

"Many, many dollars. Understand."

"You can run the boat?"

"*Sí,* it is easy. Drive for Grandfather many times."

Murdock watched the ladder come down. Two men held it while the others went up. Jaybird motioned Murdock up, pointing to his wrist. Jaybird was the last man up the ladder, now swaying on the bottom. It's twice as hard to climb with no one holding the bottom. He made it, and the SEALs inside cheered as the crew chief closed the hatch and the Sea Knight headed back for the carrier *Jefferson.*

28

USS *Jefferson*
Near Colombia

As soon as the Sea Knight came to a landing on the carrier, a formal delegation arrived with a gurney and a body bag. The SEALs stood around as Quinley's body was zipped up in the heavy black plastic and gently placed on the gurney. They all followed it to the elevator and down to the ship's hospital.

A lieutenant without a line on his young face had Murdock sign some papers.

"We'll handle your man until we get directions. I understand that the deceased has requested a burial at sea. We'll need a day's notice for the ceremony."

Mahanani took Canzoneri, Dobler, Jaybird, and Murdock to the emergency room, where their wounds were examined and treated. Most of Canzoneri's stitches were intact, but one small section had broken loose.

The woman lieutenant who treated them all stared at Canzoneri a moment longer. "I want to keep you here at least over the rest of the night and tomorrow. There's some infection starting in that broken-open section, and I want to be sure we catch it right now before it gets bad. The rest of you are released to duty."

Murdock thanked her and took the men to their quarters. They dropped their equipment in the assembly compartment they had been assigned to. Murdock had taken the stacks of one hundred dollar bills from Quinley's shirt before he went in the body bag. He whispered to Canzoneri, who dug out the bills from his shirt before they took him to a hospital room.

"Let's take out the cash, guys. No way we can keep eight million dollars. Stack it up on the table here, and we'll see if we lost any."

"Remember, we spent some of it," Ching said. "A thousand for the truck and breakfast and the guide."

"All down in black and white," Murdock said.

Everyone took out the stacks of bills and stood around as Murdock and Jaybird counted it.

"A whole shit pot full of bundles," Jaybird said. He had counted out ten and stacked them, then stacked the rest next to them. Murdock dug into his shirt again and came up with the last bundles. Murdock told the men to hang around.

He called the officer of the day and explained the small problem.

"You kidding, Commander? Eight million dollars in cash? Where the fuck . . . No, I don't want to know. I'll send two armed guards down there right now to guard it until morning."

The guards with loaded M-16s reported five minutes later.

"Eight million in cash?" one of the men asked.

"Right, and your ass will be in a forty-year-long federal prison if it isn't all there in the morning."

Murdock sent his men to bed, then used the phone again.

"Commander, can you get a flag officer down here now? A captain will do. I want this cash put in a more secure place."

"Damn, I don't see how."

"It's eight million dollars, Commander, I want it out of my hair."

"I could try the XO, Captain Wilson. Yes, I'll give him a call."

Five minutes later, the phone rang in the compartment.

"Commander Murdock here."

"Murdock, is this a leg-puller? Captain Wilson here. The OD tells me you have eight million bucks in cash you want stashed in a safe place."

"True, Captain. Fortunes of war. I want to get rid of it and have you sign off on it for me."

"Whose cash is it, Murdock?"

"Yours, I guess. It lately was owned by a pair of big shots in the Medellin drug cartel. They don't need it anymore."

"Christ. Found money. Must be some Navy reg to cover this. All right. Stay right there."

Fifteen minutes later, the captain had signed a paper stating that he had taken charge of $8,000,000 from Lieutenant Commander Blake Murdock, less about $1,400 in expenses incurred in leaving Colombia. Said cash a result of a raid on the Medellin drug cartel in Colombia.

The two armed guards stuffed the money in a duffel bag and carried it between them as they vanished up the hall with the captain. Murdock hadn't even guessed at the time. It was a little after 0400 when he dove into his bunk and slept at once.

By 1000 the next morning, he was up, dressed in clean cammies, and having breakfast when Stroh tracked him down. He brought a cup of coffee to the small table in the wardroom and pointed at the other chair.

"Okay if I sit down?"

Murdock stared at him coldly. "How does it feel to sign the death warrants of fifteen men?"

"I didn't make the decision."

"Sure, Adolph, you were just following orders. One of my men died because of you. Shot though the head. I want you at his burial ceremony just to know how it feels."

"Come on, Murdock. You've been in this game long enough. You know the odds. We're 80 percent politics, 20 percent action. The political always comes first. Always has, always will."

"Doesn't mean I have to like it."

"This is a volunteer project. The CNO told you that at the git-go. Any time you want to pick up your marbles, you can walk right out the front door."

"Then you pick another platoon leader and con him and his men about the great service to their country."

Stroh sipped at his coffee. "May I sit down?"

"Free country, in places and for some people."

Stroh sat down. "How long are you going to pout?"

"As long as it takes. After this, when we get a ride to the party, we damn better get a ride home from the party."

"Almost always works that way. Okay, twice we had a no-fly. It had to be. I fought for you right up to my retirement on it both times. I lost. I don't have the clout of the Secretary of State or the President and his advisors."

Murdock finished his three-egg omelet and hash browns before he looked up. "Just don't expect any good fishing trips."

"I won't. I'll plan to be there when the fishing's at its best. Good news. We don't have a damn thing on the fire that you guys can help us with. Unusual, but that's the way it happens."

"Good. I need to do some retraining."

"Hey, I let you go with the Bull Pups, didn't I? How did they work?"

"Good. You'll see my after-action report, which I'm writing as soon as I can find a computer. This is your price. You get us six more Bull Pups before our next outing. Bribe somebody, pay double for them. We want six more of the prototypes. Best damn weapon I've seen in twenty years of shooting. Those damn proximity fuzed twenties saved our asses more than once."

"It's impossible to get any more. They don't even have prototypes to test at the factory."

"Bribe somebody. Get them made. We need them in three weeks. They can turn them out if you put on enough pressure. We practically keep H&K in business."

"Okay, I'll try. Not promising."

"You already promised." Murdock pushed back from the table. Stroh beat him to his feet.

"Don't think it would be a good idea for you to show up at our assembly compartment. Some of the guys are not wildly enthusiastic about your hide."

"Oh, yeah." He watched Murdock. "Are you and I okay on this now?"

"No. After the burial at sea tomorrow, I want you to write the letter to the mother of Torpedoman Third Class Les Quinley, twenty-two years old. You get to tell her about the tragic accident that happened on the carrier and explain what a fine sailor he was and an outstanding person. Just lie like hell. Give it to me and I'll put it on my stationery back in Coronado and sign it. Least you can do."

Murdock walked away, leaving Stroh with his mouth open in surprise.

Murdock checked in with the men. Senior Chief Dobler walked over. He grinned.

"Hey, Commander. Sent my wife Nancy two E-mail letters this morning. My leg even feels better, and I hear that we're going to be heading home before long. Right? The men are asking."

"We get Canzoneri out of the hospital, take care of the burial at sea, and then we make the arrangements. So take a day or two off and relax."

"Oh. Guess I'm kind of anxious to get back and see Nancy. I bet she's doing fine and all. You know. I get worried about her."

"I know. We should be out of here within three days, but don't tell the men yet. I'm fighting with Stroh about chopping off our Sea Knight pickup when we finished the job."

"Hell, Skipper, we made it out. He was just following orders."

"Don't get me started on that subject. Those damn orders cost us a man KIA. Quinley would not have been hit if they lifted us out of there when they were supposed to." Murdock turned and walked away. He came back a minute later.

"Sorry, Chief. It still bugs me. How are the men doing?"

"Weapons all cleaned and ready to go. Restocking our vests with basic ammo and gear. We'll be cleaned up here in an hour."

"Our liaison, Lieutenant Commander Kenney. Has he been around?"

"No sir, but he called. Left a number."

Murdock called Kenny. "Yes, Commander, good to talk to you, too. I need your help on a few small matters. What are the carrier's regs on a burial at sea, and how do we set it up for tomorrow?"

"I'll find out, Commander, and get back to you soonest. Anything else?"

"Transport back to the States for my platoon."

"Mr. Stroh will handle that. I'll take any excess ammunition or ordnance you have, equipment, that sort of thing. Didn't I bring you some extra H&K MP-5s?"

"You did. Senior Chief Dobler will talk to you about that. He should be about ready to turn all of that over to you."

"Good. I'll find out about the burial. Sorry about your man. In this line of work that sometimes happens. I'll have something for you on this right after lunch."

Murdock thanked him and said good-bye.

He stared at the phone. He knew that Chief Dobler had Don Stroh's number. He waited a half hour, then called.

"Stroh. Sometime tomorrow morning we should have the burial of Les Quinley. Shortly after that I want to take off for the States. Please arrange our transport and have a COD on deck for our first leg to Panama or wherever we can get some land-based aircraft. Let me know if you can't make these arrangements. I'll let you know about the ceremony."

Stroh said he would get on it. "About this morning."

"What was said, was said. Let me cool off for a week or two, then I'll be able to look at the whole thing with a little better perspective. I won't hold still for my men getting killed. We can talk later."

Murdock hung up.

29

SEALs West Coast HQ
Coronado, California

Murdock eased into his chair behind his small desk in his office at SEAL Team Seven, Third Platoon, in Coronado, and tried to relax. It had been a series of good flights home. He cven caught some sleep.

As soon as they landed at North Island U.S. Naval Air Station late the night before, he and his four wounded men went to Balboa Naval Hospital to be checked over. They kept Canzoneri, not liking the way the knife slash on his left thigh looked. Fernandez was admitted. The doctors looked over his medical records that came with him and told Murdock it would be at least two weeks before they could think about releasing him.

"That chest wound isn't right. We may have to go in and find some more of the shattered round."

The doctors there checked and rebandaged Murdock's wrist and Dobler's thigh and Jaybird's arm and released them.

It was nearly 0400 by the time they got to the base and put away their combat gear.

"I'm bunking out here until morning," Dobler said. "I don't want to charge home and scare Nancy and the kids. Tomorrow morning will be better."

Murdock said he'd be in about noon and headed for his apartment. When he pulled in his parking space, he saw a light in his front window. He grinned. No burglar, this one. Murdock ran up the steps and used his key on the door. Inside, he dropped his small bag and checked the living room couch.

A long bundle wrapped in a blanket lay there. It was topped by a frowsy pile of blond hair. Murdock tiptoed to the couch, knelt beside it, and pushed the blanket back enough to kiss a pink nose.

Ardith Manchester smiled in her sleep and turned so he found her lips. He kissed them and they responded. Her arms came out of the cover and wrapped around him.

"Ha, bet you thought I was sleeping."

He kissed her again and she leaned back. "About time you showed up. You were scheduled in here at 1600 yesterday."

"We had an equipment delay in Miami." He shook his head. "How in hell did you know our flight schedule?"

She grinned at him.

"I know, but tell me anyway. You've joined the CIA."

"Nope." She kissed him quickly and chuckled. "This one you won't believe. Dad knew about your mission and followed it. Then he remembered that he had been in school with the captain of the aircraft carrier *Jefferson*. They got in touch."

She frowned and reached for his left arm. "How is that wrist? Is it healing properly?"

"Medics said so an hour ago." He laughed. "Is there anything you don't know about our work down in Colombia?"

"Only that my dad called the White House twice when they were trying to figure out if they could do another fly-over of Colombia to bring you out in a Sea Knight."

He stared at her in delighted surprise. "Lady, you might as well be in my hip pocket." He stood and held out his hand. She came up from the couch with the grace of a coiled mountain cat. When the blanket slipped off her, he saw that she was delightfully naked.

"Enough of this foreplay. Now I want you in my bed. Unless you know about our next mission and I have to fly out in less than two hours."

"No mission. I never know about them before they happen. Can't help you there. I could brief you on the trouble spots of the world and the ones that the President and the Joint Chiefs and the CIA are the most concerned about."

"Don't you dare. There have to be some surprises in life."

They didn't get to sleep for almost two hours.

When morning came, Senior Chief Dobler rolled out of the bunk at Third Platoon HQ and shaved carefully. Then he put on his civvies, backed his four-year-old Honda out of the lot in front of the quarterdeck, and headed home.

It was nearly 0730. The kids would be off to school, and he should be able to have a long talk with Nancy. He didn't know what to expect. He'd sent her an E-mail after they returned to the carrier. She knew how to receive them, but wasn't sure about sending them.

When he left, she was just out of the hospital with bandages on both wrists. If anything bad had happened, he would have heard on the *Jefferson*. Master Chief Mac-Kenzie would have tracked him down. He pulled the Honda into his parking space and looked at their ground-floor apartment. No activity. Good.

Dobler hurried to the door, tried the handle, and found it unlocked. Yes. Kids were gone. He pulled the door open and stepped inside.

Nancy came from the hall toward the kitchen. She saw him and gave a little cry of joy as she rushed forward and threw her arms around him. Tears welled in her eyes.

"So glad . . . so glad to have you home, baby. So damn glad."

"Good to be here. Kids in school?"

"Just left. You've got a good pair of offspring there, sailor."

"Should be, my beautiful wife did most of the raising of them while I played in the deep blue sea."

They walked arm in arm into the living room and settled on the sofa. It was a long, demanding kiss, and Nancy fell backward on the couch and pulled him down on top of her.

"I just want to feel you crushing me into the couch. Oh, my, yes."

Dobler was encouraged. Nancy had put on her at-home makeup. Her hair was neatly done. He figured she'd had it washed and set recently. Her blouse and slacks were ones that she liked.

"Ask me how I'm doing. Go ahead."

"Baby, how are you doing?"

"Oh, Dobe, better than I expected. The girls and I get together almost every day. We have coffee or go shopping. That Maria is a gem. Such a wonderful lady, and so good with the kids. I love her. We talk late at night sometimes on the phone."

She went to the kitchen and started coffee. He followed her.

"I said we'd talk about the Navy when I came home. Is now a good time?"

"No. I want to feed you breakfast. Bet you haven't had any. You look like you had about three hours of sleep last night. Right?"

He nodded.

"Do you know Milly, JG DeWitt's live-in? She is a marvel. So smart and classy. She works full-time, but she came over three or four times while you were gone. She had some tough things to say to me about being a SEAL's woman. Really tough. What it came down to was as women, we couldn't change a SEAL. What we had to do was try to moderate and soften some of his life. To be the one to give and bend and accommodate, so the relationship could last. That Milly is one strong woman, and I've learned a lot from her."

Nancy stood at the stove, tall and straight, her chin up and her eyes glistening. "So, swabby, some coffee, eggs, bacon, and some French toast, then it's off to bed with you for at least ten hours. After that, I have another idea what we might do in that same bed."

She grinned and turned to the stove. Senior Chief Dobler gave a short sigh. He was a lucky man. Nancy was going to do fine. They would still have the talk. He had decided right after he was shot that he was going to do what was best for his family. If Nancy wanted him out of SEALs action platoons, he would quit the next day. He could stay on the team, maybe in one of the specialty platoons. Hell, he could do two years without Third Platoon.

If she wanted him out of the Navy, he could do that and give up the retirement. Twenty years wasn't a big bunch of retirement pay, anyway. He'd see. What was best for his family was what he would do.

Family had to come first. He remembered a star baseball player who had finished his contract with the San Diego Padres. Six other teams bid for him as a free agent. He turned down a $21.5 million contract with one team to sign for $9.5 million with the team where his family lived. He said he wanted to be closer to his family, to watch his kids grow up. Yeah, what a man. Family came first with Dobler, too.

He didn't realize how hungry he was until Nancy put down the platter in front of him with the eggs, French toast, bacon, and hash browns. Dobler ate it all.

Back in the Third Platoon office, Murdock stared at his roster. Damn, he needed another replacement. He'd been averaging one man lost to the platoon on each mission. Fernandez would be back. He'd hold the spot open for him through another mission if he had to. He liked the man, wanted him on board for a little more stability. Come to think of it, he hadn't had to bail any of his men out of jail recently. There would come a time. Getting them bone weary on missions like this past one helped drain off the excess energy.

Don Stroh. That was another matter. He had considered asking to be out from under the direct thumb of the CIA. He could ask but not necessarily get away. Stroh had set up the return transport, phoned Murdock on the carrier with the particulars, and that was the last Murdock had seen or heard from him.

He didn't fly back with them as he sometimes did. It must have been partly due to being embarrassed because he had to pull the plug on the chopper. It wasn't his decision, but he had to deliver the message. By now Murdock had cooled down enough to realize Stroh's position. He was a conduit, a lead wire, an input source. He didn't make the regs or the rules or give the orders, he just transmitted them to the SEALs.

Most of the SEALs showed up at the platoon quarters by noon. They stowed their gear and sat around talking.

Ostercamp had a race to run that night at the El Cajon Speedway. A stock car. He had three wins so far this season.

Ron Holt, Jaybird Sterling, and Paul Jefferson were going to a party that night out in Santee, a slightly rural area east of San Diego.

"Hell, there's more horses and rednecks in Santee than anywhere in the country," Holt said. "I used to sleep with a broad out there last year until I got run out of town by some dude with a shotgun who claimed he was her common-law husband."

"That's when he killed you," Bradford jibed.

"Hell no. I took the shotgun away from him, fired both rounds into the air, and then broke the damn gun in half. He came at me, so I broke his arm. Last I ever saw of him."

They all laughed. "Chances are as soon as you saw the shotgun you shit your pants and ran for your car."

"Naw, he was riding a pinto pony that night," Lam shouted.

Holt grinned. "So, any more of you numb nuts want to take in a real Western party? No boots or cowboy hats required."

They passed. Then Lam said he'd like to go.

The party in the west edge of Santee, up against a hill, began at ten that evening. There was a four-piece Western band, a big patio set up for Western line dancing, and enough livestock around to make it look like a real ranch. The woman who owned it was a master programmer and systems computer analyst for a big outfit in San Diego's own silicon valley.

The four SEALs were on their best behavior. They danced, learned the simple line movements, and had enough beers to keep them happy.

About midnight, four motorcycles roared into the front of the parked cars and four big bikers got off their rigs.

Janie, the owner of the place met them with a cattle prod.

"Who the hell are you guys, and who invited you?" Janie shouted in her usual diplomatic style.

"We're the four riders from hell, and we go where we want to go, little bimbo. You ever had it twice in a row on the back of a Harley?"

"Get your ass off my property," Janie said. "I don't want you here, and I'm the honcho of this outfit. Now go."

Another one of the quartet spoke up. He had on studded leathers and a huge beer belly, but he looked as hard as a much-used branding iron.

"Little bitch in heat, we don't make trouble, we just answer it. Now step aside, and let us see your party."

Janie lunged at him with the cattle prod, which could send out a serious jolt of electric charge into whatever it hit. The tip of the prod connected with his thigh and zapped. The big man didn't even seem to notice. He grabbed the rod, jerked it out of Janie's hand, and reversed it. He found the trigger, and before Janie could scramble out of the way, he touched it to her shoulder.

Janie bellowed in pain and staggered back. The four laughed and surged past her to the patio. They helped themselves to beers and called loud sexual suggestions to the women dancing.

Paul Jefferson left the other SEALs to go for another beer. He passed just in front of the four bikers.

One of them reached out a foot and tried to trip him. Jefferson, at 6' 1" and 200 pounds, was slightly smaller than all of the bikers. He daggered a look at them and went on to the iced tubs with the beer. When he took out a bottle and turned, the four were ringed in front of him.

"What's a nigger like you doing at a nice white party like this, boy?" the biggest of the bikers snarled.

"I was invited," Jefferson said, taking a step past the four.

"Not by us you weren't, Africano," another of the bikers said.

"You got to learn your place, black man. This ain't it. This is white man's territory."

"Everyone is entitled to his own—" It was as far as Jefferson made it before the closest man whipped out a right fist and caught the SEAL on the side of the head and drove him backward. There a biker caught him and slammed his fist into Jefferson's gut. When Jefferson doubled over in agony, the biker's knee rammed upward, hitting him in the jaw and dumping Jefferson into the grass.

Somebody shouted to stop it.

One of the bikers moved his leg back to kick Jefferson, who writhed on the ground.

Jaybird and Holt saw the attack and ran through the people to the scene. Jaybird made it just in time to shoulder-block the kicker before he struck, blasting him backward so hard he sprawled in the dirt. Jaybird whirled as he sensed someone behind him. He blocked a big fist coming at him and drove his foot upward into the biker's crotch. The man dropped like a shot steer.

Holt tackled another biker and pushed him back out of the fight for a moment. When the much larger biker recovered, he slashed a fist at Holt and knocked him down. He tried to kick Holt, who grabbed the foot and jerked it forward, pulling the biker off balance. Holt lifted his boot so he kicked the biker in the stomach as he fell, jolting him to the left, out of the fight.

Lam came in late, just in time to take on the largest biker. The motorcycle rider unhooked a bike chain from his waist and began swinging it in a circle. Everyone else backed off.

"What the hell is going on here?" Janie bellowed. "I told you fucking bikers to leave. Now scat." She waved a six-gun with a short barrel. The biker and Lam didn't notice. They circled each other warily. Lam whipped off his three-inch-wide belt that had a heavy brass buckle on the end.

Jefferson wobbled to his feet and stared at the scene. He held his stomach. Jaybird grabbed him and pulled him out of the circle.

"Come on, nigger-lover bastard," the biker said. "Come get what's coming to you."

Lam darted forward, swung the belt, and smashed the heavy buckle into the biker's upper right arm.

He howled in pain and charged.

Lam had sidestepped quickly and avoided the swing of the bike chain. He kicked the biker's leg as he went by. The leg crashed into the other leg, and the biker stumbled and fell hard to the ground.

Janie fired two rounds from the revolver into the air. Everything stopped a moment, then another shot blasted into the night. Jefferson grabbed his stomach and bellowed in pain. The shot came from the crotch-kicked man. Holt was nearest him. He surged forward and knocked the gun from the biker's hand where he still sat on the ground.

"Call nine-one-one!" somebody shouted.

"I have them on my cell phone," another voice called.

The San Diego Sheriff's deputies arrived before the ambulance. They had the bikers and the four SEALs in handcuffs. They took off Jefferson's cuffs when he was strapped onto a gurney and put into the ambulance.

It was almost 1600 the next day when Murdock bailed his three men out of the county jail. They had been charged with disorderly conduct, and a trial date was set for two months away. Janie was there to help, but she didn't get to testify. She told Murdock about it in the hallway.

"Those boys of yours saved my party. The bikers weren't invited. They just barged in. They're white supremacists. They cause trouble wherever they go. Hope your man isn't hurt bad."

Murdock had been at the hospital half the night as they did emergency surgery on Jefferson and spliced back together part of his intestine and did some minor repair work.

"He'll be fine, but it will be two months before he can go back on duty," Murdock said. "We hope you'll be at the trial, Janie."

Janie gave him her full name and phone number and said it would be her primary concern. She had no idea who the SEALs were or what they did. Murdock was just as happy about that.

That same night, when Ed DeWitt came home, he saw that Milly had made it ahead of him. That meant she must have quit work early. As soon as he stepped into the apartment, he noticed the difference. Soft music played on the CD deck. The table in the small living room was set for two with candles already lit. Milly stood by the table in her sexiest dress that showed an inch of cleavage and the swell of both breasts. She called it her man-catcher dress.

"Hi there, stranger. Can I take you in and feed you and maybe give you something to drink?"

DeWitt staggered against the wall. "Anytime, anywhere."

Milly laughed at his clowning, hurried up and kissed him, then caught his hand.

"Just a few more minutes and your sumptuous dinner will be ready. How about a glass of a very nifty little Chablis first to whet your appetite?"

"Yes, and my appetite is already raring to go." He kissed the nape of her neck, and she gave him a smoldering look.

"Just a little later, cowboy. I don't want the dinner to burn."

After dinner, they left the dishes and pots and made love gently, softly, on the couch in the living room.

"I hear you've been a good Navy wife, helping to hold up Nancy Dobler."

"She's a sweet lady, a little uptight, but between Maria and me, we have her pretty well in hand. I don't think she'll have any more attempts, at least not while we have our little campaign going."

"Now that Dobler is home?"

"We'll cut back but still go out with her once a week. Maria and I worked it out. Hey, how is Jefferson? I heard on the news. They're calling it a hate crime."

"It's certain about that. They used the *N* word and everything. More than two dozen witnesses. Those four bikers are in big trouble."

"Your boys will get out of it with a fine?"

"Maybe no fine. They were defending the life of their friend."

"That Janie sounds like a SEAL herself."

DeWitt laughed. "Yes, she just might be able to do it. From what I hear, she ran a good party."

She watched him. "Ed, are you happy?"

"Deliciously."

"I don't mean right now, just after great sex. Are you happy with us, being this way? Not married. No kids. Do you want a regular relationship and a family?"

"We've talked about this before."

"I know, and I was the one who hung back. The SEAL syndrome, I call it. Women are simply scared out of their minds that on the next mission her man will be the one in the body bag come home for burial."

"You still worry that way?"

"Absolutely. I wouldn't be human if I didn't. After all, people do shoot at you quite often, try to blow you up, sink you, drown you, knife you. I have a hundred damn good reasons to worry."

"But not obsessed?"

She stared at him. Her pretty face went slack and neutral, for just a moment a hint of a smile flashed in, then it vanished. When it was gone a slow frown settled around her eyes and mouth.

"Obsessed? No, I don't think so. Not after seeing what Nancy went through. She actually sliced both wrists and took thirty sleeping pills."

"Remember, she's a five-time loser at suicide. Which could mean that she really isn't that keen on dying. She didn't slice her wrists that deep, I'm told, and she called nine-one-one herself well before she could die from the pills."

"So she's sending a signal, but she doesn't want to die?"

"I'm no psychiatrist, but that sort of thing has been known to happen. So, you're not obsessed. Good. Every SEAL in the field is concerned about getting wounded or killed. It's part of the job description. Asterisk: The body may be subject to any of several kinds of lethal objects entering it, or it may drown or be blown up by enemy fire."

Milly rubbed the purplish scar on his chest. "Is this hurting you anymore? Did it bother you on the mission?"

"No, doesn't hurt and didn't bother me. Back to you. You're not obsessed, and you're still here. How about you and I getting pregnant? If it works, then we'll thrash out the marriage idea."

Milly's eyes widened and her mouth opened in a small gasp. She hugged him tightly. Then she sat up. "Oh, yes, darling Ed. Yes, I think so. Right now we throw away our condoms and birth control pills. Hey, maybe tonight we can get pregnant."

Ed grinned. "Maybe. If we don't, it won't be for not trying."

That same night, Murdock came in from visiting Jefferson. He was feeling better. The surgery was still hurting and the pain medication didn't quite knock it all down, but Jefferson would make it. He had been cool about the fight.

"Oh, yeah, Cap. I was surprised when those four guys called me nigger and attacked me. Thought that sort of shit was over. Then when the one shot me, I was totally blown away. People don't do that anymore, I didn't think."

Murdock told Ardith about his day and the visit.

"I'm glad he'll be all right. Now you have two slots to hold open or fill. Hope you don't get a call any time soon."

"You said you have three more days. Good. Let's go rock hunting out in the Borrego Desert. About the farthest place I can think of now from the SEAL operation."

"Yes, let's. Oh, I almost forgot. I have a message from your mother. She says she's ready at any time to help you plan your wedding. Now, I wonder why she'd say that?" Ardith smiled sweetly at him.

"What a sneaky way to get into the subject."

She kissed him softly on the lips and leaned back. "Darling, I know. But we women are something of brood hens. Every time I see a cute little baby—"

He shushed her. They sat on the couch half watching a movie on TV. It wasn't that good. At last they turned off the TV and hurried into the bedroom.

"Only three more days. We don't want to waste any time."

Murdock had given the platoon a three-day leave. He took one day himself, and they drove into the desert. It was dry, it was mild. They took the ranger's tour, learned how to survive in the desert and how to find water or at least a liquid if you're that dry.

The next day, Murdock was working with the master chief, trying to dig up a replacement for Quinley. Murdock had been watching the new Tadpole training classes. The men were getting larger and larger. One SEAL Tadpole was 6' 8" and 285 pounds. He could run the forty-yard dash in 4.5 seconds.

"Master Chief MacKenzie, find me the largest, best SEAL you can. Nobody under six-four."

Murdock turned around and saw Don Stroh watching him.

"Commander Murdock, get your hat. We have an important meeting in a half hour and barely time to get there. We'll be gone the rest of the day, Master Chief Mac-Kenzie."

Murdock hesitated. Hell, Stroh was the connection, the

conduit, and the boss. He crooked his finger, Murdock and his platoon jumped. He jumped now.

"Yes, sir," he said and grabbed his cammie hat and went out the door with Stroh.

The CIA man asked Murdock to change into his civvies, then they drove in a blue Buick that Stroh always rented when he came to town. Murdock swore it was the same one, but it couldn't have been.

"An assignment?" Murdock asked.

"Not exactly."

"So what's so important?"

"Show you soon enough."

Twenty minutes later, they were over the Coronado Bay Bridge and through downtown San Diego, heading for Los Angeles. Stroh turned off to the left and headed for Mission Bay.

"Fishing?" Murdock asked.

"Fishing. They had a good bite this morning. The man on the desk said they would sail again at twelve-thirty. We have a lot of talking to do, and I owe you a fishing trip. We'll rent the tackle we need and see if we get lucky."

"So what are you setting me up for, Stroh?"

"Not sure exactly. We have three hot spots we're watching. Libya has been making waves lately now that Saddam is gone. But more of that later. I called Seaforth this morning, and they had an unusual bite of yellows. Not big ones, eight to ten pounds, but a good fight."

Murdock brightened. "A ten-pound yellow can give you lots of trouble." He paused. "Does this mean I'm speaking to you again?"

"Hope to hell it does. Otherwise, it's E-mail and telegrams."

Murdock looked at him. "Ten-pound yellows? You wouldn't tell a fish story to me, would you?"

"Swear on a stack of five-inch anchovies." Stroh grinned and looked at Murdock. "Besides, there is also Cuba getting frisky at just the wrong time and at least two Russian-made tactical nuclear weapons of the twenty-megaton variety said

to soon be on the market to the highest bidder. We hear
it's a floating sales room, but we don't know the flag or
the size ship or who is sailing her. Gives us a whole group
of things to think about."

Murdock was thinking. "Say they had something like an
old Corvette. Give you some speed, enough space, and a
few weapons for self-defense. Damn, they could go into
any port in the world and make a sale right under the au-
thorities' noses."

"Thought you'd like that one. Here's Seaforth. We have
ten minutes before sailing time. The cheeseburgers are on
me as soon as the cook fires up the grill."

Murdock scowled. "Damn, Stroh, you sure this is you
talking? Sounds like I'm about to get blindsided."

"Enjoy," Stroh said. "Just think about that floating nuclear weapon sales room."

Murdock did. From now on, he wouldn't be able to forget such a threat. He felt his blood pressure rise. He hoped
they had enough data on that ghost ship to make it their
next mission. He'd keep hoping.

The fishing report at the end of the trip:

Stroh: two barracuda, three sand bass, one Pacific mack-
erel.

Murdock: three barracuda, six sand bass, four calico
bass.

"Stroh, you promised me some ten-pound yellowtail."

"Didn't promise, just said the boat caught some yellows
this morning."

"That's as good as a promise."

"All right. Next trip I promise you three twelve-pound
yellowtail."

"Promise?"

"Promise."

SEAL TALK:

MILITARY GLOSSARY

Aalvin: Small U.S. two-man submarine.

Admin: Short for administration.

Aegis: Advanced Naval air defense radar system.

AH-1W Super Cobra: Has M179 under-nose turret with 20mm Gatling gun.

AK-47: 7.62 round Russian Kalashnikov automatic rifle. Most widely used assault rifle in the world.

AK-74: New, improved version of the Kalashnikov. Fires the 5.45mm round. Has 30-round magazine. Rate of fire: 600 rounds per minute. Many slight variations made for many different nations.

AN/PRC-117D: Radio, also called SATCOM. Works with Milstar satellite in 22,300-mile equatorial orbit for instant worldwide radio, voice, or video communications. Size: 15 inches high, 3 inches wide, 3 inches deep. Weighs 15 pounds. Microphone and voice output. Has encrypter, capable of burst transmissions of less than a second.

AN/PUS-7: Night vision goggles. Weight 1.5 pounds.

ANVIS-6: Night vision goggles on air crewmen's helmets.

APC: Armored Personnel Carrier.

ASROC: Nuclear-tipped antisubmarine rocket torpedoes launched by Navy ships.

Assault Vest: Combat vest with full loadouts of ammo, gear.

ASW: Anti-Submarine Warfare.

Attack Board: Molded plastic with two hand grips with bubble compass on it. Also depth gauge and Cyalume chemical lights with twist knob to regulate amount of light. Used for underwater guidance on long swims.

Aurora: Air Force recon plane. Can circle at 90,000 feet. Can't be seen or heard from ground. Used for thermal imaging.

AWACS: Airborne Warning And Control System. Radar units in high-flying aircraft to scan for planes at any altitude out 200 miles. Controls air-to-air engagements with enemy forces. Planes have a mass of communication and electronic equipment.

Balaclavas: Headgear worn by some SEALs.

Bent Spear: Less serious nuclear violation of safety.

BKA: Bundeskriminalamt: German's federal investigation unit.

Black Talon: Lethal hollow-point ammunition made by Winchester. Outlawed some places.

Blivet: A collapsible fuel container. SEALs sometimes use it.

BLU-43B: Antipersonnel mine used by SEALs.

BLU-96: A fuel-air explosive bomb. It disperses a fuel oil into the air, then explodes the cloud. Many times more powerful than conventional bombs because it doesn't carry its own chemical oxidizers.

BMP-1: Soviet armored fighting vehicle (AFV), low, boxy, crew of 3 and 8 combat troops. Has tracks and a 73mm cannon. Also an AT-3 Sagger antitank missile and coaxial machine gun.

Body Armor: Far too heavy for SEAL use in the water.

Bogey: Pilots' word for an unidentified aircraft.

Boghammer Boat: Long, narrow, low, dragger boat; high-speed patrol craft. Swedish make. Iran had 40 of them in 1993.

Boomer: A nuclear-powered missile submarine.

Bought It: A man has been killed. Also "bought the farm."

Bow Cat: The bow catapult on a carrier to launch jets.

Broken Arrow: Any accident with nuclear weapons or nuclear material lost, shot down, crashed, stolen, hijacked.

Browning 9mm High Power: A Belgian 9mm pistol, 13 rounds in magazine. First made 1935.

Buddy Line: Six feet long, ties 2 SEALs together in the water for control and help, if needed.

BUDS/S: Nickname for SEAL training facility for six-month course in Coronado, California.

Bull Pup. Still in testing; new soldier's rifle. SEALs have a dozen of them for regular use. Army gets them in 2005. Has a 5.56 kinetic round, 30-shot clip. Also 20mm high-explosive round and 5-shot magazine. Twenties can be fuzed for proximity airbursts with use of video camera, laser range finder, and laser targeting. Fuzes by number of turns the round needs to reach laser spot. Max range: 1,200 yards. Twenty-round can also detonate on contact and has delay fuze. Weighs 14 pounds. SEALs love it. Can, in effect, shoot around corners with the airburst feature.

BUPERS: BUreau of PERSonnel.

C-2A Greyhound: Two-engine turboprop cargo plane that lands on carriers. Also called COD (Carrier Onboard Delivery). Two pilots and engineer. Rear fuselage loading ramp. Cruise speed 300 mph, range

1,000 miles. Will hold 39 combat troops. Lands on CVN carriers at sea.

C-4: Plastic explosive. A claylike explosive that can be molded and shaped. It will burn. Fairly stable.

C-6 Plastique: Plastic explosive. Developed from C-4 and C-5. Is often used in bombs with radio detonator or digital timer.

C-9 Nightingale: Douglas DC-9 fitted as a medical evacuation transport plane.

C-130 Hercules: Air Force transporter for long haul. Four engines.

C-141 Starlifter: Airlift transport for cargo, paratroops, evac for long distances. Top speed, 566 mph. Range with payload, 2,935 miles. Ceiling 41,600 feet.

Caltrops: Small, four-pointed spikes used to flatten tires. Used in the Crusades to disable horses.

CamelBack: Used with drinking tube for 70 ounces of water attached to vest.

Cammies: Working camouflaged wear for SEALs. Two different patterns and colors: jungle and desert.

Cannon Fodder: Old term for soldiers in line of fire destined to die in the grand scheme of warfare.

Capped: Killed, shot, or otherwise snuffed.

CAR-15: The Colt M-4Al. Sliding-stock carbine with grenade launcher under barrel. Knight sound suppressor. Can have AN/PAQ-4 laser aiming light under the carrying handle. .223 round. Twenty- or 30-round magazine. Rate of fire: 700 to 1,000 rounds per minute.

Cascade Radiation: U-235 triggers secondary radiation in other dense materials.

Cast Off: Leave a dock, port, land. Get lost. Navy: long, then short signal of horn, whistle, or light.

Castle Keep: The main tower in any castle.

Caving Ladder: Roll-up ladder that can be let down to climb.

CH-46E: Sea Knight chopper. Twin rotors, transport. Can carry 22 combat troops. Has a crew of 3.

CH-53D Sea Stallion: Big chopper. Not used much anymore.

Chaff: A small cloud of thin pieces of metal, such as tinsel, that can be picked up by enemy radar and that can attract a radar-guided missile away from the plane to hit the chaff.

Charlie-Mike: Code words for continue the mission.

Chief to Chief: Bad conduct by EM handled by chiefs so no record shows or is passed up the chain of command.

Chocolate Mountains: Land training center for SEALs near these mountains in the California desert.

Christians in Action: SEAL talk for not-always-friendly CIA.

CIA: Central Intelligence Agency.

CIC: Combat Information Center. The place on a ship where communications and control areas are situated to open and control combat fire.

CINC: Commander IN Chief.

CINCLANT: Navy Commander IN Chief, AtLNATtic.

CINCPAC: Commander-IN-Chief, PACific.

Class of 1978: Not a single man finished BUD/S training in this class. All-time record.

Claymore: An antipersonnel mine carried by SEALs on many of their missions.

Cluster Bombs: A canister bomb that explodes and spreads small bomblets over a great area. Used against parked aircraft, massed troops, and unarmored vehicles.

CNO: Chief of Naval Operations.

CO_2 Poisoning: During deep dives. Abort dive at once and surface.

COD: Carrier On board Delivery plane.

Cold Pack Rations: Food carried by SEALs to use if needed.

Combat Harness: American Body Armor nylon mesh special operations vest. Six 2-magazine pouches for drum-fed belts, other pouches for other weapons, waterproof pouch for Motorola.

CONUS: The Continental United States.

Corfams: Dress shoes for SEALs.

Covert Action Staff: A CIA group that handles all covert action by the SEALs.

COB: Close quarters battle house. Training facility near Nyland in the desert training area. Also called the Kill House.

COB: Close Quarters Battle. A fight that's up-close, hand-to-hand, whites of his eyes, blood all over you.

CRRC Bundle: Roll it off plane, sub, boat. The assault boat for 8 seals.

CRRC: Combat Rubber Raiding Craft. Also the IBS or Inflatable Boat Small.

Cutting Charge: Lead-sheathed explosive. Triangular strip of high-velocity explosive sheathed in metal. Point of the triangle focuses a shaped-charge effect. Cuts a pencil-line-wide hole to slice a steel girder in half.

CVN: A U.S. aircraft carrier with nuclear power. Largest that we have in fleet.

CYA: Cover Your Ass; protect yourself from friendlies or officers above you and JAG people.

Damfino: Damned if I know. SEAL talk.

DDS: Dry Dock Shelter. A clamshell unit on subs to deliver SEALs and SDVs to a mission.

DEFCON: DEFense CONdition. How serious is the threat?

Delta Forces: Army special forces, much like SEALs.

Desert Cammies: Three-color desert tan and pale green with streaks of pink. For use on land.

DIA: Defense Intelligence Agency.

Dilos Class Patrol Boat: Greek, 29' long, 75 tons displacement.

Dirty Shirt Mess: Officers can eat there in flying suits on board a carrier.

DNS: Doppler Navigation System.

Drager LAR V: Rebreather that SEALs use. No bubbles.

DREC: Digitally Reconnoiterable Electronic Component. Top-secret computer chip from NSA that can decipher any U.S. military electronic code.

E&E: SEAL talk for escape and evasion.

E-2C Hawkeye: Navy, carrier-based, Airborne Early Warning aircraft for long-range early warning, threat assessment, and fighter direction. Has a 24-foot saucerlike rotodome over the wing. Crew 5, max speed 326 knots, ceiling 30,800 feet, radius 175 nautical miles with 4 hours on station.

E-3A Skywarrior: Old electronic intelligence craft. Replaced by the newer ES-3A.

E-4B NEACP: Called kneecap. National Emergency Airborne Command Post. A greatly modified Boeing 747 used as a communication base for the President of the United States and other high-ranking officials in an emergency and in wartime.

EA-6B Prowler: Navy plane with electronic countermeasures. Crew of 4, max speed 566 knots, ceiling 41,200 feet, range with max load 955 nautical miles.

EAR: Enhanced Acoustic Rifle. Fires not bullets but a high-impact blast of sound that puts the target down and unconscious for up to six hours. Leaves him with almost no aftereffects. Used as a nonlethal weapon. The sound blast will bounce around inside a building, vehicle, or ship and knock out anyone who is within range. Ten shots before the weapon must be electrically charged. Range: About 200 yards.

Easy: The only easy day was yesterday. SEAL talk.

ELINT: ELectronic INTelligence. Often from satellite in orbit, picture-taker, or other electronic communications.

EOD: Navy experts in nuclear material and radioactivity who do Explosive Ordnance Disposal.

Equatorial Satellite Pointing Guide: Used to aim antenna for radio to pick up satellite signals.

ES-3A: ELectronic INTelligence (ELINT) intercept aircraft. The platform for the battle group Passive Horizon Extension System. Stays up for long patrol periods, has comprehensive set of sensors, lands and takes off from a carrier. Has 63 antennas.

ETA: Estimated Time of Arrival.

Executive Order 12333: By President Reagan, authorizing special warfare units such as the SEALs.

Exfil: Exfiltrate, to get out of an area.

F/A-18 Hornet: Carrier-based interceptor that can change from air-to-air to air-to-ground attack mode while in flight.

Fitrep: Fitness report.

Flashbang Grenade: Nonlethal grenade that gives off a series of piercing explosive sounds and a series of brilliant strobe-type lights to disable an enemy.

Floatation Bag: To hold equipment, ammo, gear on a wet operation.

Fort Fumble: SEALs' name for the Pentagon.

Forty-mm Rifle Grenade: The M576 multipurpose round contains 20 large lead balls. SEALs use on Colt M-4A1.

Four Striper: A Navy captain.

Fox Three: In air warfare, a code phrase showing that a Navy F-14 has launched a Phoenix air-to-air missile.

FUBAR: DDAT FAIL. Fucked Up Beyond All Repair.

Full Helmet Masks: For high-altitude jumps. Oxygen in mask.

G-3: German-made assault rifle.

Gloves: Seals wear sage green, fire-resistant Nomex flight gloves.

GMT: Greenwich Mean Time. Where it's all measured from.

GPS: Global Positioning System. A program with satellites around Earth to pinpoint precisely aircraft, ships, vehicles, and ground troops. Position information is to plus or minus 10 feet. Also can give speed of a plane or ship to one-quarter of a mile per hour.

GPSL: A radio antenna with floating wire that pops to the surface. Antenna picks up positioning from the closest 4 global positioning satellites and gives an exact position within 10 feet.

Green Tape: Green sticky ordnance tape that has a hundred uses for a SEAL.

GSG-9: Flashbang grenade developed by Germans: a cardboard tube filled with 5 separate charges timed to burst in rapid succession, blinding and giving concussion to enemy, leaving targets stunned and easy to kill or capture. Usually nonlethal.

GSG9: Grenzschutzgruppe Nine. Germany's best special warfare unit, counterterrorist group.

Gulfstream II (VCII): Large executive jet used by services for transport of small groups quickly. Crew 3, and 18 passengers. Cruises at 581 mph. Maximum range 4,275 miles.

H&K 21A1: Machine gun with 7.62 NATO round. Fires 900 rounds per minute. Range 1,100 meters. All types of NATO rounds: ball, incendiary, tracer. Replaces the older, more fragile M-60 E3.

H&K G11: Automatic rifle, new type. 4.7mm caseless ammunition. Fifty-round magazine. The bullet is in a sleeve of solid propellant with a special thin plastic coating around it. Fires 600 rounds per minute. Single-shot, 3-round burst, or fully automatic.

H&K MP-5SD: Nine-millimeter submachine gun with integral silenced barrel, single-shot, 3-shot, or fully automatic. Rate 800 rounds per minute.

H&K P9S: Heckler & Koch's 9mm Parabellum double-action semiauto pistol with 9-round magazine.

H&K PSG1: High-precision, bolt action sniping rifle. 7.62 NATO round. Five- to 20-round magazine. Roller-lock delayed-blowback breech system. Fully adjustable stock. 6×42 telescopic sights. Sound suppressor.

HAHO: High-Altitude jump, High Opening. From 30,000 feet, open chute for glide up to 15 miles to ground. Up to 75 minutes in glide. To enter enemy territory or enemy position unheard.

Half-track: Military vehicle with tracked rear drive and wheels in front, usually armed and armored.

HALO: High-Altitude jump, Low Opening. From 30,000 feet. Free-fall in 2 minutes to 2,000 feet and open chute. Little forward movement. Get to ground quickly, silently.

Hamburgers: Often called sliders on a Navy carrier.

Handie-Talkie: Small, handheld personal radio. Short range.

HELO: SEAL talk for helicopter.

Herky Bird: C-130 Hercules transport. Most-flown military transport in the world. For cargo or passengers, paratroops, aerial refueling, search and rescue, communications, and as a gunship. Has flown from a Navy carrier deck without use of catapult. Four turboprop engines, max speed 325 knots, range at max payload 2,356 miles.

Hezbollah: Lebanese Shitte Moslem militia. Party of God.

HMMWU: The Humvee, U.S. light utility truck replaced the honored jeep. Multipurpose wheeled vehicle, 4×4, automatic transmission, power steering. Engine: Detroit Diesel 150 hp V-8, air-cooled. Top speed, 65 mph. Range, 300 miles.

Hotels: SEAL talk for hostages.

Humint: Human intelligence. Acquired on the ground by human beings versus satellite or photo recon.

Hydra-Shock: Lethal hollow-point ammunition made by Federal Cartridge Company. Outlawed in some areas.

Hypothermia: Danger to SEALs. A drop in body temperature that can be fatal.

IBS: Inflatable Boat Small. 12×6 feet. Carries 8 men and 1,000 pounds of weapons and gear. Hard to sink. Quiet motor. Used for silent beach, bay, lake landings.

IR Beacon: Infrared beacon. For silent nighttime signaling.

IR Goggles: "Sees" heat instead of light.

Islamic Jihad: Arab holy war.

IV Pack: Intravenous fluid that you can drink if out of water.

JAG: Judge Advocate General. The Navy's legal investigating arm, independent of any Navy command.

JNA: Yugoslav National Army.

JP-4: Normal military jet fuel.

JSOC: Joint Special Operations Command.

JSOCCOMCENT: Joint Special Operations Command Center in the Pentagon.

KA-BAR: SEALs' combat fighting knife.

KATN: Kick Ass and Take Names. SEAL talk, get the mission in gear.

KH-11: Spy satellite, takes pictures of ground, IR photos, etc.

KIA: Killed In Action.

KISS: Keep It Simple, Stupid. SEAL talk for stream-lined operations.

Klick: A kilometer of distance. Often used as a mile. From Vietnam era, but still widely used in military.

Krytrons: Complicated, intricate timers used in making nuclear-explosive detonators.

KV-57: Encoder for messages, scrambles.

LT: Short for lieutenant in SEAL talk.

Liaison: Close connection, cooperating person from one unit or service working with another military unit.

Laser Pistol: The SIW pinpoint of ruby light emitted on any pistol for aiming. Usually a silenced weapon.

Left Behind: In 30 years, SEALs have seldom left behind a dead comrade, never a wounded one. Never been taken prisoner.

Let's Get the Hell Out of Dodge: SEAL talk for leaving a place, bugging out, hauling ass.

Light Sticks: Chemical units that make light after twisting to release chemicals that phosphoresce.

Loot & Shoot: SEAL talk for getting into action on a mission.

LZ: Landing Zone.

M1A1 M-14: Match rifle upgraded for SEAL snipers.

M1-8: Russian Chopper.

M-3 Submachine Gun: WW II grease gun, .45-caliber. Cheap. Introduced in 1942.

M-16: Automatic U.S. rifle. 5.56 round. Magazine 20 or 30, rate of fire 700 to 950 radients/minutes. Can attach M203 40mm grenade launcher under barrel.

M-18 Claymore: Antipersonnel mine. A slab of C-4 with 200 small ball bearings. Set off electrically or by trip wire. Can be positioned and aimed. Sprays out a cloud of balls. Kill zone, 50 meters.

M-60E3: Lightweight handheld machine gun. Not used now by the SEALs.

M60 Machine Gun: Can use 100-round ammo box snapped onto the gun's receiver. Not used much now by SEALs.

M61A1: The usual 20mm cannon used on many American fighter planes.

M61 (j)1: Machine pistol, Yugoslav make.

M-86: Pursuit deterrent munitions. Various types of mines, grenades, trip-wire explosives, and other devices in antipersonnel use.

M-203: A 40mm grenade launcher fitted under an M-16 or the M-4A1 Commando. Can fire a variety of grenade types up to 200 yards.

M662: A red flare for signaling.

MagSafe: Lethal ammunition that fragments in human body and does not exit. Favored by some police units to cut down on second kill from regular ammunition exiting a body.

Make a Peek: A quick look, usually out of the water, to check your position or tactical situation.

Mark 23 Mod O: Special operations offensive handgun system. Double-action, 12-round magazine. Ambidextrous safety and mag-release catches. Knight screw-on suppressor. Snap-on laser for sighting. .45 caliber. Weighs 4 pounds loaded. 9.5 inches long, with silencer 16.5 inches long.

Mark II Knife: Navy-issue combat knife.

Mark VIII SDV: Swimmer Delivery Vehicle. A bus, SEAL talk. Twenty-one feet long, beam and draft 4 feet, 6 knots for 6 hours.

Master-at-Arms: Military police on board a ship.

MAVRIC Lance: A nuclear alert for stolen nukes or radioactive goods.

MC-130 Combat Talon: A specially equipped Hercules for covert missions in enemy or unfriendly territory.

McMillan M87R: Bolt-action sniper rifle, .50 caliber,

53 inches long. Bipod, fixed 5- or 10-round magazine. Bulbous muzzle brake on end of barrel. Deadly up to a mile. All types .50-caliber ammo.

MGS: Modified grooming standards. So SEALs don't all look like military to enable them to do undercover work in mufti.

MH-53J: Chopper, updated CH053 from 'Nam days. 200 mph, called the PAVE Low III.

MH-60K Blackhawk: Navy chopper. Forward infrared system for low-level night flight. Radar for terra-follow avoidance. Crew of 3, take 12 troops. Top speed 225 mph. Ceiling, 4,000 feet. Range radius, 230 miles. Arms: two 12.7mm machine guns.

M15: British domestic intelligence agency.

MIDEASTFOR: Middle East Force.

MiG: Russian-built fighter, many versions, used in many nations around the world.

Mike Boat: Liberty boat off a large ship.

Mike-Mike: Short for mm, millimeter, as 9 mike-mike.

Milstar: Communications satellite for pickup and bouncing from SATCOM and other radio transmitters. Used by SEALs.

Miniguns: In choppers. Can fire 2,000 rounds per minute. Gatling gun type.

Mitrajez M80: Machine gun from Yugoslavia.

Mocha: Food energy bar SEALs carry in vest pockets.

Mossburg: Pump-action shotgun, pistol grip, 5-round magazine. SEALs use it for close-in work.

Motorola Radio: Personal radio, short range, lip mike, earpiece, belt pack.

MRE: Meals Ready to Eat. Field rations used by most of U.S. armed forces and the SEALs as well. Long-lasting.

MSPF: Maritime Special Purpose Force.

Mugger: MUGR, miniature underwater locator device. Sends up antenna for pickup on positioning satellites.

Works underwater or above. Gives location within 10 feet.

Mujahideen: A soldier of Allah in Muslim nations.

NAVAIR: NAVy AIR command.

NAVSPECWAR: NAVal SPECial WARfare Section. SEALs are in this command.

NAVSPECWARGRUP-Two: Naval Special Warfare Section Group Two based at Norfolk.

NCIS: Naval Criminal Investigative Service. A civilian operation not reporting to any Navy authority to make it more responsible and responsive. Replaces the old NIS, Naval Investigation Service, which did report to the closest admiral.

NEST: Nuclear Energy Search Team. Nonmilitary unit that reports at once to any spill, problem, or broken arrow to determine the extent of the radiation problem.

Newbie: A new man, officer, or commander of an established military unit.

NKSF: North Korean Special Forces.

NLA: Iranian National Liberation Army. About 4,500 men in south Iraq, supported by Iraq for possible use against Iran.

Nomex: The type of material used for flight suits and hoods.

NPIC: National Photographic Interpretation Center in D.C.

NRO: National Reconnaissance Office, runs and coordinates satellite development and operations for the intelligence community.

NSA: National Security Agency.

NSC: National Security Council. Meets in Situation Room, support facility in the Executive Office Building in D.C. Main security group in the nation.

NSVHURAWN: Iranian Marines.

NUCFLASH: An alert for any nuclear problem.

NVG One Eye: Litton single-eyepiece Night Vision Goggles. Prevents NVG blindness in both eyes if a flare goes off. Scope shows green-tinted field at night.

NVGs: Night Vision goggles. One eye or two. Give good night vision in the dark with a greenish view.

OAS: Obstacle Avoidance Sonar. Used on many low-flying attack aircraft.

OIC: Officer in charge.

Oil Tanker: One is: 885 feet long, 140 feet beam, 121,000 tons, 13 cargo tanks that hold 35.8 million gallons of fuel, oil, or gas. Twenty-four on the crew. This is a regular-sized tanker, not a supertanker.

OOD: Officer Of the Deck.

Orion P-3: Navy's long-range patrol and antisub aircraft. Some adapted to ELINT roles. Crew of 10. Max speed loaded 473 mph. Ceiling, 28,300 feet. Arms: Internal weapons bay and 10 external weapons stations for a mix of torpedoes, mines, rockets, and bombs.

Passive Sonar: Listening for engine noise of a ship or sub. It doesn't give away the hunter's presence as an active sonar would.

PBR: Patrol Boat River. The U.S. has many shapes and sizes with various armaments.

PAVE Low III: A Navy chopper.

PC-170: Patrol Coastal-class 170-foot SEAL delivery vehicle. Powered by four 3,350-hp diesel engines, beam of 25 feet and draft of 7.8 feet. Top speed 35 knots, range 2,000 nautical miles. Fixed swimmer platform on stern. Crew of 4 officers, 24 EM, and 8 SEALs.

Plank Owners: Original men in the start-up of a new military unit.

Polycarbonate Material: Bulletproof glass.

PRF: People's Revolutionary Front. Fictional group in

Prowl & Growl: SEAL talk for moving into a combat mission.

Quitting Bell: In BUD/S training. Ring it and you quit the SEAL unit. Helmets of men who quit the class are lined up below the bell in Coronado. (Recently they have stopped ringing the bell. Dropouts simply place their helmet below the bell and go.)

RAF: Red Army Faction. A once-powerful German terrorist group, not so active now.

Remington 200: Sniper rifle. Not used by SEALs now.

Remington 700: Sniper rifle with Starlight Scope. Can extend night vision to 400 meters.

RIB: Rigid Inflatable Boat. Three sizes, one is 10 meters with speed of 40 knots.

Ring Knocker: An Annapolis graduate with the ring.

RIO: Radar Intercept Officer. The officer who sits in the backseat of an F-14 Tomcat off a carrier. The job: Find enemy targets in the air and on the sea.

Roger That: A yes, an affirmative, a go answer to a command or statement.

RPG: Rocket-Propelled Grenade. Quick and easy, shoulder-fired. Favorite weapon of terrorists, insurgents.

SAS: British Special Air Service. Commandos. Special warfare men. Best that Britain has. Works with SEALs.

SATCOM: SATellite-based COMmunications system for instant contact with anyone anywhere in the world. SEALs rely on it.

SAW: Squad's Automatic Weapon. Usually a machine gun or automatic rifle.

SBS: Special Boat Squadron. On-site Navy unit that transports SEALs to many of their missions. Located across the street from the SEALs' Coronado, California, headquarters.

SD3: Sound suppression system on the H&K MP5 weapon.

SDV: Swimmer Delivery Vehicle. SEALs use a variety of them.

Seahawk SH-60: Navy chopper for ASW and SAR. Top speed 180 knots, ceiling 13,800 feet, range 503 miles. Arms: 2 Mark 46 torpedoes.

SEAL Headgear: Boonie hat, wool balaclava, green scarf, watch cap, bandanna roll.

Second in Command: Also 2IC for short in SEAL talk.

SERE: Survival, Evasion, Resistance, and Escape training.

Shipped for Six: Enlisted for six more years in the Navy.

Shit City: Coronado SEALs' name for Norfolk.

Show Colors: In combat, put U.S. flag or other identification on back for easy identification by friendly air or ground units.

Sierra Charlie: SEAL talk for everything on schedule.

Simunition: Canadian product for training that uses paint balls instead of lead for bullets.

Sixteen-Man Platoon: Basic SEAL combat force. Up from 14 men a few years ago.

Sked: Seal Talk for schedule.

Sonobouy: Small underwater device that detects sounds and transmits them by radio to plane or ship.

Space Blanket: Green foil blanket to keep troops warm. Vacuum-packed and folded to a cigarette-sized package.

Sprayers and Prayers: Not the SEAL way. These men spray bullets all over the place hoping for hits. SEALs do more aimed firing for sure kills.

SS-19: Russian ICBM missile.

STABO: Use harness and lines under a chopper for men to get down to the ground.

STAR: Surface-to-air recovery operation.

Starflash Round: Shotgun round that shoots out sparkling fireballs that ricochet wildly around a room, confusing and terrifying the occupants. Nonlethal.

Stasi: Old-time East German secret police.

STICK: British terminology. Two 4-man SAS teams, 8 men.

Stokes: A kind of Navy stretcher. Open coffin shaped of wire mesh and white canvas for emergency patient transport.

STOL: Short TakeOff and Landing. Aircraft with high-lift wings and vectored-thrust engines to produce extremely short takeoffs and landings.

Sub gun: Submachine gun, often the suppressed H&K MP5.

Suits: Civilians, usually government officials, wearing suits.

Sweat: The more SEALs sweat in peacetime, the less they bleed in war.

Sykes-Fairbairn: A commando fighting knife.

Syrette: Small syringe for field administration often filled with morphine. Can be self-administered.

Tango: SEAL talk for a terrorist.

TDY: Temporary duty assigned outside of normal job designation.

Terr: Another term for terrorist. Shorthand SEAL talk.

Tetrahedral Reflectors: Show up on multimode radar like tiny suns.

Thermal Imager: Device to detect warmth, such as a human body, at night or through light cover.

Thermal Tape: ID tape for night vision goggle user to see. Use on friendlies.

TNAZ: Trinitroaze Tidine. Explosive to replace C-4, 15 percent stronger and 20 percent lighter.

TO&E: Table showing organization and equipment of a military unit.

Top SEAL Tribute: "You sweet motherfucker, don't you never die!"

Train: Used for contact in smoke, no light, fog, etc. Men directly behind each other. Right hand on weapon, left hand on shoulder of man ahead. Squeeze shoulder to signal.

Trident: SEALs' emblem. An eagle with talons clutching a Revolutionary War pistol, and Neptune's trident superimposed on the Navy's traditional anchor.

TRW: A camera's digital record that is sent by SAT-COM.

TT33: Tokarev, a Russian Pistol.

UAZ: A Soviet one-ton truck.

UBA Mark XV: Underwater life support with computer to regulate the rebreather's gas mixture.

UGS: Unmanned Ground Sensors. Can be used to explode booby traps and Claymore mines.

UNODIR: UNless Otherwise DIRected. The unit will start the operation unless they are told not to.

VBSS: Orders to Visit, Board, Search, and Seize.

Wadi: A gully or ravine, usually in a desert.

White Shirt: Man responsible for safety on carrier deck as he leads around civilians and personnel unfamiliar with the flight deck.

WIA: Wounded In Action.

Zodiac: Also called an IBS, Inflatable Boat Small, 15 × 6 feet, weighs 265 pounds. The "rubber duck" can carry 8 fully equipped SEALs. Can do 18 knots with a range of 65 nautical miles.

Zulu: Greenwich Mean Time (GMT). Used in all formal military communications.